DARK
SECRETS
WHITE LIES

By
C L KREGER

Copyright © 2024 by C.L. Kreger

All rights reserved. No part of this book may be reproduced or used in any manner without written permission of the copyright owner except for the use of quotations in a book review. For more information, address: clkreger dreams@outlook.com

After leaving a life of unhappy privilege in India to settle his younger brother's financial crisis in England, Clayton is held in thrall by an insatiable courtesan with tendencies to drink blood. She has plans to convert him in into her ageless lover and will NOT take NO for an answer:

And now, my Sweet. we must complete your journey." Lillian's sharp nail opened the translucent flesh at the base of her throat, and she pulled his face against the welling blood. Still under her control, he was unable to resist the rich and intoxicating smell of the deep-red droplets gathering there. Clayton fastened his lips on the building stream and swallowed. The immense pleasure and exotic promise he found within her blood swirled through his mind. He raised his head from the satin pillow and his lips twisted and became cruel. *Oh yes, my journey is complete but yours is ending.*

Anger, dismay, and remorse shape his life as he tries to cope with his unwanted vampiric nature and the constant need for blood. After twenty-odd years in England, Clayton leaves for a new life and opportunity in America. The passenger ship encounters a hurricane and is forced to land in Cuba where he is approached by a mysterious bruja crone and given an elixir that will, if taken daily for one year, allow him to walk in the sun as a Day Walker. The elixir is successful, and he remains in Cuba for several years before finally resuming his journey to America.

He becomes a successful restaurant owner in Charleston, South Carolina when his life is changed once more with an unusually strong and lustful response to meeting sixteen-year-old Mary Ellington. Four years later, he meets Mary again and falls deeply in love with her despite his dread that his blood lust might cause her death. Their brief love affair and his proposal of marriage ends with an assassin's bullet on the eve of America' s Civil War. His injuries are severe and cause Clayton to lose all memories of Mary but during the war, images of a weeping woman drenched in blood and whispering his name continue to haunt his dreams.

After returning to civilian life, he feels a strong urge to head west, still not realizing, he and Mary had often spoken of ranch life together after the war.

Mary thinks Clayton is dead even though his body disappeared the night of the murder. After the war is over and Mary has come to terms with being alone, she decides to move to Colorado and run the ranch left to her in her aunt's will. Years later, exhausted by the continued harassment of persons unknown, she decides to sell her beloved ranch, but only to the right buyer.

The lovers, separated by time and distance, continue to be drawn together as Clayton moves west towards Mary, whom he's never met and their love he doesn't remember.

This is a work of fiction. Names, characters, places, dates and incidents either are the product of the author's imagination or are used fictitiously. Brief references to actual persons, living or dead, events, or locales are used only to provide historical context within the fictional narrative.

Table of Contents

ACKNOWLEDGMENTS i
PROLOGUE 1860 ii
CHAPTER 1 BLOCKADE RUNNING 1
CHAPTER 2 WAR'S END 12
CHAPTER 3 AN EVENING'S ENTERTAINMENT 18
CHAPTER 4 A COLT NAMED KALIPH 26
CHAPTER 5 THE LONELY BOY 32
CHAPTER 6 BEST BIRTHDAY GIFT EVER 42
CHAPTER 7 OLDER BROTHER BLUES 52
CHAPTER 8 A SHORT ESCAPE 57
CHAPTER 9 A FATHER'S FUNERAL 62
CHAPTER 10 CALLED TO LONDON 68
CHAPTER 11 TERRINGTON LODGE 71
CHAPTER 12 LILLIAN'S TRAP 77
CHAPTER 13 A LIVERPOOL KILL 95
CHAPTER 14 ADAM'S MISTAKE 99
CHAPTER 15 BOUND FOR AMERICA 107
CHAPTER 16 CUBA 112
CHAPTER 17 A GOOD HORSE - A GREEDY WOMAN 125
CHAPTER 18 CHARLESTON ARRIVAL 132
CHAPTER 19 CHARLESTON'S BACK ALLEY 138

CHAPTER 20 THREE CASINO STORIES 141

CHAPTER 21 TIME AND HORSEFLESH 150

CHAPTER 22 THE FIRST MEETING 156

CHAPTER 23 TRAINING MARY 166

CHAPTER 24 FIRE AND ASH 170

CHAPTER 25 MEETING AGAIN 180

CHAPTER 26 BREAKFAST FOR TWO 187

CHAPTER 27 MR. C. NOTEWORTHY, ESQUIRE 191

CHAPTER 28 THE LOVE AFFAIR 196

CHAPTER 29 MURDER ON THE BOARDWALK 202

CHAPTER 30 WILL THERE BE WAR? 219

MARY 222

CHAPTER 31 MARY'S WAR 223

CHAPTER 32 QUEEN'S PRIDE 230

CHAPTER 33 THE SWEETWATER RANCH SOLUTION
.... 238

CHAPTER 34 SWEETWATER COWBOYS 242

CHAPTER 35 HER ARRIVAL IN GOLDEN 246

CHAPTER 36 ALOYSIUS GREY 255

CHAPTER 37 GREY'S FIRST PLAN 258

CHAPTER 38 SWEETWATER TROUBLES BEGIN ... 263

CHAPTER 39 SWEETWATER ROUNDUP 271

CHAPTER 40 NURSE MARY 274

CHAPTER 41 LOSING GILL 278

CLAYTON 282

CHAPTER 42 CLAYTON HEADS WEST 283

CHAPTER 43 WYOMING TERRITORY	288
CHAPTER 44 BEING SHERIFF	294
CHAPTER 45 WHERE'S DENVER?	309
CHAPTER 46 COLORADO	313
CHAPTER 47 THE VAMPIRE ELDER	317
CHAPTER 48 HIS ARRIVAL IN GOLDEN	327
CHAPTER 49 GREY'S NEXT PLAN	334
CHAPTER 50 SELLING SWEETWATER	340
CHAPTER 51 MEMORIES AND RUSTLERS	356
CHAPTER 52 ANGRY BLOOD	360
CHAPTER 53 GREY'S FAILURE	364
CHAPTER 54 A WEDDING AND A GUNFIGHT	367
CHAPTER 55 WOLF PACK	379
CHAPTER 56 WHITE LIES	389
CHAPTER 57 SNAKEBITE	397
CHAPTER 58 TIME	408
CHAPTER 59 MARY DECIDES	410
CHAPTER 60 EXIT STRATEGY	419
EPILOGUE	427

ACKNOWLEDGMENTS

Many thanks to my neighbor and friend, Donnie, who listened patiently while I told her of all the latest plot twists and back stories. Her encouragement and insights helped keep me on track. A special thanks to my husband, Chuck, who always came to find me after I disappeared for hours, hunkered down over my laptop fighting word battles with my muse.

PROLOGUE
1860

Mary sat on the dimly lit front porch swing of her Savannah home while her bare feet pushed its suspended wooden seat slowly back and forth. The few mourners had left earlier and now she was left with only her memories. Memories. There were no distractions now to keep them at bay. Her dreams of a life with Clayton had been buried in an empty casket three hours ago. The sodden handkerchief clenched in her hand lifted to smother the faint sob threatening to escape her throat.

She looked down at the faint sparkle of the ruby and diamond ring on her slender finger and brought it closer to her reddened eyes. *It's truly beautiful but may as well be coal, without Clayton to hold this hand. He was so sincere, so nervous when he proposed.*

A watery smile crossed her face. Clayton Masters was the most remarkable man she had ever met.

Mary continued her reflection. Their time together had been so short, but oh, how they had loved his touch, his smile, the strength of his arms around her. She had felt pure joy to see him walk across a crowded room, smiling, with his eyes focused only on her. But they had no time! Not nearly enough time together. Their love had been shattered by a crazed man's bullet.

Lost in her thoughts, Mary didn't notice the dark shadow standing motionless next to the clapboard siding of a vacant house four doors down. Its large yard, though surrounded with flowering trees, had begun to show neglect and the figure easily blended into the dense shadows cast by oversized and untrimmed shrubs. When Mary finally left the porch and closed its front door behind her, the feminine form became a mist floating outward and upward until it floated past rooftops and disappeared into the dark sky above.

CHAPTER 1
BLOCKADE RUNNING

SOMEWHERE ON THE OCEAN - 1862

It was after 0200 hours but the tired men remained alert at their posts and kept their conversations short. Though a rare chuckle might be heard, blockade running was a serious and sometimes deadly business. Another half day and the ship would be safely anchored in Bermuda. The bales of South Carolina cotton in the hold would be unloaded and after being transferred to another ship, they would complete their journey to the eagerly waiting British mills. The *CSS Advance* would return to her home port of Charleston four days later with luxury products, guns, and uniforms for the Confederacy. Hopefully, the trip would be completed before the fall weather turned against them.

The ship's senior officer, Lieutenant Commander Clayton Masters, stood near the bow as her steam engine pushed her shallow hull a smooth twelve knots. The side paddle made a rhythmic swooshing sound pleasant to his ears, so much better, he thought, than the sounds of cannon fire. The calm sea and light wind, smelling of salt, gave him a moment of peace. He used the rare opportunity to reflect on his place within the machine of war.

This war, this detestable war, men being killed or maimed, captured and imprisoned, families torn apart. Please God, let it end soon.

This was to be his last marine command before transferring back from North Carolina to the Confederate base in Charleston. He never liked the sea. Put him on a good horse with distant horizons and he was a happy man. He looked down at the curling dark waves created by the forward push of the ship and gazed up at the bright stars above. *Not much of a moon tonight. Good.*

A grim smile touched his firm lips. His thoughts continued to circle. *Can't wait to be back on land. This thirst is getting harder to control. Every man on this ship is risking his life by being on board. How much longer can I hold out before doing something stupid? Something detestable? And if that's not enough to think about, who the hell is that woman who keeps showing up in my dreams? Why is she hugging me and endlessly crying? And the blood all that blood!*

Only his daily routine of deep meditation and his self-control allowed him to tamp down his need for blood, though now after denying his thirst for the last two days, he felt his physical body finally beginning to weaken.

A freshening wind caught his attention and brought an end to his musing. Stronger whitecaps were starting to break against the bow of the fleet ship and an overhead flapping of unsecured canvas sail caused him to point a finger up to the culprit. An attentive sailor caught the gesture and immediately went aloft to tighten the lashing. As the sailor returned to the bouncing deck, he lost his balance and only a quick grab at the iron stanchion near the belching funnel kept him on his feet.

He grinned sheepishly at Clayton before resuming his work checking the mooring lines for stress or wear.

Clayton began to closely watch the distant waves with his extraordinary eyesight. The swells were building higher but there was no cause for real alarm yet. He turned and strode to the stern rail to look behind.

Heavy clouds were gathering, smearing the horizon with their thickening darkness. He had hoped to avoid any serious weather on this trip. They were heavily loaded, and rapid maneuvers to avoid Union capture could get tricky. He mounted the bridge ladder and returned to his station next to the captain.

He heard a clap of distant thunder and watched as the storm approaching from the north seemed to gather itself for an assault on their speeding ship. A series of lightning strikes followed by more cracking booms, sharply highlighted a second ship running before the storm a mile behind their own heavily loaded paddle steamer.

His Chief Mate hurried in. "Sir, we got trouble. Union gunboat closing astern. Her guns will have our range in about twenty minutes. Orders, sir?"

Clayton's clear dark blue eyes looked at the storm swells building ahead of the following ship as she plunged forward, clearly determined to catch the sleek Confederate blockade runner. His response, with its slight English accent, was confident. "Ready the ship for the storm and tell Gunny to break out the arms for the men just in case. Keep on this heading. We might still be able to avoid them once the storm hits."

The Chief Mate's reply was muffled as the ship was showered with a blast of icy rain driven almost horizontally by the strength of the gathering storm. The man braced his legs to keep balanced on the now heaving deck before carefully maneuvering himself down the bridge ladder to alert the men. Clayton stood immobile on the bridge, ignoring the frenzied slashing of the rain beating against the glass enclosure of the wheelhouse. He was mentally calculating the speed of the approaching Union gunboat and he knew the ocean was too rough now for her to use her 24-pounder howitzer with any accuracy. She had also lost the element of surprise so he wouldn't worry too much about her closing in but would fix their own efforts instead on weathering the storm.

Clayton was still looking aft when lightning flashed overhead, followed by a thunderclap loud enough to nearly deafen him. He watched a second blast of lightning strike the Union ship's metal mast and his eyes widened in disbelief when he saw the snapping bolt continue to follow two guy-lines downward and split again to strike the chain plates fastened to its wooden hull. Electricity sizzled at the recoil rail of the howitzer lashed to the forward bow. Without a safe route into saltwater and away from the ship, the dancing shaft of lightning burst inward through the wooden hull to the stored munitions below.

Seconds later the electrical charge sliced through exploding shrapnel and an orange fireball erupted. Its bright flare outlined the dark metal of an unsecured hatch as it blasted upward to the thick dark clouds above. A second roll of thunder and plumes of white steam belched skyward and outward as the ship's boiler exploded, pushing heated shards of metal into the skin of the lightly clad gunboat. The injured steamer rapidly lost momentum and began to fall behind.

The ocean storm was in full rage as heavy winds and slashing rain continued to pelt their pursuer, now wallowing helpless in the churning seas. Clayton watched struggling seamen rush to prevent the heavily pitching ship from capsizing as the towering waves continued to force their unimaginable strength against the gunboat's shredded deck. In the far distance, he could identify a second Union gunboat change course to rescue the sailors from their impending death. It would be improbable that the second ship could catch up and capture them now, so he turned his attention to the rough seas threatening to crash over the hull of his own ship.

The savage storm finally blew northeast at dawn. That afternoon the *Advance* glided into the safety of the Bermuda harbor under sunny skies and a light wind. She was guided to the north dock and the efficient crew secured the ship within minutes while stevedores swarmed aboard and quickly unloaded the bales of cotton destined for the thirsty mills of England. After completing their shipboard chores, Clayton dismissed his cheerful and thirsty crew for a few nights of well-earned shore leave. A slight smile crossed his face as he saw their eagerness to embrace what Bermuda had to offer: booze and women.

Clayton, however, needed blood and soon. He quickly strode down the gangplank and with only the occasional salute to fellow officers he sped as quickly as possible away from town. He couldn't wait any longer. Experience had taught him that an extended delay led to ravenous beastlike behavior, and he was *not* that beast. The virus in his veins was demanding sustenance and could not be ignored any longer. He needed a successful hunt *now*.

Just a few more streets and alleys to cross. He was too weak to use any of his higher skills, but he could still sprint a good distance. He rapidly left Nassau behind and reached the overgrown and partially burned and abandoned sugar plantation he had discovered during an earlier visit. He paused in the shadow of a storm-blasted pine before silently approaching a slovenly dressed man seated on the chipped concrete steps of the mansion. Pure instinct caused the man to stand and throw a knife at the intruder, but the throw was clumsy, and Clayton was blindingly fast. He grabbed the would-be killer and sank his fangs into the exposed throat. A short guttural scream was followed by silence.

Thick blood laced with laudanum coated his tongue and he swallowed quickly, determined to finish what he had started but knowing he would need some time to remove the drug's effects. He moved back to the blasted pine and sat in its shade with eyes closed, waiting for his body to cleanse the toxins from his blood. His mind calmed and he was determined not to dwell on this last bit of abhorrent behavior. What was the point?

Within a half hour, he felt well enough to dispose of his victim and return to town.

The strong island sun had lessened, and he became more comfortable as he walked along the shaded boulevard towards the guesthouse he always used when in town. It was a weathered, gingerbread ramshackle of a house that he preferred because it had three floors and sat back from the street. Overgrown bushes crowded themselves next to the peeling paint of the front porch and two mammoth oaks guarded the red brick pathway leading to the crumbling steps. Brilliant flowers in hues of red, yellow, and purple grew untended in the large Grecian style urns placed on each side of the sun scorched porch door. Clayton paused in the middle of the pathway and stood just for a moment looking at the house. *Even unkempt, this old lady of a house has charm.*

He rented his room three months at a time and since he paid in advance, the ancient landlady was more than happy to ignore the odd hours her English gentleman lodger kept. She was holding her dust mop and waiting for him in the dimness of the wide vestibule of the house. Her voice was amused as she took in his brine-soaked uniform, "Welcome back, sonny. Had a good trip, did yah?"

Clayton was gravely courteous with his reply. "Ran into a storm, but no damage. Everything was delivered and in tiptop shape. How are you, Mrs. Hunt? You're looking mighty fine today."

The tiny woman pretended to cough and shrugged her bony shoulders, "Oh you, yer such a charmer. That reminds me. A real fancy lady showed up after dark looking for you a couple nights ago. I didn't say anything about yer arrival time, but she said she was staying at the Paradise Hotel."

Two hours later, after a refreshing shower and change of clothes, he found his friend Thalia relaxing in her darkened room on the second floor of the hotel. Heavy drapes had been pulled over the one window facing the harbor and she had covered her regular clothing with an Arabic caftan as added protection from the sun. It was a shame really; she was old enough and strong enough to remain awake during daylight hours but would never be able to enjoy the outdoors during the day.

He closed the door behind himself, walked towards her and took her hands in his. "Madam, you are as beautiful as ever." She just smiled up at him and said nothing, overcome with the pleasure of seeing her good friend Clayton.

The older woman was an exquisite beauty of middle age. Her skin was pearlescent and had tiny laugh lines peeking out next to her perfectly defined rose-colored lips. Blond hair shot with silver strands had been swept up into a seemingly careless knot twisted at the crown of her head, artfully escaping curls framing her still perfect jawline. Her body was described by her many enchanted lovers as "Rubenesque" rather than sylphlike and it still matched the loving portrait Rubens had painted of her in 1632.

Clayton and Thalia caught up on each other's news until the tropical sun had set, and it finally turned dark enough for her to leave her room to feed. He offered to keep her company while hunting but she insisted on going alone. Her passage back to England was confirmed for later in the evening, so she had just enough time to hunt, finish packing and board the ship before it left. He never mentioned his blood-filled dreams and she never mentioned his lost love.

Clayton left Thalia standing on the wraparound porch of the hotel and strolled along the darkly shadowed alley between it and the saloon next door. He knew of a run-down camp area where the homeless hung out and sometimes planned their next mischief. Had anyone been watching, they might have seen a humanlike blur flash out from the alley and into the campground seconds later.

After his flightless sprint he slowed and moved into the trees surrounding the campsite.

Broken wagon wheels, a few mis-matched chairs, shabby tents, and piles of unidentified trash dotted the weed infested field. In its center, a fire sporadically lit the faces of the poorly dressed shadows relaxing around it. Someone was softly playing a guitar and faint smells of grilling fish floated through the air mixed with the scent of unwashed bodies and wood smoke. A few small children played in the dust at a woman's feet as she held a baby to her breast and sang softly. Clayton tried to ignore the haunting melody as he picked out a female seated away from the bright firelight. She was slumped round-shouldered on a log and her knees were spread to form a place for her hands to hold a half empty bottle of dark island rum. He could smell her sickness from where he stood, unobserved, at the tree line. He approached, breathing easily as he sat down next to her. She reared back on the log and tried without success to focus on his face.

He smiled at the deeply lined visage and bent to whisper into her ear, "I have my camp set up over by the trees. How about joining me for a late supper?" She nodded blearily at him and painfully staggered to her feet. A few women seated near the campfire glanced over, nodded in their general direction, then resumed their conversation while staring into the depths of the fire's embers. The two shadows walking towards the trees were quickly forgotten.

Clayton half supported the skeletal form of the aged female as they began to walk from the firelight and into the darkness of the surrounding forest. Her hair was knotted and matted with dust. A few gray tendrils escaped the scarf carelessly tied around her ears and the ragged hem of her skirt threatened to trip her stumbling feet. He could tell her death from a failing liver was only a day or so away. The yellow tint of her eyes, the jaundice of her skin and her swollen belly spoke of a very hard life that would soon end.

Inside the dark periphery of the trees, he stopped short when she said in a soft voice, "You know, mister, I'm not very hungry after all. Might we just sit a bit?" Her voice was hoarse and filled with phlegm, but it still held evidence of cultured breeding. Against his better judgement, he allowed his mind to meld with hers and peered into her thoughts. He briefly felt her strong love for a handsome young sailor followed by anguish and years of loneliness. He quickly retreated but, in her eyes he saw her defeated acceptance of his embrace before lowering his mouth to the pulsing vein of damaged blood.

She began to struggle weakly in his arms as his fangs pierced her throat, but she was so lost in an alcohol daze that she hardly noticed as his kiss deepened. He sent a feeling of love and comfort into her dying mind and her chapped lips smiled while she fell into warm darkness to meet her sailor-boy. Clayton's soft, "Thank you", drifted away into the nighttime wind.

He carried the lifeless body further into the woods and gently laid her head against the base of a towering pine. Crushed pine needles scented the air, and he used a drift of twigs and dirt to partially cover her well-worn shoes. He folded her hands over her breast and scraped more forest litter over her threadbare clothing. He knew it wouldn't be long before scavengers would arrive to feast on the nearly bloodless corpse and if she was eventually found, her death would be attributed to misadventure.

Three hours later, a rejuvenated Clayton sat at a small table at the rear of the Parrots Roost tavern with a stoneware mug of untouched wine before him on its knife-scarred tabletop. He was reflecting on his earlier kill, trying to rid himself of the image of the victim's fear before his mouth fastened on the wrinkled skin at her throat. He had made the unusual choice of opening her memories to him after hearing her voice and her story saddened him. He knew he made her accept his deadly embrace, but there was that single moment—just before his piercing kiss and he knew it would always be this way. His need for blood had to outweigh sympathy for his victim.

Other customers in the smoky interior of the saloon jabbed quick looks at the handsome loner dressed in white linen and gray light wool trousers. They noticed he stared down at his wine but never drank, and there was something about that stony blank face and ice blue eyes that discouraged any hearty welcome from their group. All decided it would be best to leave him be. Even the barkeep allowed the stranger the full use of the corner table rather than berate him for not drinking while taking up valuable space.

CHAPTER 2
WAR'S END

LIVERPOOL, ENGLAND - 1865

Unfamiliar mental exhaustion filled Clayton as he looked out at Liverpool's crowded harbor. Low ocean swells carrying refuse from a dozen ships slapped gently against the piers of the port city. A strong onshore breeze carrying scents of burning pitch, rotting hawser ropes, seaweed and dead fish stirred the uncut hair escaping the confines of his CSS Navy cap. He turned his head to gaze toward the far end of the pier where the sweating crew members of his last command stood at attention. The late afternoon sun threw his profile into high relief. Dark hair, razor clean strong jaw, narrow straight nose, and dark blue eyes confirmed what countless women had thought for almost half a century, the man was incredibly handsome. When he pulled his cap lower, the luminous glow of his unnaturally smooth but lightly tanned countenance subsided.

He had captained the *CSS Advance* and successfully evaded the Union blockades between North Carolina and British held Bermuda fourteen times. The operation had been turned over to a different captain and he had heard that the *Advance* was now in Union hands. It was a year ago when he was reassigned as the Lieutenant Commander of the *CSS Shenandoah*. He sighed. *And here I am again after an assignment I didn't want. Back on English soil after three quarters of a century.* The magnificent *Shenandoah*, scourge of Union whaling ships, rested in the Liverpool harbor, her cannons removed, her flag struck, and the American Civil War ended.

He threw the tattered remnants of his half-smoked cigar into the oily water below. Putting his musings aside, he straightened his uniform over his broad shoulders and strode toward the far end of the pier. Final inspections of the *Shenandoah* and all the official ceremonies were over. Now he could bid a farewell to his men and release them to their future, hopefully one free from war. Immediately after, he would complete the resignation of his Naval commission and begin a new life as far from this ocean and all wretched wars as he could get.

Away from the horrific rubble that was all that remained of Charleston.

Two hours later, Clayton smartly saluted his long-time friend and superior officer, Admiral Thomas J. Wilson. The corpulent man grinned through his generous walrus-like mustache as he rose behind the gleaming mahogany desk. The men shook hands and he gestured for Clayton to sit on the nearby leather sofa.

Wilson's southern voice was gruff, "I understand you wish to leave us, Lieutenant Commander. Well, I am sorry to see you go. In these last few years, you've been a credit to this man's navy. Your leadership will be sorely missed." The admiral's official voice changed to that of a friend. "I hope you have time for a brandy with me while you tell me of any future plans?"

Clayton walked to the nearby sofa and dropped his six-foot two-inch frame onto its welcoming plumped up cushions. He removed his cap, set it next to him and slowly stretched out his long legs with a stifled groan. Wilson smiled at him and walked over, placing a glass with a generous amount of brandy into his outstretched hand. Both looked down at the clear amber liquid, gave a mock salute to each other and swallowed the rich, smooth tasting alcohol.

Wilson seated himself across from Clayton in the sofa's matching overstuffed armchair, raised his eyebrows and observed his friend sprawled on the sofa. He cleared his throat and began to speak. "You know, Clayton, we've gotten to be pretty good friends over the last thirty years, and it may be years more before we cross paths again, so, I thought I'd share a few of the more outrageous comments said about you." He smiled before saying, "Consider it entertainment and understand, I don't personally believe much of it, but here it goes. It was said you would stand motionless for hours during your night watch. Your strength has become legendary especially during heavy seas. Even an officer said your eyesight and hearing were extraordinary during one of their more brutal sea chases." Clayton said nothing but took a healthy swallow of his brandy. The admiral cleared his throat again and continued, "Rumor has it that you've kept your youthful good looks despite years of salt air and sun because you smear animal blood on your face." He sniffed before adding, "Hell, I don't believe THAT for one second."

Clayton's face registered surprise mixed with dismay but before he could respond, Wilson began to retell a story being passed around. "The best story? Well, it seems an injured seaman swore he saw you get hit with at least four enemy bullets. He even saw several chest and stomach wounds bleeding heavily as you staggered past him to the ship's leeward rail. The medic treating that same injured seaman confirmed that you didn't show up at his clinic until the next night. By that time, the medic found only barely discernable scratches on your chest." The admiral heaved a sigh and said, "Well, you guessed it, that poor sailor was teased unmercifully by his pals as trying to make up the story for free drinks." He gave a short laugh and sipped his brandy while his gaze sharpened on the face of his friend reclining on the couch. The respect he had for Clayton wouldn't change but he had to admit to himself, the man was definitely covering up something.

Clayton shifted uncomfortably and didn't quite know how to respond. Was Admiral Wilson questioning his age or something darker? His memory surfaced.

The two men had met while Wilson was on shore leave as a twenty-two-year-old midshipman raising hell in Charleston and they had shared some raucous times at Clayton's restaurant and gentleman's club. He always appreciated Wilson's respect for his personal boundaries. The man never asked for explanations. He knew Wilson had heard the local gossip about unusual success with the ladies, but even when he was pumped for more information about Clayton, he refused to talk.

Clayton smiled into the tired eyes and deeply lined face of his friend and felt the few tense moments change to companionable silence softened by their shared memories. The office darkened as shadows began to edge the book-lined walls, and as they looked at each other, more smiles tugged at the corner of each mouth.

Wilson shifted his bulk deeper into his massive armchair and waited for his friend to speak his mind.

Clayton took another sip of brandy before breaking the silence. "Well, now that the war is over, I've decided to go back to America. There's lots of country to see and I keep thinking about their wild West. Not making any firm plans until I find somewhere I'd like to settle. Maybe I'll try my hand at ranching or become a gentleman gambler on the Mississippi River. I'm well suited to the night life, don't you think?" He grinned and threw back the remainder of his brandy as he stretched again. The admiral stood, grabbed the decanter, and replenished both of their glasses.

The conversation changed again as they began to reminisce of hard-fought battles, won and lost. It was after seven o'clock before the admiral thought to order a light supper. Thirty minutes later, an orderly returned with meals for the two men, who continued their discussion of world events as only good friends can do. Clayton picked at the food on his plate and apologized for his lack of appetite which he attributed to tiredness and Wilson said he understood.

Finally, and with a show of regret, Clayton stood and adjusted his uniform. It was time to leave.

Admiral Wilson smiled as he rose from the table. "I wish you well and do try to stay in touch. I'd like to hear from you occasionally. Send me some pictures of that 'wild West'". Clayton nodded but made no reply as he looked at the deeply lined and weathered face and shook his hand for possibly the last time.

Still saying nothing, he bent to grab his cap and walked to the office door. He paused with his hand on the doorknob and looked back at his friend. He was leaving one of the best men he had ever had the occasion to meet. It was never easy to say goodbye, but time and his hidden nature demanded it. Thirty years of white lies with his friend or *any* good relationship had its limits before serious consequences occurred. He stepped through the door and closed it behind him.

Admiral Thomas J. Wilson shrugged and took a final sip of brandy. He was thinking that one should never compare one's own portly and aging body with that of his good friend Clayton. Even now, that man's frame was as slender and supple as it was thirty years ago. The man hadn't aged a bit. He looked back over his shoulder at the stack of unread reports still waiting on his desk and sighed. He was just too tired to work anymore. They would have to wait until tomorrow.

CHAPTER 3
AN EVENING'S ENTERTAINMENT

After leaving his friend, Clayton's outraged stomach finally lost its contents in the fetid darkness behind a busy saloon. *I can NEVER, and I mean NEVER allow this to happen again! Wilson, I blame you, your brandy, and your friendship. You made me feel all too human tonight.* He immediately felt much better after the purge and returned to his rented room on the second floor of Mrs. Smith's Boarding House for Gentlemen. The room itself was smallish but comfortable enough, with an easy chair next to a small coal burning fireplace. It also had the luxury of a private water closet with flush toilet and sink courtesy of water provided by a cistern on the roof. A round wooden table with two chairs, a chest of drawers and a double bed with brass headboard completed the room's furniture. As a Lieutenant Commander, he had the option of using the officers' quarters in town but considering his lifestyle, he preferred privacy as much as possible.

Sitting on the edge of the bed he decided to change into evening clothes and stroll over to the bar at the Commodore Inn. It had been a few days since he had satisfied his hated blood craving, and he couldn't delay any longer. He quickly pulled off his close-fitting naval uniform with a sigh of relief. *I'll figure out what to do with it when I get back.* He tossed the loosely folded outfit and cap onto the bed and began to dress in his usual black evening jacket and vest. He decided on a silk cravat instead of a newly fashionable bow tie and secured it with a four-carat black diamond bound in silver filigree. He fastened his onyx cufflinks to the cuffs of his crisp white shirt and slipped a narrow knife into its special sheath strapped to his ankle. The knife always came in handy if forced to fight in close quarters surrounded by a yelling mob of drunken men. His smile was brief. *Better to slice than bite.*

After setting his top hat at a rakish angle, he grinned as he looked at himself in the mirror and saw a fashionably dressed, trim and fit handsome man of thirty-five. *Not too bad for an old man over a hundred plus years.* Satisfied and his ego intact, he closed and locked the door behind him. He whistled a jaunty tune as he clattered down the uncarpeted stairs to the front lobby.

Clayton entered Liverpool's Commodore Bar a little after 10:00 PM. The tables were filled with the after-theater crowd enjoying one last bit of entertainment before heading home. Two musicians played current love songs on a grand piano and violin, and the competition between conversations, music and laughter grated on his overly sensitive ears. It had been a while since he entered the chaos of such a closely packed and highly perfumed gathering, so he tuned them out before being overwhelmed with a flood of discordant sounds.

He handed his hat to the hat-check girl and stepped further into the noisy room. A youthful waiter saw him at once and eagerly approached through the light haze of cigar smoke to take his order. His handsome and still beardless face glistened with a light sweat from the overheated salon and when he saw Clayton's unblinking gaze raking the length of his body a flush stained his cheeks.

"May I take your order, sir? Or would you prefer to stand at the bar, uh, sir?" The soft-spoken waiter stumbled to a halt as he stared up into Clayton's face, his mouth slightly open. He shook his head as if coming out of a daze, and finally lifted his pencil to write the order.

An amused Clayton stopped teasing the boy about some possible blood sport and responded, "Thank you, I'd prefer a quieter corner I think and a bottle of your best claret and two glasses." He gestured and said, "You can find me over in that area by those drapes." He effortlessly moved through the packed crowd as if they didn't exist, his body seeming to move them aside as he approached. He stopped near the window hung with dark red velvet drapes and stood quietly facing the crowded floor. Conversations and the scent of expensive perfumes continued to float through the air. There were several beautiful women holding drinks and laughing as they flirted with their escorts. He particularly took note of the ones who stared at him a little too long, their appreciation mirroring his own on their painted faces. Pouting red lips smiled at him as if confirming their invitation and he smiled to himself. *A veritable cornucopia of deliciousness.* Clayton began planning his evening.

As he stood waiting for his drink order, Clayton remembered the lessons learned while sitting at the feet of his old Buddhist friend (and teacher) in the outskirts of Bombay. The deep-seated anger he initially felt at being *turned* while in London so many years ago was beginning to fade as time and his ability to meditate balanced the rollercoaster of his lifestyle. Those lessons didn't particularly seem at odds with his *otherness,* and he usually felt comfortable focusing on the present and this life of being not quite human.

Normally, his need for blood could be satisfied by stalking and taking the blood of the human flotsam that floated around the underbelly of any city. Sometimes he fed on those few souls who were about to die, but he hated its necessity and took little pleasure from any of it. Tonight, however, would be different. He would indulge the darker side of himself.

The young waiter brought his drink order, looked down at the floor and mumbled, "Thank you," as Clayton signed the charge slip. The server *was* thankful to be stepping away from the tall too handsome customer with the piercing ice blue eyes. He was one scary guy. He was glad to have other customers gesturing from across the room and he sped away to take their orders.

A small side table became vacant nearby, and Clayton moved towards it with bottle and glasses in hand. As he approached the table, a woman elaborately dressed in red satin for the evening pointed her gloved hand to him and to the table, her eyebrows raised in question. He nodded, put glasses and the bottle on the table and gestured for her to sit as he pulled out a chair for her. He knew the diamond necklace at her throat was paste but it sparkled in the light of the chandeliers and looked perfect surrounding the slender column of her neck. Her gown was draped seductively over generous breasts, and he truly admired the view as she drew closer.

Mahogany hair framed her oval face and the luminous glow of her creamy light brown skin seemed to beg for his undivided attention. Her slightly accented southern voice was husky velvet as she asked, "Are you enjoying your evening? I couldn't help but notice you the moment you walked into the room. You didn't stop to greet anyone, but you certainly *noticed* the ladies."

She rested her chin on her hand as her elbow rested on the tabletop. A wicked and confident teasing smile crossed her pouting scarlet lips as she continued, "And I'm *so* glad you noticed *me.*" When she leaned forward, his enjoyment of the view increased immensely.

Clayton tried to ignore how his lower body responded (the night was still young) so he shifted back into his chair and smiled as he poured two glasses of wine and handed one to her. He said, "Well, yes. I couldn't help but *notice* the most beautiful woman in the room."

Her sultry response was quick and to the point. "I would love to sit and chat with you but there is one important question I *must* ask will you ask me to dance?" Her deep breath caused her perfect decalage to rise and his hardening interest below rose with it. He knew this southern belle belonged to him for the night and he would thoroughly enjoy the experience.

The two glided around the crowded dance floor with ease and such a mastery of the steps that other dancing couples paused to watch. Clayton heard the excited whispers, "Why, it seems like they might be floating on air." He smiled to himself. *Indeed, we ARE floating on air*. At last, his companion jokingly complained of exhaustion, so they left the dance floor and Clayton escorted his companion to their corner table before stepping away to make other arrangements for his evening entertainment.

The Commodore Inn personnel knew Clayton well and he was able to obtain a key to his usual suite for a two-night stay, with a minimum of fuss. In his hotel room, champagne and seduction mixed with easy laughter and delightful intimate explorations created the perfect evening. Hours later, the lady slept next to him as he relaxed in the darkened room on a confusion of pillows, sheets, and bedspread. He yawned. Yes, his hunt was successful, and his blood lust completely satisfied.

The sky was just beginning to lighten when Clayton left the hotel and headed back to his own room. He smiled to himself as he thought of the lady finding herself alone in the soft bed. Her exhaustion would probably be forgotten when she spotted the diamond and sapphire brooch he placed next to her pillow and, with a bit of luck, she'd never notice the several tiny spots of blood staining the strap of her chemise. His post-hypnotic suggestion should keep her in bed and safe while her body replaced the blood he had taken. He had enjoyed himself immensely but knew there could never be a repeat of the erotic games they had played. Repeat performances led to mistakes.

Back in his room, he removed and carefully folded his evening attire before placing it into the steamer trunk with his other clothes. He chuckled to himself as he put on a robe. *Clothes are a lot easier to put on and take off nowadays.*

He was beginning to feel the sluggish pull of sleep but ignored it while he carefully packed his personal papers into an oilskin envelope. After dressing for the day, he methodically went around the room deciding what to take and what to donate to the poor. He would *not* be returning.

Finally, he pulled out a small, locked box from beneath the bed. The ebony box gleamed with its high polish. An inlay of narrow gold surrounded the image of a snarling wolf with eyes of blueish diamonds. This item was the one thing he was most concerned about. The box held his father's signet ring, wooden prayer beads, and a silk embroidered sachet enfolding a handful of earth from India.

These mementos were all he had, connecting him to his previous and totally normal life. He put the box into the steamer trunk, closed its lid and locked it. He would ignore the urge to sleep no longer. He opened the hinged lid of the second iron bound trunk and lowered himself to rest, curled up on the welcoming soil inside.

It was dusk when he settled accounts with his landlady. He knew his two trunks would remain safe with her until he returned for them. She personally liked Clayton and was happy to accommodate his request, though his offer of money equal to a month's rent in advance helped seal the deal. His bank had already sent a letter of credit to their New York branch in America. He wasn't quite sure yet when he wanted to head back since there were still plenty of interesting places to see if he remained in Europe. He also knew ocean-going steamer packets left Liverpool every week, giving him a wide choice of transport for the first leg of his journey if he decided to head America.

CHAPTER 4
A COLT NAMED KALIPH

Clayton was thoughtful as he walked the damp streets of Liverpool in the early morning. *Typical misty start of the day, rain this afternoon and probably won't clear for a week. I definitely need a change of location. And I still miss you, Saladin. Our fast rides into the countryside. That sun, that hot wind in my face. I do miss you, buddy.*

The old memory sparked a recalled conversation with a deckhand on the *Shenandoah*. There was supposed to be a stud farm somewhere south of Liverpool that bred and sold Arab horses. He should investigate it to see if he could find another Arab mount before returning to America.

He pulled a small notebook from his pocket and found the address for the stud farm. It was time he seriously entertained the idea of replacing his beloved Saladin with another Arab stallion. Well, there was only one thing to do, travel the hundred miles south to the village of Hastlemere by coach and check out available stock at the Al Sabir Arabian Stud. It would have to be an impressive horse to replace his old friend.

Two days later, Clayton boarded the weekly mail coach that would pass through Hastlemere. On its scheduled return to Liverpool, the coach driver promised to pick him up. The fee was reasonable for the round trip and the man seemed happy to have the company of a well-dressed Englishman sitting up front and beside him occasionally. The driver had a nice little side business going with the mail coach route. After all, the driver thought, what's the harm in making a few extra pounds from my own private passenger service?

The mail coach clattered to a stop at the farm's gated entrance after picking up a second passenger and delivering packets of mail to several villages. The sign over the gate proclaimed *AL SABIR ARABIANS* so Clayton grabbed his valise, climbed down off his perch next to the coach's driver, and approached the locked gate. He waited there as an older man garbed in a headscarf and burnoose hurried down the narrow road to greet him.

The greeting was warm as the gate was unlocked and opened. The man happened to be the owner of the farm and after a few gracious exchanges and introductions, Clayton was invited to dine at the family compound. As they walked along the narrow road to the residence, he told the sheikh of his youth in India and how his horse, Saladin, had been his best friend. He would not entertain the idea of replacing him with a different breed.

The two men entered the home of the sheikh where a servant took Clayton's carryall, coat, and hat. He entered a beautifully appointed living area and after the two seated themselves, the same servant brought a tray of tea and small bowls of dates and honeyed bread. They continued talking as they warmed themselves with cups of tea.

The sheikh's accent was softly Middle Eastern. "Mr. Masters, it would be my pleasure to show you our stock. Our broodmares have genealogy charts going back four hundred years. I'm sure you're aware the bloodline is charted through the mare, not the stallion, yes? And what are you looking for? It is not our normal practice to sell an animal destined for America I'm sure you understand. The casual mixing of bloodlines is not such a desirable thing to us." The message was clear. Clayton would have to be approved before an animal was sold to him.

Clayton was quick to respond. "I can assure you, any stallion under my control would not be bred to an inferior mare. I respect the breed. I would never compromise that."

The old sheik nodded. "Very good. Well, let's go see the ladies we have in the fields first." Both donned oil slickers against the light rain and headed out towards a neatly fenced pasture that paralleled the road the mail coach had used earlier.

As they walked toward the pasture, the owner regaled Clayton with the back stories of his mares, their histories and how he came to open his stud farm in southern England. It was fascinating to listen to, but the moment he stood leaning on the pasture fence, his full attention was taken by the beauty of six Arab mares galloping towards the fence, eyes shining, tails raised like flags whipping in the wind. All six mares crowded up against the fence demanding the sheikh's attention and he responded with whispered endearments as he stroked each velvet nose.

Sheikh Mohammed Al Suliman continued the tour with Clayton until they entered the extravagant stable housing four proud stallions, each one standing in his own spacious box stall. The sheikh explained to Clayton that these animals weren't for sale. His stallions were mature studs of at least seven years of age and were needed to continue his breeding line.

He gave Clayton a questioning look. "However, if you would consider an untrained colt? I have one in particular you may like. He is fiery like his mother but will not behave as we prefer. I can't use him as a stud because of his bad temperament, but he *is* a beautiful black two-year-old. He might grow out of his bad manners with more time, but if he doesn't learn to behave, he will have to be gelded and that would be such a shame." The two men left the stable and walked towards a small paddock near the side of the building.

An attentive stableman was asked to bring the colt to the paddock for viewing and Clayton watched as the youngster was brought out on a long lead rein. The colt was tossing his head and it seemed to Clayton that he was trying to throw off his halter to show resentment at being lead against his will. Splayed legs and crow hopping against the pressure of the long rein continued as the stableman tried to restrain the temperamental colt. As he checked out the perfect conformation of the young stud, he thought he might just be able to use this fiery independence.

Clayton turned away from leaning on the paddock fence and faced the sheikh. "May I approach this bad boy?"

"But of course. Please be careful, I cannot promise his good behavior."

Clayton opened the gate and let himself in. The barn worker's eyes widened as he handed the lead line of the skittish animal to Clayton. He gave a small bow and hurriedly ducked back behind the safety of the paddock fence.

The two, man and youthful horse, stood in the middle of the small corral. Neither moved a muscle. Clayton sent soothing thoughts to the colt as he approached and introduced himself by blowing softly into the horse's nose as he stroked the black velvet neck.

The colt pricked up his ears, shook his head and nickered as Clayton reached to scratch his forehead and rub his neck and ears. He draped the lead rein over the horse's neck and with his back to the colt, made a slow walk around the circumference of the pen. The horse obediently followed behind, his tail flicking back and forth. When Clayton stopped, the colt stopped, when Clayton began to walk again, the colt followed right behind. He turned around and faced the youngster. They stood looking at each other. The horse nickered softly and thrust his head into Clayton's chest. Their connection was obvious.

The sheikh seemed astounded with the change in the colt's behavior and the stableboy's mouth hung open. This had never happened before. Ever.

Clayton was smiling as he asked, "What's the name of this handsome lad?"

The sheikh laughed and slapped his hip. "He is called *Kaliph al Zahar* or *To Command* would be a close translation in your language."

"I like that name. Okay, Kaliph, would you like to stay with me and go on an adventure to America?" The two men laughed as the colt seemed to agree by bobbing his head up and down several times as he pawed the ground with a hoof.

Clayton paid for the animal and stayed as a guest of the sheikh until the mail coach arrived on its scheduled return north. During his time at the stud farm, he worked with Kaliph and talked to him endlessly. The two began to form a strong partnership.

It was time to head back to Liverpool and cross the Atlantic to America. First, he arranged for the horse to be taken to Liverpool. Once there, Kaliph and he would spend some leisure time getting reacquainted before traveling to America on one of the new steamer ships that traveled weekly between Liverpool and New York City.

One month later the two disembarked at New York's busy harbor. Kaliph wasn't used to the noise and unending cacophony of clanking trolly cars, booming machinery and houses crowded so closely together and Clayton was anxious to start his newest adventure, so as soon as possible, the two left the city for St Louis, Missouri. Referred by many as the Gateway to the West.

CHAPTER 5
THE LONELY BOY

INDIA – CHILDHOOD - 1762

"I hate Mother, I hate Father, I hate Brother, I hate Nanny and I *hate* green peas!" Twelve-year-old Clayton stamped his feet as he shouted the dire litany after leaving his mother's solarium and heading for the door. He was never allowed to do *anything* on his own except study, play his piano, read some stupid books (except the ones he managed to get smuggled in) or wander by himself in the gardens. Even there, there was usually an adult skulking somewhere about. His stupid baby brother got to do anything he wanted including grabbing Clayton's old but still favorite toys, (which he always managed to break). Clayton wasn't even allowed to make friends with the native boys his age. Some kind of grownup excuse of "class difference" (whatever that was).

Sometimes the unfairness seemed overwhelming, and he would retreat to his small room next to the third-floor nursery. He would read for hours until his father lowered the hammer and demand his 'return to civilization' before throwing Clayton's current book across the room.'

'Be nice to your baby brother and share your toys' his mother would say with a flavor of disinterest. Clayton knew his two-year-old brother was becoming spoiled rotten and really evil, but nobody seemed to notice or even care.

Clayton's lower lip jutted out as he flung himself out the front door, barely avoiding the attentive servant trying to open it before being trampled underfoot by an angry little boy. Once outside, he saw their gardener working along the compound walls raking mulch around a drift of dark pink bougainvillea. He marched up behind the gardener, grabbed a rake lying unattended on the lawn cart and targeted the hapless bush nearby, striking repeatedly at its innocent blossoms. "Take *that,* you filthy scum!" he shouted. Blossoms went flying and the startled gardener stepped back, speechless as the boy flung the rake with all his might at the inoffensive bush. Clayton's sight blurred with angry tears as he continued to vent his anger by stomping down the gravel path toward the small stable at the back of their compound.

The personal guard currently assigned to keep track of the young master was lounging at the stable door, intent on kissing the pretty new laundress. His attention was completely focused on her physical charms, and he didn't notice the angry hellion marching towards them. Clayton stopped a few feet away and just stood, hands on hips, waiting for them to finish. The two, alerted by the loud raspberry from pursed twelve-year-old lips, pulled apart. The blushing laundress picked up her basket of clean linens and fled into the rear entryway of the house.

The guard's wide grin as he looked at the retreating backside of the new girl became solemn as he looked down at Clayton and said, "Uh, can you keep this a secret? Just having a bit of fun. But what brings you here Young Master? What can I do for you?"

From the scowl on Clayton's face, and gleam in his eye, the guard knew blackmail of some sort was in the offing. He thought quickly. Possibly an adventure outside the compound. It's daylight so it should be okay. Hopefully we'll get back before supper and I can get another chance for a kiss from the new girl.

Clayton stomped his booted foot. "There's nothing to do around here. I'm going crazy. Take me outside and I promise not to tell Father what I just saw." The young voice ended with a wheedling note, and the bodyguard breathed a small sigh of relief.

After telling the mayordomo of their plan, the guard returned to Clayton waiting impatiently at the compound's gate. They began to walk along the shaded avenue towards the daily market several blocks away. The afternoon's moist heat was intense despite the trees shading the cobblestone walkway and Clayton's linen shirt was soaked with sweat before he completed walking the first two blocks. Anger at the unfairness in his life began to lessen as he felt the sheer joy of escaping from the eagle eyes of the house servants. He figured his bodyguard wasn't so bad, and he never told secrets. He did his best to ignore the man who followed a few yards behind, still smiling he knew, from his kiss with the new laundress. He picked up a stick and whomped a few weeds foolish enough to spring up between the cracks of the cobblestoned street.

Jim, the bodyguard, was lost in thought and muttered to himself, "Lord, I've forgotten her name. I'd better find out if I want another kiss." Planning how to get the young lady's name without embarrassing himself took his attention away from Clayton, and he fell back even further.

The two arrived at the open-air bazaar and the moment the guard's attention was captured by a hand painted picture of a half-naked temple dancer, Clayton escaped into a crowded alley that opened onto the next street.

Clayton forgot about the bodyguard as he happily patted the pale tan colored Brahman cows ambling their way along the pathways, casually dropping their dung as they strolled unconcerned among the crowds. Long chains of marigolds swathed each neck like tiny suns. He watched a trader lead three camels in a stately parade towards the public water trough at the center of the open plaza. He admired the long streamers of brilliantly colored cotton hung from crossed lines stretching from balcony to balcony overhead. Exotic smells of spices clashed with the ever-present cesspool odors of human and animal waste in the gutters that ran down the middle of the streets.

Tightly rolled grass carpets, and newly woven baskets were piled next to vendor stalls of roasting meat and bubbling curries. Shiny brass teapots crowded next to wood carvings and leather bags. Men carrying large urns of coconut water on their backs offered their buyers a dipper for a rupee. Women dressed in saris sat on the ground with their heaped baskets of fresh vegetables almost blocking the aisleways to the more permanent shops. Electric blue peacocks screamed their unearthly calls from their perches above crates of live chickens and ducks. Monkeys ran along rooftops and hurled monkey insults to the throng below. He knew better than to get too close, an excited monkey could sling a handful of their filth with deadly accuracy. Strident voices of hundreds of sellers attempting to attract hundreds of buyers created a wonderfully confused babel for his youthful ears and Clayton continued to walk along the cobbled street, thinking the market was the perfect place for the day's adventure.

He turned to examine a display of bright red and yellow glass bangles, when he felt a hand lightly brush his shoulder. As he turned to see the hand, his pocket was deftly emptied of its wallet. He grabbed the hand and pulled as hard as he could, but the pickpocket had a helper who made a quick grab for the wallet and scampered into the milling crowd.

Turning to give chase, he ran smack into the saffron-covered belly of a rather large monk who had been standing behind him. He looked up, ready to apologize, but the monk's twinkling eyes, and wide smile radiated humor instead of offense. Clayton decided that here was another adventure just waiting to happen. His wallet and its theft would have to wait.

"I'm so s-sorry sir," Clayton said, "just got my wallet stolen and didn't see you behind me."

The monk's voice was a cheerful baritone. "So, young master, what are you doing here by yourself? Looks like you've been taken advantage of by that young thief and his partner. Aren't you going to chase after him?"

Clayton shrugged, "No, there wasn't much in it, and he probably needed it more than me but I'm 'kinda embarrassed to be robbed like that." He looked down at his boots and sighed. "Guess I should try to find that old bodyguard and go home before it gets too dark." His earlier anger had softened, and he was feeling a bit tired from walking in the steaming heat of the market crowds.

The monk recognized the boy as the eldest son of Robert Masters Jr., one of the richest merchants with the East India Company. He also knew the general area where the family lived though he never had occasion to visit, and he personally thought the British were overly haughty and class conscious, though he tried his *Buddhist best* not to be judgmental.

He said, "I will go with you since we seem to be walking in the same direction. As we walk, perhaps you can tell me of your other adventures today." Clayton's animated conversation ended with the Abbot inviting him (with his bodyguard) to visit the Buddhist ashram in the nearby countryside at some future date.

Jim caught up with the walkers just as they drew near the gates of the compound. His voice shook with suppressed anxiety. "Young Master, you can't just run off like that. Your father would kill me if you got lost or kidnapped."

The ever-impudent Clayton grinned and winked at the man. "But I *wasn't* kidnapped, and I *wasn't* lost. I knew where I *was all the time!*" His face lost its grin and became solemn as he turned to gravely offer his hand to the monk. Clayton remembered to keep his grip firm, just like his father had taught him. Afterwards he marched past the reddened face of the still breathless guard and entered the compound through its massive iron-bound gate.

Retracing his steps, the monk smiled to himself and thought that small hand belonged to a rather remarkable young man who had a great future ahead.

Clayton rushed into the house to tell his mother about his latest adventure and meeting the monk. He figured he'd get punished for running away from his guard and losing his wallet, but this news was just too big to keep secret. He found her sitting alone in the garden under the awning that shaded the cane chairs from the late afternoon sun and heat. A tall bubbling fountain dominated the center of the small courtyard, and the moist air was heavy with scents of daylilies, daisies, hollyhocks, lavender and rose bushes. He thought, why does mother want an English garden in Bombay anyway? He just didn't understand why she spent so much time in the garden either, when there was so much to explore outside.

He stood unnoticed in the doorway and watched her reading a letter she had pulled from the thick packet in her lap. Her head was bent and her hand trembled as she reached for the cup of tea on the small wrought iron table next to her. He continued watching, unnoticed, as she sipped the tea, folded the letter, and put it in the pocket of her day dress. She sat motionless, her hands in her lap, sighed, and began to open the next one. Finally, his excitement got the better of him and he walked toward her, spilling out the details of his adventure as he approached.

She turned to him with a vague smile, and he saw the blank disinterest in her gaze. "Oh that's nice, Clayton. Don't forget to wash before dinner."

His adventure remained buried in his throat as he turned away. "Never mind, Mother. I'll tell you later." She didn't respond, but looked beyond him, towards the high stone walls surrounding the garden.

When he reached the door, he looked back, and he saw that her eyes were shiny with unshed tears. Must be some kind of grownup mystery, he thought. His shoulders were slumped as he walked down the cool dark hallway towards the rear of the house.

Clayton's good mood was ruined, but there was still time before dinner, so he decided to visit the stable and talk to his best friend, Saladin. He visited every day even though he wasn't allowed to ride the young stallion anywhere except the local exercise yard and only with his personal riding master. He loved his horse and knew that one day he would be old enough to ride outside on his own. He vowed they would ride like the wind and never come back to this stuffy old place.

Saladin whickered softly when he heard Clayton's voice at the stable entrance. He stamped a hoof, impatient for the treat he knew was coming. Saladin was a coal black stallion with an unusually friendly disposition towards the young boy. At four years of age and fifteen hands at the shoulder, the elegant Arabian looked every inch a blooded prince of the desert. The rare horse was a gift from a rajah who owned an impressive stable in Rajasthan. Clayton's father had made some excellent trading deals for the rajah who showed his appreciation with the gift of Saladin as a foal. Horse and boy developed a strong bond and Clayton hoped Saladin would be his friend forever. His father hoped the stallion would become very profitable in stud fees.

Clayton unlatched the stall door, entered, and stroked Saladin's velvet muzzle. He pulled a carrot from his pocket, broke it in two and gave him half. He whispered, "Hey, boy, someday I'll grow up tall and be with you all the time if I want to." He laid his forehead against the warm shoulder of his friend.

A month later a bored Clayton wandered to the far back of their family compound. It was an area he seldom had reason to visit, and he noticed a cleared area of pounded clay partially covered with woven mats. He was astounded to see their newly hired Japanese gardener making odd motions with his hands and legs. There was a rhythm to his movements that was almost hypnotic, and he couldn't stop watching. He stared at the dancelike moves with an open mouth until the gardener drew to a stop, bowed to the air, and folded himself into a kneeling position, one hand on each thigh. The man's back was to Clayton, and he spoke softly, "You are here, young master. What do you see?"

Clayton was entranced and gulped his reply, "Sir, what I just saw is beautiful. Almost like a dance. If you have time, I'd really like to watch you do it again or try to learn it. You can ask my tutor. He'll tell you I'm a good student and I promise to behave. What were you doing, anyway? Can I learn it too? Please, please?"

The gardener was amused by the boy's earnestness. "Come, sit and we will talk. I am samurai from a faraway country called Japan. You saw an exercise for unarmed combat we used a long time ago. It is no longer taught, and I am old now, but I remember and with my memories, I feel alive again when I do these movements. I have done this for many years. Learning takes time and much practice."

For the next ten years, while Clayton worked hard to master the jujutsu movements, he also built an inner calm readiness and confidence at the ashram that became an integral part of his persona.

CHAPTER 6
BEST BIRTHDAY GIFT EVER

INDIA – TEENAGER - 1767

Clayton was sitting by himself in his mother's garden, long legs stretched before him, fiddling with the Chinese puzzle box his father had given him for his seventeenth birthday. He had finished his jiujitsu lesson and practiced for three hours until the muscles in his arms and legs screamed for mercy. He had taken a quick bath and was now bored to death. He could only meditate so much and now he thought his brain would wither away in his skull due to lack of interesting stuff to do.

Seemed like his father was always tied up in business or extolling the virtues of the East India Company and how lucky the family was to be a part of it. A very lucrative part, his father often reminded him. His mother always seemed to be missing in action and his precious little brother Adam continued to be a pain in the neck.

His dark thoughts were interrupted by smothered giggles from behind the garden gate and its pathway just outside the enclosed compound. He looked directly at the gate but said nothing and made no effort to open it. He heard whispers and giggles again and the sound of crunching gravel. He continued to watch the gate and saw the hinge lock jiggle. A small white hand folded around the edge of the door as it was pushed open. A pretty face peered around the door and smiled at him as he continued to relax on the bench.

Clayton yawned a greeting, "Hullo, who are you?"

The girl opened the door wider and stepped into the garden, her hands clasped before her. "I'm Betsy, your mum's new personal maid." Clayton noticed the Irish accent and decided it was cute. She waited for his response but other than a raised eyebrow, he said nothing.

Not to be ignored, Betsy continued with her introduction. "I just started on Monday, and this is the first time I was free to see the garden. I have your mum's permission of course." He shifted on the bench to sit straighter as he also noticed the nice little package the young woman presented underneath the gray cotton uniform worn by his mother's female staff. *She has some serious curves and a really nice bosom.*

His heart began to race as he smiled and did his best to keep his voice calm and firm when he asked her to join him. Betsy seemed hesitant at first, though she walked the path toward him until she stood at his side in the shade of the small awning overhead. As she moved closer, Clayton realized she was older than he had first thought. He smelled her light musky sweat overlayed with a floral perfume that sent his teenage senses reeling. His lower body reacted without his permission, so he turned to hide his all too evident interest and managed to put his recent gift on the bench without dropping it. Clayton tried to hide his rising excitement at meeting Betsy. *She's so pretty, and that Irish accent sounds like music. I wonder if she considers herself a "woman of the world" because of her travels. Wonder how old she is? Will she like me enough to let me kiss her? Oh lord, has she noticed the tent in my trousers? Stop it, stop it!*

He said, "Would you like a tour of the garden? It's larger than it first looks."

Betsy appreciated what she was looking at. Not only was he quite handsome and well built, but he was also the family's oldest son. She pretended not to notice his obvious sexual excitement. Experienced as she was, she had seen it all before. She fluttered her eyelashes and looked straight at his mouth, and up into his dark blue eyes. She made her voice low and seductive as she teased, "And just how far does this garden go? We won't get lost, will we?"

She placed her hand lightly on his arm. Clayton had never experienced a grown woman flirting with him before. In fact, he never had the opportunity, but he knew it when he saw it. His face flushed when she caught his hand in hers and teased, "Maybe you should hold my hand, so we don't get separated as we walk?"

He took a deep breath. "Okay," was all he could say. They began to walk along the graveled path that led to the denser foliage at the end of the walkway.

A huge willow tree grew outside compound's cement wall and its fronds draped thickly over the wall's spiked top and into the garden. Betsy gently pulled a stunned Clayton underneath the shelter of the fronds and moved his hand to her hip with a grin. His heart pounded and his mouth dried as his hands instinctively moved to circle her waist. *I don't know what to do. Should I try to kiss her, or should I wait till she kisses me*? He had no chance to decide as she reached up, put the palms of her hands on each side of his face, and thoroughly kissed him.

He pulled her into him and lost himself to her experienced hands and mouth. He couldn't seem to get enough of her kisses, and his cock had a mind of its own, until she stepped back, glanced down, smiled, and said, "Ah, now, you needn't be a'hurryin about it."

His mouth felt swollen and warm as he stood rooted to the spot. He needed to catch his breath and decide what to do next. He certainly wanted more but was unsure of her expectations. All became clear when she reached to pull his loose cotton shirt over his head and tossed it to the ground. Without words, she smiled as she removed her full apron, and it quickly joined the shirt. She smiled again as she undid the buttons on her blouse and waited for him to understand her silent invitation. He reached out and slowly pushed the blouse completely off her shoulders, exposing her generous breasts for his stunned and breathless approval.

Betsy cautioned him, "Gently now," as his hands gripped both globes and his thumbs rubbed the erect pink buds. Clayton thoughts whirled. *Bet she knows I'm a virgin, but this part seems right.* He leaned down to gently suck each nipple. His erection felt rock hard as it pressed beneath the thin linen of his summer trousers. She reached down to grasp it in her left hand as her right rubbed against the smooth heat of his chest. The size of his youthful equipment underneath the fabric brought a delighted smile to her lips.

Betsy gently bit his earlobe and murmured softly into his ear, "Maybe we should lie back a bit, I'll just spread yer shirt and my apron over here and—" She knelt and patted the ground beside her where his shirt lay. Clayton swallowed, dropped to his knees, and sat next to her, still unsure of how to continue. She motioned for him to lie back on the discarded clothes and when he did so, she lay on her side next to him and began to stroke his chest and lightly tease his nipples. He shivered as she reached down and with one experienced hand, undid the two buttons at his waist. As she had hoped, he was naked and fully aroused beneath his linen trousers.

Clayton shuddered as she moved her hand slowly down his belly to the dark thatch surrounding his straining cock. Her teasing hand returned to grip its warm hard smoothness and a pearl of moisture glistened as she slid her palm up and down against the shaft. He gasped at the pleasure her slow stroking caused. *It's so much better when* she *does it*.

Betsy removed her hand, smiled at the awestruck pleasure on Clayton's face and licked the light sweat on his chest. She wanted his first sexual experience to be the best she could offer.

He reached for a breast and cupped it in his hand. It was wonderfully heavy and warm in his palm. Betsy began to breathe a little harder, shifted upright on her knees, and moved both her hands to lift her breasts towards his flushed face. She murmured, "Why don't I just sit on you a bit so you can have double the pleasure?" He could only nod. She re-arranged her skirts and began to lower herself onto his abdomen. Clayton removed his hands from her breasts and gripped her hips to help her balance. She looked into his eyes and reached her hand past her skirts to his thighs beneath her. She smiled down at his flushed face and teased, "Shall we continue?"

Clayton was barely able to think straight but managed, "Yes yes," while continuing to explore the generous pink mounded landscape beneath his mouth and hands.

He could feel her own heat build above his groin as she told him to put his hands under her skirt and push down his trousers. He felt a little awkward but quickly did as she asked and laid back. He could feel her hot wetness glide forward against his engorged shaft as he reached again for her breasts. The heat and the friction from her slick sheath became too much and he bucked upward and exploded in an unexpected release of pure sensual power.

He could tell Betsy didn't seem upset with his quick release and Clayton's heart slowly regained its normal rhythm. His breathing calmed but his thoughts raced. *Maybe this happens to a guy for the first time. I wonder if she has to leave right away. I should ask if we can do this again. Or should she straighten herself up and return to the chores waiting for her in the house? Did anybody see us walk over here?*

He decided Betsy would let him know if she had to leave and sat up, holding her in place with his hands around her waist. She was still on her knees, her bottom resting on his outstretched legs and her hands gripping his shoulders.

He grinned up at her. "Do we have time to try again?"

She braced her hands on his shoulders as she rose higher, then lowered herself directly onto his straining erection. It was too awkward to continue, so they stretched full length and she raised and lowered herself over his length until the warmth in her core flamed and released her with waves of hot pleasure. He climaxed again with a gasp and held her bottom tightly to him as several pulses pushed against her drenched inner softness.

Both were silent while their breathing slowed. She rolled aside and rested her head on his outstretched arm. He shifted to look down at her and pulled the uniform's parted cloth to cover her breasts. He nuzzled her neck and kissed it before kissing her flushed cheek.

He whispered, "Thank you for the gift. I mean, I've never I'll leave first so you can put yourself back together. Will you be okay?"

Instead of a reply, she stood up and appeared to admire the view of a sexually satisfied and very handsome young man. His trousers had been pulled up and he was shaking out his shirt.

She said, "I'm fine and you're welcome. 'Twas a rare treat for me to spend a bit of private time with you."

He stood up and faced her as he drew on his shirt and began to button it before asking, "Will I be able to see you again?"

She smiled as she rearranged her apron. "To be sure but we must be vera' careful with the hows and the whens." A distant voice interrupted. "Betsy, are you back there? The mistress wants you." Betsy gave Clayton a quick kiss and dashed away to answer the summons of her employer.

Clayton stood alone under the shelter of the willow and thought of what had just happened. He wanted to laugh out loud at this new and delightful discovery. He wanted to hide Betsy in his room so he could enjoy her even more. Smiling at his foolishness, he slowly walked back to the garden bench and sat in the fading sunlight while reflecting on his best birthday gift. Ever.

It was several hours before he could excuse himself from the family's modest birthday celebration. Once he entered his room, he locked his door against a possible intrusion by Adam and flung himself onto his bed. His thoughts were of Betsy and how wonderful she was. So what if she were older? She was beautiful and he knew in his heart that she must love him just as much as he loved her, or she wouldn't have even let him kiss her. He began to plan their next meeting and was still smiling when he fell asleep.

Over the next six months, Clayton and Betsy managed to sneak away to different hidden spots where they enjoyed each other immensely. He found that drinking a little brandy beforehand even added to the thrill and challenge of avoiding discovery. He continued to raid his father's brandy supply and stopped only when his father mentioned he thought a servant was helping himself. Sometimes Betsy introduced a new position to her *student lover* and if it didn't work, they laughed together. When it did work, they enjoyed each other with even more enthusiasm. Clayton turned out to be a fast learner and he became more and more confident in his methods of pleasing Betsy. The former *student* became the best lover she ever had.

One day, it all came crashing down. Clayton noticed the servants were whispering to each other as he passed, and his mother was scowling at everybody, her lips compressed into a thin line. She looked directly at him and said with icicles dripping from every word, "I had to let Betsy go this morning. The chit was pregnant. No sense at all." She glared at him but said nothing more before lifting her chin and swirling away in a dark cloud of cotton chintz and perfume.

The stark probability that the baby was his flew through his mind. He was still only seventeen, but if the child *were* his, he would marry Betsy right away and take care of her. First though, he had to find her. He cornered Betsy's best friend, Susie, to ask if she knew where she might have gone. The friend tried for several days, but Betsy had disappeared into the human maelstrom that was Bombay.

A month later, Susie quickly pressed a letter into Clayton's hand and fled to the servants' quarters.

My darling boy. Don't worry about me, I have found a good job and a home with a Christian missionary couple. They have hired me to be a nursemaid for their two-year-old daughter. After my baby is born, we can remain with the household. If I want to leave, they are willing to adopt the baby. I'm not sure what I will do yet, but all is well with me. Please don't try to find us as it would be pointless and heartbreaking to see you again. We shared something wonderful, but it is time to let go. I will keep the memory of you in my heart.

With fondness,

Betsy

P.S. Dear Master Clayton: I wrote the above letter for Miss Betsy, but she signed it herself. Please take time to reflect on your carelessness and I'm sure God will forgive you if you ask Him to.

Your Most Humble Servant,

Pastor George L. Cruthers

* * *

With time, Clayton's guilt about Betsy softened as he reluctantly became more involved with the family business. The rough lesson learned from Betsy's pregnancy stayed with him and he vowed to never finish his act of lust inside a woman's sweet heat again.

Two years after the birth of her baby girl, Betsy was introduced by the missionary couple to an Irish widower with young twin boys. Mr. Timothy Kelly was immediately taken with her lively spirit, and he viewed Betsy's baby girl as the perfect addition to a future family. On their wedding night, he was delighted with Betsy's bed sports (his former wife having been a disappointment), and the next morning he swore to the new Mrs. Kelly that he would make her happy for the rest of their lives.

CHAPTER 7
OLDER BROTHER BLUES

INDIA, ELDEST SON - 1776

"Get out of this house and don't come back!" The thundering voice of his father followed twenty-six-year-old Clayton as he angrily hurried down the stairs from his father's office. Once again, he was being blamed for the actions of his younger brother. He rushed through the front door entryway and swung himself up and onto Saladin being held by a servant waiting at the bottom of the entryway steps.

In his office above, Robert Masters clasped his hands behind him and muttered to himself before turning to his youngest son. His voice was icily calm. "Adam, I expect you to tell me exactly what went on last night and don't lie to me. I've had it with your irresponsible behavior, and you are both ruining the reputation of this family. I won't have it."

Adam turned slightly away from his father and tamped down the smirk threatening to show. "Dad— Hearing the sharp intake of his father's breath, he said instead, "Father, I made some new friends at the club, we had a few drinks and decided to play some cards. Some ladies joined us, so we had a few more drinks and continued to play. That's all. Just simple fun."

Mr. Masters took a deep breath. The scorn in his voice was palpable. "Was *Lillian* one of those *ladies* by any chance?"

His shoulders were rigid, and his face was mottled with anger at his younger son's misbehavior. He had been relaxing at his club and overheard another member telling this story to an enthralled group of men. As usual, Lillian provided plenty of grist for the gossip mill and Adam had the common sense of a bean when it came to attractive females.

Lillian was a well-known courtesan with a cruel sense of humor, and a heart of ice. Equally adept at cards and the bedroom, she was a favorite with the men, and generally ignored by their wives. It seemed that she had been around for ages and many a husband had succumbed to her charms. Whispered gossip about her activities in the bedroom continued to be passed among the men. Her skills were legendary. The mystery surrounding her origins added to her popularity with the younger set and it was not unusual to see her in the evening. The blond-haired beauty was always gaming with a group of friends, at the theatre, or on the arm of a gentleman.

"Well yes," Adam stammered, "things got a little out of hand when Lillian was accused of giving me betting signals. Of course, that wasn't happening, and I was merely defending our honor. I *was* winning on my own. I wasn't cheating, I just had a strong run of good luck."

His father interrupted. "And during the scuffle this extra playing card fell onto the floor?" He held the damning evidence aloft.

Adam's voice became shrill. "No sir. Clayton showed up at the door, barreled in and pulled the other players away from me. The card must have fallen from someone else, not me! I swear." Adam looked down at the floor, shoulders hunched over, and managed to create a look of outraged innocence on his face. *The damn card should have remained safe in my pocket*. He figured his denial would be good enough, since it usually was. After all, he was the favorite, and the baby of the family.

Mr. Masters stared at the humble stance of his youngest boy and knew it for the lie that it was. He felt defeated and thought to himself, *almost eighteen years old and still behaving like a child. Julia spoiled him since birth, but what can I do? And Clayton with his pride he will never even try to defend himself against his baby brother.*

His voice became a disgusted basso rumble. "All right, go to your room and get some rest. You are to stay away from that club and no gambling. You two have created enough gossip between you to last a lifetime. Out, out!"

Adam escaped from his father's wrath and softly closed the office door behind him. Quietly humming to himself, he sauntered into his bedroom, shoulders up and a grin on his lips. He figured he had plenty of time to bathe and change before dinner. Afterwards he could sneak out to meet his dockside buddies and check out the newest working girl at Miss Electra's.

An hour later, Mr. Masters pulled the servants' cord and ordered a dinner tray to be brought to his office. He just couldn't sit and face Julia at the dinner table while she prattled on about how Adam shouldn't be punished for such a minor incident. He already knew what she would say, "'boys will be boys'" and then blame Clayton for adding to the ruckus.

He grew thoughtful. *What is it about her constant defense of Adam while practically ignoring Clayton, our firstborn? Well, no time to investigate. I've got to finish these letters tonight and get them sent out on the next packet to the London home office.*

A servant delivered his dinner tray and put it on the desk. He was told not to return for the emptied tray. There were several letters to finish, and he didn't wish to be disturbed. Bowing his head in acknowledgement, the servant withdrew and gently closed the door behind him.

He continued writing letters to members of the East India Company questioning why they continued to ship opium along with the cotton, silk, spices and other trade items currently being offered. Lucrative or not, he felt opium was a two-edged sword that would cut both ways.

He had seen the cursed results of opium addiction down by the docks and it wasn't a pretty sight. He suspected that his youngest son was spending too much time with a rough crowd down there, though there were no reports of him using the stuff. Thoughts crowded him, *I must keep an eye on that boy. Better yet, get him married.*

Just as he finished and signed the last letter, the fountain pen slipped from his suddenly nerveless fingers. He grabbed the corner of the desk and tried to stand, but the sharp pain coursing down through his shoulder bent him double. He gasped for air and sank to his knees beside the desk and onto the oriental carpet. Dark spots danced before his eyes.

He tried to fight through the dizziness, his voice choked, "My God! It's too soon! I have so much to—" The spots merged, and blackness descended. All thought drifted away.

Several oil lamps remained lit throughout the night and shone gently on the surface of the crowded desk and its scattered papers. In the shadows near the outer wall, the crumpled form of a heavyset man lay motionless on the rug.

CHAPTER 8
A SHORT ESCAPE

Clayton was furious with his younger brother for manipulating their father once again. Adam was a great liar. He always managed to fold enough truth around his lies to make any excuse or explanation plausible, and almost impossible to disprove. His anger mounted as he rode Saladin at a brisk clip along the shaded streets of Malabar Hill. This northern part of Bombay held an enclave of wealthy British expats working for the East India Company. High brick and concrete walls, topped with broken shards of glass, surrounded spectacular gardens and the grand homes hidden within. Here, the servants departed at dusk unless further service was required. Very few were lucky enough to live in the crowded quarters at the rear of the compounds.

He spent scant attention to where he was going until he realized Saladin was tossing his head nervously, pulling at the bit. He had passed deep into the poorer part of Bombay and was about to be surrounded by a mob of chanting people streaming towards the southernmost city-government offices. He knew Bombay was not exactly a safe place for a single white man so rather than trample some of the crowd with a galloping out of control stallion, he pulled Saladin's reins sharply to the right, edging closer to the buildings lining the streets. Once there, he was able to find an open alley and quickly traversed it to a quieter street. He slowed and stopped when he recognized his surroundings. With a few strokes of his hand, and using a soothing voice, he was able to calm the excited animal.

In the distance he heard angry chanting and a gunshot.

His heart raced as he continued to head north, away from the city. Riots were becoming more common in the slum areas due to political and religious differences. Food supplies were also becoming a problem. One or two bad harvest years, and the people would be seething with anger. He urged Saladin to a quicker speed and left the city behind.

Sometimes, late at night when the oppressive Bombay heat wouldn't allow him to sleep, he thought of his future within his father's trade business and its relationship with the East India Company. As the oldest son and presumptive heir, he was expected to build the family's trading empire even higher. He felt the chokehold of the strict rules laid down by India's caste structures. Rules of the EIC. Rules of his father. Rules to be followed when proud mothers introduced their daughters (or nieces or younger cousins) with a "suitable" marriage as their goal. Perfect for Adam, impossible for him. He was so tired of their hypocrisy and was ashamed of how the English elite so often treated their household staff or even the tradesmen. Their arrogance and sense of entitlement even embarrassed him at times.

Outside the city gate, the crowds were less packed, and he saw brightly clad, sari-dressed women, some accompanied by servants, giving coins or food to yellow garbed monks. Small, ragged, and unfed urchins ran through the shifting crowd and descended on any

Westerner who looked slightly confused or who stood too long in one place. Their treble voices were always chanting, "Please mister, please! Coins for us. We show you around to best places. Cheap!" When ignored, the urchins surrounded their victim and shouted taunts or ran to their next prospect and repeated their shrill calls.

Clayton shook his head and kept Saladin moving at a slow but steady pace. The pedestrians always managed to move out of the way of the sharp hooves and stone-faced Englishman. Some only grudgingly backed away, and he noted scowls quickly hidden by pointedly turned backs. He was sensing a change coming to the relations between Britain and India. Westerners had better guard their property and their pockets or they might lose everything.

Clayton rode on, lost in thought. He knew from many past arguments that his father's temper would burn itself out by the evening. He also knew his younger brother would once again escape any real punishment. Their mother would intercede on Adam's behalf and plead for their father's forgiveness while chastising Clayton's lapse of judgement in allowing Adam to gamble at all. Clayton felt he and Adam were so unalike in temperament and looks, one of them must have been adopted. He grimaced at the thought.

At last, he reached the outer edge of the city and approached the closed gates of the familiar ashram. He hoped his Buddhist friend was inside and available to see him. He desperately needed to talk and hopefully spend the rest of the evening in quiet reflection. He had been able to receive a few lessons in Buddhist philosophy and it sat well with his other beliefs, but he also knew that in-depth study was needed to achieve even the first level of enlightenment. He would never be able to manage that, given his circumstances.

A monk with a shaved head, dressed in faded saffron robes, silently greeted him in response to his impatient door pounding. With a smile and a hand gesture, the monk took Saladin's reins and directed Clayton to the visitor's courtyard. He would wait there until the abbot could greet him properly. Just sitting alone in the courtyard calmed Clayton's spirit and his pulse quieted in tune with birdcalls and burbles of a low water fountain nearby. Fourteen years had gone by in such a flash after meeting Balakrishna when he was a boy and it had been over a year since he last saw his friend. This visit was long overdue.

Sitting in the solitude of the courtyard, he reflected on his place within his family. He knew his father would expect his return the next day. He had been thrown out of the house so many times it had become a post-argument pattern. He really needed to have a heart-to-heart conversation with his father about the family and its financial ties to the East India Company.

The Masters family had made a fortune over the past fifty years beginning with his grandfather, but lately the English parliament was becoming very unhappy with the growing wealth and influence of the upstart commoners. After seeing the growing mob tonight, he also had a strong feeling that his parents should leave India and return to the safety of English soil.

His thoughts wandered. Saladin had turned out to be the profitable stud his father wanted, but it was almost time for Clayton to step up and semi-retire his old friend. He smiled at the mental picture of his horse happily grazing or rolling in the sand as he was wont to do right after a good brushing.

A hand on his shoulder startled him out of his reflections, and looking up, he saw Balakrishna's wide smile. "Welcome, Clayton. Please join us at our meal. It's been too long since we've had the pleasure of your company. I look forward to hearing of your adventures in the outside world." His open smile warmed Clayton and did much to ease the tension in his shoulders.

After their meal, Balakrishna asked Clayton if he had continued with his physical training and still found enough time to meditate with any regularity. His eyes twinkled as he remembered the eager British child sitting at his feet as he taught his acolytes lessons of The Four Noble Truths.

Clayton replied with a smile, "Well, it took a bit of doing, but yes. With the help of my bodyguard, the stableman, and my valet, I was able to escape the house for my jujutsu lessons. Still no idea how that Japanese gardener came by his training, but I'll be forever grateful to him. It still seems strange that physical combat combines so well with a mental and spiritual side. I benefited from both I think."

Balakrishna heard the confidence in Clayton's voice and saw a healthy well-muscled body accompanied by a very sharp mind and a heartfelt compassion for others. It seemed that his protegee had done well in many ways and he hoped his future would be a good one.

CHAPTER 9
A FATHER'S FUNERAL

The next morning, a refreshed Clayton arrived back at the family compound. He still resolved to have that heart-to-heart conversation with his father as soon as possible. After handing off Saladin to one of the servants he bounded up the concrete steps to be greeted by the hang-dog visage of their majordomo. "What?" His question was interrupted by the muffled sound of wails from the servants inside.

"Sir, your father has p-p-passed away." The majordomo stood aside with head bowed, as Clayton shouldered past him and sped up the marble staircase towards his mother silently standing on its upper landing. He tried to wrap his arms around her shaking shoulders. "Mother?" In response, she stepped back and out of his attempted embrace.

Her reddened tear-swollen eyes managed to glare up at him and her voice was cold. "Your father was found dead in the office early this morning. Where were you? The servants, the constable, even your brother oh, for God's sake *everybody* has been looking for you since dawn!"

Clayton tamped down the mixture of hurt and anger at her clipped response. He kept his voice calm. "Mother, I'm sorry I wasn't here but just tell me what happened."

She sniffed into her handkerchief. "The maid brought his morning tea and paper and found him on the FLOOR!" She paused, straightened her shoulders, and raised the now sodden handkerchief to swipe at her wet cheek. "He was found on the floor beside his desk. The doctor said he passed away last night sometime after supper. He ate in his office because he had paperwork to finish and didn't want to be disturbed. He laid on that carpet all night! All alone!"

She began to cry in earnest and turned away. Her voice became cold gravel. "Go to the office. Your brother and our solicitors are there. I can't bear it anymore. I'll be in my room if anyone needs me." Her lady's maid put a light shawl over her shoulders and led her away.

A stunned Clayton sped up the stairs and opened the door to his father's office. His brother and the two solicitors who served his family with their personal and business needs rose to their feet to greet him. Adam's face had a shuttered look, but he said nothing as he looked at the floor and sat down again. The two solicitors stepped forward, shook his hand, and stiffly conveyed their sympathy for his recent loss.

Clayton moved to the rear of his father's massive mahogany desk and sat in its empty chair. He looked at the three men in turn and waited for someone to start talking. When nothing was forthcoming, he gave himself a mental shrug and began. "So, what's been done so far?" Other than a throat being cleared, silence answered him. He picked up his father's ink pen. *Guess it's up to me to start the meeting.*

"Okay, I'll start. We'll want to inform the press of our father's passing, but not until arrangements have been made for a very private funeral. Let me make it clear, the funeral service will be kept small. I will not let father's death generate a circus of speculation." Under his breath, he said "Though it probably will." *But maybe a small service could be held before the more public gathering Mother is sure to demand.*

With input from the two solicitors, Clayton and Adam proceeded to decide the more important items to be handled immediately and those that might be handled later. All four men in the room knew the vital importance of a swift transition in the power structure of Masters and Sons Shipping. Their family business held strong financial and political positions within the East India Company and had done so since Robert Masters Sr. joined the EIC in 1718 and moved his family to Bombay. After the death of his first wife, he returned to England and remarried. He never returned to India and very little was known about the reclusive owner. The company now employed over three hundred British clerks, sailors and local stevedores who were dependent on their salaries and shareholdings within the Masters and Sons Shipping Company.

Much later in the afternoon the solicitors departed, and the house reverted to an almost tomblike silence.

Clayton spent several hours writing letters to family members detailing the death of his father. His request for his father's replacement as the current Director General was added to the growing pile of correspondence to be taken by the next cargo ship bound for England. If all went extremely well, he should have a reply within three years but as the eldest son he would have to run the company as best he could. His stomach clenched.

He began to read after pulling files from desk drawers and ledgers off shelves. It was after midnight when he finally stopped. With blurred vision and clenched jaw, an emotionally exhausted Clayton decided that he didn't like the business and political trends he had uncovered. If he were to save the company from the machinations of the British Crown, he would have to quietly divest most of the family shares in the East India Company and move some of their wealth to other investments like steam engines. Perhaps increase their stock in the Bank of England.

The public funeral service ended up being much larger than he wished, since his mother had made it clear that the family business needed to show their commitment to the East India Company and their own Masters and Sons Shipping.

Everyone from board members and long-time shareholders down to the newly hired EIC employees attended. The politically connected stood near Indian Maharajas from two neighboring states and on the steps of the vast church, Buddhist monks prayed and burned incense for the soul of the late Robert Masters Jr.

* * *

Almost four years passed before their company ship returned from the London headquarters with a response to Clayton's news and requests. It included a lucrative return on investment since the contents had sold easily on the British market. Shareholders were thrilled with their profits, and each employee received a bonus. The EIC's Court of Directors acknowledged the death of

Clayton's father, and since Clayton was not interested in the position, the Company appointed Mr. Henry Addison. He arrived on the ship as their new Director General for the usual two-year term. As expected, Adam and his mother decided not to sell their EIC shares. Adam was offered a position on the board of Masters and Sons Shipping, but he declined due to his youth, and frankly, to his disinterest.

A surprise waited for Clayton with the ship's arrival. His mother informed him there was a special passenger and she would only feel comfortable if Clayton were with her to welcome her guest. Clayton was introduced to Freddie, a gentleman of modest means but impeccable breeding and business connections. She explained that Freddie was an old friend from her time in an English boarding school. He faintly remembered Freddie visiting while he was just a child, but he had stayed for only a month and left suddenly. His nine-year old mind took little note at the time, and his father had dismissed the abrupt departure as a business necessity. He still remembered his mother disappearing into her room and crying for days afterward.

He stepped forward and gravely welcomed his mother's old friend. *I might be looking at a much older version of my baby brother, Adam. Ahh the mystery of the "favorite son" is solved and finally explains all those letters.*

The Board of Directors for Masters and Sons Shipping pleaded with Clayton to remain in charge for at least two more years. A member of the board had an older son who, with Clayton's training, would be ready to run the business. Clayton agreed after a raise in salary and meeting the son's pretty younger sister. His romance finally died a natural death after she accepted the fact that he would not propose marriage. She easily found his replacement and married within three months. The scandal caused gossip for weeks.

* * *

Rumors began circulating in the clubs and salons. Adam amassed huge gambling debts and had formed an addiction to opium. He was found badly beaten near one of his favorite waterfront bars and, unable to bear the gossip, his mother and her new husband moved back to England. Shortly afterward, Adam managed to escape his creditors and joined them.

Clayton sold all his trade stocks, dividing the sales between several EIC investors. After putting aside a sizable amount, he created a second account under an assumed name and those funds were split between promising investments and the safety offered by the Bank of England. He resigned from the Board of Directors at Masters and Sons Shipping and began to think seriously about his future. At age thirty he had limitless free time.

He had made no promises of marriage.

He had wealth and he was still exceptionally good looking.

Clayton was now able to pursue his own interests, but he was tired. The efforts to keep the business profitable and growing had taken a toll on his mind and body. A stay at the ashram of his Buddhist friend might bring the peace and renewal of Self he desperately needed.

CHAPTER 10
CALLED TO LONDON

INDIA – THE ASHRAM - 1780

The early morning air was perfumed with the scent of lilies and wisteria. Pungent incense slowly drifted up in the stillness and the faint chanting of Buddhist monks created a perfect counterpoint. Clayton sat with crossed legs beneath an acacia palm in the center court of the initiates living quarters. Sun beams slipped through the leaves to caress the calm of his upturned face.

The ashram had provided the peaceful environment he sorely needed after dealing with the sometimes-brutal job of running the family business, but he knew it would soon be time to leave. Even after his mental and physical training there was still a small bubble of discontent buried deep in his mind that proved he could not make the complete commitment needed to pursue more studies. It would be useless to stay.

His reflections were interrupted by a young initiate in yellow robes who stood without comment at the outer edge of the garden. The boy held out a letter, so Clayton gestured for him to approach but said nothing as it was placed in his outstretched hand.

Letters from England usually contained bad news, so he wanted to be alone when he read it. In the dusky shade of his cell, he saw the letter was water stained, and its return address had blurred, but Clayton could read his brother Adam's name and return address well enough. He contemplated not opening the letter, but he still felt a connection to his family and began to read the dreaded correspondence.

It seemed that his younger brother had been in trouble again. Gambling, bad investments, and his growing addiction to opium had eroded his fortune to almost nothing. He continued to read:

Mother has refused to help this time, no doubt encouraged by Freddie, that beast of a husband. Mother's reputation will be ruined forever if I don't make good on some overdue loans. If you come to London, I know your reputation will help ease the pressures on Mother and together we can put things right! I promise that with your help, I'll quit the drugs, get some kind of respectable job and pay you back. Please, dear God, I need your help! I'm out of options and I might even be killed! Here is their address but I need

The letter continued along the same lines of begging and promises. It had already been well over a year since the letter had been written so he had no clue about Adam's current situation or that of his mother. Clayton sighed. It seemed that the decision to leave the peaceful ashram had been made for him. Family still came first, dysfunctional, or not. He needed to speak with his abbot, arrange transportation from India to England and contact his solicitor in London. The Cape Route meant a almost a two-year delay but there was no other way to cross the 11,000 miles of ocean. He hoped to find Adam at his mother's country estate mentioned in the letter. Terrington Lodge in Bedford, England sounded stuffy. He thought it was probably an old mausoleum of a house with leaky roofs, drafty rooms, and poor plumbing.

Clayton made ready to leave.

He dreaded the next thing he had to do. Saladin would not be making the long journey to England. He would be willing to go, but the thousands of ocean miles were just too much to consider. His old friend deserved a comfortable semi-retirement at the Royal Espadrille Turf Club. Lady Cheswick-Monmouth, a good family friend, promised to have him well cared for and his royal linage as an Arabian stud would be great advertising for her own stables.

Early morning haze hung overhead as Clayton unloaded Saladin from his travel trailer and walked him to the opulent stables behind the mile long racetrack and viewing stands. He groomed and curried him until his black coat caught the rising sun's rays. Once finished, Clayton grabbed a handful of mane and threw himself on Saladin's broad back. They trotted to the racetrack and the excited Saladin broke into a full gallop with Clayton clinging to his neck and mane. The stable boys gasped and said the man was crazy to ride without a saddle or bridle!

The twelve-year-old boy, hidden inside the man, and his best friend Saladin fulfilled his childhood dream as they flew like the wind.

CHAPTER 11
TERRINGTON LODGE

BEDFORD, ENGLAND – 1784

Clayton was thoroughly sick of travel. All he wanted right now was to stop moving. The past two years by ship to Portsmouth, England, followed by a very wet seventy-five-mile journey north by coach to London had worn him out. The roads were muddy, the rain incessant and the hostel food during the trip was awful. Why couldn't the English make a good hot Indian curry? He signed the hotel register and shuddered at the thought of climbing the three flights of carpeted stairs to his suite on the third floor. He was in luck. Two porters were available to haul his luggage up to the room while he warmed himself with a brandy in the hotel's bar. He really needed to straighten out the kinks in his back caused by the bouncing coach.

After a second brandy Clayton felt more human and less icicle. He nodded to the attentive bartender wiping up spills from an earlier customer. "Do you happen to know how far the town of Bedford is from here? Or any available transportation to it?"

The morose looking bartender continued to swab his counter but replied, "Coach comes through every three days you just missed it." When he saw Clayton's raised eyebrow and questioning look, he grinned through his handlebar mustache. "It was the same coach you just got out of."

"What about mail service to Bedford?" Clayton wanted to let his mother know of his arrival in advance.

Now the face behind handlebar was deadpan. "Yep, it's every three days from the postal office down the street you just missed it."

Clayton shook his head, sighed in disgust, and stiffly climbed the stairs to his room.

The wet weather continued for another three days. He gave up alerting his mother about his arrival and boarded the public coach. Midway to Bedfordshire County, the coach broke an axle, and he was forced to hire a private carriage. After following some very involved directions they finally approached the signpost marked *Terrington Lodge*. Two large stone pillars stood as sentinels guarding the opened iron fence and the driver turned into a well-kept graveled road winding through manicured lawns and oak trees. He saw a small reflecting pool surrounded with Greek statuary as they continued to follow the curved path past a stand of pruned cedar trees. The full glory of Terrington Lodge was revealed.

Clayton was speechless. To his eyes, it was the ugliest piece of architecture rendered by man. The massive manor house boasted unmatched turrets at either end, a dismantled portcullis acted as an extended entryway. Neither added to the beauty of the brown brick three-story house and the many windows marching across its facade seemed out of scale for the size of the building. Were those crenelations along the roofline for defending archers? So, what happened to the moat and drawbridge? Clayton shook his head and decided not to ask about its history.

The carriage pulled to a stop and his musings were interrupted by the arrival of his mother and her husband Freddie on the front porch steps. Servants rushed to empty the carriage and as Clayton stepped down, his mother walked forward, her hug stiff and brief. Her sixty years of age sat well on her, but he noticed her gunmetal eyes were blank as always. Shiny with unshed tears perhaps. But not for him. Never for him. Only for her favorite but feckless son, Adam. Freddie shook his hand and tried to make up for the awkward greeting given by his wife to her oldest son. His large smile seemed a bit forced and the handshake a bit strong.

Freddie's voice was also a bit loud. "Welcome, Clayton. What's it been three four years since we've seen you? Ah, you look great!" The man's jovial greeting seemed too hearty since he was here only because Adam might still be in real trouble.

Clayton just smiled at Freddie. "Yes, it's been a while and quite the trip. Won't want to repeat it any time soon."

With the strained greetings over, mother, son and Freddie entered the great room of the house. It was a nice surprise for the eyes. Flowered chintz was everywhere, lots of colorful pillows, comfortable upholstered furniture, groupings of plants and several small tables, topped with knick-knacks, welcomed the tired traveler. A large marble fireplace was the focal point of the room and the cheerful fire within radiated welcomed heat.

His mother seemed nervous and began to prattle on about the house. "I didn't know about it until Freddie and I returned to England. But your grandfather purchased the house and farm in 1735. Seems he made it rich with Masters and Sons Shipping and the EIC, so he bought it when he returned from India. Family papers say he became a recluse when his second wife died after childbirth, and he worked from this very house until he passed away in 1758. Your father was that baby, but he never lived here, and I never even heard of the place while growing up.

I suspect your grandfather, Robert Senior, ignored your father's existence until he reached his majority. We married your father and I, then he sent us to India." She paused to take a breath. "We were never notified of his death, either oh, this is so confusing. Anyway, my solicitors contacted us when we returned to London. We saw Terrington Lodge and just fell in love with it despite paying a horrible amount of inheritance tax. But still, it's a working farm so the place pretty much pays for itself."

Julia finally stopped her nervous chatter and looked down at the clenched hands resting in her lap. Freddie reached over to take her cold hand in his warm one and smiled with encouragement while an uncomfortable silence filled the room.

Clayton felt angry and frustrated with the long trip and the cold welcome from his mother. He put his hands on his knees and leaned forward. "Mother, I don't give a damn about this house or father's unhappy family history. You *know* why I spent over a year trying to get to England. So, tell me, where is "the wonderful and perfect" Adam? Does he even know I'm here?"

His mother looked stricken and said nothing. Finally, the loud ticking sound of the gold and glass clock on the mantlepiece seemed to provide her with the perfect excuse to leave the room. She stood up abruptly and said, "It's late. I'll arrange for tea."

Freddie looked sheepish at his wife's behavior and with a nod towards the back of his retreating wife said, "I'll have a servant to show you to your room. Please forgive your mother. Adam's behavior has become even more irrational than before, and she suffers from almost continuous anxiety." Clayton was too tired to comment and decided to skip the tea and just have dinner sent to his room.

It was three days before Adam burst into the breakfast room while Clayton enjoyed a final cup of coffee with his newspaper. He rushed around the table with a whoop and hugged his older brother who tried unsuccessfully to stand up. "Clayton, you're here! You're really here! Wow, you look great!" he gushed.

Clayton couldn't say the same about his brother's appearance. "Yes, well, I'm here all right. So, let's talk. Let's fix whatever the problem is so I can get back to London. The welcome from Mother has been a bit cool to say the least."

Adam ignored the reference to their mother. He gave his usual cherubic-like smile and said, "Ahh, you just got here but give me time to clean up a bit and I'll take you to the best Irish pub in Bedford." He spun out of the room and up the stairs before Clayton could respond.

An hour later, they were sitting in a private booth tucked away from the curious eyes and ears of the other patrons. The tankards of Guiness sat ignored as Adam offered excuse after excuse for his misfortune with business and cards. It became clear to Clayton that his younger brother was mentally unstable. His eyes were reddened, and he seemed feverish with a slight sweat on his forehead. He was twitchy and restless. After two hours of sporadic conversation, he promised to help Adam pay off his gambling debts and would also repay Freddie any loans he had made to Adam. Any new debts were his alone and there would be no future brotherly business ventures. Out of the question.

Within two weeks, the debts were settled, and Adam disappeared. Again. Clayton felt like an unwelcome houseguest and his mother made no attempt to put him at ease. Freddie spent most of his time at the farm and though he was cordial, he made little effort to act as a host. Clayton ate breakfast alone and suffered through another week of silent dinners before giving up on Adam's return. He left the house and returned to London as quickly as he could.

CHAPTER 12
LILLIAN'S TRAP

LONDON - 1784

Lillian stood in the ornate gilt covered balcony looking out over the crowd of theatre goers below. Well-bred chatter and muffled laughter drifted up through the light haze of smoke from the oil lamps placed on the edge of the stage. The orchestra had just finished tuning their instruments and began to settle themselves for the evening's performance. Her sharp gaze restlessly searched for a tall man amid the stylishly dressed crowd. Behind her she felt a stir of air and heard the whisper of expensive silk. Exotic perfume assailed her nose as she turned to greet the older beauty silently standing beside her. Neither member of their special sisterhood said a word as they nodded to each other before moving to the edge of their first level balcony.

Male heads turned up to gaze with hot eyes at the well-known courtesans, their evening escort duties temporarily forgotten. Both women smiled faintly down at the crowd as if in acceptance of the homage being offered. Both ignored the heartfelt sighs of the disappointed men below when they flicked their fans open and moved back to sit on the cushioned chairs provided.

Moments later, a young man, an acquaintance of Lillian's, appeared with glasses of champaign and an assortment of chilled sliced fruit and cheese. He hoped to win the lady's favor and join her for the evening's performance. Unfortunately, he was sent away with only her smile and a promised invitation to her next house party.

Lillian was looking for Clayton Masters. According to local gossip, he had left India to be with his family on their country estate and his arrival in London caused a torrent of speculation about his reasons. She frowned thoughtfully. Despite her invitation and obvious interest, he continued to refuse to visit her weekly salon and was rarely seen at the season's balls.

When she did manage to snag his attention, he was unfailingly polite but remained uninterested in her several attempts at conversation. He said he remembered her in India but refused to say more on the subject. Her lips thinned as she thought of that cool perfectly modulated voice continuing to discourage her best attempts at flirtation. That was an insult she would not let go. She wanted to make him hers with a fierce hunger she had never experienced before. The thoughts of his final submission and erotic nights they would share brought heat and blood to her pale cheeks.

The lights were dimmed, and the orchestra began to play their musical introduction as she caught a small stir at the far-right aisle on the mezzanine level. He was here! Her breath caught and her hands grabbed the railing in front of her. Tonight, she vowed, she would have him. All of him.

Thalia had already agreed to help with the first phase of her seduction, so she and Lillian left immediately while the theatre troupe took their final bows. The two hurried to a quiet corner of the street and watched as the crowd of theatergoers dispersed to local restaurants or other forms of evening entertainment. They stood watching Clayton chatting with an acquaintance before gesturing for his waiting closed carriage to approach. With blinding speed and a swish of silk skirts the two women entered the opposite side of the carriage as it drew to a stop.

He had barely climbed into the darkened interior when strong hands grabbed him and held him immobile as a cloth soaked with chloroform stole his breath. Hands and feet were tied tight, and a dark hood was pulled over his unconscious head. The two abductors looked at each other and Lillian smiled so wide, Thalia could see the tips of her fangs.

* * *

Clayton woke with a splitting headache and slowly realized his aching wrists and ankles were tied with silk rope. After carefully turning his head, he saw the rope looped several times around all four posters of an immense canopied bed. Carefully lowering his chin, he could see that he was spreadeagled and held immobile on a pink satin bedspread heaped with feminine throw pillows. A white cotton sheet was carelessly draped over him from hip to knee and his face flushed when he realized he was completely naked under it. Muscles strained as he pulled on the twisted silk at his wrists. He tried flexing his feet in the hope those bindings might loosen but twisting against the ropes brought more bruising and the silken ties remained tight. He began to thrash and yell with anger, but a tomb-like silence was the only response. His throat was raw, and he became aware of being very thirsty. The headache continued to feel like dull hammer blows on the back of his skull until he finally admitted defeat, eased back on his pillow and closed his eyes with a low groan.

What time is it? How long have I been here? Where in the hell is "here"? Just as he was about to start thrashing and yelling again, the bedroom door opened and a slender blond woman wearing a face mask approached the bed. She was dressed in an elaborate negligee that left little to his imagination, but thirst and a very uncomfortable twinge in his abdomen dulled any carnal thoughts her attire might raise. Her steps were light and made no sound as she glided toward the bed.

Her sultry voice was barely above a whisper. "I'll untie you and allow you the privacy of my washroom if you promise to behave yourself." She knelt on the side of the bed and held a glass of water to his lips. "Your clothes are securely stored away and there is no leaving this bed unless or until I allow it. Will you agree?" He took a small sip and tried to see who was behind the mask.

"Seems so." His voice was heavy with sarcasm, but he swallowed the rest of the cold water gratefully. She nodded and proceeded to untie the bindings before pointing to her adjoining washroom. Clayton grabbed the cotton sheet, rose from the bed, and quickly wrapped it around his middle. His back was to her, so he missed seeing her nostrils widen or hearing the sharp intake of her breath when she smelled the scent of his blood as he shuffled past.

Clayton returned to the bedroom feeling refreshed and ready to do battle with whatever this situation was. His question was asked with a sneer. "Am I allowed to sit?" She nodded but said nothing as she gestured to a chair and handed him another glass of water. He gulped down half its contents before grating out, "So what do you plan on doing with me? Am I a prisoner being held for ransom?"

The voice behind the mask was melodic. "I want you to sleep in that bed for tonight and the next two nights. After that you're free to go whenever you wish." Her dark glare through the mask's eye openings challenged him to ignore her once again. Not *this* time, she thought.

She removed her mask.

"Lillian!" Clayton gasped. "How what are you doing here?" He rose from the chair and was about to force his way past her and out of the room but once again his head began to spin. A strange half darkness fell around him as he felt himself easily lifted and placed in the middle of the bed. Silken ties were gently re-wrapped around his swollen wrists and the cotton sheet was pulled away and replaced with a coverlet from the bed.

In his daze, he felt her slip beside him, her cool body not totally unwelcome against his heated length. He lost the mental battle of trying to reconcile Lillian's beauty in Bombay with her unchanged beauty of today as her hand stroked his forehead and lingered on his lips and chin.

"Such a handsome man," she murmured as she ran her sharpened fingernail down the side of his face. The hand moved to his neck and lowered to stroke his shoulder. The cool touch traveled to his chest and paused while she gently pressed her moist lips to his nipple, sucking it into her mouth. His breathing quickened and he realized that he couldn't move a muscle if he had wanted to. The drug was in the water, he thought, as it continued its course through his veins.

Her lips lit fires on the surface of his skin as she licked and kissed her way back up to the side of his neck. Unwanted visions of lewd possibilities and sensual abandonment seemed so real he couldn't help but cry out while digging his hands into the mattress beneath him. He groaned deep in his throat when her cool hand reached down and grasped his hardening cock.

His thoughts whirled as he tried to move with the arousal building within him, but the restraints and the effects of the drug kept him almost motionless while Lillian deepened her kiss at the throbbing vein in his neck. His heart began hammering in his chest and he gasped at a sharp pain. Even as he cried out, the pain became erotic, and his body convulsed as the first throbbing wave of release engulfed him.

Lillian drank his pulsing blood and smiled as the sweet copper and honey elixir threaded its way into her body. It was exactly as she knew it would be, coming from this man, so dark, so rich and oh, so satisfying. After drinking deeply, she licked the wound at his throat, and it immediately closed. She sighed and laid her head on his shivering chest. She would be back again before morning to take just a small sip before dawn forced her to retire. She rose, straightened her elaborate night shift, and drifted to the doorway to change for the evening's entertainments. Her quiet, "I'll see you later." was barely heard and her promise drifted through the dimness of the room. With a quiet chuckle, she glided through the open doorway.

Clayton laid on the bed, his mind clouded with the aftereffects of the drug. He tried to rise but the soft unrelenting restraints still at wrists and ankles allowed very little movement. He became aware of a soreness in his neck, and rising anger swept away most of the drug's effect. He had been taken against his will to serve the insane demands of that woman. Despite the adrenalin rush, he couldn't fight the drowsiness threatening to overtake him. As he began to succumb, he remembered the incredible rush of pleasure. The faint remnants of her scent on his pillow stirred his cock to hardened life once more. He managed to whisper, "Oh Buddha." before his awareness dimmed, and he fell again into darkness. Time passed.

Lillian stood at the doorway viewing the sleeping man on her bed. Shadows and light heightened the planes of his cheekbones. His jaw, lightly covered in whiskers, made him look even more handsome than before. His sensuous lips promised to reveal hidden delights if she could take him to her without the bindings keeping him restrained. With a flick of her hand, the bindings removed themselves as she lowered herself to his side.

"You're mine again and I'll make you enjoy it," she whispered in his ear as her mouth descended to his throat and her hand caressed his still sleeping body. She bit deep.

Clayton awoke with a start, pain again mingled with almost unendurable pleasure. Lillian's perfume surrounded him, and he shuddered as her cool hands easily stroked him into arousal. He became dimly aware of the missing cuffs even as he turned aside and reached to draw her into his embrace. He quickly mounted her and with mindless need plunged into her body. Her velvet heated moistness erased all thoughts of escape.

She reached up and pulled his face to hers, eyes luminescent with the heat of her desire. Her lips closed on his neck while he screamed for his release. Again, the pain and pleasure rose to almost unendurable heights as he lost his control and climaxed deep within her a second time. Shuddering with the aftermath, he tried to push himself off, but steely arms held him captive as sweat and blood mingled in the bedsheets. He fell to her side, exhausted, but a determined Lillian rolled on top of him and lowered herself onto his still hardened and throbbing cock.

"Enough!" He tried to throw her off and used both hands around her waist to still her hard plunges. He thought of pushing her away but in his weakened state he was too slow, and she grabbed the nearest wrist and sank her fangs to drink. He screamed as he helplessly climaxed again. She looked down at him and smirked, her fangs retreated beneath her blood reddened lips.

Clayton gasped for air. "What in the hell are you doing to me?" he whispered.

"Anything I want," she responded, "and I promise that you will enjoy every minute of it." He tried to push himself aside, but a sudden weakness overtook him. "What are— " The question remained unasked as he fainted onto the strewn bedclothes.

Lillian rose and smiled down at the sleeping man. *This will be so much fun. Another night and you'll not even think of leaving me*. She hummed to herself as she left to seek her rest in the hidden chambers of the next room. She decided she wanted more than a mere three nights.

The days and nights merged into a haze of lust and pain for Clayton. Unwanted memories crowded against painful reminders of his unwilling surrender to her relentless demand for his blood and his body's craving for this unusual sexual release. Hunger became secondary and the fruit juice he was offered seemed just enough to keep him going.

After her most recent bout, he stumbled through the door of the bathroom and peered into the mirror. He saw his haggard reflection as he leaned against the porcelain sink and he realized that he had eaten practically nothing since his abduction. He was weak, but still on his feet. Barely. He touched the faint marks at his neck and both wrists. Bruises on his ribs and along both arms and inner thighs spoke to some very rough sex. He cursed her as he fully realized he was Lillian's unwilling sex slave. *Thank God, tonight, is the third night. The woman is crazy!*

He continued to stare into the mirror over the sink. Something in the back of his mind kept intruding. His face turned cold as he considered: how could he be released fully knowing what had happened between them over the last wait how *many* days and nights?

Though he felt weak from the loss of blood and lack of solid food, if he kept his wits about him, he might be able to prevent her voracious lust from overtaking him. He finished washing, wrapped the cotton sheet around him and stumbled back to the canopied bed. The sheets had been changed again and the room refreshed as it had been for the last three nights. Tonight, he vowed to drink nothing.

Lillian entered the room at midnight with a teasing smile on her lips and a carafe of red wine and two crystal goblets in her hands. She held the carafe out to him. Her voice was flirty. "We must celebrate your last night here. As I promised, you can leave tomorrow morning. Your clothes are waiting for you in the last room down the hallway. But before then, let's drink to pleasures shared and pleasures to come." She poured the wine and handed one glass to him before climbing onto the bed and sinking back onto the multiple pillows.

He took the glass in his hand and carefully placed it on the nightstand. He looked at her as her gown parted to reveal the pale marble of her naked flesh beneath. He reached over and pulled the front of her gown together. He didn't want any distraction.

"Lillian, I don't know what you think you're accomplishing by keeping me a prisoner. It won't work. I'm sure my family has been looking for me and once the authorities have been alerted, your scheme will be discovered. Your reputation ruined. A jail cell will probably be the result of this stupid charade of yours."

Instead of looking worried, she archly replied, "Oh, I don't think so. You're dead. Your poor burned body was found in an abandoned warehouse near the docks. So burned in fact, other than your signet ring, you were hardly identifiable oh, by the way, it's on the bedside table and it hasn't been three nights, it's been *five* wonderful nights of pure pleasure." She paused and in a voice of command she almost snarled, "So lay down lover. Let the fun continue."

Clayton's mind stuttered to a halt as an unseen force pushed him against the bedframe and pushed him back onto the pillows. The sheet was yanked from his chest by unseen hands. Shock and disbelief at what he had just heard and what he was now seeing robbed him of speech and coherent thought. He barely realized his hands and legs remained untied.

Lillian drank from her glass of wine before she slowly removed her nightgown and nestled against his body. She stroked his chest with the emptied glass. Her dark eyes drew him into their depths of promise and once again, helplessly mesmerized by her and unable to resist, he removed the glass from her hand and placed it next to his on the nightstand.

He turned towards her and smoothed his hand down her hip. Her cool hands removed the sheet entirely and her finger stroked his belly and lingered below his swelling erection. She shifted and lowered her face to engulf the velvet softness of the crown. Her tongue and lips stroked and sucked at it until he grabbed her head and pulled her away, trying to delay the inevitable.

She rubbed the length of her cool body against his building heat as her lips found the junction between his neck and shoulder. Fangs descended and pierced the throbbing vein as she fed deeper and longer than before. He bucked with gasps of pain and pleasure as he slid his cock into her slick and heated core, triggered her own shuddering release for the first time. Her body demanded more, and she easily flipped him on his back to ride his hardened cock until dark warmth pooled again in her abdomen. Clayton met her thrusts with his own until his climax shattered all coherent thought.

The rising tide of Lillian's stolen pleasure swept through her, and she used her inner muscles to prolong the erotic spasms. With a last gasping breath of pleasure, she released her grip on his sweated shoulders, leaned over and licked the slowly seeping wound at his neck. She knew she would want him forever and would do what it took to keep him at her side.

Lillian's voice purred, "And now, my Sweet we must complete your journey."

Her sharp nail opened the translucent flesh at the base of her throat, and she leaned forward to pull his face against the welling blood. Still under her control, he was unable to resist the rich and intoxicating smell of the deep-red droplets gathering there. Clayton fastened his lips on the building stream and swallowed.

The immense pleasure and exotic promise he found within her blood swirled through his clearing mind. He circled his hands around her waist and steel arms gripped her tight as he drank again. He shifted and easily flipped Lillian on her back against the satin pillows. He stared down at her and his lips twisted and became cruel. *Oh yes, Lillian, my journey is complete but yours will end soon.*

She saw the look in his arctic-blue eyes and tried to pull away, but with his growing strength he easily held her and drank again from the scarlet fountain. The sheer glory of her blood slipping down his throat caused him to almost scream his pleasure. Images of her hundreds of years passed through his consciousness in a tumult of fierce desires and heat. He dimly felt his loosened skin begin to tighten and fill as her blood threaded through veins and arteries. Incisors lengthened unnoticed while bruises disappeared from his flesh. His mind sharpened to pinpoint clarity. He was no longer under her control.

He realized he actually enjoyed the taste of her filling his mouth even as she whimpered, "N-no—" and tried to push him away. Her plan to dominate was beginning to evaporate as her body betrayed her. She began to weakly thrash from side to side but his hands and arms held her prisoner as her blood continued to merge with his. His anger gave him even greater strength to hold her immobile while he continued to drink from the slowing trickle. She convulsed and he felt her body grow limp. One final swallow. He released her throat and licked his lips, tasting the last smear of her lust. His smile was cruel. *Oh yes, my journey is complete but yours has ended.*

He roughly shoved her away and, leaning on his elbow, looked down at the motionless monster beside him. Her twisted face was waxlike, and she remained unmoving, but her neck wound sealed itself as he silently watched her. His mind seemed removed from his body and no emotion crossed his face as he continued to gaze at her. He had gotten a sort of revenge in draining her body but what should he do next?

He rose from the bloodied bed, entered the washroom, and thoroughly cleaned himself. After locating the neat pile of his clothing, he dressed hurriedly and returned to the bedroom. His legs suddenly gave out and he fell to his knees. *Oh my god, what just happened? What have I done?* His mind was completely his now and his throat constricted at the memory of the last few days.

He was unable to speak or move with the knowledge that he had drunk the blood of a vampire and might possibly become one himself. But was this even possible? He drank blood and loved it! No, he hated it! This being this horrible woman had not only raped his body but raped his mind. The horror of the last week stunned him, and he tried to organize his whirling thoughts.

He shuddered as he saw Lillian's foot twitch against the blood-spattered fabric of the bedding. Her pale hand moved slightly, her neck twisted toward him, and her eyes opened slightly to look straight into his.

He scooted back towards the doorway, unsure of what he was seeing or how to stop it. He knew he couldn't allow her to seduce other wretches and who knew how many victims she had drained of blood in the past.

The bedroom door opened behind him and the beautiful older woman he had seen at the opera softly closed it behind her. Her delicate perfume entered with her, but her posture and grim set of her mouth told him she was feeling anything but delicate. She moved towards the bed and looked down at Lillian's now twitching body and casually flipped the satin bedsheet over the naked woman and turned towards Clayton.

He managed to stand and prop himself against the bedroom wall. The stranger turned to him and said coolly, "You'll have to kill her. If you don't, she'll make your life a living hell as she did mine." She drew a large wooden hat pin from her purse and handed it to him. His nerveless fingers dropped it to the thickly carpeted floor. His throat was so dry words could not be said aloud. Her eyes looked intently at his face, but she remained motionless as if calculating what his response would be.

Clayton remained silent as she turned to the slowly re-animating corpse lying on the bed. She bent and picked up the long wooden hatpin as she said, "I'll help you with her, but we must act quickly."

She moved swiftly to the side of the bed and after raising her gloved hand high, she shoved the pin forcefully into Lillian's naked breast. Lillian shrieked thinly, her body spasming on the mattress, heels drumming convulsively, fingers becoming claw-like as they tried to pull out the pin lodged in her heaving chest. Her shriek abruptly stopped when her body began to turn to ash and mingle with the spots of blood on the twisted sheets.

His savior's voice held cold satisfaction. "Good riddance to bad rubbish. Always hated that woman. A self-styled queen with the morals of gutter scum. Pretending to act like a lady. Hah! A selfish and self-centered a creature as I've ever met."

The woman turned from Clayton and heaved a sigh as she approached the ashes and removed the wooden hatpin, placing it back in her purse. "You have a lot of questions, I'm sure, but I will tell you this right now. You need to rest, and you will need me to help you survive the next few weeks. You may call me Thalia, and don't even *think* about seducing me. I don't need the bother."

Clayton remained leaning against the wall while his mind tried to process what he had just seen and heard. He could feel his muscles strengthening, he could see every tiny detail of the room's damask wallpaper. He could hear a mouse scurrying between the bedroom walls, and someone was walking past the house three floors below. He looked down at his hand and marveled at its shape and admired its masculine beauty as his fingers lengthened slightly. Each hair and vein were clearly visible. The bruising had already disappeared and the puncture wounds on his wrists healed as he watched with fascination. He ran his tongue along his teeth and two small fangs descended, startling him with their sharpness.

His mental review was interrupted by a sharp twinge in his stomach pulling his full attention back to the present. He noticed the graying of the light outside through the bedroom window and felt a strong need to lie down and hide from it.

Thalia was standing as before, and her eyes were stern, her mouth set in a frown. "We must leave this room *now*!" She shoved open a window and gestured towards the bed. The mound of black ashes whirled about and vanished through the gap. She placed her hand on his wrist, her voice was sharp. "If you want to survive, come with me *now*."

He shuddered but followed her through the open doorway. She led him to the room Lillian had used earlier. It was bare except for two low beds placed in its center and he noticed the lack of windows. For some reason, it felt comforting despite the building discomfort in his belly and the strong urge to sleep. She motioned to one of the beds and said, "Lie down for a bit, I'll be right back." She moved quickly from the room as he fell, half senseless, upon the bed.

A few minutes later Clayton twisted to his side and gasped as his stomach heaved and he started to spew a noxious black mixture onto the floor. Two feminine hands holding a large copper pan caught the fluid before it could damage the carpet and a soft voice reached him, "Don't worry, you'll feel better soon." Her soothing voice became dreamlike as he fell into a much-needed sleep.

* * *

The year passed quickly as Clayton, with Thalia acting as his mentor, worked his way around the streets and alleys of London always avoiding people who might think him dead. She refused to share her real name and cautioned him to reveal little about himself to anyone. Darkness was his best friend, and until he became more adept with his new lifestyle, the rising sun or even a cloudy day would be his enemy. He learned how to select a target and take his blood meal without leaving a trace of himself behind. He abhorred the idea of taking a life, but his need for fresh blood drove him to kill and the different tastes were almost seductive. The thought of drinking from a human being sickened him to his very soul and he hated Lillian with a vengeance.

Evening's shadows were beginning to retreat, and both could sense dawn's approach while they stood together at the back entryway of Lillian's house. They had been together for a year and Clayton was finally more comfortable with the disgusting routines needed for his survival.

Thalia looked fondly at him and hugged him briefly then her voice became earnest. "Don't forget that you've drunk the blood of a very, very old vampire. You have abilities now that you might have never discovered on your own. You should be able to control the urge to drink. Practice denial until you know how long you can go without damaging yourself. And remember, never continue drinking after your victim dies." She paused, "My final wish for you is to, in time, find a love to share perhaps forever." Her sad smile pierced his heart as she turned away.

A moment later she was gone in a swirl of perfume and dark mist.

Clayton remained at Lillian's house for another year. He was seldom seen outside and became known locally as a recluse with an extreme allergy to the sun. He already had new papers for identification. Several years before, he had put money aside under another name thinking, if things in India went sour, he would have enough capital to start over at whatever took his fancy. Now, he could withdraw from those funds any time he needed them.

He was beginning to be concerned with someone identifying him despite his reported death two years before. He didn't particularly like London, and Liverpool sounded promising. With his newest skill of flying, he could hunt in both Liverpool *and* London. He shrugged. *Ah well, time for me to move.*

CHAPTER 13
A LIVERPOOL KILL

LIVERPOOL – 1786

He was angry! He had a right to be angry! His hatred for Lillian renewed every time he had to give in to his insufferable thirst. For the past two years he fought against his body's need for blood and for two years he lost the fight. Sometimes his still-burning anger with Lillian's betrayal caused him to be extremely rough, but usually his better nature asserted itself and his empathy allowed him to bring acceptance, if not ecstasy, to his chosen victim. If he were a stronger willed man, he would just seek oblivion. But he was not strong-willed enough and tonight he found himself walking through the stink of Liverpool's waterfront in search of the night's victim.

Clayton's thoughts continued to darken. He would have to remain a monster, a blood drinker he abhorred every day since his creation two years ago. A man needing to slay another human being just for his own survival. His throat clenched at the thought.

The night around him matched his mood. The stench of burning coal mixed with the ever-present nightly fog drifting through the streets. The gas lights at each street intersection struggled to cast their feeble light for pedestrians unlucky enough to be walking in the fetid dark.

Determined to become the remorseless hunter that he needed to be, he adjusted his evening cloak closer to his body, straightened his shoulders and began to whistle softly into the night. He twirled his ebony cane and continued to whistle through his teeth as if not paying the slightest attention to his darkened surroundings.

He felt a whisper of air behind and to the left of him when he turned into an alley as though taking a short cut to the next street. He ignored the overflowing garbage cans and the stink of rancid grease. Human waste and the sharp odors of spilled beer and rotting cloth added to the sweltering stench assaulting his nose. Steps quickened behind him, and he heard a rough intake of breath when the would-be thief lifted his iron bar to begin its downward strike on Clayton's unprotected back.

With blinding speed, he turned and used his cane to savagely strike the thief's raised arm. Clayton glared into the shocked and widened eyes as he grabbed, twisted, and tossed the iron bar to the ground behind them. Grabbing the thick neck with his left hand, he pulled the startled man close to his chest. Whiskey breath and bad hygiene blended with a sharp tang of fear and sweat as the man's broken arm became useless.

Trying to pull away, the man's feet scrabbled uselessly on the slick garbage-strewn cobblestone as he was lifted and pushed against a soot covered brick wall. Ignoring the pain of his broken arm, the burly man continued to use his considerable strength against the slender nightmare but now his only thoughts were to get away from the hell promised on that emotionless pale face before him. Strength drained away as he helplessly watched incisors elongate and the piercing blue eyes become pools of blackened death. Strong hands held the man immobile as the cruel mouth descended. His muffled shriek became a soft gargle.

The hunter had become prey, and it was time to feed. In his frenzy, Clayton bit multiple times, tearing flesh and swallowing the crimson tide without thought or enjoyment. His simmering anger at Lillian's betrayal burst into flame and turned his body into a mindless killing machine.

Clayton looked at the human wreckage in his arms and carried the last emptied corpse towards a pile of wet and rotting carpet laying at the side of the alley. He figured the carpet, shattered wooden crates and dark shadows would probably hide the body for several days until its stench drew the attention of a passerby. Any unhealed wounds would be blamed on the hundreds of rats infesting the area.

Without Thalia's calming influence, three more luckless pedestrians became victims before his sense of humanity returned and his savage anger cooled. He was sickened at his loss of control and swiftly returned to his darkened apartment facing Liverpool's Lord Street.

After double locking the heavy apartment door, Clayton threw himself down on the threadbare couch in the center of his living room. He stared at the empty fireplace and thought of his reckless behavior. *I can't continue like this. It makes no sense to kill for the pleasure of killing. I don't need to kill every night to survive. And, what if I get caught? Then what? I can just imagine the screaming headlines: VAMPIRES ARE*

REAL AND LIVING IN LIVERPOOL. Better get a handle on this, and soon.

He felt his body begin to slow and knew it was time to sleep. In the corner of the room almost empty of furniture stood a heavy chest of drawers. The lowest two drawers were combined into one and shared a false front. He pulled a handle and the drawer opened and slid towards him. Laying himself down, he pushed a release and the drawer slid closed and locked itself. As he began to fall into his usual deathlike sleep, he remembered the deep meditation techniques used in India. Maybe they could help him delay his need for blood every night deny his thirst until his body finally *demanded* that he take the dark drink. That's it, he thought, meditation might be the answer maybe. His excited thoughts grew quiet, and Clayton slept.

CHAPTER 14
ADAM'S MISTAKE

LONDON 1790

Adam slowly climbed up through the fuzzy and half formed gloriously pink stairway to full awareness as a bony claw of a hand continued to pluck at his shoulder. He tried to tell the hand to "screw off" but could only croak "ackkk" before his parched throat closed in protest. He levered himself up on his elbows after a tin dipper of water was held to his cracked lips. He gulped the cool liquid and managed to whisper, "More please." The water threaded itself through his dehydrated body and his mind began to drift. Again, the claw smacked him on his chin. No doubt the claw belonged to the aged voice with its simple command, "You go now. You no have money, can't stay here. Alla' time buy, buy, buy but money gone. You go *now*."

The heavily accented Chinese voice brought him to sharper awareness. As he slowly swung his legs over the edge of the wooden bunk, the room tilted, and his suddenly heavy head dropped into the palms of his hands. His eyes squeezed shut against the pain grinding its way into his skull and he groaned but the ever-present claw pulled and poked him, and he heard that screeching voice again, "Go! You not come back. Getting too sick. No die here!"

Adam's vision slowly cleared as he focused on the face floating before him and on the dimly lit room surrounding him. He smelled his own rank sweat and ran his hands through his lank unwashed hair as he managed to stand up and stumble to the door. The opium den held two rows of wooden bunks with an aisle between them. The two tiers of benches where he had lain could handle four men easily and further back in the shabby tenement, another two rows were fully occupied. The cloying smell of opium clotted his nose and stuck to the back of his throat.

Adam looked down at his tiny tormenter and asked, "How long?"

The small, wrinkled face scowled up at him. "You be here four and half days. Too long. No eat. No drink. You die. Now *go!*" The tunic-clad proprietor raised his hands to push against Adam's back, as if he might hasten his departure using force. A gnat pushing against a heavy wind had a better chance of success.

Moments later, Adam found himself kneeling alongside the den's street curb. He had just emptied the contents of his stomach into its gutter and began to feel the strong tearing pull of his addiction. He just couldn't leave like this. A little pull on the pipe would set him straight. Get himself cleaned up then go talk to Clayton. Big brothers should help. Shouldn't they?

He found his silver pocket watch, a special birthday gift from his father, and offered it to the old man. "Take this, it's worth a lot! Please?" Hopeful eyes followed the twig-thin hand as it reached to take the offered watch. He was handed a small, wrapped package in return and the old man turned and scuttled through the tenement's still opened door.

Adam stumbled along the damp cobblestone street until his rubbery legs refused to support him. Was he hungry? No. Thirsty? Not really. He lowered himself to the concrete steps of an unopened dry goods store and took a deep breath.

Misery at his current situation flooded his thoughts. *Everything I try to do ends in failure. The woman I thought to marry gets engaged to another man. Even the whores on the waterfront avoid me like I have the plague. Okay, I had a bout of syphilis, but the sweat treatments and mercury doses have cured me! Clayton is even more wealthy than before with his business acumen, but will he hire his own brother to help manage even just one of his businesses? No! Will he help his younger brother start his own business venture? No! It's not my fault that the markets dried up or my cheating partner ruined my company.* Adam knew his reputation was ruined and even his own family would probably refuse to help him. He had asked for their help too often. Self-pity and self-loathing washed through him with a tsunami of "what ifs."

Adam opened the packet of opium and swallowed it all. A moment later, he was rewarded with the quiet pink rush of euphoria. Now, he could see how things might get better if he could just get one more chance to start over.

He smiled, stretched out his legs and nodded to his boots. *I'll talk to my brother.* M*aybe he—* Adam quietly died in the doorway of the shuttered building with the emptied opium packet clutched in his hand.

Clayton was nearing his apartment when he heard the piercing whistle of constables a few blocks away. Boredom and curiosity made him sprint towards the noise. A small crowd of excited onlookers surrounded a lifeless form sprawled face up on the doorstep in front of a still closed dry goods shop.

The constables were questioning two rough looking longshoremen who admitted to knowing the victim but only as a drinking and gambling pal. They had found him collapsed on these very steps. Yes, there was a well-known opium den nearby, but they never used the stuff. The constables moved on to question another possible witness.

Clayton smelled death as he moved closer. He saw the body sprawled on the low steps. There was something about— At first his mind refused to believe, but it was his brother Adam, and he was dead.

He felt a passing sadness for the brother who was never able to fulfill his dreams of wealth and prestige. He had always sensed that something was broken in Adam's nature. He had tried and failed to fix him more than once. He drew a breath, and approached the police who were continuing to question the gathering crowd. As he approached, the curious onlookers faded back, as if to give him plenty of room.

A sergeant turned towards Clayton. "Do you have anything to say about this?" The man's voice was tired, but his sharp look took in the tall, elegantly dressed man standing before him.

Clayton's response was politely cool. "Sir, the man at your feet is my younger brother Adam Masters. Please allow me to contact my family before details of his death get printed in the papers. Here is my card. I'll make myself available for further questioning, but I really must get to my mother first, to prepare her for the news."

The sergeant glanced at the calling card and recognized Clayton's name. The family was well known and there would be no problem letting him leave the scene. His voice was respectful. "Well, sir, if you could come to the station house to wrap things up, that would be fine. It doesn't seem to be the result of an assault, more like he took his own life or overdosed by mistake." The sergeant realized the callousness of his remark and mumbled his apology immediately. He gave a nod to Clayton, turned away and began to disperse the crowd.

After his brother's body was loaded into an ambulance, Clayton strode away from the area with a clenched stomach and a dark mood. *Mother and Freddie are in the city staying with Aunt Mildred for the London season, but I am not going to rush over to break the news of Adam's overdose and death.* He already knew how the scene would play out. First, Mother would wail about the loss of her precious son, then she would faint. Gracefully. If there was an audience, she could go on for hours.

He had loved his younger brother, but the family was always in an uproar due to his crazy and sometimes dangerous behavior. Was he a bad older brother to feel just a touch of relief now that Adam was dead? Adam never apologized for causing mayhem for the family. Not ever. With a conscious effort, Clayton shut off the endless litany of his brother's failings. He needed a distraction, and he already knew what worked the best.

Strains of laughter and music pulled him towards one of many of the dockside pubs found on the edge of the city. Pale streetlights highlighted his small smile when two young streetwalkers crossed the street to approach him.

The older of the two flirted outrageously and pressed her hands against her breasts as a further enticement to the handsome stranger. Her strong cockney voice was meant to be temping. "Hey handsome! How about spending some time with us? Yer a cutie, you are. Me and my friend Jennie will give you a good time tonight. Only a few shillings for a good romp. Maybe a two fer one?"

The younger Jennie grinned at him, "How about a bit of fun? A little of the grab and tickle will put everything to rights, mister. What do yah say?" The timing of their invitation was the perfect solution to his bitter thoughts, and the sheer cheekiness of the women with their cockney accents amused him. With his charm fully engaged he said, "Ladies, if you will do me the honor of your company?" Clayton tipped his hat before offering an arm to each young prostitute. They both giggled and each clutched an arm with slightly soiled gloves as they entered their usual bar with their latest gentleman friend.

Molly thought that with luck and the barkeep's help, she might make enough money to take the rest of the night off. Her mouth firmed slightly as she considered her options. If he was stingy there were other ways to empty his wallet.

Clayton was amused while he watched the bartender pour and spike the rotgut that served as the house special and only smiled when the ladies used their own diluted drinks to toast his health. They both began to caress his shoulders and lean into him, their teasing voices promising erotic delights. Two was always better than one. He motioned for the bill, paid, and looked pointedly with a raised eyebrow at the stairs leading to the rooms above. The bartender shrugged and held out a dirty hand for the price of the room. He knew he'd get his cut later. Still giggling and chattering, the two ladies led him up the dark stairs.

The trollops wasted no time, leaping onto the stained bedding of the room's narrow bed. Each posed as if advertising their wares and with fake seductive smiles, encouraged him to join them as they began to pull the blouses from their shoulders and hiked skirts above their knees.

Clayton stood there looking down at the poor wretches trying to make a living the hard way. They were both too thin, somewhat soiled, and overpainted in their poor attempt to generate interest. He decided to be generous. He would only drink from the older woman and let the younger one escape into dreams. No one would die tonight.

He slowly took off his evening cape, unwound the cravat at his throat and tossed it aside. He was still dressed as he moved towards them and positioned himself against the brass headboard of the bed, comfortably wedged between the two doxies. He smiled into the face of one after the other, and his calm measured voice suggested they relax. Both complied easily as their eyes became blank and breath softened. He turned to the older of the two and kissed her neck as he murmured endearments to her. Her pleasure at the unusual kindness was beginning to build as a sharp nip at her throat heightened her pleasure even further. She became lost in a dreamlike vision of love and family as the blood was drawn from her slowly pulsing vein. He finished quickly and after kissing the slight puncture, it immediately closed. With his hand under her head, he gently moved her aside to rest and dream of a better life.

The younger of the two streetwalkers remained curled on her side dreaming of the puppy she had owned as a young child before cholera had struck down both her parents.

He re-tied his cravat and after settling his cloak on his shoulders and grabbing his cane, he looked down at the old-young faces while pity etched his own. He placed a generous handful of banknotes next to the guttering candle and left the room. Guilt flooded his mind. He had taken blood, not as a necessity, but as a distraction from his own unhappiness. He shoved those feelings deep, not wishing to dwell on his failures.

It was best to head home before sunrise.

CHAPTER 15
BOUND FOR AMERICA

LIVERPOOL - 1807

It was 4:00 a.m. and the early morning darkness was warm and humid. Clayton timed his arrival to be at Liverpool's dockside while dawn was still a few hours away, but he remained in the sweltering heat of the airless coach while the hired driver and his own struggling servant handed off his luggage to the sweating stevedores loading the ship. His first-class passage had been paid weeks before and the ticket was snugged securely in the inner pocket of his jacket.

He had found another employment position for his servant. He had given him an envelope earlier with six months' wages and figured it should help to soften the blow of leaving his strange but interesting employer.

Excitement was higher than usual. The paddle steamer at the dock was one of the newest and fastest ships of the British Steamship Lines. The *Calliope* would carry 56 passengers and a crew of eight. Their departure scheduled for April 23 was confirmed and if all went well, they should arrive in American in less than 23 days. Clayton smiled to himself as he looked at the paddle steamer. With its single smokestack, side paddles and two fully rigged sails, the ship looked rather comic, as if the engineers couldn't decide whether steam or wind should power her forward across the Atlantic.

The cement pier was loaded with bulging sacks of potatoes and onions, tins of sugar, tea, and coffee. Boxes of canned goods, fresh fruit and vegetables nestled close to each other, and bottles of wine and liquor, tightly wrapped with cloth and fitted into boxes filled with sawdust, were carefully loaded onto pallets, and rolled up the service gangplank. The waiting crew manhandled the pallets and quickly wrestled them to the storage areas below deck.

Slabs of beef, pork and mutton were bundled in swaths of muslin and stacked high within slatted wooden boxes. Rapidly melting ice underscored the need for a quick trip to the refrigeration units near the ship's galley. In another designated area, away from the confusion of provisions being loaded, mountains of tagged luggage belonging to the passengers still waited to be carried aboard and dispersed into their assigned cabins of the ocean-going steamer.

Clayton sat forward and opened the window slightly to peer out at the bustling crowds carefully avoiding the two nervous coach horses. The smells of salt water, sweat, horse dung and burning coal assailed his nose and his eyes smarted with the noxious smoke belching from the smokestack amidships.

After twenty-odd years in England, he was ready to leave it behind, but he did not look forward to the three-week trip at sea. Too many people in a very small area. He needed to keep a low profile if he were to feed his thirst and survive the trip. He shook his head, pulled on his kidskin gloves, and grabbed his cane.

A few passengers waiting to board, noted his arrival and saw a tall, handsome man sporting a pair of the new, darkened eye spectacles. His dark gray three-piece suit was cut in a classical Italian design that set off wide shoulders and narrow hips. Going against current fashion, he remained clean shaven with close-cut sideburns reaching his jaw. His stylish hat shaded most of his face, but the dark blue spectacles complemented the pale porcelain skin while emphasizing strong cheekbones and chin.

Clayton's white teeth flashed as he touched the brim of his hat to acknowledge a young woman boldly staring at him with fascination. She was standing in the shadows of the loading sheds with her companion, and she blushed when he caught her eye. A slight bow and his small smile sent in her direction completed the quick flirtation and he knew she would be providing him with a delightful and very special after-dinner drink. These small drinks, carefully taken from crew and passengers, should be enough to tide him over until they reached South Carolina. He might be weakened but he'd survive the trip. The thought of losing control during the euphoria of draining his victim's blood turned him cold, knowing that if it should happen, an "accident" resulting in death from a nasty fall would have to be arranged.

Most of the passengers had boarded the ship so Clayton was able to walk up the ramp at a rapid pace. He feared the early morning light and felt himself becoming more and more sluggish as he followed the white coated steward to his first-class cabin on the foredeck of the ship. Once inside his cabin, he ignored his unpacked luggage and threw himself into the tiny windowless bath closet and locked its door. Within minutes, he was deeply asleep.

For the rest of their ocean crossing, he kept to his room during the daylight hours after explaining to the purser that he was highly allergic to sunlight. Since he was seen each evening in the grand salon, no major rumors were passed around about his health. Some of the women even offered their own ointments to ease those irritations caused by any brief exposure to the sun.

Still one hundred miles from the safety of the American harbor at Charleston, the ship was struck by a hurricane with a ferocity never experienced by the ship's captain or crew. Passengers were put into life jackets and herded below with instructions to remain in their cabins. All kitchen fires were doused and anything that might shift, or cause injury was quickly stored or secured to the nearest upright. All the ship could do now was ride out the storm and hope for the best.

The gale winds and surging seas finally overcame the attempts by the crew to maintain the pressure of the ship's steam boiler. Using only the smallest bit of sail and rigging, the captain was able to keep the ship facing into the waves but, without power, the ship was now at the mercy of the storm as it blew southward and angled west towards the barrier islands off the Florida coast.

In the darkness of the storm, Clayton was unseen as he easily climbed the slippery metal stairs to the wheelhouse. He mesmerized the captain into letting him remain and stood with him and the navigator while calming their unspoken fears with thoughts of his own. He admired the captain's bravery, but saving the ship and its passengers would be challenging. If they were lucky, the ship would avoid gutting herself on a reef or getting stranded near an uninhabited coastal island.

Time seemed to crawl slowly but finally the hurricane loosened its deadly grip on the *Calliope* and veered to the northeast. The strong winds lessened, and the crew was able to raise both sails until the boilers could be brought back online. With the wind now in their favor, the captain was able to maintain a southwest heading while the cabin crew reassured passengers and cleared away clutter. The musicians played their brightest songs while the hungry passengers enjoyed their first hot meal in twenty-four hours. The remaining crew began to repair what damage they could to the rest of the ship, but the boilers remained inactive.

The sun was about to break through the early morning clouds and Clayton hurriedly complimented the captain and retreated to his darkened room. Sleep was claiming him as he stumbled into the bath closet that would hide him safely until dusk. He slept deeply and rose at twilight after hearing the deep blasts of the ship's horn.

Land was sighted but the passengers' joy in their arrival faded as the captain confirmed that Cuba was their next port of call.

CHAPTER 16
CUBA

HAVANNA - 1807

The shaken passengers clustered together in small groups and stood silent as the crippled ship was escorted to Havana's nearest available dock. Hawsers were thrown and made fast, the passengers' gangplank lowered, and the ship's crew moved through the crowd with encouraging words. There would only be a few days' delay while other transportation was arranged to get the passengers to their original destinations and the steward assured them that all efforts would be made to deliver their luggage into proper hands.

Havana's mayor boarded the ship and spoke briefly to the captain. Until the Calliope's departure, rooms in Havanna's finest hotels would be available. The passengers could continue their travel to Charleston, South Carolina or, if they preferred, Spanish-held St. Augustine in Florida. Since both destinations were served by the ship's company the adjustment wouldn't pose a problem.

Now that they felt reassured, the passengers became restless and called out questions to the captain and mayor. Someone in the crowd yelled that he would not stay another minute on a sinking ship and attempted to rush from the bow onto the gangplank. He was pulled aside by an alert crew member and escorted away from the agitated crowd, but the remaining passengers surged towards the side, anxious to leave, and it was only with determined effort that the ship's captain and crew managed to avert a panic.

The last of the passengers and their sodden luggage had been taken off, placed into pony carts, and taken to the designated hotels before Clayton emerged from his darkened cabin and walked on silent feet towards the deep shadows at the stern of the ship. He briefly considered taking a small drink from an idling crewman smoking a cigarette as he leaned against an enormous pile of twisted wire. No one would see the attack and his damnable thirst was making itself felt. No, he thought, No, too soon. Best to get off the ship immediately.

Once onshore, Clayton asked one of the town volunteers to take his luggage to the hotel assigned to him. He would register later after things had calmed down a bit. The volunteer shrugged, took his luggage, and disappeared into the small group of remaining onlookers and longshoremen.

Clayton forced himself to walk at a normal speed as he wove through the Cuban crowds enjoying the beautiful early evening. Pulsing music from one open area drew a small crowd of partygoers and several couples held each other tight as they danced. Cantinas had their doors and shutters open to the cooling breeze from the ocean. Everywhere he looked, it seemed people were laughing, talking, drinking, or dining on the delightfully pungent food.

His thirst continued to slam against his control before he found a quiet side street that looked like it might take him towards another area of the waterfront, an area not as well-lit as the town's busy square. His nose took him to the fish market where the buildings were shabby, and rats were busy dining on the offal escaping the garbage bins. A night-shift worker was pushing his bloodied broom towards a trench-like drain cut into the middle of the alley. A tall water tank and hose stood ready to sluice the smelly mixture down its length and into the bay. Clayton shrugged at the sight and thought, it's a smelly but effective way of keeping the walkways clear.

Clayton could not deny his building thirst any longer. With blinding speed, he launched himself towards the unsuspecting broom pusher, grabbed him from behind and pulled him into a darkened doorway. His thirst left no time for niceties as he drove his fangs into the side of the man's neck and drank deeply. The rush of pumping blood to the back of his throat made Clayton almost insane with the pleasure he had to deny himself while onboard the ship. He pulled the man even closer into his arms as he continued to drink. It was only when he felt the heart was failing that he released his victim, a pitiful heap of limp flesh in dirty coveralls.

Remorse filled Clayton as he looked down at the near empty husk of a once living human being, but he forced his feelings aside as he picked up the inert body, slung it over his left shoulder, and leaped up to the catwalk circling the water tank. His whispered "Thank you" before dropping it in was heard by only a few seagulls. He looked down at the body as it floated briefly until water soaked into the clothing and it sank from sight. He knew he would never survive if he dwelt on things he couldn't change and with a twinge of regret, he dropped off the edge of the water tank's catwalk to the cement below.

Since the night was still young and he felt refreshed with the new blood being absorbed into his body, he decided to walk around, look the town over, and enjoy the sights. If he got lucky, he just might meet a willing young thing for a bit of fun. It had been a while, and a man had certain "needs". He smiled to himself, thoughts of blood forgotten, replaced with a vision of soft willing flesh and perfume.

Several nights passed and he treated himself to everything Havana and the outlying towns had to offer. He toured the churches and opulent gardens and was invited into many of the stately colonial homes. He casually introduced himself to the city's prominent members during a town hall meeting and entertained them later at recommended restaurants. He listened to local gossip and to stories told around late-night fires. He pretended to drink the island rum while encouraging the locals to tell stories of their island life.

He learned Cuba's rich soil, heat, and moisture was perfect for growing sugarcane and tobacco. He learned of the damnable but lucrative slave trade routes between Africa, Cuba, America and even England. It seemed obvious to him that slave labor meant enormous profits, but it felt so wrong to him. He had read about the English parliament discussing a slave trade act and wondered if it might finally vote to abolish the practice. It was past time but only the future held the answer to that hotly debated question.

It was evening. Clayton had fed earlier and was restless with inaction and no discernable goals for pleasure. He wandered toward a group of locals seated around their bonfire and nodded at a few faces he recognized. They made him welcome by offering him the last of their local rum and a vacant place on one of their logs. Legends and ghost stories seemed to be the entertainment for the evening, and now it was after two o'clock in the morning. Most of the group began to shuffle off to their homes and the fire was beginning to die to embers when a very old woman of indeterminant lineage joined those remaining.

One hand gesture from the new arrival, and the rest stood up and hurried away. Her sharp eyes fastened on him, and she moved towards his log. She sat next to him without invitation and said nothing while making herself comfortable. She began to speak. Her voice was cracked with age and held an accent completely foreign to his ears. "I haven't seen you around here before. What do you think of our little island? Lots of history, lots of mystery."

Clayton said nothing but looked at the ancient face and found it strangely fascinating. Her scent did absolutely nothing for his senses. How could this be? So unexpectedly strange.

The old woman continued, "Did you hear the story about our famous ceiba trees tonight? We call them kapok trees, though. In fact, there's one right over there." She smiled and pointed her bony finger at a massive trunk surrounded and supported by exposed roots the size of small whales.

Clayton was captivated by the voice and manner of the stranger and his interest was piqued after being bored for the last few days. He was ready for this unusual entertainment and said, "I haven't had the pleasure. So, what's the story that goes along with their fame?"

She began to speak as she looked, not at him, but at the surrounding darkness. Her soft voice told of the tree's value. She explained how its fruits provided soft fibers used to stuff pillows and mattresses. She paused and poked the embers of the fire with her wooden cane before looking straight into Clayton's eyes and began to tell the story of a tree that was very special to her Mayan ancestors.

He was entranced as he listened to her and watched the shifting rainbow-like aura glowing around her tiny body. She spoke of an ancient culture who believed that the giant ceiba tree was a symbol of the Universe. The roots reached down into the underworld, the trunk represented the middle world where humans lived, and the branches represented the upper world or heaven.

She paused again, stood up and straightened her back. "But that's not all I wanted you to hear."

He shifted on the log and stretched out his legs towards the dying fire and said, "You want me to hear what?"

The crone didn't answer but withdrew a handful of pale white dried twigs from a satchel and threw them onto the glowing coals. Green fire ignited, rose high and quickly died. As she leaned forward to gaze into the remaining embers her face seemed to glow a hellish red before returning to its natural dark brown. The night's soft breeze stopped suddenly.

"I *know* what you are, Clayton Masters, and you don't live in *any* of those special places. You exist *between* life and death. Heaven will never receive you unless your deeds outweigh your undead nature. I can feel your clouded and unhappy past, but I see a possible future that *can* be a good one." Clayton could not say a word in response, but he knew for sure, he had *never* told her his name.

"I will offer you this future because I sense a deep regret and anger at what you've become. You did not make this choice yourself, so I will give you another, though there will be a small sacrifice on your part."

He was amazed at what he heard and wanted to believe every word she said. He lowered his head. A few tears, faintly tinged with blood, dropped onto his clasped hands. She waited patiently for him to compose himself and reached for his hand. She grasped his fingers and he saw the shiny blade of a small knife lightly pressing against his wrist. Surprisingly he didn't try to pull away. "W-what are you planning to do?" he asked.

Her voice was almost a whisper. "I can help you, but I will need some of your blood to begin."

Clayton was tempted to pull his hand away. *Wait a minute my blood? Can I trust her?* He finally nodded his acceptance knowing he was damned if he refused to trust her, but remained damned if he didn't accept the promise of change.

A sharp slash of her blade and she caught his dripping blood into a tiny bowl held in her hand. She covered the bowl tightly and placed her hand over the cut on his wrist, pressed and withdrew. The blood ceased to flow at once, and he watched the wound disappear.

The old woman struggled to her feet and walked towards the huge tree. She used her bloodied knife to scrape bark from the kapok's massive trunk and drew a series of glyphs into the exposed cambium. A white feather coated with his blood appeared in her hand and she began to paint over the deep scratches. When she finished, she looked over her shoulder at him.

"I'm called Mother Isabella. If you want to hear more of what I have to say, come to me here at midnight five nights from now. I will be nearby watching for you. If you don't come, you will not see me or this blood again. *Ever.*"

Clayton tried to make sense of what had just happened and said nothing as she shifted her satchel onto her shoulder and slowly walked away. The few streetlamps lining the city park seemed to avoid casting their light on her stooped form, and she faded into nothing as he silently watched from his log perch next to the dead ashes of the fire.

Several times the following week, Clayton sought the brothels, and the madams provided only their best working girls available. The shrewd businesswomen soon learned he was very generous with his money, and the girls had no complaints. It was puzzling to them, though, that he had no favorites like other customers. He entertained each temporary companion with dinner and other amusements before taking them to his own rooms for the rest of the night. The ladies were always politely returned before sunup with memories of intense pleasure. They figured a slight bruise on the neck or wrist was worth the price paid for an entertaining and lucrative evening.

He managed quite well with taking only the small drinks to slake his thirst, but his need for blood was like a toothache that wouldn't heal. He was determined to use only those professional ladies of the night because he vowed never to fall in love with someone he might hurt with his passion. He admitted to himself that anger at Lillian's debauchery sometimes caused him to go too far and with his anger and blood lust out of control, he drained his victim to the point of death.

His dilemma still had no solution on the final night Mother Isabelle had told him to meet her. He lingered at the foot of their kapok tree watching for her, his mouth dry with anticipation. He saw her look directly at him from a distance and he saw her smile and nod though he knew he was completely hidden in the shadows. She slowly walked towards him, her aura shining brightly.

She lifted her arm and crooked a bony finger towards him. "Come." Without saying another word, she turned and walked toward the far end of the same field where they had shared the bonfire before. He followed, almost compelled against his own will to keep pace with her rapidly disappearing figure.

After walking for a half hour, they stopped at the foot of the largest kapok tree he had ever seen. The roots digging into the soil were higher and wider than two men standing side by side. The leafy canopy of the two-hundred-foot tree rustling in the night's soft wind could barely be seen even when he looked straight up its vast length with his preternatural eyesight. He peered closer at the smooth bark at the base of the tree. Hundreds of glyphs had been etched into its flesh, and some of them seemed very, very old.

"Sit." She demanded and motioned for him to sit on the ground between the two largest roots that extended wing-like for several yards.

"A woman of few words," he mumbled as he carefully lowered himself. He was mildly surprised when his shoulders didn't touch either of the massive roots and saw they were quite higher than his seated self. He rested his back against the tree's smooth trunk as he straightened his legs and waited for her to speak again.

Mother Isabella knelt before him and opened the woven sack she had been carrying on her back. "You have traveled many dark roads, but now I will give you the way to shed light on those roads. You can become a day walker."

Clayton was stunned to silence at what he was hearing. Day walker? He had never heard of such a thing. He realized he was very young in vampire terms, but surely, some stories would have made the rounds. He nodded at Mother Isabella. "Please ma'am, please explain what you mean."

She smiled at his politeness. "I know you are the undead but there is an aura surrounding you that says you are deeply unhappy. I can't remove your need for blood, but I can make it possible for you to enjoy the sight and feel of sunlight on your body. You will be almost human but there will be some small discomfort. It will be tolerable." She paused to take a breath while arranging a few items on the emptied sack.

She handed him a small brown glass bottle and gave her instructions. "Once you take the first sip of this elixir, you must continue to take a small sip every morning just before you sleep. You must do this for one full year. She paused for breath and continued, "If you miss even one daily dose you must destroy the bottle when you rise for the night but at least you will be able to live as you do now. Nothing will be changed but there will be no second offer."

He looked closely at the bottle. It was a clear brown color, and the size of a pint that usually held brandy or whiskey. There was a cork stopper and a label with strange writing and symbols on it. He raised his face questioningly to her but said nothing.

Her hands reached into the satchel again and she handed him a piece of parchment. "These are the instructions for making more of this elixir and a list of the ingredients. If someone else tries to read the label or the parchment, both of these will turn to ash. Remember, once you begin to take this elixir you must take it for one full year. After that, you can greet the sun every day without fear. You will seem like other men but you will still need to take the blood and there may be a little discomfort. Two things to remember: this elixir will not work for another such as you and if you miss one dose, destroy the bottle and parchment immediately after you rise."

Clayton's mind was spinning, "Wait what do you mean about 'a little discomfort?'" She ignored his question as she struggled to her feet, gathered the scattered items, and placed them in her satchel. He heard her faint laughter followed by a "Don't worry!" as she moved away into the darkness. He looked at the small bottle in his hand as he sat, still trying to understand her surprising offer. A frown settled on his lips.

Should I continue my so-called life as it is now, or should I become a slave to this elixir for the required year? And what if it doesn't work? What if I'm forced to miss a daily dose? Is the chance to walk again in the warmth of the sun worth my possible death if it doesn't work?

Questions without answers continued to swirl around in his head until the darkness began to dim with the promise of a misty dawn. He pulled himself up and stepped away from the roots of the tree. His feet barely touched the ground as he sped towards the town and the promised safety of his room at the hotel. He knew he had waited too long before returning.

He felt the sun on his gloveless hand when it gripped the doorknob to his room. A quick searing pain, and he was inside his darkened retreat. The bright morning sun drenched the front of his hotel with the first of its heat as he was shutting and locking the door behind him. He fought to stay awake as he stumbled towards the bed, slid underneath, and pulled its dark covers back into place.

Sleep was threatening to draw him down, and with his last bit of conscious energy, he managed to sip from the brown bottle and plug it again with its cork. The bottle, still gripped in his hand, landed on his chest as deep sleep overtook him.

The blackout curtains were tightly closed, and the hotel's staff were aware of his unusual sleeping patterns. No matter, they thought, the poor man was highly allergic to the sun, and he paid extremely well. Plus, he treated the staff favorably and didn't make any odd requests, only that they never interrupted him during the day.

Clayton continued to follow Mother Isabella's instruction for the required year, but he never saw her again. On morning three hundred sixty-six, he prepared to move to his usual sanctuary under the bed when he realized his body wasn't demanding that he sleep. He moved the blackout curtain aside, gritted his teeth and put his hand out the opened casement window just as the sun made its usual robust appearance. A tingling sensation but no pain! He withdrew his hand and looked closely. There was a slight coloration on his skin, but it looked more like a very light tan rather than the deep burn he expected. His thoughts whirled as he dressed quickly, eager to face the day with his new ability.

The manager of the hotel greeted Clayton with a surprised, "Oh, good morning! Is everything to your liking? Are you well?" He stopped polishing the registration countertop as he smiled his welcome to his unusual guest.

Clayton's response was almost jaunty, "Yes, thank you. I'm fine now and look forward to many more of these sunny mornings. Your establishment is quite satisfactory, and I'd like to extend my stay for another month if possible."

The manager quickly replied, "Oh, yes of course, Señor. It is no problem at all."

CHAPTER 17
A GOOD HORSE - A GREEDY WOMAN

A week later, Clayton dressed in a light cotton shirt and linen pants similar to what the local plantation owners wore. He stepped into the morning sun and was almost run down by a man shouting for his horse to behave as he sawed on the reins and cursed. The horse was sweating, and blood trickled from the bite of the cruel bit in his mouth. Foam and blood spotted the heaving sides of the animal from wounds made by the silver spurs on the man's knee-high leather boots, and the horse's eyes were wild with pain and fear at the harsh treatment it was receiving.

The horse was pulled to a stop and Clayton looked up at the man with a frown. "Señor, what are you doing to this fine animal?"

The panting horse shuddered and lowered its head. The rider looked down his nose at Clayton's question and sneered as he answered. "It is none of your business what I am doing. But since you asked oh so politely, I will tell you. I am Estacio Carlos d' Escobar and this "fine animal" as you say, will not obey his master. And *that* would be *me*."

Clayton wanted to pull the arrogant man from the saddle but said nothing in reply as he stepped back to view the sweating horse from a different angle. *This animal is a beauty but obviously has been mistreated in the recent past, probably by that idiot sitting in the saddle.* He mentally centered himself before asking, "I'm unfamiliar with this breed, what is it?" He resisted the urge to put out a hand to calm the sweating and still nervous animal.

Estacio's obvious sense of superiority rose with each word, "Well, if you must know, it's a Hanoverian stud, given to me by my very good friend the Duke Franz Zelenski of Prussia.

He is a warmblood, registered as Noble Haus von Mecate's Prince." The disdain while speaking to the rude commoner threaded throughout his reply.

Clayton couldn't hold back anymore and with cold calmness said, "Well, Estacio Carlos d' Escobar, if you continue to beat that horse into submission, you'll only have a corpse left to bury. This proud Prince will never willingly respond to such ill treatment."

Surprise at the arrogance of the Englishman's comment as he gently touched the animal's lathered neck, crossed Estacio's face. Nobody could speak to Estacio Carlos d' Escobar like that! Without waiting for another word, he dug his spurs into the bloodied sides of the horse and charged up the street towards the Governor's palace.

Clayton stood lost in thought. That horse was a beauty, and he didn't deserve such a terrible owner. A plan began to form in his mind, how might he rescue the horse without drawing the wrath of Estacio Carlos d' Escobar or his family? A competition, a card game? Or, on the other hand, accidents can happen in the most unlikely places.

A week later, Clayton finalized the purchase of twenty acres of land and ordered a small barn and corral built. A well was quickly dug and would supply plenty of fresh water for the cement horse trough built nearby. Five acres of the property were enclosed with sturdy white fencing and the short road to the barn was lined with fast-growing flowering shrubs. The teams hired by Clayton were excited to be working on such a project and for such a compatible employer. They finished in record time and Clayton started the next phase of his horse rescue.

While the property was being made ready, Clayton learned all he could about the proud d'Escobar family and its financial holdings on the island. Estacio loved to gamble and made wagers that were reckless and costly, he would also cheat occasionally and was rarely challenged about it. The young man was spoiled to the point of cruelty and his horse wasn't the only thing to feel the whip. Field slaves sometimes disappeared from their plantation without explanation and local gossip hinted that they were probably beaten to death and buried in the muck of a black- water swamp a few miles away. Parents cautioned their daughters to never be alone with him but sometimes one heard of a daughter quietly sent to distant relatives on the mainland or married quickly into a less desirable family.

Clayton's plans included a party for his acquaintances. He reserved the ballroom at Havana's largest hotel, had it lavishly decorated, hired musicians, and set up a buffet that could feed at least a hundred hungry guests. There was a small open room adjacent to the ballroom that women sometimes used to refresh themselves away from the crowded dance floor. This time it was converted to a gambling area and was made more inviting with decks of cards placed on the baize covered table. Various bottled liquors, cigars and one strikingly beautiful woman would serve the guests who chose to use them. Clayton was ready for his big show.

What happened next kept the city's gossip grapevine active for weeks. Estacio Carlos d'Escobar lost Prince, his best horse, to Clayton Masters during a high-stakes poker game. One witness breathlessly told his version to anyone who listened, "Estacio kept drinking afterwards and kept saying he was cheated. He just would *not* listen to reason. He kept yelling at Mr. Masters, drew his pistol, and shot him, point blank! That pistol ball looked like it hit Mr. Masters square in the chest, but it couldn't have been *too* severe. He was up and walking around the next day." The other card players and those observing the previous game knew that cheating had not taken place. Definitely *not!*

Several days later, Estacio Carlos d'Escobar was found by his plantation foreman hanging from the lower branches of a young kapok tree. The suicide note detailed how sorry he was for the shame he had caused his family. The town mortician thought it strange that the body lacked much of its blood but said nothing. Nobody other than his immediate family really cared. Estacio was not well liked and was a known liar and bully. The town was well rid of him.

The head of the d'Escobar family insisted that Clayton accept Prince since the family's honor demanded it. The father hated the horse anyway because it reminded him of his son's foolishness, and he wanted him removed from the estate as soon as possible.

With Clayton's patience and simple re-training during the next several months, the intelligent Prince regained his original temperament and began to trust his new master. The two were often seen on the boulevard, the Englishman sitting straight but relaxed in the saddle, the horse proudly showing his different dressage gaits.

The town fathers happily accepted the donation of the twenty acres and added another thirty to create a small equestrian park where everyone was welcome to ride or picnic.

* * *

After two years in Cuba, Clayton felt it was time to leave and continue his trip to America. This was his last evening. His ship would leave for Charleston, South Carolina, on the next tide. He relaxed in the gathering darkness, smoking one of his slim cigars, his hired companion for the evening sitting on his lap and whispering sweet suggestions into his ear. His hunger was beginning to stir. Clayton caressed her cheek. "Anita, would you care to walk with me to the beach tonight? Just look at that moon! Since tonight is my last evening here, it'd be a shame to ignore it."

Anita put down her mug of iced sangria. She was only too happy to walk with the handsome Clayton Masters. He always paid so well. Calculating thoughts circled. *Such a fine man and so rich too! Maybe he'll give me a going away present. Maybe a nice expensive going away present!* This time her smile wasn't forced and in her light Spanish accent she murmured, "Oh yes, Señor, I shall like to walk the beach with you."

She held his arm as they slowly walked down to the beach. They strolled along the firm sand gently being touched by lapping waves and they continued to walk in silence until he stopped and smiled down at her, his teeth gleamed in the moonlight. He gestured towards a small grove of distant pines, hugging the edge of a sharp cliff rising above the crashing ocean waves at its base. "Shall we walk to that cliff before turning back?"

She looked at him with a knowing smile on her lips. "Of course, Señor."

They continued to walk in silence, stopping occasionally to kiss and tease until they reached the end of the beach. He held her hand as he led her up the shallow steps cut into the face of the limestone cliff. After following the steps winding back and forth, they finally stepped into the shelter of the small pine forest. Fragrance of pine and ocean drifted across his face and Anita's musky scent combined with jasmine sent his senses reeling. He wanted to take *everything* from her tonight.

He bent to taste Anita's moistened lips but changed direction slightly to tease and nibble at her neck. She groaned as she responded by pulling his face back to hers and plunged her expert tongue deep into his mouth. She was surprised to feel herself becoming unusually aroused and soon forgot about expensive presents or extra money as she felt his lower body respond to hers. She pressed herself full length against him, trying to satisfy the unexpected lust that was quickly building.

Clayton stepped back, removed his linen jacket, and dropped it. He swept Anita off her feet and lay her down on the jacket spread on the cooling sand. He stretched out beside her and spread her dark hair against the pillow of his arm while one hand reached through the thin cotton of her blouse and caressed her breast. After pushing the fabric down, he licked and kissed the dark pink nipple exposed to the moonlight and murmured lovers' nonsense into her ear. She shivered with heated anticipation and reached her hand to the hard length of his cock, her impatient gasps reflecting her urgency to be filled completely.

He ignored his own building lust and moved his hand to the rich moisture between her loosened thighs. She twisted against his hand and moaned in response.

"Delightful," he murmured into her ear before biting deep.

Anita's blood was rich with iron and reflected the hot warmth of the Cuban sun. The lust-filled beat of her heart pushed it into his eager mouth, and he swallowed rapidly until the beats slowed. Sanity slowly returned when he pulled his lips away from the seeping wound and watched closely as the heart stuttered to a complete stop. One last stroke of his tongue and the two puncture marks closed completely.

He felt some regret but not too much, the woman was greedy and had a reputation of cheating her customers. But still it was a life cut short. He carried her limp body to the edge of the cliff overlooking the ocean and threw it easily into the surging water below.

A few hypnotic suggestions back at the at the cantina and his last walk with Anita was forgotten.

CHAPTER 18
CHARLESTON ARRIVAL

CHARLESTON – 1809

South Carolina's heat and humidity hammered Clayton like a fist as he prepared to leave the covered deck of the steamship now resting in the Charleston harbor. Just moments before, he had said his good-byes to several of the passengers he had met onboard. In the shadowed overhang of a steel walkway, a very pale and slightly dazed young woman was seen crying into her handkerchief as he held her close and seemed to whisper into her ear.

The matrons sniffed at such a public display of emotion. The men wondered what caused such a fine-looking woman to cry on Mr. Master's shoulder. The observers politely looked away and resumed their exodus from the ship to the waiting pier. Clayton dabbed a tiny smear of blood from his lower lip and suggested that she forget all about him and their special last night together.

Their ship was one of several that plied the Atlantic between Cuba and Charleston or the more regularly scheduled New York City-Charleston route. Other ocean-going vessels were loading or unloading, and the piers were crowded with milling people gathering their luggage, hugging family members, or hailing porters. Frazzled mothers grabbed curious children before they were trampled by excited horses or fell into the low swells of the filthy water splashing against the pier's cement columns.

He deadened his hearing to a bearable level and looked around for an empty cab. After seeing one at the far edge of the crowd he beckoned to its driver and motioned him over. In a moment, the man was offering to take Clayton to a highly recommended hotel and for a modest daily fee he would be happy to provide his personal services full time.

The "highly recommended" hotel had seen better days, but its location was perfect. It was away from the main thoroughfare and surrounded by buildings partially filled with tenants or businesses that usually closed by seven o'clock. Charming pocket parks and well-kept brick lined alleys with bright flowers or trees in pots could be seen as the carriage neared the hotel. Once inside the Charleston Inn, Clayton signed the register, had his hand luggage moved to his room, tipped the porter, and returned to the pier to make sure Prince would be safely unloaded.

As the carriage approached the loading docks, he heard Prince scream with fear. He cursed, jumped from the cab, and pushed his way through the small crowd beginning to form. They were watching a beautiful horse being unloaded from the steamship in a harness contraption that now hung over the open space of water between the ship and the dock. The huge horse was thrashing wildly and might injure himself or worse, might manage to break free and plummet into the dirty water surging below.

As Clayton approached, the crowd seemed to clear a path between him and the terrified horse dangling above the water. He broadcast his thoughts to the distraught animal. "Prince, be still. I am here. I see you. We will be together soon. Be still. Be calm. Soon now." The horse may not understand his master's words, but his soothing voice calmed the animal. He ceased his frantic kicks which allowed the stevedores to pull the sling over to the dock's solid surface and gently lower the hawsers to the concrete below. Trembling, but safe on all four hooves, the sweat-lathered animal lowered his head and heaved such a breath that several onlookers chuckled quietly to each other. "Yep, that horse is happy to be back on ground again and ain't he a beauty!"

Clayton approached Prince and removed the canvas material binding his eyes. The horse whickered softly and lowered his head to nudge his shoulder. He stroked the velvet muzzle as he spoke, "Hey, boy, you're okay now and I think you're going to like it here." The close bond between the horse and his master-friend remained.

Mr. Early, Clayton's hired cabbie, recommended a stable fairly near the hotel. He dumped the horse's tack into the back of the cab and a lead-line was attached from Prince's halter to the iron ring set into the rear. They moved at a walking pace down several quiet side streets and took some short cuts to the stable so Prince could regain his balance and loosen his tight muscles from the ocean voyage. A short while later, he was happily ensconced in a box stall with fresh hay and a bucket of clean water.

After saying goodbye to Mr. Early, Clayton left the stable and decided to stretch his own muscles by walking the three blocks to the hotel. He climbed the two flights of stairs to his room thinking, Prince isn't the only one who needed to stretch his legs.

He looked around after closing the door to Room 207. It was large and well-appointed, though he observed some slight wear on the bedding and lush oriental rugs. A small fireplace already held coal that could be lit if the evening became cool. He smiled to himself thinking how nice it was not to worry about temperatures. His body accepted what nature sent him. The freezing cold of winter or the exhausting heat of summer rarely made a difference. His body felt the temperature and accommodated itself without a problem. Daylight was tolerable if he was careful, and his dark blue tinted sunglasses were a definite plus. The itch created by exposure to daylight he considered a small price to pay when compared to this newfound, and very special, skill.

The sun lowered in the west as he washed the travel grime from his body in the bathing area attached to his room. Worth the extra cost rather than sharing the common bathing room at the end of the hall, he thought. Unpacking and hanging up his clothes took only a few minutes, and he became aware that his cursed thirst had strengthened to the point where he couldn't ignore it much longer. With a sigh, he prepared to leave the room within the hour.

Clayton saw his guide waiting at the hotel's curb, "Ah, Mr. Early, thank you for waiting. I'm not familiar with Charleston. Can you drive around a bit and show me the sights?"

"Of course, sir! Is there anything in particular you'd like to see? Theaters, restaurants, gambling halls saloons? And I know a place where the ladies are fine to behold and more than willing to entertain a gentleman." The last bit of information was said with a wink.

"No thank you, let's just drive about, while I get my bearings."

Clayton sat back on the comfortable cushioned bench of the open carriage and let the soothing early evening air pass over him. His body relaxed but his vision remained sharp as he studied his surroundings and noted where people gathered, what they wore and how they behaved.

Music spilled into the streets from several open doorways, some taverns more raucous than others. He made his mental choice when a very drunken sailor almost fell under the wheels of their passing vehicle.

Mr. Early pulled the horse to a sharp stop as the drunk stepped back onto the curb with a curse and a hiccup. Clayton continued to watch as he stumbled to the side of the building, sat against its wall and fell asleep. He was ignored by passersby and when his buddies emerged from their chosen saloon, they laughed at him before moving to the next entertainment being offered further down the street.

"Mr. Early, you may take me back to the hotel now. Please pick me up tomorrow at two o'clock and take me to the Bank of Charleston. I believe it's on Meeting Street. I'd also like to purchase a vacant lot or a building, so if you know of a local sales office, I'd like to go there afterwards.''

"Yessir, Mr. Masters, I'll have the carriage at the hotel doors at two sharp." Mr. Early chirped to his horse and the carriage moved smoothly into the traffic.

CHAPTER 19
CHARLESTON'S BACK ALLEY

Clayton stepped down from the carriage and entered his hotel, climbed the stairs to his room, and moved to its side window. In a flash, he had the casement window open and jumped to the rooftop of the neighboring building. He quickly made his way to where he last saw the drunken sailor. And there he was, still sprawled on the sidewalk, still being ignored by passersby.

He dropped lightly down to the rear of the alley and strolled towards the lighted sidewalk fronting the saloon. He leaned over the man to put his arm under his shoulders, and with little effort, heaved him up to lean against the building's wall. Anyone who even noticed would think the drunk's buddy was taking care of him when the two moved into the shadows of the alley.

Clayton's need to drink roared through his veins as the drunken man's odor of cloying soured beer filled his nose and lapped at the back of his throat. He couldn't delay any longer. "Forgive me." The words were barely heard by the victim as fangs punched through the soft tissue of his neck.

Clayton fed deep and the rush of new blood almost made him dizzy with the hated but sheer pleasure of the moment. He pulled back just seconds before the man's life drained completely away. Filled with new strength, he tossed the drained corpse over his shoulder and climbed the rough bricks of the building to its tarpapered roof. Pounding piano music and shrill voices below buried the slight noise of his movements and dark shadows concealed them both.

From the saloon's high roof, he could easily see the layout of the city's streets and alleys. Most of the city seemed to be made of wooden structures with an occasional brick building lording over its neighbors and rented townhouses stood pridefully next to retail businesses. He even saw some houses attached together, similar to London's row houses. Most of the nearby alleys separating the buildings were quite narrow, only the width of a horse and wagon. The houses were spaced further apart as one left the bustling downtown area and those alleys might present a problem later if he needed to leap a greater distance with his burden. The possibility of being seen was greater.

Clayton ended his evaluation of the residential area and looked north towards the warehouse district aligning the river. He thought those rooftops might provide the concealment he needed until he could safely drop to the ground. The decision was made, and he began to sprint from rooftop to rooftop until he was unable to continue along the elevated route.

He dropped to the tall reeds growing against a quiet warehouse and waded further into the black muck of the river's shoreline before heaving the corpse into the rushing waters making their way into the bay. He stood and watched as it floated like a bobbing piece of rotten wood for a few moments until it finally sank beneath the dark swirling currents. Only now, did he allow himself a few seconds to regret the taking of a life in order to support his own.

Clayton was nearing the outskirts of the entertainment center of the city when he looked down at his pant legs. They were still covered with black mud and stank of rotting weeds. A smile touched his lips and he laughed outright. *I guess I'll have to call it a night and just go back to my room. I look like a drowned rat!*

A dark mist entered the second-floor window of the Charleston Inn and reformed into its usual guise of a handsome six-foot-two-inch male. Thirst satisfied and any regrets of stealing another man's life buried deep within his conscience, he was ready to relax and spend some time planning his future in Charleston.

CHAPTER 20
THREE CASINO STORIES

CASINO STORY ONE

Every day, Clayton made a point of riding Prince about the city as dusk was beginning to settle on the wide boulevards and giant live oaks. It was the best opportunity to become familiar with the streets and alleys. Families taking a final stroll after the dinner hour gave friendly greetings as they admired the beautiful Hanoverian stallion. Everyone knew that Mr. Masters was English and extremely wealthy. Everyone with a marriageable daughter hoped to catch his attention.

During the greetings and small talk, he let it be known that he was looking for a property close to the bay. In fact, he let it be known that his first choices would be Church Street or Bay Street. As he slowly jogged Prince down Bay Street, he was hailed by an earlier acquaintance.

"Mr. Masters, Mr. Masters!" The gentleman tipped his hat and smiled at Clayton as he approached the restless horse.

"It's Mr. Brownell, isn't it? Yes, I believe we met the other night. And how is your lovely wife? Not with you this evening?"

Mr. Brownell looked wary as he responded. "My Amelia is just fine, thank you. Are you still looking for property in the city? I have an acquaintance who would like to sell one of his buildings and I think the place might interest you. I can give you his card if you'd like to contact him."

Clayton reached down, took the card from the man's hand, and looked at it in the fading light. "Yes, I'm still looking for the right place. I'll call on him later tomorrow. Thank you."

Mr. Brownell hesitated for a moment and asked, "Excuse me, but could you tell me what business you might be interested in? In case I hear of more available properties."

Clayton responded gravely, "Yes, of course. I plan to open an establishment with a restaurant, full-service gentlemen's club, and private rooms for overnight guests. I hope to offer nightly entertainment and card games. If I added a ballroom, do you think the ladies would enjoy it?"

With that question, Mr. Brownell knew he would never re-introduce his wife to this suave and overly good-looking man but hid his concern and offered up a toothy smile. "Sir, your new establishment would be most welcome in our little town of Charleston! Here, take another of my cards, and if I can be of any service, please call on me at any time. My window draperies are known to be the best in the South!"

Clayton smiled faintly at the man's blatant self-advertisement as he tipped his hat and continued his evening tour of the city. He was thoughtful. *Things are shaping up very well. At this rate, I'll have to start making lists. And I really should throw some type of party to meet other business owners and, who knows, maybe an investor or two.*

CASINO STORY-TWO

Clayton looked around him with satisfaction and began to walk through the newly decorated rooms. After nearly three years, a lot of hard work and a few shipping delays, his Sapphire Restaurant was finished and open for business. Three chandeliers hung from twenty-foot ceilings and gaslight sconces were placed along three of the four walls with military precision. Crisp white tablecloths dotted with dark blue linen napkins and heavily engraved silverware graced each table. Gilt covered chairs with seats and backs covered with rich blue and gold tapestry were placed around each table in groups of four or six. Facing the fourth wall, tall movable panels painted with *trompe-l'oeil* scenes of a French countryside could be pushed aside to open an additional space large enough to handle over a hundred people.

Four great windows faced the tree lined boulevard and were swathed with rich blue jewel toned velvet. Walls were painted with a pale blue that shimmered in the candlelight. Several fluted columns, four feet in height, stood against the walls, their vases holding fresh flowers that sent their mild fragrance throughout the room. The hardwood floor was polished to a high gloss and elaborate handwoven carpets from India were spread casually about.

In the center of the room, a white marble fountain with tiny cherubs holding urns, tinkled fresh pale blue tinted water into its open bowl. The unit was surrounded by masses of small tropical plants and there was even a caged Macaw to provide surprise entertainment to curious children.

His smile turned into a grin as he moved down a wide hallway to a smaller room that was designed for card games and the enjoyment of a good cigar. *That* room would not be opened until after the dinner hour and every attempt had been made to keep the patrons comfortable while they lost (or sometimes won) at cards. The full bar offered top-shelf whiskeys, brandies or any liquor requested, and two waiters dressed in black with long white aprons would serve drinks to the tables. Card games needn't be interrupted. The third floor of the building contained six lavishly decorated rooms for overnight guests.

He turned to Sam, his General Manager, "Okay, in one hour, open the doors. The reservations should prevent too much mayhem but if you run into any major problems, I'll be in my private apartment but I'm sure you can handle anything that comes up." He smiled at the man who had become his majordomo, who knew everything there was to know about the running of the new enterprise. Clayton took out a slender cigar, lit it and walked towards the carpeted stairway leading to his third-floor private office suite. He didn't want people to see him too often, familiarity led to questions that he didn't want to answer. He would come down later to greet the guests.

Once in the privacy of his living room, he took off his jacket and loosened his vest. Kicking back on his couch he reached for the wine glass waiting for him on the glass-topped table next to a chilled bottle of champagne in a silver bucket. He wasn't much of a drinker. The alcohol (like any regular food) unsettled his stomach, but he liked the idea of occasionally sharing a drink with friends. He popped the cork and poured the pale golden liquid into the waiting glass. He propped his boots on the glass table and saluted himself.

It felt good to be the boss.

CASINO STORY THREE

Life and work at The Sapphire Restaurant had its special rhythm and after a few years, Clayton was able to relax and think about what else he might do with his free time. So many options in this vast America, so many places to see. He was alone but not lonely. Female companions were easy to find, he just had to control his thirst that might lead to questions.

And avoid determined mamas with marriageable daughters.

There was a firm knock on the door of his private living room and he felt the strong presence of another undead member of their special community. A cold chill touched his veins and a decision had to be made quickly. Run or respond? Before he managed to get off the couch and open the door, it slammed open and he heard a surprised gasp followed by an, "Oh, dear!"

An extraordinarily beautiful redhead dressed in an evening gown of dark blue satin decorated with black jet beads glided into the room and smiled warmly at him. She gracefully held both white gloved hands up towards him with open palms.

Her voice was throaty and low. "Mr. Masters, I really *do* come in peace. I've been waiting for you downstairs, but my need has made me impatient." Clayton was thinking he would never turn away a lady in *need*. He gazed at the perfection of her face and put aside his unlit cigar, but his wine glass remained, unnoticed in his hand.

Clayton didn't know who the lady was, but her sadness was almost visible and damned if he could identify her scent. He had seen several of his kind over the years and they usually avoided each other, but this woman was very, very old and her slight accent was intriguing.

His voice was thoughtful. "And how may I help you? I doubt there is anything you can't do yourself. I was about to enjoy a glass of champagne my one self-indulgence after a busy day at the Sapphire. Won't you join me?" He began pouring champagne into another glass and handed it to her without comment.

She smiled, raised her glass, and said, "We don't *really* need to drink this do we?"

He gestured for her to join him on his couch before saying, "No, but I like to follow some of the rituals. Your name, for a start, would be nice."

She said softly, "I'd prefer not to give you my name, it's really not important."

One eyebrow lifted as he replied, "Very well, what can I do for you?"

"I want you to kill me."

Clayton was stunned as she pulled a jeweled stiletto from between her breasts. Even though he was very young in vampire years he considered himself sufficiently sophisticated when faced with the unusual. He had seen and done a lot during the last half century, but this was a total surprise. He sat back against the cushions of the sofa, crossed his leg, and kept his face calm as he very carefully put his untouched champagne next to the silver bucket. She continued to stand in the center of the room, her regal stance and fabulous beauty took his breath away.

"Why?" was all he could say.

Her silken voice continued. "You obviously know what I am, and I've been aware of you since India. And Lillian remember her? She and I were acquaintances for centuries before you released her to her final death. It was well that you did, she was a real pain to be around, and Thalia and I are more than grateful. But I'm tired, I've seen and done everything I want to do."

She glided forward and sat next to him on the sofa. "I've survived plagues, been worshiped as a Pacific Island goddess, danced with kings, corrupted emperors, and seen the rise and fall of dynasties." She folded her hands and looked down, "But I've lost too many people that were dear to me. I'm tired but too scared of failure to create my own final death. I want you to make love to me then end my existence. I promise not to take your life. You are so beautiful to my eyes, and what better way for me to leave this world then while being held in your arms?"

Her face was a study in porcelain surrounded by the incredible red halo of fire that was her hair. A crystal tear crept from the corner of one dark green eye and lodged in a corner of her scarlet lips as she smiled at him and removed her opera length gloves.

Still speechless, he tried to make sense of her outlandish proposal. Saying nothing he stood and moved a step away from her. He needed some distance from this temptress to clear his head and think about what she had said. She stood and without seeming to move across the room, he felt her press her body against his back. She gently laid her head against his shoulders and sighed as she put her arms around his waist. He could do nothing except turn and pull her closer. She was taller than most women and she fit him perfectly.

He had no will or reason to deny her, and her beauty seemed incandescent as he slowly slipped her gown from her shoulders. She wore nothing underneath except pale silk stockings and crystal studded slippers. He kissed her shoulder and felt her shiver slightly under the soft caress of his lips. As he carried her to the bed, her arms circled his neck, and her mouth found his lips with a kiss that burned away all anxiety about taking her life as she wished. He would do whatever she wanted.

He tried to prolong their lovemaking as long as possible. He wanted to stroke and caress each inch of her perfect body. Her skin radiated an unusual heat and a light flavor of cinnamon wherever he touched her, and it was almost exquisitely unbearable. She returned his caresses with her own until he lost his sense of self within the emotion she poured forth. He felt an emotion unlike anything before when, at last, he plunged completely into her scorching heat and welcoming wetness. He moaned deep in his throat as his fangs pierced the marble whiteness of her neck.

She sighed faintly and held him while he drank deep and continued to worship her body with his hands. As she promised, she did not drink from him but the visions within her blood saturated his thoughts with love, lust, and immense power. He almost screamed with his first climax and unable to stop he pushed even deeper into the glory of her and bit again. At the last, he gazed into the depthless green and gold of her eyes and gasped with his second even greater climax, willingly overcome in the perfect union of spirit and body.

Moments later, she smiled up at him, closed her eyes, and died.

Clayton refused to think as he rose from the bed, picked up the stiletto from the low chest next to the bed and plunged it into the perfection of her breast.

A full moon streamed through the second-floor window to highlight the crumpled form of a dark blue satin gown. Crystal studded sandals were carelessly lying next to the glass table holding a partially emptied champagne bottle. One slim white arm draped over the side of the counterpane, and the wealth of tangled red hair looking like spilled blood, almost hid the flawless pearl white face.

Within minutes, silver flakes of dust began to rise from the body and whirl above the bed, the moon's light reflecting off their tiny pieces.

He quietly stood in the darkness watching as her body dissolved. He opened the casement window, and the tiny stars streamed out into the darkness beyond. He felt the dark heat of her blood continue to rush through him, its incredible age and embedded skills suffusing his body with knowledge and inhuman strength. A parting gift from his goddess who was dead as she truly wished.

Pink tears glistened on his cheeks as he realized that keeping in touch with his humanity would be harder than ever before.

CHAPTER 21
TIME AND HORSEFLESH

CHARLESTON – 1850

Clayton felt time was passing so fast. Railroads were expanding the length and width of America. Communications and even the changing rules of society kept him alert. Men's clothing seemed fairly stable but ladies' fashion? He'd never understand it.

Two flush toilets had been installed next to the public rooms of the restaurant. The expense was worth it, almost as good as advertising. Regular customers brought their visiting friends, which generated even more income as the reputation of the Sapphire Restaurant grew. In the ballroom, Samuel Morse had lectured to an audience of avid listeners about his astonishing invention, the telegraph. Clayton was able to attend a scientific convention in New York City with Alfred Nobel as a guest lecturer. Nobel's paper centered on the growth of explosives from black powder to nitroglycerin and included his newest interest; his laboratory work to invent an explosive he wanted to name 'dynamite'. Clayton still smiled at those memories of night-long discussions and political arguments for and against its use.

He was forced to retire Sam after many years of service. His employee gratefully accepted Clayton's offer to move him closer to his daughter living in New York City. This simple remedy removed the probability of the man noticing a distinct lack of aging for Clayton and he decided that all his managers should be encouraged to retire after twenty years. He would offer each a generous financial motive to move elsewhere. If the incentive to move failed, he would have to take other measures to ensure his secret *otherness* remained undiscovered. He truly didn't want to do that.

The restaurant and gaming room were huge successes, and the ballroom was reserved for gala events well beyond the next year. Baron, the grandson of Noble Haus von Mecate's Prince, was eight years old and a stunning copy of his grandsire.

In 1855, the city of Charleston celebrated New Year's Eve with a costumed ball at the Sapphire Restaurant. Both the restaurant and ballroom had been lavishly decorated with blue and silver tissue paper. Streamers of tinsel hung overhead, and the underwater fantasy featured mermaids and a larger-than-life sized statue of Poseidon holding his 16-foot trident. The party was considered a huge success but now, Clayton was at a loss. The party was already two months ago, and he felt at loose ends with little to keep his interest. What could he do next? *Time, I have so much of it. Will it be a blessing or a curse?*

He decided to watch the men in Sapphire's popular card room. It was a great place to pick up pieces of gossip or catch up on the current situation regarding slavery (which he abhorred). He looked through the light haze of tobacco smoke toward the crowd of men standing at the bar. All four tables were busy with players worshiping Lady Luck with their games of poker.

It seemed to him that the customers he knew in the past were being replaced with the new generation of their sons. The sons played with a recklessness that only inherited wealth could bring. Some had already lost small fortunes to poorly placed bets, yet they continued to play, hoping for better outcomes.

Nature also changed the lives of the townspeople. He knew that some folks disappeared when their wealth dissolved due to low cotton prices or poor land management. A year earlier a hurricane caused severe flooding and breached the levies used to maintain the rice fields. Rebuilding those levies took time, was labor intensive, and needed an investment that was slow to show a profit.

Bad harvest years caused plantation lands to be divided and sub-divided, usually among family, until some tracts of land were auctioned off to raise money. Finally, there was nothing left to sell. Several families had already lost their land and made their permanent homes in the city. Some of the more famous families moved out of state rather than show their humiliation of bankruptcy and some stayed but mostly hid behind heavy curtains and closed doors.

A brash young man interrupted Clayton's musing, calling out from across the room. "Hey, Mr. Masters, come on over here. Need to settle a bet." The voice was slurred, and his eyes were reddened from too much drink. "I gotta bet going with my friend here that my horse can beat his horse. I wanna' match between em' that's fair and square. What do y'all say? Hold the purse and call the winner!" All eyes turned to the two young men seated at the table and the room quieted.

Clayton's attention was captured with the idea of a horse race. *Why not? The house will benefit by a percentage since it holds the event and provides security.* He raised his voice, "All right, how does this Saturday sound? The race can take place at the armory field. One and a half miles. No-limit bets. Winner takes all."

The combatants shook hands and the room erupted into chatter as men placed wagers on their favorite horse and rider. Clayton stood near the door and marveled at the insanity taking place in front of him. He would not place a wager lest someone accuse him of cheating.

Saturday dawned clear with only a slight nip in the air. The late morning turned warm enough for the men to remove jackets and walk around in shirtsleeves. The women sat on benches or chairs placed in the sun and many of them began to fan themselves when it rose directly overhead. It was a perfect time for folks to gather outdoors for a picnic or a walk in the parklike woods of the Charleston Arsenal. The crowds continued to grow as more and more people arrived and their excitement seemed contagious.

A course for the race had been set up with little flags attached to poles at regular intervals. and Clayton could smell the sweat of horseflesh as their riders cantered along the track to familiarize themselves with the course. Wagers between the onlookers grew even more heated as the horses began to line up at the starting posts.

Clayton turned to George, his current hotel manager and asked, "What's the wager between these two?"

George shook his head and replied, "One side bet five thousand dollars, the other didn't have cash and was probably too proud to lower the amount, so he bet his plantation. It's lost value for the last three years. Bank is about to foreclose. The idiot doesn't know how to manage the estate at all after his parents died. But if he wins, the money keeps him afloat for another couple years. If he loses, well, I doubt he's even thought about that possibility."

The two men walked over to the starting post and stood on a low wooden platform. The rules and the two wagers were loudly announced by George, but the restless crowd barely heard him. Finally, he called for silence and Clayton fired his Navy Colt into the air. The excited mob roared with enthusiasm and surged forward to get better views of the race.

The horses charged forward with each rider crouched low in the saddle. As they came around the track at the one-mile mark, the sorrel gelding was slightly ahead of the bay. Both riders used their crops in a frenzy to demand faster speed from their straining mounts. At the final marker the sorrel and the bay were even but, with a final push, the sorrel passed the finish mark, and won by a nose.

The crowd went wild with both glee and consternation. Who won? It was so close! Clayton's preternatural eyesight clearly saw which horse won, but he knew the loser would be very upset and contest his loss. Trouble brewing, he thought.

The riders dismounted, and their heaving and sweat streaked horses were led away by two boys who would cool them down and walk them a bit before giving them water.

Clayton motioned for the two riders to join him on the platform. He dreaded what was about to happen but what could he do about it? His own boredom had made him the arbiter of a wager that would probably mean a bitter future for the loser.

He gathered himself mentally to announce the winner of the race. "The sorrel wins by a nose." All hell broke loose as half the crowd jumped and yelled for joy, pounding on the backs of their friends as they congratulated each other. Most of the remaining crowd good naturedly accepted their loss. Those standing close to the last post confirmed that the sorrel had won, if only by a little. The race was fair.

His loss enraged the twenty-year-old and he swore that he would get even some day with the fool who called his horse the loser. Yes, it would give him great pleasure to put a bullet into Clayton Masters someday! He stomped off after slamming his plantation papers into the open hand of the winner who wisely said nothing except, "Thank you."

"Go to hell," was the only reply.

CHAPTER 22
THE FIRST MEETING

CHARLESTON - 1855

Miss Mary Lydia Ellington was almost giddy with excitement. She and her mother joined the small group of pedestrians waiting to cross the boulevard. Her face was radiant as she grinned at her smiling mother. They were going to the best restaurant in town for dinner and would be celebrating her sixteenth birthday. She felt like a grownup in her very first full-length dress. Not to mention her hair was no longer in pigtails but stylishly pinned into a chignon at back of her neck.

Mary chattered happily as they began to cross the street. With her anticipation of the special event crowding her thoughts, she didn't see the black Hanoverian stallion and his handsome rider come to an abrupt stop only a few yards away. Mary was blissfully unaware of the near collision and cheerfully followed her mother's quick yank on her hand.

Her mother noticed Clayton, however, and frowned as she recognized him as that scoundrel owner of the restaurant they were about to visit. Well, she couldn't really accuse him of anything, but he was so handsome, he just *had* to be hiding lascivious behavior of some kind. She gave herself a mental shrug and frowned at him again before continuing to guide her daughter along the sidewalk of the shaded boulevard.

Clayton sat motionless on Baron as he breathed in the most incredible scent he had ever experienced before. The light floral aroma mixed with soap and healthy young female made him almost shiver with delight. His nostrils flared as he drew in the heady mixture. He turned his head to find the source and realized the scent belonged to the pretty young woman crossing in front of him. He sifted through the scents again and had no doubts at all. That smiling female was the source of the truly delightful smell. Seconds later, the scent was more than merely delightful, his body responded outrageously as pure lust threatened to make his fangs lower.

After the two women had passed safely to the sidewalk, he nudged Baron into a slow canter and continued to make his way down the boulevard. His mind was busy trying to sort out what had just happened. He had grown used to being temporarily overwhelmed by scents, sounds, and sometimes sights, but he knew how to quickly tamp down overloaded sensations without appearing to be distracted. But this was something new. His whole body was reacting in a way unfelt for years.

As he continued his evening tour, he was greeted by acquaintances but only smiled and nodded as he made his way towards the alley leading to the back of his restaurant. The restaurant's private stable was fifty feet from the back door of the kitchen and one side of it served as storage for his personal carriage. He rode Baron into the yard and a stable boy rushed out to take the reins and lead the horse into the shelter. Clayton thanked him and climbed up the back stairs from the kitchen to his private rooms on the third floor of the building.

He threw himself into his armchair. Good lord, what was wrong with him? A child on the verge of womanhood drove his senses into freefall! He had to find out more about her. Obviously, she was a little too young to approach, but he already knew that she would be very special to him in the future. If he couldn't have her yet, he would at least keep an eye on her and protect her. Time was most certainly on his side.

After returning home, sixteen-year-old Mary found herself pleading with her mother in the drawing room of their townhouse. "I'm sorry, Mother, but the only thing I want to do is become a nurse. You know how I helped Mrs. Johnson when she had pneumonia. She said I had a true gift for taking care of the sick. And Mrs. Boyde, the grocer's wife with the sick baby? I helped her too." She clenched her teeth and looked straight at her mother. Her blue eyes signaled her readiness for battle.

Mrs. Ellington tried her best. "Mary Lydia, I know you want this. You've always wanted to fix things even when you were a child. But nursing isn't a proper occupation for a young woman of your station. What would our friends think? Just the thought of seeing blood gives me the willies. You should be thinking of a husband and motherhood."

She blotted the corner of her eye with a tiny lace handkerchief as she shuddered. She knew from experience that her daughter was stubborn, and when she made up her mind it was difficult to change it. She sighed. The only thing to do would be to find the best and safest opportunity for her daughter to fill her dream of nursing the sick, but she would delay the inevitable for as long as she could. Maybe Mary would change her mind as young girls often do.

Her voice was resigned. "Well, at sixteen you can't be tied up and locked in your room, but I do wish your father were still alive to deal with such a misguided daughter.

Mary Lydia decided that waiting for her mother to find what she considered a proper nursing position was out of the question. After a week with no result, she decided to search on her own. She visited several of the local doctors and after their initial shock at hearing her request, they always gave her a resounding "No!" before ushering her to the door.

Mary was in low spirits while seated in the waiting room of Charleston's leading physician, Dr. William Bradford. She tried to stay positive, but he was her very last hope. A slow half hour passed before Dr. Bradford called Mary into his office and motioned to the chair used during consultations.

She had filled the early promise of beauty, and her manner of dress and self-confidence made her look several years older than her sixteen years. He knew her family and knew she wanted to be a nurse. He was more progressive than others in his profession and believed that Nightengale was on the right track about hygiene and hospital cleanliness. Better *he* should give Mary the training she so desperately wanted rather than some quack with a bloody apron and dirty hands.

Dr. Bradford sat behind his desk and steepled his hands while resting his elbows on the desk's polished marble top. He pursed his lips before saying, "Well,

Miss Ellington, word has gotten around that you are interested in the nursing profession. Do you realize that sometimes it can be exhausting, messy and downright disgusting work? It's not even considered a respectable job for ladies like sewing or teaching." He frowned at her over his spectacles.

"I don't care, Dr. Bradford. I just feel it's something I'm called to do. I want to help sick people get well and the only true and right way to do it is with proper training. I'm begging you to take me as your student. I'll study, I'll work hard, and I'll never complain." She reached into her purse. "Oh, and I do have references for you." She began to hand him her letters of reference.

Dr. Bradford smiled at her. "Your references won't be necessary. I've already heard from your patients. You not only carefully administer their medicine, but you tend to the actual comfort of the patient. It's a true gift. So, if your mother approves, I'll accept you as a trainee. It's a three-year commitment and will be challenging because I have my practice and have patients in the hospital. I expect you to be always available, and if you can't take the pressure, you're out. No excuses. No pleading for another chance. I don't have time for female theatrics. Agreed?"

Mary's face glowed with joy as she stood up and offered her hand to the doctor. "Agreed, Dr. Bradford, I'll be the best student and make you proud of me!"

After she left his office, Mary couldn't contain her excitement. She decided to take a short cut through one of the pretty cobblestone alleys to her house two streets over. She couldn't wait to see her mother and share her good news. Well, she thought to herself, my good news maybe not so much for Mother. A giggle burst forth with the sheer excitement of beginning to train for her heartfelt desire. She was on her way to a real nursing career.

Mary's exuberance ended when two poorly dressed young men came from the shadows and stood before her, their legs spread for balance and intimidation. Their eyes gleamed with malice, and one pulled a knife as the other maneuvered to stand behind her.

"What you doing little lady? Sounds like you're having fun. And all by yourself, too! How about you share some of that fun with me and my friend here? Jack, you grab her and pull her over to that big doorway over there and I'll keep watch."

Jack rushed towards Mary, and she dropped her purse as she stumbled backwards. He pushed her roughly against the splintered wooden door and began to fondle himself with one hand while he held his knife against her neck with the other. Fear closed her throat, and she was unable to call for help. She couldn't breathe, her stays felt like iron bands around her ribs and her mind began to cloud as she slumped sideways. Jack moved aside to grab an arm and tried to hold it twisted behind her, but his position became useless when she dropped sideways to the dirt. He tossed his knife aside and wasted no time pulling her skirt above her knees. He reached for the drawstring of her ruffled pantaloons as his pal Rusty abandoned his post and moved closer to watch with avid interest.

Rusty never felt the blow on the back of his head from the hoof of Clayton's stallion. In a flash Clayton was off his horse and grabbed Jack, the would-be rapist, by the back of his neck and shook him like a piece of dirty carpet. He snarled into the fear struck face, "If you want to live, you leave this city before midnight. I know you now! I will find you and I will kill you as easy as squashing a bug. Understand?" The stench from the young man's fear clogged his nose as Clayton threw him halfway down the alley. He grabbed the semi-conscious Rusty by the back of his filthy shirt and threw him so hard into the side of the building that the mortar between the bricks showered onto the cobblestone below.

The young thug groaned as he got to his knees, slowly stood up and staggered down the alley towards his rapidly departing partner in crime. Rusty believed the warning given to his friend Jack and planned on leaving the city as soon as he possibly could. He knew his uncle had a place a couple miles north where he could stay. He used his sleeve to wipe the blood dripping from his nose as he muttered to himself, "That old man is crazy strong."

Clayton reached down to help a still dizzy Mary to her feet. He brushed her skirts to remove some of the clinging dirt, but she pushed his hand away and with a quiet but slightly shaky voice said, "Thank you, but I can do it myself." She bent down to pick up her purse and swiped at the remaining grit on her skirt.

He took hold of Baron's reins and breathed in the wonderful aroma that was so uniquely Mary's. He forced himself into check against the wild urge to pull her into his arms. He wanted to bury his face in the tousled hair that had become unbound and massed at her neck. He remembered she was only sixteen, but the siren song of her innocent scent and seductive young beauty almost drove him to lose control. He wanted to kiss that tender neck and drink her blood's heavenly essence, even if was just a little sip. He stepped back a few paces and stood leaning against the solid and unmoving shoulder of his horse as he gained self-control.

Mary looked up at her rescuer. Her eyes widened as she recognized the owner of her favorite restaurant. She whispered, "You're Mr. Masters, aren't you? I've seen you so many times on your beautiful horse. What's his name?" *Mr. Masters is sooo handsome! Oh no, he's looking at me like I'm on the dessert cart and he wants a bite!*

Clayton read her confusion, so he calmed his own inner turmoil before replying, "His name is Baron and yes, I own the Sapphire. I've seen you there with your mother. Is she doing well?" *Of all the inane questions, I'm losing my mind! This child was almost raped and I'm asking about the health of her mother?*

He started again. "Are you all right, Miss? Why on earth are you in this alley and walking alone?"

"I took a short cut to our house. It was stupid of me, and I surely won't do it again. I know who you are, so let me properly introduce myself. I'm Miss Mary Lydia Ellington." She gave a prim curtsy. "Thank you again for your rescue. I'm almost home and quite safe now, I'm sure." She turned to begin walking towards her street, which was still one block away. Her skirts swayed slightly with each step and the tight bodice hinted at a girl on the edge of womanhood.

Clayton couldn't bear to let her go so soon. With his most attentive and sincere smile fixed in place he said, "Please allow me to escort you, at least to the front of your house. There are ruffians all over the city and I'd hate it if you ran into more trouble." *Oh God, help me resist.*

Mary was charmed by being treated as an adult. She looked up at his incredibly handsome face and was immediately captured by a pair of deep sapphire eyes surrounded by lashes any girl would be proud of. She said without hesitation, "Thank you. It's not far, and I do feel a little shaky." S*trange that I feel so safe with him. I hope I can see him again. He's kind of old, but I'm getting older too, so—* Before she could finish her adolescent dreams about Mr. Clayton Masters, he was depositing her at the front steps of her house.

The housekeeper opened the door and saw Clayton tip his hat, gracefully remount his horse and canter away. She also noticed Mary's bemused face and faint smile as she slowly climbed the steps and entered the front hall. Of course, she recognized Mr. Masters. The whole city knew of his somewhat questionable reputation. "Trouble ahead," she muttered, "but it ain't my place to interfere." She closed the front door and continued to dust the entryway table.

Mary replayed her encounter with Mr. Masters hundreds of times and her vivid imagination supplied multiple, albeit chaste endings. *He's the one, he's the only one I want. Somehow, I'll have to run into him, casual like. And I'll say Oh, fancy meeting you here. No that won't do too artificial. Got it Mother, we must dine at the Sapphire more often.*

Clayton was thoughtful as he slowed Baron to a crisp walk as they continued down the empty alley towards the boulevard. His heart was still beating triple time and his teeth were clenched with the effort not to turn around and simply grab Mary and make her completely his. The image of her slender throat surrounded by her honey-streaked brown hair had his thirst raging and his lust rising.

It took time and a good gallop out of town before Clayton was able to calm his thoughts. Mary was special and deserved to be treated with care and respect. No doubt, he would see her occasionally maybe a smile and a nod a brief public conversation get her used to his presence. If all went well, he'd court her when she was a little older.

It would be very hard to wait.

CHAPTER 23
TRAINING MARY

CHARLESTON - 1855

Mary's heart was thumping with excitement as she waited for Dr. Bradford at the entry steps of Charleston Community Hospital. *My first day of nurses training! My very first day of becoming a professional nurse. Life is wonderful.*

Dr. Bradford hurried up the granite steps to meet her. "Well, Miss Ellington, here you are and right on time! Let's go inside and I'll introduce you to our head nurse. She will be very helpful to you. She knows just about everything there is to know about nurse training and the running of this hospital."

They entered the reception area of the hospital together and Dr. Bradford guided Mary over to a tall woman standing nearby. "Miss Ellington, I'd like you to meet Mrs. Helen Pritchett, our Head Nurse." He paused, "Mrs. Pritchett, may I present Miss Mary Lydia Ellington our nurse trainee?" Mary gave a small curtsey and held out her hand.

Mary saw the tall stiff-backed woman and swallowed her dismay. She stood almost six feet tall, with her iron gray hair parted in the middle and severely pulled back into a bun, so tight, it seemed to scream for release. Two deep lines bracketed her mouth, and the thin bloodless lips were compressed into a straight line as she looked down at Mary and sniffed through a very narrow beak-like nose.

Nurse Pritchett bent her head to acknowledge the introduction but continued to grip a bundle of papers with both hands. "Doctor, if you'll excuse me, I need to get these papers to administration. If you like, I'll take Miss Ellington with me. She will need to be fitted with a nurse's uniform and given a tour of the patient wards."

"Of course," Dr. Bradford replied and turned to Mary, "and after your tour please come to my office and we can discuss a course of training for you." Introductions over, he strode rapidly down the long hallway toward the ward containing several of his post-operative patients.

Head Nurse Pritchett walked slightly ahead of Mary and tossed out short descriptions of each room they passed on their way to the nurse's parlor and changing room. She saw the first-floor reception/registration room, four public wards, a large operating room, a small operating room, and a staff lavatory. They walked through the dining room and past the kitchen situated at the back of the building. Rather than climb the stairs to the second and third floors, Helen described them as each having four wards including a linen room and a lavatory for the ambulatory patients though bedpans, of course, were used as needed. All wards were designated for men and women separately.

Mary thought she'd never be able to find her way around but at last, her guide came to a halt and pointed to a large double door and said, "That door leads down to the basement. Don't ever go down there without a doctor's permission. It's used for autopsy and surgical training. You aren't ready to see that yet, anyway."

They retraced their steps until Nurse Pritchett paused before the entrance of the nurse's parlor. "Well, that's it for today's tour. I'm usually very busy but let's get you an apron and cap and sit for a cup of tea. I'll give you a quick list of your duties as a trainee."

Mary followed instructions for pinning and tying the apron to her dress and managed to pin her hair up and stuff her curls under her nurse's cap. Helen motioned Mary to sit and she did so with an expectant smile, ready and eager to take notes about anything her teacher would say.

Nurse Pritchett began. "Besides the lessons from me or Dr. Bradford, your daily duties will include housekeeping chores as well so take notes."

The chill voice continued. "One. Sweep and mop each ward floor. Two. Bring in a hod of coal for each ward's stove every morning. Three. Light is important so bring a kerosene lamp with you to each bedside. We supply the lamp but you're responsible for keeping it full and clean. Four. Keep good notes on each patient's condition. Our doctors need these notes, they're very important. Five. Work hours are from 7:00 a.m. until 8:00 p.m. and you'll be provided with lunch and a light supper. Dr. Bradford usually takes Sunday off. You can have Sundays off as well unless he needs you. Finally, we expect our young nurses to act with decorum. Any behavior that reflects badly on this hospital or on Dr. Bradford will result in your dismissal. Do you have any questions?"

Mary's earlier excitement evaporated under the verbal assault of Helen's rules. She felt out of her depth so quietly finished drinking her now tepid tea before responding. Her voice was low but without a tremble. "Not really. But how shall I address you?"

"You may call me Mrs. Pritchett. Now, it's time you return to Dr. Bradford. I'm sure he'll fill you in on your training schedule, but please come to me with questions or problems with patients. I'll introduce you to the rest of the staff at lunch tomorrow and you'll be assigned to the wards you'll be responsible for. Good day, Miss Ellington." With that polite dismissal, the head nurse stood and sailed out of the parlor under a cloud of lavender and rubbing alcohol. Mary put the used cups and saucers into a wooden bin (used for that purpose she hoped) and began her search for Dr. Bradford.

Mary continued to learn nursing for the next three years. Dr. Bradford was so impressed with her intelligence and medical curiosity that he went beyond his original curriculum and added actual medical procedures as part of her training. She continued to excel and several improvements to patient care were the result of her suggestions. Mary was nineteen when she received her certificate as a Nurse Generalist, fully employed at Charleston Community Hospital.

CHAPTER 24
FIRE AND ASH

Mary:

It was just before midnight and Mary was preparing for bed after a long day in the hospital wards. After covering a second shift for a fellow nurse, her shoulders ached, and her feet were ready for a nice long soak in hot water. Her brain felt fuzzy, but cleared at once when she heard heavy fists pounding at the front door. Unmindful of propriety and trained to respond to medical emergencies, she threw open the door just as her mother came down the stairs to join her.

Mary's voice was calm. "Mr. O'Connor? What is it? What's happened?"

Their disheveled neighbor, covered in soot and sweat, leaned against the door frame. His tired voice was filled with gravel. "Fire, Miss Mary. Big fire north of here. Dr. Bradford sent me to get you. There's a first aid station being set up in front of the school. I'll bring you to him soon as yer ready."

Mrs. Ellington gave Mary a brief hug and urged her to quickly dress and join the doctor. She herself would wait with friends next door until they were told to evacuate. Mary flew up the stairs and quickly donned her nursing outfit and a pair of sturdy shoes. She pulled her hair into a loose knot at the nape of her neck and stuck her nursing cap on her head with a pair of hat pins. "It will just have to do," she muttered and grabbed her medical bag before rapidly descending the stairs to the waiting Mr. O'Connor.

Ten minutes later, Mary was confronted by a milling crowd of desperate victims and crying families. Several people sat on scattered benches waiting to be seen by doctors. Their faces seemed shrunken and stonelike in their shock. She caught sight of Dr. Bradford sewing up a long gash on the arm of one of the volunteer fire fighters and hurried towards him.

"How can I help?" she asked the overworked doctor.

His response was hurried and distracted. "Everything's getting mixed up. Folks keep moving around and it's hard to tell who needs what or who comes first. Grab someone and start to separate the injured from the merely curious they're causing confusion and getting in my way."

Mary asked a policeman to set up a makeshift barricade to separate the injured from the onlookers and weeping families. Once finished, she directed that any empty cots and extra blankets be placed in orderly rows. After getting Dr. Bradford's permission, she arranged for any critically injured to be sent directly to Charleston General Hospital and the medical staff waiting there.

She approached one of the other nurses. "Can you ask the others to pin notes to the patients after they're interviewed? Like we do in the wards. I think it will really help the doctors." The nurse passed on the suggestion and a rhythm emerged.

A few hours later, attending the fire's victims had fallen into a procedure and Mary was able to treat several patients by herself. There were burns, broken bones, a few open wounds and one pregnant lady about to go into labor. That lady made it to the hospital just in time and was delivered of a baby girl.

Mary's last patient had burns and a broken arm after jumping from a second-story window to the street below. She had just finished setting the bone and was beginning to wrap it when an aide came to her side with a message. She gravely nodded to the messenger and continued to finish wrapping the patient's arm in a cast of plaster-coated strips of muslin. When she finished, she approached Dr. Bradford. He gave her a brief hug and agreed that she should leave immediately.

Clayton:

Clayton stretched out on his bed at midnight after several high-stakes poker games had finished and the gamblers had left for home. The special black-out drapes had been pulled shut over the two windows in his room and the doors were double locked to assure his safety while he slept. The building's doors were closed and locked, all candles and gaslights were extinguished. The kitchen staff wasn't scheduled to arrive for several hours. He smiled to himself at his mental images of bread and rolls rising in their baking pans and fresh fruit being chilled prior to being sliced and served. Sapphire's Sunday breakfast buffet was considered one of the city's jewels. Families seemed to enjoy the buffet after church and the shaded boulevard provided the opportunity to settle their meal and greet friends.

His eyes closed and he was about to slip into the deeper stage of healing sleep when ghost-like tendrils of smoke crept into the room through the closed casement window frame. FIRE!

Clayton threw himself off the bed and sped to the window, shoved it open and looked out over nearby rooftops to the orange and red flames beyond. It seemed like his restaurant was in its direct path and would probably be burning within an hour. He threw on boots and his heavy coat before jumping through the open window to the roof of the next building.

After crossing several buildings, he swooped down to the sidewalk below and sprinted past a small pocket park. A very young boy saw a fantastic figure with a flaring black coat land unhurt, but before his shrill voice could be heard, his mother pulled him into a waiting carriage about to leave for the safety of the southmost riverfront.

Clayton arrived near a swirling mass of men, hoses, and firefighting equipment. As he stood at the edge of the confusion, he heard a shout from the top floor of a smoldering building at the end of the block and raced towards it. No one else was near enough to hear the agonized call for help, their attentions were on the blazes immediately before them. Looking around, Clayton noticed he stood alone and unseen by the volunteers, so he gathered himself and jumped three stories up to an open window and grabbed its shattered frame to steady himself.

Thick black smoke and gouts of flame began to boil through an opened hallway door into the room, seeking an exit past Clayton and through the open window at his shoulder.

An old man's eyes were glazed with pain, but he still managed to hold a tiny child close to the window, away from the smoke and the room's rapidly thinning oxygen.

His voice was faint with exhaustion. "Mister, take the baby but I don't think I can make it. Bad lungs and that broken glass cut m-m—" He fell to his side unconscious.

Clayton grabbed the child as the old man slid to the floor, the deep wound on his stomach slowly pumping a trickle of scarlet. *No, you can't give up yet.* He ignored the hellish call of fresh blood as he bent and lifted the old man over his shoulder. He held the baby pressed to his chest with the other arm and jumped free of the window, pushing away from its smoldering frame. As he leapt, the building's roof buckled and crashed into the smoke-filled room with a roar of intense heat and flames.

Clayton felt red heat flash over him and smelled cloth and his own flesh burning as he sped away from the fire toward a group of volunteers wielding shovels. Several men spotted the approaching figure and shouted for more stretchers. He gently laid the old man down and watched as a nurse ran to tend to the motionless baby and the old man. *Oh, please God, let them stay alive. Let them live well.* Before more help arrived, Clayton walked quickly away, sight unseen. He couldn't ignore the intense pain from the burns crossing his back any longer. It was breaking dawn when he lowered himself onto the healing soil kept under his bed.

Luck was with Clayton. More volunteer firefighting units arrived and fought like demons to contain the blaze to a three-block area and an unexpected heavy rain drenched buildings and rooftops surrounding his restaurant. The fire was finally contained and guttered out two buildings away.

Within an hour his burns healed, and Clayton entered the restaurant kitchen. It stank of wet wood, ash, and smoke but it hadn't suffered any real damage. When his kitchen staff arrived, he directed them to make plenty of coffee and sandwiches for anyone who asked. Baskets of food and jugs of coffee and water were taken back to the exhausted firefighters putting out the last of any remaining flames. He walked over to the temporary medical area near the school.

Clayton thought he saw Mary Ellington working beside a doctor within a cordoned off area set up to help the victims. She would be almost twenty now, he thought, as he stood back to watch her slim form. She bent to deal with the burns of a man whose broken arm had just been set when another nurse hurried up to her and spoke into her ear while she still held the muslin dressing. He saw her straighten up, brush off her skirt and return to dressing the injury in front of her. She finished quickly and briefly spoke to the doctor she had been assisting. He nodded, hugged her, and she hurried away. Clayton was curious about the sudden departure and followed at a distance to an area set aside for any victims past recovery.

Mary's mother was dead of smoke inhalation. Unmarked except for a dusting of soot, she had been found inside their locked front door, obviously overcome by the dense smoke generated when the fire reached their kitchen. The rest of the house was spared thanks to the efforts of the firefighters, but they had been too late to save her.

It was over. Three whole blocks of downtown Charleston had various degrees of damage. Five businesses had burned almost completely to the ground, and many had smoke and water damage. Five town houses would have to be razed and rebuilt. One stable was destroyed with two horses unable to make their escape. Three people had died, twenty-nine people sustained injuries and many were temporarily homeless.

Clayton's rescue was successful. The baby was fine and the old man, though badly injured, was expected to recover.

* * *

Mary was still in shock over the death of her mother when a letter arrived from an aunt who had fallen ill and wanted her to come to Savannah as soon as possible. The dated letter was already two weeks old when she received it, so Mary had no idea what the aunt's health might be. She was also mystified, what aunt? She was still trying to come to terms with her mother's will. The contents of the house were hers, but the house itself was deeded to a distant male cousin in New York since women (her mother) couldn't own property.

The will included a short note written in her mother's hand. Evidently, her mother had a younger sister, Polly. They had a falling out when both sisters fell in love with the same man, a rancher from Colorado. Sixteen-year-old Polly left for Colorado on the arm of her much older husband and the two women never spoke again.

Mary would be happy to be leaving Charleston and its version of hell behind. She needed to meet her Aunt Polly, needed to understand why her mother never mentioned her. She needed comfort and hugs and soft encouraging words from real family.

Mary was granted a leave of absence from Dr. Bradford after explaining her need to visit her Aunt Polly in Savannah.

* * *

Aunt Polly was dead.

In Savannah, Mary sat by herself in a quiet park hugging the river. She had just turned twenty and realized she was barely prepared to live by herself. She knew next to nothing about running a household, her family had always depended on servants. She had arrived in Savannah with the hope of resting and getting to know her Aunt Polly. She simply needed time to catch her breath and make some plans for her future.

She sat and reflected on her current situation. A concerned neighbor told her that Aunt Polly had died and had been buried before her letter had been found and mailed. The kind woman handed Mary a business card and said, "I was at the funeral and some lawyer gave me his card. Probably because I lived next door to your aunt for years. Anyway, guess you might want to get in touch with him. His name is Noteworthy, and he's been at the house a couple times." The woman sniffed, "Don't seem right, his coming around so often to that empty house. Don't like his sort at all looks shifty if you know what I mean."

A day after Mary's conversation with the neighbor, Mr. Noteworthy showed up on her aunt's front porch and proceeded to unlock the front door. He jumped back in surprise to see Mary standing in the open entryway but recovered quickly and introduced himself as her aunt's lawyer. He handed her his business card.

Mary did not like him at all but invited him in and Mr. C. Noteworthy, Esq. lost no time explaining the situation. "Miss Ellington, I'm sorry to have to tell you this, but your Aunt Polly left no will. I encouraged her to have one drawn up, but she was so stubborn. Why, she never even told me she had family in Charleston! Without a will, you'll have quite a fight on your hands if you expect to inherit and to be honest, even if you *do* inherit from a will, you should sell this house. It's far too much of a responsibility for you I mean, your being unmarried and so young and all."

The more Mary heard, the angrier she became. Finally, she had enough, "Mr. Noteworthy, please leave. I haven't had the opportunity to go through any of her papers yet. If I find anything of note, you can be sure you'll be contacted. Now please be kind enough to leave." She rose from her chair and escorted Noteworthy to the front door. He was still talking when she slammed the door shut behind him.

She heaved another sigh. There *was* a will after all. She found it stored in a box with other legal looking papers. The house, a healthy bank account, and a working ranch somewhere near Denver Colorado had been left to her by her Aunt Polly.

She would have to meet with that nasty lawyer tomorrow at one o'clock and the bank was expecting her in an hour. She could stay at the Savannah house while her aunt's estate was settled, and since she had taken a leave of absence from Charleston Community Hospital, future employment shouldn't be a problem.

Mary stood up from the park bench and straightened her skirt. Time to meet the bankers.

At 2:00 p.m. Mary sat in the visitor's chair facing the bank's manager. Her face drained of color as she leaned forward. "What did you just say? What do you mean, I withdrew the funds and closed the account? She passed away only three weeks ago! I've never been here before! Here, this is my aunt's will, and this is my signature!"

The banker looked at her with a professionally sad smile and very cold eyes. "I'm sorry, Miss Ellington, but the money has been withdrawn and the account has been closed. According to our bank records, there's nothing left in the account there is nothing we can do for you, perhaps you should speak with your lawyer."

Mary grated out, "Oh yes, I'll just *do* that." She stormed out of the office and angry tears threatened to fall. What should she do? What *could s*he do? She had enough money to last a few weeks but after that, she would have to find work. Either return to Charleston or stay in Savannah and continue nursing. But she had no friends in Savannah and just wasn't ready for such a change yet and why had she never been told of an aunt? She'd probably never know.

CHAPTER 25
MEETING AGAIN

SAVANNAH - 1858

After almost losing his restaurant to the fire in Charleston, Clayton decided that a buying trip to Savannah was in order. His city was rebuilding at a breakneck pace and wood was in high demand and short supply. He would make his purchases, fix up the place and donate money or building materials to anyone who needed help.

Dark shadows crept into the alleys while Clayton enjoyed stretching his legs along the town's main street. Gas lights were being lit along the walkways and the restaurants and saloons were doing a brisk business. He strolled along the sidewalk, casually looking into shop windows still open for any late sales. He was looking closely at a poorly done rendition of a horse and rider chasing a fox, when a young woman, arm swinging a hat box and humming a popular song, collided with him.

The box flew into the air as her feet flew out from under her. Clayton instinctively grabbed the woman with one arm as his left hand caught the box's twine handle before it hit the ground. His arm closed around the tiny waist even as she managed to hang onto his other arm still holding the box. The song's lyrics were replaced by a loud gasp.

Clayton was unnerved by her delicate perfume flooding his senses as he settled her onto her feet. He finally realized he still had his arm around her and forced himself to loosen it. He wanted to bend his head to her neck to continue inhaling those rich and promising aromas. The sent was so familiar

The distraught young woman began to apologize as she took a step back while attempting to straighten her skirts and reach for the box he still held by its twine, but she stumbled again when the heel of her walking boot caught on the hem of her skirt. She grabbed his arm and tried again to maintain her balance and her dignity.

Embarrassed and breathless, she looked down and saw a pair of highly polished boots attached to a very well-shaped trouser leg. Her eyes slowly raised upward to the perfectly tailored dark suit fitted to a tall athletic frame. Slightly tousled hair, black as night, framed his chiseled jaw with modest sideburns and touched the edges of the starched white collar of his shirt. Her thoughts scattered when she recognized the silver and black-diamond pin on the jacket's lapel of a perfect and incredibly handsome man.

Mary's voice was flustered, "Mr. Masters? What are you doing here? I mean Oh, I'm so sorry! I was heading home, and I didn't realize it was so late. And I wasn't paying I mean I didn't see you in front of me. I- I don't usually bump into people." *Oh, he is beyond handsome, he is simply gorgeous.* She stuttered to a stop as she continued to gaze up at his pale face and almost forgot to breathe.

He leaned into her slightly and deeply inhaled her scent, his eyes almost closed with rapture. The perfectly sculpted lips were still threatening to smile as Mary's heart began to beat erratically. The gleam in his eyes seemed to promise a deviltry about to be delivered.

Erotic thoughts filled her head, and her knees grew weak as a flush of pure desire coursed through her. This is *not* a normal reaction to a good-looking man her practical mind cautioned her and after taking a deep breath Mary managed to say, "Uh, Mr. Masters? My hatbox, please? You may return it now."

Clayton's mouth twitched again seeing her discomfort. He knew exactly what was causing her to blush and stammer. He had sent her his message loud and clear, and he was confident that he could have that lovely throat at once if he wanted it. He could hear her heart wildly beating beneath her corset's confining layers of cotton and whalebone. He stood completely still with slightly narrowed eyes, watching as she won her internal fight to regain her control and modesty.

He noticed she remained focused on an empty spot just over his shoulder. The encounter took only seconds, but now he knew it was young Mary and all grown up. Oh, yes, he remembered her quite well and the perfection of her scent was making his head spin.

He loosened his grip on her arm holding the hatbox. "No harm done Miss Ellington. But please allow me to carry your package. It's late and I'd be happy to get you a carriage."

The cultured voice soothed her rattled nerves. Her thoughts were still a bit confused, but home wasn't that far away. In a slightly breathy voice, Mary managed to reply, "A carriage really isn't necessary." She pointed a finger, "I live in that yellow house in the middle of the next block." Clayton kept hold of the hatbox while the two of them walked in stilted silence to her front gate.

After setting the box on her front porch he turned back to her and said, "I remember meeting you in Charleston. Did you become the nurse you wanted to be? I would guess you've been busy. I haven't seen you around Charleston since the fire and I was sorry to hear about your mother's passing and *here* you are in Savannah."

His implied question gave Mary a chance to collect her thoughts. She cleared her throat. "Thank you. Yes, it's been a hard few weeks, but I'll survive. Savannah will be home for a while. The Charleston house belongs to a New York cousin now and I didn't want to stay there anyway. And it seems I had a family member here in Savannah that I'd never met." Her voice changed and became brisk, "So, thank you for walking me home. It was very nice to see you."

He brought her hand to his lips and lightly pressed his mouth over its delicate wrist. He saw soft blue veins pulse beneath the tender skin and the pupils of his eyes expanded as heat coursed through his body. He reluctantly dropped her hand, and he could still feel the press of her flesh on his lips. He was startled at the strength of his attraction to her after their years apart. He decided to rethink his length of stay in Savannah. He wanted to know her a little better. His heart was telling him it would be worth it.

He said, "I'd really like to continue our conversation. I would be honored if you would accompany me for a late breakfast. Perhaps tomorrow morning at the Waterfront Cafe? We can play catch-up with all the gossip." His voice held a hint of laughter, smooth and low with its touch of English accent. He continued, "Shall we meet at ten o'clock?"

Mary stood still, admiring the perfect voice framing an invitation to breakfast and totally forgot that a response was expected. She finally managed to breathe a short, "Uh, yes, thank you. I will meet you there at ten o'clock." Her quivering legs climbed the steps to the porch, and she managed to open the heavy door, enter, and softly close it behind her.

She leaned backwards against the door's wooden comfort but quickly realized her mistake and murmured, "Oh, rats I forgot to bring in the damn box." She felt stupid and embarrassed while she waited for him to walk away. Finally, she yanked open the door, grabbed the box off the porch and retreated to safety.

Clayton stood unseen in the shadows, hearing and watching the comedy of the flustered female and her hatbox. He smiled slightly and began walking along the sidewalk away from the house. He remembered their first meeting years ago when she was sixteen and tonight's strong attraction to her told him it was time to renew their acquaintance. His brain insisted on imagining her unclothed until his desire flamed and refused to burn out with just a sedate nighttime stroll. He broke into a pounding run *away* from temptation.

Mary stumbled up the stairs to her bedroom as she recalled meeting him in Charleston. *It's just too good to be true. Clayton Masters, here in Savannah? Interested in me? No! Impossible!* But even with her denial, the tiny pearl buttons on her jacket resisted her shaking fingers' attempt to release them as she readied herself for bed.

Would she be able to even hold a coherent conversation with him tomorrow? Should she cancel? *No, darn it! I can do this! I'm a nurse and I can handle anything!* She removed the rest of her clothing and stood in front of the dressing table mirror assessing her face and almost naked body. Too tall, bosom larger than fashionable, waist didn't need a corset, but the hips seemed a little too slim. The face? Pretty but not beautiful. Good cheekbones and chin. Thank goodness for good hair! *I don't look like the lady's catalogue pictures but I do okay. Well, at least I have a brain, and* that *should count for something.*

After slipping her plain cotton nightshift over her head, she sat in front of her dressing table and pulled the pins from her hair. She gave it the usual hundred strokes with her brush, braided it and climbed into bed. Her cheeks burned with the memory of his lips on her wrist. And those eyes and that kissable mouth! Her stomach tightened with the idea of seeing him again and a feeling of warmth pooled in her abdomen.

She touched the nipples on her breasts, and they hardened into pink points when she thought of his mouth— *No, stop it! You'll drive yourself crazy.* She drew a few deeps breaths and finally calmed. She had to admit that his charms would be very hard to resist, and she wasn't even sure if she wanted to. The faint smell of his cologne still remained on her wrist, and she couldn't help but happily breathe it in.

Clayton tried to resist Mary's seductive scent by sprinting as fast as he could through the neighborhood and as he passed a few late pedestrians, they felt a cool breeze ruffle their hair. His resistance lasted less than ten minutes and he soon found himself outside the house again. For another hour, he remained comfortably seated on the open sill of her second-story bedroom window. Any guilt over his voyeurism disappeared as he watched her brush her hair and tame its length with a braid. Why did he find her so fascinating? She wasn't a conventional beauty, but something about her eyes and mouth hinted at intelligence and sensuality. He almost lost his perch when he watched her hand drift slowly over her two perfect breasts, down to her waist and hips. He knew she couldn't see him but if he wasn't careful, any noise might draw her to the window.

His predatory instinct was demanding he choose. Drink now or leave now. He shook himself free of her allure and with a small sigh, drifted down to the shadowed lawn and fled again through the darkness to find a safer place to hunt.

Mary heard the wind moan briefly outside her window. She felt restless and sleep was slow to come but she became drowsy and thought of him again before she drifted off. The hint of Clayton's cologne brought dreams so detailed and intimate that when she woke the next morning, she was blushing and damp between her thighs.

CHAPTER 26
BREAKFAST FOR TWO

Clayton decided America was a fascinating place to be. *Or is Miss Mary Ellington the fascinating place to be?* He chuckled at the thought. One final look in the mirror and he was ready. He acknowledged to himself that this type of anticipation was unusual, but for some reason, he really *did* want to know her better.

He was across the street from the restaurant waiting for the morning traffic to clear and saw her sitting at a table near the window of the café. She was dressed in a fashionable dark green dress that complimented the color of her skin. Her dark hair had honey highlights that caught the bright morning sunlight and a gold clasp at her throat accented the graceful line of her neck as she raised her coffee cup. He stood motionless and watched her drinking, totally engrossed in a newspaper article.

As if sensing his nearness, she looked up and directly at him through the café window and he began to hurry towards her from across the street. She smiled a greeting and gestured to the empty chair across from her as he entered the warm steaminess of the small restaurant.

He sat himself in the chair across from her as she folded her newspaper and laid it next to her cup. A waitress quickly came to the table for their order. He looked at Mary and smiled. "Miss Ellington, what would you like for breakfast? I've heard that the food is very good here. Please go ahead and order."

She nodded, smiled, and addressed her request to the waitress. "I'd like an English muffin with marmalade if you have it, two soft-boiled eggs and more coffee please."

"Yes, miss." The waitress turned to Clayton. "And for you, sir?" The hand holding her pencil stopped midair as sensual heat flashed through her body.

His voice was casually slow. "Just coffee, thanks." He broke his mental connection with her by nodding and turning to Mary.

Jillie the waitress felt her face heat again as the blood rushed to it. She shook her head, tightened her grip on her pencil and retreated to the kitchen counter. Her hands were shaking as she handed the breakfast order to the cook. She didn't want to return to the table with their order. That man made her so nervous! He was way too good looking, and her grandma had always told her to beware of men with a devilish grin and dark blue eyes.

As promised, Mary's breakfast was good. She was so engrossed with how well their conversation was going she never noticed Clayton took only a sip before ignoring the coffee in front of him. They spoke of life in Charleston and Mary's training as a nurse. They spoke briefly about the fire, and she began to tell him of the recent loss of her Aunt Polly.

She concluded her story with, "And I never knew I had an aunt. I got here too late to say good-bye to her and the inheritance money has disappeared." Mary sat back with a small sigh of relief after telling her tale. His look of compassion and encouragement had made telling it so easy.

A look of alarm crossed her face. "Oh no! I almost forgot. I have a one o'clock appointment with that nasty lawyer I mentioned. Here I've been chattering on and lost track of the time." She rushed on, "I'm so sorry but please excuse me and thank you for breakfast!"

Her face flushed pink as she quickly gathered up her purse and newspaper. Clayton stood up and smiled as he said, "I've enjoyed the "chatter" as you call it, but I have no particular place to be this morning and if you'd like some company, I'd enjoy walking you to your appointment. Maybe I can even provide moral support for you if you battle against that *nasty* lawyer fellow."

Mary heard the teasing in his voice and was eager to continue their acquaintance. "Actually, I'd appreciate the company. I don't trust Mr. Noteworthy. There is something about him that sets my teeth on edge. His office is just up the street, but I've never been there." *If walking beside this handsome man starts tongues wagging, then so be it.* Her heart skipped a beat when he tucked her hand under his arm and smiled down at her.

Clayton was happy to be seen walking and talking with such a delightful and pretty woman. Her scent continued to drive him to distraction, but he held himself in check with thoughts of a much better and, with luck, a much longer relationship.

As they walked, he remembered seeing her skipping along the street as a little girl. Her determination to become a nurse. Even the aborted attack in that alley didn't scare her enough for her to abandon her training. She didn't let the untimely loss of her mother, or her aunt defeat her. Not to mention, here she was, her reputation intact despite her choice of a previously unsuitable career. Times were changing and a career in nursing was acceptable nowadays.

But this feeling I have? She's perfect and I want her with me. Always. Am I falling in love with her? He gave himself a mental shake. *No way! I can't let this happen. If she's in my arms if I lose control—*

As he struggled with his thoughts, the handsome couple walked towards the lawyer's office. Mary had visions of their life together, but Clayton could only see her possible death at his hands.

CHAPTER 27
MR. C. NOTEWORTHY, ESQUIRE

Promptly at one o'clock the two stood outside the office of Mr. C. Noteworthy, Esquire. She laughed softly at the pretentiousness of the name and title displayed on the door's tarnished brass nameplate. Clayton, meeting the lawyer for the first time, was not prepared for the amazing amount of dust and clutter displayed before him as they entered the office. He managed to keep his face blank as he viewed the nightmarish rat's nest on display. *This disorganization can't possibly encourage trust in the man.* He quietly closed the door behind him as Mary delicately sneezed into her lace handkerchief.

The warped wooden floorboards creaked faintly underfoot despite the best efforts of the threadbare carpet to muffle the sound of their footsteps. Sunlight struggled its way through the cracked dirty window facing the street and dust motes floated in the air as if invited to a dance. Ill-used books and scattered papers were loosely stacked on a five-tier bookcase to the right of the entrance and dozens of brown file folders, each tied with frayed string, tilted near the edge of an overly crowded desk.

Spilled liquid of some kind had left its mark on the top folder and Mary thought it would be interesting indeed if they fell off the edge should a door be slammed shut. A fly-specked picture of George Washington hung in the middle of the wall behind the desk that faced the door and Mary noticed a crack in the width of the picture frame bisected George's nose. Poor George, she thought. There were two brown leather chairs with sprung seats facing the desk. Clayton escorted Mary to the cleaner looking leftmost chair but preferred to stand slightly behind her to her left. His hands rested on the chair's high back, and he resisted the urge to caress the back of her neck.

Mr. C. Noteworthy, Esquire, stepped around his overly large desk and the scent of mildew, unclean linen and recent cigar smoke followed him. His thinning hair was parted low on the side and combed across the shiny dome in an unfortunate (and unsuccessful) attempt to hide his baldness. It also seemed to be held in place with just a little too much pomade. He inclined his head as he greeted Mary with a smile marred by a missing incisor. His voice was a basso rumble seemingly at odds with such a short toad-like stature.

"Ah, Miss Ellington. Indeed, a pleasure to see you again, but I believe our business was concluded last week, yes? A sad business to be sure. Did you want to discuss the sale of the house?" He finally took notice of Clayton. "And, if I may ask, who is your gentleman friend? I don't believe we've met." He took a step forward and held out a pudgy hand to shake.

Mr. Noteworthy's oily voice sputtered to a halt as Clayton ignored the hand and stood motionless, his ice blue eyes coldly staring at the lawyer. He was thinking that the man's voice sounded a bit froglike, and his blood probably tasted like the bottom of a cesspit.

Clayton said softly, "You recently reviewed the estate of Miss Ellington's aunt. Miss Ellington asked my advice on a few items that seem to have been overlooked. Perhaps you can clear up any potential misunderstanding of what exactly her inheritance includes and what exactly are the financial arrangements made according to the will?"

The lawyer's face turned crimson as he tried to gain control and dominate the conversation by drawing himself up with his chest out. Unfortunately, the attempt was marred by a rather large gravy stain from an earlier lunch. Buttons strained on the bullfrog's vest and Mary turned her face away to stifle another sneeze behind her handkerchief.

Noteworthy's voice rose to a whine. "To the best of my knowledge, Miss Polly Ellington had left no will at all! When Miss Mary *did* find the document, I offered to help again, *pro bono* you understand, and I am offended, sir, that you think I might have taken advantage of this poor young lady's loss!" His chubby hand gestured in her direction as he paused to take another breath. "Why, I even met her at her home to save her the trip downtown to this very office!"

"Mr. Noteworthy," Mary interrupted, "I spoke to your assistant the same day I discovered the will among my aunt's papers and found your business card on the kitchen table. Yes, you graciously offered to come to my home to explain its contents to me, but you spoke so quickly I barely understood what you were saying. After you left, I went to her bank with the will to prove I was a legitimate heir. Imagine my surprise to find her account was emptied and closed."

Mary took a deep breath, straightened her back, and continued, "Sir, what happened to the five thousand dollars mentioned in the will? It is clearly written that I am to have the house, a working ranch in Colorado and five thousand dollars and, sir, it wasn't *me* who withdrew that money!"

Silence crowded the shabby room. Mr. Noteworthy's face began to redden and swell with indignation at the implied threat to his honor.

Mary ignored him and pulled open a small leather case to remove several pieces of paper. Her voice remained calm and clear. "Well, we know one thing, don't we? Someone pretended to be me at her funeral while I was still in Charleston. That person forged my name to withdraw the money and closed the account within a week of her death. I have that note and signature right here. I even hired a detective to do some research. If I'm not mistaken, isn't the bank president your brother-in-law?" She leaned forward in the chair and her eyes bored into the flushed and sweaty face of the short stout man in front of her.

Dead silence greeted Mary's confident announcement. The lawyer's face became chalk white, and his eyes looked haunted. He shifted his feet on the threadbare carpet and looked at the office door as if getting ready to run. Mary remained quiet and composed, her hands and leather case resting in her lap.

Clayton remained completely still as he watched Mary maneuver through this difficult and emotional situation. He was prepared to step in if she needed moral (or physical) support, but he was impressed with her courage while dealing with this scum of a lawyer.

Mr. Noteworthy looked crestfallen and finally accepted his defeat. He already knew the forged signature wouldn't pass a close examination. His brother-in-law had warned him, but greed had overcome his common sense. Finally, he said, "Yes! I admit it. I didn't know your aunt that well and she only spoke of you when she became bedridden. I found an unmailed letter addressed to you and when you didn't show up for the funeral, I figured you didn't care. I promise to return the money. My reputation will be ruined if this gets out!"

Mary rose to her feet and tucked her papers into her leather case. She kept her face carefully neutral as she stood next to Clayton. The man was a rat, and she would never forgive his actions. The upset lawyer seemed ready to grovel at her feet and plead some more but was interrupted by a sharp knock at the door. Clayton raised an eyebrow and Mary nodded to him with a faint smile. He stepped aside to open it for the two blue suited policemen who stood waiting there and asked them, "Did you hear everything?"

"We did sir, and we'll take it from here." As they approached him with handcuffs, Mr. C. Noteworthy, Esquire sank into the vacant armchair and with a low sob, covered his face with his hands.

CHAPTER 28
THE LOVE AFFAIR

A month later, Mary sat on the front parlor sofa of her Savannah home nervously waiting for Clayton to arrive for their dinner date. She loved being with him and looked forward to their dates, though those dates were seriously lacking in romance. Her heart did a double-quick beat as she continued to think of him. *Tonight, I'm going to make him kiss me. Kiss me on my lips! He's such a gentleman but enough is enough. He's been calling on me for a month without so much as a kiss on my cheek! Am I just not attractive enough? Is there something wrong with me? Or, heavens forbid, is something wrong with him? No. Absolutely, not. Other than the lack of a kiss, we get along so well. Yes, tonight is the night! And if he refuses to take the hint, I'll just flat out ask him why or maybe just kiss him myself. Hah! Take* that, *Mr. Clayton Masters!* With her plan of feminine attack in order, she settled back to wait for his arrival.

Clayton pulled the carriage to a stop in front of Mary's porch a few minutes before eight o'clock. He had been driving aimlessly for almost an hour waiting for the time to pass. Supper reservations at the Hilton House were for eight-thirty and he figured they would take the long way to the restaurant while she was forced to sit close to his side.

Memory of her scent caused his pulse to race with the thought of pulling her into the circle of his arms with her breasts held captive against his chest. He would finally be able to kiss the sweet spot just below her ear. His fangs threatened to drop at the image of her blood welling up into his mouth as his kiss deepened. His cock began to harden with the thought of entering her moist and welcoming heat. He tried to slam his mental door shut on those particular thoughts.

Oh God, help me keep a safe distance from her. She's becoming so hard to resist. Just being near her is driving me insane. Those lips need kissing, and that tiny waist needs my hands around it... and those perfect breasts— I want her. I need her. I want to feel the waterfall of her hair on my chest as we make love. His cock hardened and lengthened until it pressed tightly against the waistband of his trousers.

Mary continued to sit on her sofa while she adjusted her skirt for the hundred-and-first time and thought of stolen kisses. Those thoughts were interrupted by a firm knock on her entryway door and with her determination to get a kiss somehow, she marched to the door and pulled it open with a little too much energy. It slammed against the wall with a resounding bang, startling them both.

Clayton stood in the doorway, his tall form blocking the streetlight and his face shadowed. He gazed unspeaking at her, his pupils enlarged, and his fangs threatened to drop a second time. Sheer will kept them hidden as he stepped forward and swept her into his arms. Her toes barely touched the floor as he bent his head to kiss her eager lips.

His kiss deepened as her mouth opened to receive his heat. His tongue began to ravage her mouth and she responded with a heat of her own. Her arms rose to encircle his neck and pull his head lower as he put his hands around her tiny waist. Easily lifting her off her feet, he took two steps into the entryway and kicked the door shut behind him with his boot. His voice was amused and a little breathless. "Let's not set fire to the neighborhood, okay?"

She felt his hardness through the fabric of her skirts and yearned for more. Her body was on fire with the need to finish what they had just started, and she pushed into his lean form with mindless urgency. Liquid heat pooled low on her belly, and she rubbed against him, mentally cursing the skirt that kept her from reaching her goal.

Clayton pulled her hips closer to his rampant cock and whispered into her ear, "Are you sure you want this?"

Realization of what she was about to do swept through her and made her pause. Common sense had almost deserted her, but even with weakened knees, she managed to take a step back and pushed her hands against the granite wall of his chest. She gazed up to his face trying to catch her breath. Those brilliant blue eyes held her captive, and his arms now acted like steel bands circling her back. He said nothing, but with a regretful sigh, finally loosened his arms and released her. He gripped her elbows and moved her away from him to safety. She never noticed the narrow tint of red encircling the dark sapphire of his eyes.

She blushed and said, "Whew! You simply take my breath away, Mr. Clayton Masters." Her smile was quivering with her efforts of trying to lighten the mood and her eyes sparkled with new knowledge. She was right, this man was the one she wanted, and his kisses proved he wanted her just as much. Her feminine attack plan had been unnecessary after all.

Clayton breathed her unique woman's scent deep into his lungs and was entranced by her swollen lips and the sound of her pounding heart. *Oh yes, she's perfect for me.* He gave himself a mental shake before returning her smile. He reached for her shawl and draped it over her shoulders but let his hands linger there as a promise of intimate moments to come.

His smooth voice held frustrated desire touched with humor. "My pleasure, Miss Ellington. Shall we go to dinner now?"

The drive to Hilton House was quiet as both mentally reviewed what had just occurred between them. Mary realized now that she would have to be very careful not to arouse Clayton's passion, not to mention her own. She had been so close She wanted the feel of his heated skin on her own. To feel his lips, capture her own. To stretch her naked length on him and make him *fully* her own.

Clayton was intensely aware of Mary's breath quickening as she shifted in her seat. He refrained from pushing a lewd thought or two into her mind but continued to drive quietly, pretending his full attention was on the carriage horses, while Mary collected her thoughts. He reached for her hand, and she clasped his in response while smiling to herself. She was confident that their relationship would continue to build. Slowly.

It was after midnight by the time Clayton returned Mary to her front porch. After saying a long goodnight filled with kisses and heat, he left her standing in her entryway flushed and trembling. It was hard for him to leave, but his future and her life depended on his maintaining control of his unholy thirst for blood, not to mention his building physical need for her body.

As he drove away, he thought about their easy companionship, their shared love of books and the theatre. Sometimes they played chess in her front parlor until all hours and damn, if the woman wasn't improving her game! Enough. He needed to hunt, and he had put it off almost too long.

It was still dark, and Clayton had fed well before returning to his rented apartment. Thalia was waiting anxiously for him inside. She hugged him briefly and lost no time in explaining her visit. He and Thalia had blood ties from the day she rescued him in London years ago and she had come to Savannah with a warning.

Her voice reflected her distress. "Clayton, you remember the losing rider of the Charleston horse race. Well, he's shown signs of madness ever since. He continues to rant about being cheated out of his plantation and he's vowed to hunt down and kill you even if it takes forever. Can't you do something?"

"Well, it wouldn't be right just to kill him. He's too well connected with family and too many people will remember me and that race even if it's been almost five years ." Clayton's voice trailed off.

Thalia's voice was thoughtful. "At least the Charleson crowd remembers that the race was fair. I've heard that they've practically quit trying to convince him of such, so they're just ignoring or avoiding him and his outbursts." Her face showed genuine concern.

"Please, Clayton, be careful. I'd hate to lose a good friend." The topics changed and they talked of old times and current events until it was time for her to leave. The morning sun was *not* her friend, so he walked her to the door and quickly hugged her goodbye. After hugging him back, she kissed his cheek and left in a swirl of satin and mist.

* * *

Days and weeks flew by as Mary and Clayton continued to see each other. He escorted her to the many entertainments Savannah had to offer and sometimes they just walked in the park or had a picnic by the river. He taught her how to ride an English saddle after she commissioned a riding habit with an unusual split skirt from her favorite seamstress. The society matrons were appalled at the reckless behavior of Mary and Clayton as they cantered their way to the outskirts of town. Riding astride like a hoyden and without a chaperone? What possible good would come of this behavior? Her reputation would be ruined! To themselves, however, the matrons had to admit that the two made a handsome couple.

CHAPTER 29
MURDER ON THE BOARDWALK

SAVANNAH - 1860

Clayton and Mary strolled arm in arm along the Savannah River boardwalk. The early evening was softening to hues of gray and pink in the western sky. Streetlights were being turned on and their soft glow graced the night mist rising off the slow-moving river.

He was thinking of their time together as he split his presence between Charleston and Savannah. They agreed that their age difference wasn't an issue, and he was going to ask her to become his wife. He knew beyond a doubt that she was the woman for him. Forever. He wanted the marriage as quickly as could be arranged because he felt war between the North and South was going to happen soon, and he wanted Mary to be wholly his before he was forced to leave Charleston for good. *Fifty years in one place was way too long for explanations. Once the war is over, we'll reunite and move somewhere else maybe that ranch in Colorado. It sounds like the perfect place to put down roots for another fifty years, anyway.*

He turned towards Mary, still holding her hand in his. He cleared his throat before he said, "Mary, will you consent to be my wife?" Her startled look caused him to rush on. "I can't imagine my life without you. We can move out west to the ranch in Colorado if you want to and I have plenty of income so we can make a very good life together."

Mary remained quiet and a look of near panic crossed Clayton's face. "Well, please say something, I'm feeling like a schoolboy."

Mary smiled up at him, her face glowing in the lamplight and her voice was soft. "Oh, Clayton yes. Of course, my answer is yes. What else would it be?"

Completely undone by her reply, his shaking fingers managed to find and pull a small box from his jacket pocket. He opened it and removed an engagement ring from its snug ivory and velvet lining. The three-carat diamond was nestled between two blood red rubies in a silver setting and reflected the overhead gaslight as he gently placed the ring on her finger. Her eyes grew huge as she realized the wealth it represented and she lifted her hand to admire it before saying, "It's absolutely beautiful." She put her arms around his waist and hugged tightly while pressing herself against him before lifting her face for his kiss.

After at least a million kisses later, Clayton placed her hand into the crook of his arm, and they slowly continued along the riverside walkway as it turned from sturdy boards to tightly packed gravel. His voice was quiet as he said, "Mary, we have to talk about something else. War is coming, and I'll probably be called up by the new Confederate Navy. I'll be based out of Norh Carolina but should be able to get shore leave to see you sometimes if you continue working at the hospital. I know it's going to be rough to be apart from each other, but I don't want to wait any longer. I love you so much and I need you to be my wife." He stopped to pull her into his arms and bent his head to kiss her again.

Clayton promised himself that he would make a good life for her for as long as she could be by his side whether it was for a day or for a thousand years. He would do what it took to keep her happy and if old age meant she must go, then he would stay by her side and comfort her so she could leave this world without sorrow. He could *never r*eveal the monster within him to this wonderful woman. He would continue to keep his dark secrets.

From the darkness, an enraged scream of, "Found you, you bastard!" was followed by the loud crack of a gunshot. Clayton felt a burning coal pierce the back of his neck, and his shoulder felt the punch of another bullet as a second shot rang out from behind. The assassin wasn't finished yet as his third bullet plowed through his abdomen, and narrowly missed a kidney.

A shout, a curse, and the sounds of running feet faded as he helplessly fell to his knees and toppled to his side. The gravel pathway began soaking up the blood draining from the bullets' three entry and exit wounds. He faintly heard Mary shriek his name as she dropped down beside him and pulled his shoulders onto her lap, his head resting there while his blood drenched her skirt and smeared their engagement ring with scarlet.

Several passersby chased and grabbed the assassin and wrestled him to the ground. One grabbed the man's pistol and held it pointed down at him as another tied his wrists behind him with the assassin's own necktie. The man was laughing hysterically, "I gottcha! I finally gottcha! You lied! I won that race, fair and square! I said I'd make you pay, and I just d-did!"

Mary was sobbing as she watched life drain from Clayton's open eyes. She cried, "No! No! Please don't die! Don't leave me!" Clayton could hear Mary's words, as if she were shouting to him from down a deep well. He saw pitch black clouds rushing towards him and tried to speak words of comfort, but the whispered words died on his lips and his darkness became complete.

Minutes later, an older, finely dressed woman appeared at Mary's side and placed her hand on her shoulder. Her cultured English accent murmured, "He's gone my dear. Get up now, let the police do their job." Mary was too grief stricken to make sense of what the woman was saying, but reluctantly rose to her feet when two strong silken clad arms lifted her upright. She was led away and made to sit on a nearby bench. Lost in her personal hell, Mary wasn't even aware when the unknown woman left her side.

Thalia left Mary quietly weeping on the bench and remained unnoticed when she followed the ambulance with its lifeless burden to the city morgue. In the darkness of its entryway, she was easily able to unlock the security door and after casting a bit of glamour, pass the night-duty morgue attendant writing up the recent delivery. She gathered her skirts and sped along the dimly lit hallway until she found the door that opened to the cool autopsy room.

His motionless body, covered in blood, was still dressed and laid out on a granite surgical table. Without a pause, she used her fingernail to slice the skin at her wrist and held it above Clayton's mouth. There were no immediate signs of revival, but as her ancient blood began to drip onto the still lips, their marble whiteness turned a pale pink. She pushed her wrist against his mouth and the pressure opened it slightly to receive the steady red trickle. She only had a few minutes before the coroner arrived for the body, so Thalia closed the wound at her wrist and grabbed some clean cotton pads stored on a nearby shelf. She pushed a handful against the shredded skin and muscle left by the bullet's exit at his shoulder and hip. Once done, she quickly located long linen bandages and quickly but carefully wrapped Clayton's gaping wounds at neck and throat. The bullet had entered so close to the top of his spine; she prayed her movements weren't making the injuries worse.

Thalia's heart was in her throat as she easily picked up Clayton's lifeless body and ran lightly down the empty corridor to the back of the building. No one stood to guard the exit door and she pushed through it in an instant. Still tightly holding him in her arms, she lifted up into the darkness overhead and flew towards her home on the outskirts of Savannah.

Thalia fought the urge to panic knowing that she had to get more blood into him as soon as possible so he could begin to heal. She rushed through the opened kitchen door of her house, and down the basement steps flinging off her hat and shawl with one hand as she went.

She gently laid Clayton on the basement floor and rushed upstairs to change into a simple gardening dress. Her fingers felt like stumps as she tied on a full-length apron. It wouldn't do to have blood showing if she needed to answer the door or leave the house. She quickly filled a kitchen pan with warm water and returned to the basement with towels and sheets for the unused cot stashed in the corner. She removed the blood-soaked jacket and shirt from her unconscious friend and tossed them aside, she would have them burned or buried later. She began to sponge off the drying blood, careful to avoid turning his head or neck.

Once the blood was sponged away, Thalia's (collected over hundreds of years) knowledge of the human form helped her to assess the wreckage left by the bullets. The second bullet had caused damage to the muscle and pierced the shoulder blade but avoided any arteries and nerves. The third bullet had narrowly missed a kidney and no other organs were hit; so, she knew he'd heal from those wounds given time. She peered closer at his neck and prayed that the first bullet hadn't severed his spinal column but even with a doctor present only so much could be done now.

* * *

Later that evening Mary still felt numb with grief. Her love's dead body had been taken to the morgue and she knew she needed to have it transferred to a funeral parlor. She was standing in the darkened hallway of her home trying to clear her mind so she could handle the arrangements when there was a sharp knock. She was startled by the sound and moved stiffly towards the front door as if in a dream. Her cold hand fumbled with its latch before she managed to pull it open.

The police were standing away from the door as she stepped out. They appeared nervous and unsure what to do with the caps in their hands. The older of the two began to speak. "We wanted to let you know the shooter confessed. Turns out he was a gambler from Charleston who insisted on a high stakes horse race. Mr. Masters judged the other guy as the winner and this loser vowed revenge. He tracked him down and shot him." Mary's face remained blank as she stared into the distance and said nothing in response.

The officer swallowed twice, looked away from her and stammered, "There's something else Your gentleman friend, Mr. Masters, he seems to have disappeared. We don't know how it could have happened what with our security in the building but, he's missing." Both looked down with embarrassment as if there were something fascinating about the porch's painted wooden floor.

Mary stood frozen in disbelief at the last bit of news. Black sparkles swam before her eyes, but she fought against fainting and gripped the edge of her doorway, breathed deep and remained upright. Her voice was flat. "Please notify me immediately when you find him." She turned, closed the door, and calmly mounted the stairs to her bedroom before falling fully clothed onto her bed.

In the darkness across the street, the same older woman who had helped Mary earlier watched in silence, before turning away. She knew Clayton would definitely need help while he healed. She only hoped the young woman he loved so much would be able to move past the ugliness of his murder and live a decent life. It never worked well when a vampire and a mortal loved each other. Thalia heaved a sigh and wished them her the best.

The Lieutenant Captain of Savannah's Police Department felt it was best to downplay the news of a stolen corpse. Keep both the murder and the theft out of the news as much as possible. It put his department in a very bad light and there was an election coming up in six months - the victim wasn't a local after all. He demanded everything about the assassination and body theft to be buried amidst the hysterical news of the pending war between the north and south.

Two days passed as Thalia worked feverously to save Clayton. She fed herself at night from the usual supply of human detritus that littered the underbelly of Savannah. After she fed, she'd return to the basement beneath her house and minister to him with small blood exchanges. The wounded shoulder and abdomen were doing okay, but he remained unconscious and the vicious wound at his neck was very slow to heal. He had lost so much blood! She knew that his spine had been severely injured but not completely severed so she believed the chance of his survival with moving limbs was good.

She became impatient with the slowness of his recovery and decided on a more old-fashioned cure. She changed into a pair of men's overalls, grabbed a shovel, and began digging in the dirt floor of the basement. In a matter of minutes, she created a space deep enough and long enough to accommodate his unconscious body.

After wrapping Clayton in several clean sheets, she picked him up and easily moved him to the edge of the hole and carefully laid him down. She took the shovel and poured a thin layer of dirt over him, enough to thoroughly cover him, but just enough so she would be aware of any movements during his healing progress. She sighed. It was up to him now. She had done all she could.

Another night passed with nightmarish slowness while she sat alone in her kitchen remembering all the delightful moments she had shared with Clayton. They had argued, laughed, and even cried together but nothing affected her more than this last threat. Thalia was afraid he had lost so much blood it might permanently affect a complete recovery. If the spinal cord was unrepairable, it might even result in his final death. She held back her tears, set her shoulders back and decided to fight even harder to keep her friend alive.

The fourth night had fallen when she heard a faint sound coming from her basement.

Her heart was pounding as she rushed down the wooden stairs and found an alert Clayton sitting on the edge of his cot, his naked body swathed in dirt-stained sheets. He looked at her with a faint smile and pushed his dark hair from his face with a thin hand. His blue eyes were dim and his face was puzzled as he asked, "What's happened? Where am I and what are you doing here?"

Thalia rushed over to Clayton with a huge smile on her face and carefully hugged him. "Oh, my! Just look at you! You're alive! ... Well kind of alive."

A smile quirked at the corner of his mouth but he said nothing as he grabbed her hand and kissed it. His voice was hoarse. "Lady, I know I owe you. I *am* alive and I'm really, *really* hungry."

She smiled and said, "Here, take this until we can go outside to hunt." She presented her wrist against his mouth and felt a slight sting as his lowered fangs pierced the skin. She felt her blood being pulled through her veins and into his mouth. After a minute she breathed,

"Enough!" She pulled her wrist away and stepped back while smoothing the puncture marks with her hand.

"Now talk," he demanded. "I remember the fire in Charleston. I planned on getting building supplies in Savannah. I remember that's about it." He cautiously rubbed the back of his neck. "That's all I remember but I think I'm missing something important."

Thalia stared at him but shuttered her thoughts. She decided not to tell him about Mary Ellington and his funeral. She didn't want him to remember the attempted murder or agonize over his lost love. It would be best if he didn't remember her at all, these mixed relationships never worked out.

His face grew thoughtful, and he pulled the sheet closer around his body. He shook his head. "No, wait Who's looking after Baron?"

"Baron is fine. Your Hanoverian royalty is in a private stable outside of town. I've checked on him every night and he's eating again. I think he misses you, so best you go get him as soon as you can."

Thalia's next words were brisk. "I'm going to pick up some clothing for you and when I return, we'll get you sorted out. You still have more healing to do, and you need a lot more blood, more than I can share with you right now. There's a lavatory upstairs. Towels and soap are already laid out so help yourself. I'll be back as soon as possible. Oh, and once you're ready, please, *please* wait for me in the back parlor, it's the darkest and won't be seen from the street." Clayton remained seated on the cot as she turned and hurried back up the stairs with a swish from her calico skirts.

Thalia 's fresh blood circulated in his veins and his mind was becoming clearer, so he rose, re-wrapped the sheet around him and began to mount the stairs. By the time he reached the bath on the second floor of the house, he felt his strength begin to ebb. He placed a hand on the wall and managed to reach the bathtub before falling to his knees in a half faint. When his head cleared, he turned the faucets and hot water began to flow. He climbed into the swirling water with a satisfied groan and shut his eyes. He struggled to stay awake while the tub filled and finally reached out to turn everything off before lying against the warmed porcelain back. "Pure heaven," he muttered. One hand still gripped a washcloth as he fell deeply asleep.

Thalia arrived back at the house with an arm full of packages from the all-night second hand store several blocks from her neighborhood. She had been able to use the measurements from Clayton's bloodied garments, so she figured they would be a good fit. She also had to think how to retrieve the rest of his things from his Savannah rental without too much of a fuss. Maybe go alone to remove any references to Mary, and later return with him to finish emptying the place. Maybe encourage him to stay with her in Savannah while healing. Her plan in place, she unlocked and opened her front door.

After removing hat and gloves, she called out, "Clayton, are you up?" There was no answer. She quickly moved through the house and down to the basement but didn't find him. She was becoming alarmed and rushed up the stairs calling as she went, "Clayton, are you okay?" Again, no answer. She knocked at the bathroom door and gently pushed it open. Escaping steam swirled around her and into the dimness of the hallway. She stepped into the vapor and beheld the most handsome man she had ever met, lying fast asleep in the slightly bloodied water of the bathtub. She smiled at the sight and shook her head. They had known each other for so long and it was a real shame that circumstances had made him a younger brother rather than a lover. She sighed.

"Clayton, wake up." Her soft voice startled him, and he sat up so suddenly the water splashed over the sides of the bathtub and onto the floor. He looked at her over his shoulder and a blush rose to his face. He started to cover himself with the inadequate washcloth when she entered the room and grinned at him but crouched forward instead.

"You ain't got nothin' I haven't seen before," she purposely drawled. She winked and turned her back as he leaned forward to pull the plug from the tub's drain. "Dry yourself off. I have some clothes here for you. They're used, but clean, and you can replace them when you get home." She walked through the still opened door and pulled it closed behind, her laughter spilled into the hallway.

"I'm too old for her nonsense," he muttered as he struggled out of the tub and stood on the wet floor.

It was late when he finished dressing, and he was savagely hungry as he flew through the chill and mist of the night sky. He passed two late night strollers. They were obvious lovers and the sudden ache in his chest made him hesitate. He continued his search until he heard rough laughter from inside a shuttered factory near the edge of town. He landed without a sound on the roof, and peering down from a partially broken skylight, he could see three men playing cards on a slab of wood balanced on an empty beer barrel. The men looked like brutes and were carelessly dressed in dirty clothes. He could sense their callous disregard for each other or even the small child at their feet. A very young boy lay on the rough concrete floor nearby. Clayton could easily see that he was gagged and bound with lengths of rope, whimpering as his terrified and helpless eyes fixed on the men seated at the makeshift table.

With a crash, Clayton dropped from the skylight directly onto the table below. His weight shattered it and the men scrambled to avoid the splintered pieces of wood. He grabbed the nearest gang member and hurled him against a steel pillar holding up the roof's framework. Even as the man's head hit the steel with a resounding crack, he grabbed the second man and with one blow of his fist, knocked him unconscious. The third man pulled out the pistol tucked in his waistband and started to aim it at Clayton. This one was more in control and fired as Clayton grabbed the hand holding the pistol and broke the man's wrist. Before he could scream a curse, Clayton's fangs found his throat and crushed it. The man was losing blood but alive.

Remembering the child, he turned away before sprinting into the distant shadows with his unconscious victim. Anger at the callous treatment of the tiny boy unleashed his usual control and he savagely drank from the crushed throat. After drinking his fill, he quietly dropped the corpse at his feet and wiped his face and hands on a clean handkerchief before approaching the boy.

He knelt beside the trembling child and untied the cruelly tight ropes before pulling the dirty cloth away from his tiny mouth. He said, "Hush now, I won't hurt you. Can you tell me your name? Or where you live?"

The small child was too traumatized to whimper anything except, "Bobby."

Clayton kept his voice low and soothing. "Bobby, I'm going to pick you up and take you to a safe place. I'm sure your parents already miss you and are looking for you. They want their boy back home. Is it okay if I help you up and take you home or somewhere safe?"

Bobby fell into the calm well of the stranger's voice and allowed himself to be picked up. The voice became a distant caress as Bobby's tired eyes fell shut and he slept in Clayton's arms.

He swiftly carried the sleeping boy to the closest police station after carefully sending mental pictures of angels and peace into Bobby's traumatized mind. He brought the child into the building, and gently put him on the bench against the wall. He nodded to the shocked constable standing behind the counter and said, "I found him in that abandoned warehouse on East Fourth Street. I heard the fighting from outside, seems there was a gang fight. He said his name is Bobby."

With a nod to the speechless constable, he turned and quickly left before he could be questioned. The constable scratched his head and immediately dispatched a second man to the home of Bobby's parents. The parents arrived to find their son happily sitting on the edge of the counter drawing pictures. But where was the gentleman hero?

Clayton sped back to the warehouse. The two gang members were still out cold on the dirty glass-strewn cement. The rest of the gang hadn't returned yet, so he hauled the dead torso of the third gangbanger to the darkest and furthest part of the empty warehouse before digging a hole deep enough to bury it. He easily picked up and moved some nearby metal scraps and broken concrete to cover the disturbed oil-soaked soil. He knew it would be weeks before any decay would be noticed. If ever. No, he did not feel bad about killing this useless being. Someone who would harm a child? The world was better off without him.

A siren wailed in the distance. Time to leave.

Newspapers reported the capture of the notorious Black Hands gang that had been abducting children and holding them for ransom. The first man had a severe concussion from hitting the steel roof support, the second man insisted, through his wired jaw, that he had been hit by the devil himself. True or not, the man's jaw had been broken by the strength of the blow, and it was slow to mend. The third man was never found. After they recuperated in the hospital, the men were transferred to prison. Within a month, both died at the hands of other prisoners who wouldn't stand for anybody hurting children.

Bobby's parents gently questioned him about the kidnapping, but other than swearing that a dark angel rescued him, the three-year-old could tell them nothing.

* * *

A week after Clayton's *empty casket* burial, Mary was finally ready to deal with his furnished apartment. She let herself in with her extra key and moved about the three small rooms in a daze, barely able to remember why she was there. She drifted from room to room until her mind cleared and she felt able to fill a small box with only the most cherished and personal souvenirs of their short time together. The furniture stayed with the apartment, everything else could go to charity. Her eyes were dry, and her mind was blank as she let herself out the door and went home.

It was early dark when Thalia watched Mary leave Clayton's apartment carrying only a small cardboard box. Her hired movers rapidly packed his personal belongings into tagged boxes and moved everything out to a waiting wagon. The apartment was empty of anything relating to Mary just as Clayton arrived after having fed several miles away from town.

He looked around but he saw nothing to trigger his memory and the place seemed curiously vacant. Thalia moved quietly around the rooms and once, when his back was turned, she stooped to snatch a tiny handkerchief laying underneath a chair and quickly tucked it into her pocket.

"Clayton, why don't you stay with me? My place is certainly large enough and it will be easier for you to return to Charleston on short notice if you only need to move your clothes but you really should avoid the Sapphire, just in case—"

"Yes, I guess I'm supposed to be dead, right?" Her offer sounded good, but his gut told him leaving this apartment would change his life. He was about to close the door a final time when a very faint scent of jasmine teased his nose. Why did he think it was familiar?

Clayton was careful to avoid being seen in Savannah lest anyone recognize him after his murder by that crazed man from Charleston. He was still rooming with Thalia when she handed him a letter from the Confederate Naval Command. He was to appear before Admiral Thomas A. Johnson at the North Carolina naval base in two weeks to receive training and accept his commission in the newly created Confederate Navy.

CHAPTER 30
WILL THERE BE WAR?

CHARLESTON – 1861

No one noticed the black mist floating through the open third floor window of the Sapphire Restaurant.

Two hours later, Clayton placed the day-old newspaper on the corner of his desk and was trying to relax in his private office suite on the third floor of the restaurant. More and more articles were being written about a possible war between the North and South. He hated the idea of any war but this one would give him a perfect exit. He had spent too much time in Charleston.

Alex, Sapphire's current general manager, walked into the office carrying his usual morning coffee and almost dropped it when he saw his missing boss calmly sitting at his desk.

"Boss? Is it really you? They said you were shot and died of bullet wounds in Savannah! Even a small article in the paper! W-what—"

Clayton's voice was hypnotic and persuasive, "Those accounts were vastly overstated but I need you keep quiet about my survival. It's important Alex that you say *nothing*. I'll clear up the record when I return. You must say *nothing* about me being here."

His voice became teasing, "Have some coffee? Help yourself, it's on the sideboard."

Alex's hands shook as he poured himself another cup before lowering himself to the chair opposite Clayton. He took a sip and stared at his boss, waiting for him to speak.

"So, Alex, do you think there will be a war soon? Possible war is what all the papers are writing about these days. What are your thoughts?"

Alex cleared his throat, put down his coffee cup. "Yes, I think there *will* be a war. I sincerely hope not but the North is vehemently against slavery. My cousin's boy has already signed up for the army and my nephew is talking about it, too. Thank heavens he's only fourteen and can't go." He sighed and continued, "Guess it's going to be Union fighting Confederacy if our government keeps drawing lines in the sand." He grimaced, "I'd sign up myself but with such a bum leg, I doubt if they'd take me."

"You're also a little too old for a call to arms," Clayton reminded him. The grin directed at his office manager took any sting out of his comment. He shifted in his chair and said, "I have something important I need to do for the navy, and I leave tomorrow. Remember what I'm telling you. Don't say anything about seeing me alive. I'm taking only a few clothes and my horse. Everything else I'll leave to your stewardship, and I'd like to propose something to you."

Not waiting for a response from Alex, he continued, "You know I've been away from the Sapphire for a bit, checking out business opportunities in Savannah. You've done a great job here in my absence so I'm offering you a partnership. If anything should happen to me, as a partner, you'd have one hundred percent of the business."

Alex was momentarily speechless. "A partnership? Truly? Where do I sign?" *Hell, yes. Me and the missus can finally put aside a little savings for the two grandchildren. Maybe do some traveling once things settle down.* He sat forward in his chair, coffee forgotten.

Clayton smiled at his eagerness. The papers had already been drawn up and were only waiting for Alex's signature. Everything was taken care of. Alex had been with him for quite a few years and deserved the chance to run the restaurant and hotel empire by himself. Assuming Charleston survived the war intact.

Later that evening, Alex and his wife were talking about their good fortune. When he had gotten the job offer, they had already heard about Clayton's thorough training program and generous retirement plan. He grew thoughtful and started adding up the years the Sapphire had been in business. Could it really be fifty years? Impossible, the man didn't look more than thirty-five but since nothing could make sense, he went to bed and refused to question his good luck anymore.

Alex kept his promise and told no one of Clayton's brief re-appearance.

MARY

CHAPTER 31
MARY'S WAR

SAVANNAH – 1866

It had been six miserable years since Clayton's murder and disappearance. Mary sat on the park bench and stared down at her gloved hands as she rolled pathway gravel beneath the toe of her boot. Her dark gray walking dress matched the bonnet perched on her head. A package of day-old bread rested next to her, but the pigeons would have to wait for their late morning treat. Her reddened eyes reflected her sorrow, but the clenched jaw showed a strong helping of frustration seasoned with bewilderment. Her thoughts drifted back to the war and her shock at the almost complete destruction of Charleston. Even her beloved hospital had been leveled to rubble.

Her hands clutched in her lap as she remembered.

* * *

Charleston is being bombarded! Mary's mouth opened in a silent scream as she heard the deep-throated roar of the nearby cannon fire. It was only moments later that the sounds of shattering windows and falling brick walls reached her. She whirled and raced up the steps of the hospital to check on her patients and share her disbelief with the other nurses. The Union army was firing on a civilian population! Never heard of such a thing! Shrill screams from some of the younger nurses reminded her to first calm them before trying to find out exactly what was going on. An hour later, she had just completed caring for the patients in her charge when Dr. Bradford found her and motioned to follow him into his office.

Dr. Bradford's usual spotless jacket and pants were covered in dust and one lapel had a smear of mud. His face looked worried, but his voice was firm. "Mary, I received a message that the Union has decided Charleston is the 'symbol of rebellion', and as such, they will probably destroy this city. Our troops will defend us as much as possible of course, but it's entirely possible we will need to move our patients to a safer place. No doubt the civilians will be encouraged to leave as soon as they can. Any ideas for moving us out?"

Mary's face was grave, "My concern is for my patients of course, and our nurses and doctors should be protected as much as possible. Do you think a cease fire might happen so we can get everyone to safety?"

Dr. Bradford's voice sounded tired. "I have heard that might be the case. I need you to help arrange for transportation of our patients and assign a couple of nurses to pack all medicines and equipment needed for a field hospital. I'll give you a location when I hear from the general. Oh, and try to keep everyone from panicking while you're at it." He gave her a faint smile as he rose to leave. "I'll be meeting with the mayor and whoever else is available, so until you hear from me, please do whatever it takes to keep safe. I'll try to get back before nightfall." He left quickly, knowing that Mary would organize everything necessary, the staff respected her and would follow her directions.

Night had fallen and the angry cannon fire finally stopped. Mary leaned against the pillars of the hospital's front entryway and looked out at the devastation wrought by the blasts. A day earlier, the patients and supplies had been safely transported out to the field hospital several miles west of the city. Her body was begging for relief and her eyes felt on fire from the dust and grit stirred by the constant barrage of offshore cannon fire. Earlier, an endless stream of silent grief - stricken women and children plodded past the hospital followed by wagons filled with whatever fit and might be useful. She was about to return to her temporary office when her attention was caught by a slight disturbance a block away. She knew that some looting had already started but she had been warned to stay away. Stay safe.

There it was again. Someone was pushing a heavily loaded cart away from the mostly damaged private home she knew had been boarded and abandoned earlier in the week. He sure looked like a thief, she thought, hiding from the moonlight like that. She strained her eyes to see better when a dark shadow fell from the roof of the house and landed on the exposed back of the would-be looter. She heard a stifled cry cut short as the two images merged into one. Only seconds later, the shadows parted, and a body shaped mound lie motionless on the ground. The second body stood tall and unnaturally still and looked straight at her. Her senses screamed for her to run but her muscles seemed to be locked in place. Her thoughts were frantic. *Another minute and he'll probably kill me too!*

Mary's wide eyes caught the movement of something large and manlike leap an impossible distance from the roof of the boarded-up house to land directly between her and her would-be murderer. Both lunged into each other and in an instant, the two grappled and wrestled their way back into dense shadows. Mary's terror loosened its grip and she fled to safety behind the heavy doors of the miraculously untouched hospital.

The next morning was eerily still and quiet. A heavy fog covered Charleston's harbor saturating the tattered confederate flag still affixed to the hospital's flagpole. Mary descended to the street with her medical bag and the sad sense that the building might not be there waiting for her return at the end of the war.

Nervous sweat gathered at her throat, but she wanted to confirm what she thought she saw the night before. The cart had tipped over and its contents, though scattered, remained untouched. She took a deep breath and forced her feet towards a pile of rumpled rain-drenched clothing lying at the foot of the abandoned house. She approached slowly and a shudder passed through her when she saw the contorted and nearly empty husk of what had been a human being. She stumbled back on shaking legs, unable to accept the results of what she had witnessed the night before. Emotionally and physically exhausted from her nursing efforts Mary's body did the next best thing it could do. It fainted.

* * *

Unseen by Mary, a tall form detached itself from the roof of the abandoned house, quickly grabbed the victim's corpse and returned with it through a shattered window on the second floor. Clayton was muttering to himself, "Damn that stupid blood-drinker. Scaring that woman half to death and leaving a drained corpse to stir up the locals." *At least the arrogant SOB won't harm anyone else.* Contemptuous sapphire blue eyes looked down at a small pile of damp ash and a few shreds of cloth on the floor, all that remained of the luckless vampire. He would dump the thief's remains into the harbor after nightfall, and head back to his ship. He assumed that the woman would quickly regain her senses and leave the area. She was dressed as a nurse and should be pretty tough-minded. He briefly wondered who she was and what she would do when she realized the corpse was missing.

* * *

And Mary remembered—

With trembling hands, the stained cotton sheet was pulled over the young man's face. He had been one of her favorite patients, but despite her efforts, the 16-year-old artillery gunner had died, and she felt his death as her personal failure. She looked around. The lingering smell of gunpowder mixed with the scents of gangrene, blood, urine, and poor hygiene rarely registered with her anymore. As she raised her head and straightened her aching back, she noted the still overcrowded ward. She called for an orderly to remove her former patient and moved toward the next cot. Another traumatized young soldier lie there, blank eyes staring up at nothing, even as his left hand plucked at the gap left by his missing right arm. A massive bandage encased the stump of his right leg. Below the knee, there was nothing.

THE WAR IS OVER! Faint cheers could be heard from the surrounding wards filled with wounded soldiers. She couldn't find such excitement within herself yet. She had managed to get by on only a few uninterrupted hours of sleep each night. Caring for the sick and wounded men, attending the physicians when they needed her experienced hands, and following the suggestions written by Miss Florence Nightingale had finally taken its toll on her mental and physical health. She was one of the walking wounded herself but without visible scars.

During the following month, the field hospital slowly emptied, and she hoped the recovered men could make their way safely home to their loved ones. She continued to assist in the surgery as needed, tending the post-operative patients, and writing letters home for the men. Inventories of supplies and the constant cleanup required for good recoveries kept her busy with little time to dwell on her own needs.

Finally, the work was finished, the field hospital dismantled, and Mary was free to find her way home. She joined a company of returning soldiers and was able to snag a ride on a wagon carrying their scant supply of food and medical supplies back to Charleston. The men felt lucky to have an actual nurse with them and they treated her with respect. Their week on the road was slow and Mary took care of the soldiers as best she could. Each evening they sang together or told stories of family and hopes for the future. One by one, men left the group as they passed by familiar fields or distant homesteads. Hopefully there would be someone left to welcome them back.

When the wagon reached Charleston, Mary was stunned to see how little was left standing. She went straight to the military hospital set in a cleared area where their hospital used to be and slept uninterrupted for twenty-four hours. When she finally woke, the morning sun was bright and a light breeze from the harbor promised a beautiful day. Her body was rested, and her mind was clear. She decided to return to Savannah. If her aunt's house was still standing, she would move there immediately.

CHAPTER 32
QUEEN'S PRIDE

SAVANNAH - 1866

Mary was tired of sitting around doing nothing. The thought of reading more magazines or taking pointless walks to nowhere didn't appeal to her at all. She was so involved in her dark thoughts that a knock at her front door startled her. Her heart leapt into her throat when she saw a dark shadow through the lace curtains. Who on earth could be calling on her so early in the morning?

She peered through the curtain. *Oh, it's only Harold. Well, his company is better than sitting and stewing about something I can't change.* She straightened her shoulders and opened the door. "Good morning, Harold. What brings you to my front door this morning?"

"Well, M-Mary, I have a new rig and I thought you might like to take a drive in the park with m-me. If you're not too busy this morning or this afternoon?"

Mary's smile was forced, and she tried not to sigh. "Okay, just let me get my shawl."

He waited on the porch for her, thrilled with the idea of sporting around town a bit with Miss Mary Ellington sitting beside him. He wished his mother liked her as much as he did. He thought of their many arguments about Mary in the past. He mentally reviewed the hated list. Mother didn't approve of her nursing career during the war at all. Why, she would have seen men *actually naked*! And too forward speaking. Too smart. Way too pretty. Trouble on that account for sure. She'd probably flirt with men every chance she got and make him miserable. No, Mary was *not* the right wife for him according to his mother.

Harold silently helped Mary onto the seat of the carriage. His tongue seemed to be stuck in his throat, so he just smiled at her, climbed aboard and flicked his whip at the horse.

Mary appreciated his silence. She should tell him soon that she could not accept his attentions anymore. It wasn't fair to let him think there was a future for the two of them.

He was so distracted by her presence that he miscalculated the direction to the city park and ended up passing through the slaughterhouse district as he corrected his error. Harold sped up the carriage to quickly pass the stench of spilled and rotting blood drifting from the open windows of the buildings. He noticed Mary put her handkerchief to her nose to block the smell and was furious with himself for causing her any distress.

Mary suddenly shifted around in her seat and grabbed his arm. Her voice held excitement. "Look, Harold, over there. Isn't that a horse tied to that post? That poor thing. I'll bet they're going to kill it too! Pull up, I want to see better."

Harold was reluctant to stop, but Mary's command and her pull on his arm really left him no choice. He barely stopped the carriage when she jumped down and ran back towards the sad looking animal hitched to a post.

She slowed and approached the horse as she held out a hand while softly talking to it. Its mane and tail were clotted with burs. Bot flies had made nests in the ears and were matted tightly on the legs and belly. Ribs showed through the mud splattered coat and the hips were thinned. There was no doubt in Mary's mind that this horse had been maltreated and was about to be slaughtered. The head hung so low with drooping ears that Mary easily put her hand under its chin and gently lifted it. Her heart thundered. *Good lord. This mare is pure Arabian*. She ran her hand slowly along the sunken withers looking for more damage. There were some recent scars, but this horse might be saved if she could rescue it quickly.

"Hey you! Whatdaya think yer doin? Get away from that animal!" The man's shout was loud and as Mary took a step back, keeping her hand on the mare's neck, the animal raised her head and looked at her. The gentle brown eyes seemed to ask for nothing more than an end to her pain.

Mary, however, was having none of it as she repeated her mantra: '*I can do this! I'm a nurse and I can handle anything!*' This horse could and would be saved.

Within the hour, Mary purchased the horse for an outrageous sum of twenty-five dollars. A curious youngster loitering nearby earned a dime by running to the local vet to tell him of her emergency and her urgent need for a vacant stall for her horse rescue.

Harold stood with a slack jaw and watched Mary turn into a whirlwind of activity as she handled the broken-down nag and the angry manager of the slaughterhouse. It seemed to him that he was only a bystander to this drama and would never have a part to play in it. He also realized he wasn't the kind of man who could stand up to her if her mind was set on something. His mother was right after all.

Mary was about to walk away, leading the horse to the stable, when she remembered Harold patiently waiting for her. A crimson blush rose to her face at her obvious rudeness. "Oh, Harold, I'm so sorry. It's just that—" She searched his face and saw the end of their relationship, such as it was. Her eyes were bright with unshed tears and said gently, "Harold, thank you for the morning drive. Go on home. I'll get someone to drive me back when I've finished up here. It will probably be a while before I see you again."

Harold shook his head and his voice turned into a vicious whine. "I don't think so. You're just like what my mother warned me about. Anyway, good luck with that bag of bones, you're going to need it." With a final sneer, he turned his back, climbed into his waiting carriage, and left her standing alone.

Her hand continued stroking the horse's neck as she whispered encouragement. Harold was already forgotten.

The veterinarian was out on an emergency house call when the two arrived at the stable used while treating sick horses. Mary demanded that the single box stall be cleaned out and fresh straw laid down. Her tone of voice let the doctor's assistant know she was not to be ignored and delay was not an option. When it was ready, a bucket of fresh water and an armload of hay was placed inside. She led the mare into the clean stall. At first, the mare just stood with her head down, but the lure of fresh water drew her to the bucket. She pushed her muzzle into it and began to drink thirstily. Mary continued to talk to her and stroke her mud-covered neck.

The vet arrived and was astonished to see a beautifully dressed young woman talking to the dirtiest and saddest looking excuse of a horse he had ever seen. The dusty sunlight through the stable's high window created a halo of gold on the highlights of the honey-dark hair as she stood stroking the horse and quietly talking to it.

The vet decided she wasn't an angel after all when she turned to him, and he saw the front of her dress strewn with bits of straw and dirt. He nodded towards the horse, "Well, it looks like our work is cut out for us. I'll tell you what needs to be done and my assistant will take notes. Sound all right with you?"

She leaned on the wooden door of the box stall and listened as the assistant wrote the list of instructions. She paid close attention to the vet's review and was grateful that she had enough money to heal the sad looking animal. She knew there was beauty under the filth and obvious neglect.

The vets voice continued, "We need to treat the bot flies, especially her ears. Use some baby oil on the mane and tail and they won't need cutting. Might take a while to work all the burs out but it'll be worth it to save the length." He bent to lift each hoof for a closer look. "You'll need a farrier for the hooves especially that split. Doesn't seem too deep so it'll grow out in time with a metal plate screwed in."

The vet continued, "See the swollen belly with the longer hair underneath? She needs to be dewormed. I also recommend some warm, wet beet pulp to get her diet balanced. Lots of water and quality hay. Lots of good grooming and you'll have yourself a fine-looking Arabian mare." He looked up and smiled as he straightened. "Are you going to name her?"

Mary replied, "I'm going to name her Queen's Pride. She *will* be a queen and proud again when we're finished."

The mare continued eating the hay as her ears twitched at the soft conversation. The vet was repacking his bag and prepared to leave as he continued to give final instructions to his assistant. Mary stepped away from the horse and was about to join him when the mare raised her head, took a step forward and rested her head on her shoulder. Her heart melted, and she whispered to Queen's Pride, "We're going to be friends forever."

It took over a month to easily see the improvements in the mare. Daily grooming brought her coat to a gleaming dappled gray. Each hoof had been trimmed, and a metal band screwed in place to allow the one split to heal as it grew out. The mane and tail remained full and long due to Mary's slow and careful removal of the imbedded burs. The best improvement of all was the mare's attitude. She whickered a greeting whenever Mary approached, her ears perked forward and eyes shining.

Finally, the day came when Mary decided to ride her, and she dressed in the riding habit she used when riding with Clayton. She had ridden many times as a child in Charleston, and during the war she grabbed and rode any horse available if she needed to help the injured still in the field. It was time to see if Queen would allow her to mount. She brought the horse out of the stable and into the small paddock. The horse followed her around the pen until Mary stopped at the mounting block near its gate. Okay, Mary thought, will you allow this? She grabbed a handful of mane and swung her leg with its split skirt over Queen's bare back and settled herself.

Queen shivered and swung her head around to see what was happening but remained quiet. Mary pressed her heels and gave her a gentle signal to walk forward. Another signal and the walk turned to a short trot. Another press of her heel and the trot turned into a slow canter which made Mary feel like she was sitting on a rocking chair. She knew she had rescued a gem of a horse and vowed to give her the care she deserved.

An older gentleman's attention was captured by the sight of a young woman working her horse through its paces without saddle or reins. He stood leaning on the paddock fence and admired the obvious connection between the Arabian mare and her pretty rider.

He called out, "Excuse me miss, may I have a minute of your time?" Mary checked Queen to a halt and looked down at the stranger, a question in her eyes. She said, "Yes? Do I know you?"

"My name is Charles Hilton, I'm a reporter for the Missouri Journal, here's my card." He continued, "Just passing through town, but I'm pretty sure I've seen your horse before, an Arab, isn't she?"

Mary was terrified at where this conversation might lead. "Why, y-yes. I rescued her from a slaughterhouse. As you can see, she's fully recovered, and I have her papers. What's your interest?"

"Well, it's quite a story. But there is a man in New York, name of Henry Bergh, who is interested in protecting the welfare of animals and has founded an anti-cruelty society. I think it was called the ASPCA. I wrote an article for my paper about abuse and his organization. Well, I saw this little beauty several months ago in Charleston and located her owner. Nasty man, not a bit of shame when he was caught beating on her when she couldn't pull his coal wagon. I gave him a good licking in the article I wrote, but the horse disappeared before she could be rescued. Figured he took her away to sell for dog meat or tallow without public interference. I always wondered what happened to her. Well, it looks like she's found herself a good owner. Meeting you this way will provide a positive note for a follow-up article and I thank you for that. You have yourself a good day, Miss." The journalist smiled, tipped his hat, and walked away.

To Mary, seated on Queen's Pride, the day seemed even better than ever.

CHAPTER 33
THE SWEETWATER RANCH SOLUTION

I can do this! I'm a nurse and I can handle anything! Any time Mary was feeling overwhelmed or challenged, she recited her personal mantra of capability. Vivid images of the war and its aftermath still haunted her dreams and she continued to mourn for Clayton and his mysterious disappearance. Tears threatened to fall again but she knew she must take control of her life and move forward.

She decided moving to her inherited ranch in Colorado might offer a solution to her feelings of abandonment and loss. She and Clayton had discussed the possibility of living at the ranch many times and it had been fun to plan the trip out west together. What they might find when they got there and what they might do at the Sweetwater Ranch provided conversations that sometimes lasted into the wee hours of their nightly dates.

Finally, eyes still reddened, but cheeks wiped free of tears, she walked to the telegraph office on Park Street. Before entering, she straightened her skirt, patted her hair back into place and rearranged her hat to its proper tilt.

The telegraph operator was a wizened twig of a man with a pair of round rimless glasses perched on the top of his shiny bald head rising above a nest of puffy white chin whiskers. He saw her standing in the doorway and immediately put aside his newspaper and stepped closer to the counter.

His voice was a friendly tenor, "Yes, miss, what can I do for you?"

Mary stepped closer and replied, "I'd like to contact a ranch in Colorado. I don't have any particulars except its name, the Sweetwater Ranch near the town of Golden City, Colorado. It's outside of Denver, I believe."

"Well, we can try to send a telegraph directly to the Golden City office the name of Sweetwater Ranch is probably known thereabouts so, if need be, someone can take the message out to the ranch. Does that sound about right to you?"

Mary passed her filled-out form to the operator. "Yes, and please send this soon as you can."

He put his glasses on his beaklike nose and blinked rapidly. "Oh, you're Miss Polly's niece! I'll send this right away. It might take a while to hear back but I'll send a boy to your place with any reply."

She smiled and reached into her purse. "Thank you so much. How much do I owe you?"

"Miss Mary, your aunt was very well thought of around here and I remember her talking about her Sweetwater ranch, even after she lost her husband. Nope, there's no charge today." He smiled at her and turned away to the telegraph machine mounted on a sturdy side counter. Mary swallowed the lump in her throat at his generosity, nodded and quickly left the office.

The operator read the message several times before keying it in.

AUNT POLLY PASSED 09/21 STOP WILL VISIT

SWEETWATER RANCH SOON WITH WILL AND TITLE STOP

PLEASE WIRE PARTICULARS TO THIS ADDRESS STOP

MARY LYDIA ELLINGTON. STOP.

Well, a bit wordy the operator thought but the poor thing seemed to be pretty confident about heading out to Colorado by herself. He shook his head and thought, "Yep, she's got gumption." He began to tap out the message.

Four days later, Mary answered the door to find a boy proffering a telegraph envelope. Mary grabbed her purse, dug out a few coins and pressed them into his hand. He touched his finger to his cap, jumped from the porch and scampered off, clutching his treasure.

She tore open the yellow envelope with shaking hands. *This is it! Oh God, what if it's a mistake or—* Her heart was beating rapidly. So many things could go wrong. She gathered her courage and unfolded the paper with its glued strips of message.

SAD NEWS STOP COME TO RANCH EARLIEST POSSIBLE STOP

SEND ARRIVAL DATE STOP

GILL NILSON FOREMAN SWEETWATER RANCH STOP.

Well, *that* was to the point! Of course, at the current cost of ten dollars per word, she understood its brevity. At least her aunt's name was known at the ranch. She figured she would be able to leave Savannah in about a month after securing transportation and renting out her furnished house until she decided what to do with it. Thankfully, her lawyer would handle the details. Thomas A. Johnson, Jr. had been a friend of her aunt's and had moved his legal practice to Savannah a short time ago. She felt she could trust him.

The month passed in a flurry of dress making, house cleaning, moving some personal items into storage, and saying good-bye to a few friends. Queen's Pride had been trained to walk up and into a cattle car like the one that would be used on their trip west. She shuddered at the thought of spending so much travel time between Savannah and Denver but there was no help for it.

Finally, everything was ready, and a wire was sent to Golden City, Colorado with details of her arrival date and time in Denver. Queen's Pride would be stabled there while Mary traveled the last fifteen miles from Denver to Golden City. Those miles would be by stagecoach and hopefully, someone would be on hand to welcome her.

CHAPTER 34
SWEETWATER COWBOYS

THE RANCH - 1867

Mary's first wire caused an uproar at the ranch. The cowhands were all wondering if she were pretty, if she were young and single, if she could she cook. What if she was stuck up and too fancy to talk to them? Or maybe she wouldn't last a month but would turn around and head back east where life was easier. Bets were made on all possible attributes the mystery lady might have and the real possibility that she might not even stay.

Gill, the ranch foreman, was keeping his opinions and questions to himself. He figured any lady from the east wouldn't last a year with the heat and hard work of ranch life. Work was hard, profits were unreliable. On the other hand, the boss's wife had stuck it out for a long time until the babies He shut down his introspection. He would take a wait-and-see attitude until Miss Ellington actually showed up.

That evening, Gill lit a cigarette and sat on the front porch of the bunkhouse, reflecting again on some of the history of Sweetwater. Miss Polly had met and married his boss after a whirlwind courtship in Savannah. The two moved west together and built the ranch on nine hundred acres of rough country. They were extremely lucky to have discovered the small lake was spring fed and each year they managed to add to their acreage until they reached their goal of twelve hundred acres nestled against the foothills of the mountain range.

They were happy together for several years but the harsh demands of building a successful ranch caused her to lose two babies in the eighth month of both pregnancies.

She was heartbroken and ill when she returned to Savannah and her husband's family. The boss stayed behind at the ranch and visited her as often as he could, but the travel distance was a huge problem at the time. Their monthly letters seemed to keep the marriage strong until the day he died of a broken neck. His horse showed up at the ranch with an empty saddle and it took almost two days before his body was found near the shriveled remains of a trampled rattlesnake.

Miss Polly made the long trip from Savannah and stayed only a month. She spent most of her time with Gill as they rode around Sweetwater and discussed its future without her husband. She became an absentee ranch owner but maintained close contact with him through the years. Their relationship was based on mutual trust, and he had always assumed that the niece, Miss Ellington would inherit the property after Miss Polly's death.

It was almost a month later when Gill opened Mary's return wire detailing her expected arrival in Golden City. Gill groaned aloud, "Oh no. She's going to be here in three days." Always on the lookout for rustlers on the upper range, fixing the windmill's pump on the far side of the lake and saddle breaking twenty-five wild horses for the U.S. Army had delayed trips to Golden so the telegraph wire was hand delivered to the ranch.

"Cookie!" he yelled, "round up the boys and get em' to the Big House!"

Within minutes, Cookie and the ranch hands were assembled in front of the neglected house. Some were smoking, some lounged against the corral fence, some were sitting on the front porch chairs. All were unusually quiet. One of the older hands asked Cookie, "What's up?" Cookie just shrugged his shoulders. "Not a clue. Maybe it's about that eastern gal." He quit talking as soon as Gill walked up.

Gill took off his hat, swiped it against his leg and said, "Okay boys, Miss Mary Ellington arrives at Golden in three days. We gotta get the place spruced up so I'm assigning some special jobs. Cookie, double check the food supplies and add some stuff that ladies like to eat."

Cookie suggested he hire extra help to clear out and clean up the Big House. After their boss died, it became unused and had been closed for years. The guys preferred their bunk house which was large but cozy, and no one complained about muddy boots left on the floor.

Gill liked Cookie's idea. "Okay, just make sure those cleaning ladies finish their work by Wednesday. The men can help move furniture." He paused then continued, "Duke, you and I will return the cleaning ladies home and pick up Miss Ellington for the return trip back to the ranch. Rusty, check out the little cabin. If it has leaks, grab Sam, and fix what you can and make sure there is plenty of firewood and water close to hand. Clint, bring in Sunny from the herd. I know she's been saddle broke, but gentle her out some and clean her up.

When you all finish, go about the rest of your chores." He grinned, "And let's make this the prettiest little ranch in Colorado!" The men chuckled and moved away to work on their assignments.

The three days passed with a frenzy of activity at the ranch. The cleaning women attacked each room in the Big House with brooms, dusters, buckets of water and bars of lye soap. Bedding was aired and clean sheets laid on, curtains removed, shaken clean and rehung. As a final thought, a bouquet of wildflowers was put in an empty mason jar of water and placed in the middle of the kitchen table. The place smelled clean and fresh as the door closed behind them.

The trip into Golden with Duke driving the buckboard and Gill riding beside was uneventful. The ladies spoke little. They were tired plus the sun and heat made them a bit sleepy. Gossip could wait until there were no menfolk around. Each was dropped at home as promised and the two men continued their ride into town.

CHAPTER 35
HER ARRIVAL IN GOLDEN

A very tired and dusty Mary Ellington stepped down from the stagecoach after accepting the helping hand of a co-passenger. Her only thoughts were of relief from the unending jostling inside the coach and of finding at least a gallon of water to drink. She also wanted to change out of her dusty clothing and rid herself from the clutch of her lightweight corset.

Her two travel trunks were handed down and hauled over to the dusty wooden sidewalk in front of the stage office on the outskirts of Golden's sprawling boom town. Goodbyes were said between the passengers and in a short while she was left standing alone as the horses and coach were led away. Hoping for relief from the sun, she moved into the shade offered by the covered porch of the stagecoach office. It wasn't any cooler, but at least the sun's glare was lessened. There were several dog-eared notices displayed and it appeared the town fathers had recently renamed Golden City to Golden.

She looked up and down the street. Her thirst was building, but she was afraid to leave her shelter to look for water. She didn't want to miss her ride out to the ranch. Other than dust devils flying in the distance there was nothing moving in the scorching heat and the few curious onlookers had disappeared into the unpainted houses facing or dusty two-story brick buildings. She tried to swallow some spit to ease her parched throat, but it didn't help much, and her lips felt rough and dry.

She muttered out loud to herself, "Golden, Smolden after all this traveling what if I die of dehydration?" The irony of being so close to the end of her journey then dying of thirst, had her shaking her head. She focused her reddened eyes on the distance again and tried to ignore the headache beginning to grow behind her eyelids.

A small dust cloud from the west was moving closer, and when Mary squinted her eyes against the sun's glare, she could see someone driving a buckboard and a tall slender man wearing a huge hat riding next to it on horseback. The buckboard pulled to a stop a few yards away and another light coating of dust filmed her skirt and coated her already dry lips.

The two new arrivals looked hard at her. The man on the horse dismounted, walked towards her, and said, "Miss Mary Ellington? We're from the Sweetwater Ranch. We're here—" She nodded, smiled, and fainted gracefully at his feet.

Duke jumped off the buckboard and rushed forward to help, but Gill was already kneeling beside her. "Duke, get her some water from Mr. Wilson's store."

Duke ran to the opposite side of the street and returned with a large cup balanced in his hands. He carefully handed it to Gill who used an arm to brace Mary's head on his shoulder while pressing the cup to her lips. She gulped the water, sighed with relief, and gulped again.

At last, she struggled to her feet with Gill and Duke each holding an elbow. After she shook out her skirts, she looked at both and said, "Yes, I'm Mary Ellington and I need to get to the Sweetwater Ranch. Are you my escort by any chance?"

Struck with shyness, Duke could only tip his hat to Mary and mumble, "Yes ma'am." Gil, being older and very polite, introduced himself as the foreman of the Sweetwater Ranch and offered his arm to Mary. "Miss Ellington, why don't you wait in Mr. Wilson's store while we load up the buckboard. It's a mite cooler in there and you need to drink a lot more water before we head back to the ranch, it's a two-hour drive." Mary nodded without comment and the three walked across the street towards the store.

Gill held the door for Mary as she stepped inside the slightly cooler gloom. She stared at the wildly piled assortment of dry goods resting on shelves, counters, and floor. A skull and horns of a Texas longhorn steer, mounted on the far wall, lorded over the chaos. Her eyes widened. *Those horns must reach more than six feet from tip to tip!*

The heat was still oppressive, but Mary ignored it. Some of the items in the store were strange and she moved down each of the three aisles closely examining every single one. In the dimness at the back, several wide brimmed hats hanging on pegs caught her attention. Were these the famous cowboy hats she had heard of? She already realized her fashionable hat wasn't enough to protect her face from the scorching sun, so she approached Gill with her question. He hesitated just a moment before agreeing that she needed a new style. Definitely. He hid a grin while he watched her try on every available hat before selecting her favorite. She fell in love with a pearl gray Stetson and decided she would be able to at least look like a westerner if given half a chance. Mr. Wilson offered more water and solemnly agreed that Mary's choice of hat was perfect.

Duke and Mr. Wilson loaded the buckboard with Mary's two trunks and miscellaneous items needed at the ranch while Gill entered the post office/telegraph office to pick up a week's worth of mail and newspapers. After watering the horses, they left the town of Golden, population three thousand two hundred and five.

Their return ride was a quiet one. The men had little to say to each other and Mary was too busy just trying to hang on to her side of the bouncing bench seat. The rattling buckboard finally crested a low hill, and while the horses rested, she saw the Sweetwater Ranch for the first time.

She caught her breath at the beauty of the snowcapped mountains in the background. The foreground held a fair-sized lake reflecting the cloudless blue sky above and a light breeze occasionally teased its surface with tiny ripples. Several cottonwood trees dipped their roots into the lake's edge, and she could see cattle grazing near a tiny cabin nestled against a large stand of white pine. Mary sat quietly. *Maybe Aunt Polly used it to get away from all those males at the ranch. A woman always needs a little privacy for herself after all.*

Gill cleared his throat and shifted on the saddle. "Well, that's the Sweetwater. It's a small spread, about twelve hundred acres. Grass and water practically all year except dead of winter so good grazing for the herd until October or November. We get a ton of snow and the spring runoff from the foothills helps water the grass. Don't let the distance fool you, it's still five miles away."

Mary's mouth dropped, twelve hundred acres is considered *small*? She pointed a gloved finger towards the distance and asked, "What's that adorable little log house used for?"

Gill straightened his hat. "Oh, that was built specially for the boss's wife as her hide-away your Aunt Polly, I think? Got tired of being around men all the time, I guess." Gill pointed to the right of the cabin, "Not too far up the side of that other hill with those trees is the family graveyard. From there, you can see quite a way. Beautiful place to rest if you ask me." Gill fell silent as if a little embarrassed by saying so much to a stranger, even if she was family.

Mary looked at him and asked, "Is it livable? I mean, do the men use it for anything, like storage or for extra workers?"

"No, Miss Ellington. Nobody uses that place since the boss died. His missus got her after the funeral. She used it one last time then had it boarded up against the weather. Ain't been opened since." He cleared his throat. "Well, I mean, we opened 'er up because you were coming to see the place. The roof needed some minor repairs, but the well works just fine and the boys laid in some firewood." He cleared his throat again and fell silent.

"Thank you, Gill, I look forward to seeing everything and it's so beautiful out here."

She turned to the silent Duke, "Oh, I almost forgot! I have a mare boarded in Denver. Queen's Pride came out with me from Savannah, but I didn't think it wise to ride her to Golden after such a long journey in a rail car and I didn't really know the distance. I'd like to bring her to the ranch as soon as possible if that's okay."

Duke just blushed, tongue-tied in the presence of a pretty female so Gill answered instead. "I'll ask a couple of the men to ride into Denver and pick her up. We'll need papers to prove ownership, of course, but the Sweetwater Ranch has a good rep so I'm sure there won't be any trouble. They can leave early tomorrow and be back in a couple days. Only about thirty miles total each way. We'll take care of everything. Not to worry."

Gill kneed his horse forward and the buckboard team, knowing they were close to home and their supper, moved at a quicker pace.

As the trio approached the two-story ranch house, Mary saw men walking towards its front porch. *Oh, there are so many of them! And I don't know a thing about ranching. How am I supposed to handle this?* She realized, finally, the huge responsibility she had taken on by deciding to move to Golden instead of remaining in Savannah and selling the ranch, sight unseen.

She clasped her hands in her lap and repeated to herself her special mantra. *'I can do this. I'm a nurse and I can handle anything!'* Yes, she had handled a lot of responsibilities during the war, had seen the gruesome side of warfare, and had survived the hells of the operating theatre. She would just have to move forward and do her best. Hopefully the ranch hands were a good group of men who would continue to work for such a greenhorn.

The buckboard pulled to a dusty stop in front of the house. The waiting men were speechless as they removed their hats and gazed at the new owner. The slender and fashionably dressed young lady on the buckboard was wearing a huge gray cowboy hat and holding a frilly pink sun parasol over her head.

Mary smiled at the men as Cookie came forward at once to extend his large meaty hand to help her down from the buckboard. "Welcome to the Sweetwater, Miss Ellington. I'm Mark Jones, but everyone calls me Cookie. We're all glad to see that you arrived safely. Your room is ready here in what we call the Big House. Maybe you'd like to freshen up a bit before being introduced to the men." Cookie's mother trained him well when he was a kid, so he knew just how to treat a lady.

Gill and Duke stood dumbfounded as the "oh so polite" Cookie grandly led Mary up the steps and into the entryway of the two-story ranch house. The two men shook their heads, grinning at each other in silent acknowledgement. They had rarely seen Cookie behave like such a gentleman.

The rest of the ranch hands grabbed the travel trunks and quickly unloaded the kitchen supplies. Four suddenly shy and tongue-tied cowboys deposited Mary's trunks in the largest bedroom upstairs and quickly left, their boots thumping against the uncarpeted hardwood stairs. The buckboard and tired horses were led to the barn by men grinning ear to ear.

The front yard was quiet again with only the sound of chickens scratching in the dust.

Only Cookie remained and stood in the front hall doorway, his hands threatening to crush the hat he held between them. "Miss Ellington, would you like me to show you the rest of the house? Or uh, can I bring you anything?"

Mary collected herself, she had to put her new staff at ease. "First of all, Mr. Cookie, my name is Mary, or if that's too informal for you, please call me Miss Mary. Yes, if you don't mind, please show me around." Suddenly, she realized how prim she sounded so she twirled around in the center of the room with her arms flung outward. "I just *love* this place!" She let out a giggle, and Cookie's face flushed with pride at what they had accomplished getting it ready for the newest owner of the Sweetwater.

He shyly responded to her outburst, "Uh, Miss Mary, my name don't start with mister, it's just Cookie."

Mary followed Cookie from room to room as he gave a short description of each. The house was beautifully designed, and each room seemed to welcome the viewer to step in and relax there. The last room was the first-floor kitchen, and Mary was slightly disappointed. Its fixtures were out of date, and it seemed rather small.

When she mentioned the size, Cookie explained, "Well, Miss Mary, most cooking is done in the cookshack next to the bunkhouse. When Miss Polly lived here with the Boss, they usually ate with the men. The kitchen is used mostly when we got guests needing coffee or a quick bite to eat." He paused, "And that's about it for the house tour and I gotta' get supper started. Is there anything else I can do for you?"

Mary hesitated and asked, "Could I eat with the men where they usually eat? I can meet everybody at once and maybe hear about what everybody does and if there any other things I should know about." She shyly added, "Like cowboying."

Cookie's hand reached up to hide his grin at her last remark and nodded, "Yes, ma'am, someone will come get you when it's ready."

She climbed the stairs and found water waiting for her in the washroom adjacent to the large bedroom. After cleaning face and hands and loosening her corset, she managed to take off her walking boots before falling across the welcome softness of the bed.

CHAPTER 36
ALOYSIUS GREY

DENVER, COLORADO -1867

Aloysius Grey relaxed at his office desk, digesting his delightful though somewhat heavy luncheon at the Cattleman's Emporium down the street. Lunch had been delightful due to the company of Miss Della Timberlake, locally known as Red Della. The lunch though, sat heavy because he couldn't resist the second slice of apple pie. He had plans for Red Della tonight and hoped the heaviness disappeared soon. He rubbed his crotch and smiled at the thought of Red Della's soft mouth on his cock.

He pulled his accounting ledger from its hidden space beneath his desk and thoughtfully paged through it. Very few of the accounts were still open, but his plans included closing those remaining accounts as soon as possible, either by property deed or the judicious use of force. The railroad's local representative had assured him the Union Pacific's southern route would come through Golden on its way towards Denver. He planned on reaping huge profits by selling this accumulated property for its pre-determined right-of-way.

Only one major ranch remained stubbornly free of his grasp. The Sweetwater Ranch. If he could get Polly Ellington to sell it at the right price, he planned on re-selling the front half to the railroad for their right-of-way and use the back half for his special military force.

He smiled to himself. Special military force or outlaw gang. Same thing. Working and winning with his railroad scheme was only the beginning of his rise to power. The governorship of this territory wasn't impossible for a man of his means and his attempt to change the name of Golden City to Golden had recently won the approval of the city council while gaining him name recognition.

Grey continued his meditation. *But Widow Polly always refuses to sell Sweetwater. Her husband is long dead. She lives in Savannah, and I hear the ranch continues to lose money. Why the hell is she keeping it? And now that the war is over, that property is even more valuable because the railroad needs it. Why is she holding out? What don't I know?*

He shifted his bulk more comfortably and thought some more. *Just might have to make a trip to Golden to check out the property again. Been a year or so since my last visit and offer. Might have missed something by working so much in Denver. Yep, that's what I'll do. Make that trip soon as I can.*

A week later, Aloysius Grey arrived in Golden and registered at the Golden Nugget Hotel. He reserved a suite of two rooms on the second floor with the idea of using one room for personal purposes. The second room would serve as a temporary office (and cover) for any legal or semi-legal business he might drum up. There was a definite need for lawyers in Golden. The town was practically lawless, and he had heard about celebrating cowboys shooting up saloons, getting into brawls and sometimes even shooting each other. Nowadays, even old water rights and property titles were being fought over.

He was about to head out for Sweetwater, when his number one henchman, O'Grady, confirmed the rumor of Miss Mary Ellington's arrival. The grapevine was in full force with the news that she had inherited the Sweetwater Ranch from her Aunt Polly and already arrived at the ranch.

His thick fingers pulled a fresh cigar from the carved wooden humidor resting on his new desk. Within a minute, a thick cloud of smoke floated through the open door of his hotel office.

His thoughts tumbled about. *Well now, that little eastern flower of a gal won't be able to handle the rough and tumble of ranching in the scorching summer heat around here. I'll make a better offer and if she refuses like Miss Polly, I'll just have to arrange a few welcoming parties. Add some reminders like cut fences. Or a missing herd. Probably should send out O'Grady with notice to the gang. Get the boys ready for a hoo-raw at the Sweetwater.*

He heaved his girth out of his office chair and moved to the door. He kept the smoldering cigar clamped between his teeth as he grabbed his bowler hat and thumped loudly down the carpeted stairs to the hotel lobby. The Wildcat Saloon was directly across the street from the hotel, and he wouldn't be surprised if just about all the news of the territory filtered through that bar. Some of it might even be helpful.

CHAPTER 37
GREY'S FIRST PLAN

The following morning, O'Grady shuffled along the wooden walkway in his broken-down boots to the livery stable down the street from the hotel. He was in a foul humor. His own damn horse was lame after the last herd had been chivvied over to the next territory from the T-Bar ranch. Hell, any outfit that couldn't keep track of their own cattle deserved to lose em'. Thinking about his cut from the recent theft just made him angrier. After paying his feed and saloon bill, his share of the take was hardly enough to keep him in booze and grub for a week.

He managed to hire a decent animal for the ride out to the hideout, and still angry, savagely dug spurs to horsehide. The horse wasn't used to such mistreatment. The big buckskin gelding threw his head down and began bucking and crow hopping to show his displeasure. O'Grady wasn't prepared for an argument from his rented ride. He went sailing ass over teakettle and landed on his rump in the middle of the street. The horse, now free of the painful jabs, ran full steam back to the safety of his stable.

When the stable hand saw the blood on the side of the sweating animal, he swore he would never rent out any horse to that stupid excuse of a man again. That O'Grady was a real bully. He shook his head as he led the still shaken horse into the stable for a good rubdown and extra ration of oats.

O'Grady got up and dusted himself off. He saw a few drinking buddies hanging around outside the Wildcat and they were grinning from ear to ear at his discomfort. O'Grady ignored their grins, "Hey, you guys, you got a mount I can borrow for a couple days? I'll make it worth your while." One of the men spit into the street and offered his horse but only if paid in advance. O'Grady dug into his pocket and gave the man two dollars. He privately considered it too much, but he was a man in a hurry. Mr. Grey was not kind to people who didn't follow his orders.

O'Grady and his replacement mount did a very respectable canter out of town and headed towards the hideout in the foothills north of Sweetwater Ranch. He followed the well-marked road for several miles and turned off onto an ill-defined trail that wound around several stands of sagebrush. The trail appeared to end at the foot of a low cliff. After he dismounted, he whistled loudly, to avoid getting shot by a lookout. When he heard the answering whistle, he pulled the horse behind him and maneuvered down the slope of a dry wash dotted with boulders and brush. The wash continued for a half mile and opened into a deep box canyon.

The eight-acre canyon was large enough to hide a dozen men and their horses. It also held a small shack and corral and seemed naturally designed to prevent smoke from being seen by any passersby. A steady stream of water fell from a granite rockface into a hand-built cement pool at its foot. Most of the grass had been trampled to dust years ago, so hay and grain were painstakingly brought in whenever the gang was in residence.

As O'Grady walked in leading his horse, the lounging men stood up and reached for their guns. They only relaxed when they recognized him as one of their own. The youngest ran to the shack and returned with their boss, Big Bill.

Nobody remembered how Big Bill got his name, and no one wanted to tangle with the five-foot three-inch fire breather. He was built like a barrel cactus. One eye seemed to wander where it wished, and a poorly healed scar ran from his hairline to his bearded jaw after making a neat traverse over his flattened nose. He had a reputation of shooting first, then knifing, stomping, and (maybe) asking questions later. Their boss-man was one ugly dude with a temper to match.

The men gathered and shuffled in place while they stared at a sweating O'Grady. They didn't like him one bit, but he was their only connection with their employer in Denver. They had good luck working for Grey. The jobs always paid well, and usually went off without a hitch. But they were getting bored now and were ready for some paid action. Even the nightly poker game had lost its luster. Seemed that nobody had any extra money to bet with and playing for toothpicks or matches just didn't seem quite the same.

Big Bill strolled up to O'Grady and spit a stream of tobacco juice close enough to splatter near his dusty boots as he stood, still holding his horse's reins. He growled, "So? What do you want?" His basso voice totally unmatched the size of his torso.

O'Grady swallowed first and said, "Mr. Grey needs the boys to be ready for a tangle at the Sweetwater spread. The old lady died, and the new owner showed up. He wants that ranch land really bad. Willing to pay good money to run her off."

The men remained standing near O'Grady but said nothing. Big Bill slowly took off his sweat-stained hat, swiped it against his jeans, and spit at the ground again, just missing O'Grady's boot a second time. He grated out, "Me and the boys are going to need a little extra in the pot. Everybody knows that the railroad is coming through the Sweetwater, and we'll get blamed for any trouble at the ranch. Anybody gets hurt, we got to stay low till the heat passes. So, Grey's got to pay the regular cost plus an extra five hundred. That'll cover it." There would be no argument with Big Bill about the price.

O'Grady gulped at the cost but nodded his head. "I'll tell the boss what you said. I'll be back with his plan." He pushed through the loosely gathered men towards the canyon's exit. After leading his borrowed horse through the rocky wash, he re-mounted and rode slowly back the way he came. He felt like he had escaped with his life.

Heat still simmered on the baked sands of the trail back to Golden. O'Grady drank from his canteen, but its tepid water didn't quench his real thirst, so he reached back into his saddlebag and pulled forth a fresh bottle of whisky. Still riding slowly, he uncorked it, threw back his head and tipped the bottle for a drink. One drink led to two and by the time he reached town, O'Grady was completely drunk.

Aloysius Grey stood waiting in the Wildcat's shadow and watched as O'Grady slid from the tired horse and staggered into the hotel lobby across the street. He sneered, turned around and re-entered the batwing doors of the saloon. He refused to meet O'Grady when he was so drunk.

CHAPTER 38
SWEETWATER TROUBLES BEGIN

Two hours after falling onto the bed, Mary woke to the shrill sound of a triangle calling the ranch hands to supper. She hurried to put on her boots, and with a few hard pulls, her corset was back in place. She was about to rush down the stairs when there was a knock at the front door. From her vantage point at the top of the stairs, she could see Gill through its frosted glass.

"Come on in," she called, "it's open!"

Gill was standing at the foot of the stairs with a small smile and laughter in his eyes. He truly admired the view of the slim, well-dressed Easterner as she descended the uncarpeted flight of stairs. Her hair had been restored and her gray eyes sparkled out of a freshly washed face. The large gray cowboy hat was firmly placed on her head.

He drawled, "Miss Mary, would you do me the honor of escorting you to supper?"

She began to laugh at the man's silly attempt at over-the-top politeness when he offered her his arm. "Why, thank you, kind sir. It would be my pleasure." She put her hand lightly on his arm and they descended the porch steps and walked towards the meal and the men waiting for them.

Later that week Queen's Pride was delivered as promised and adapted quickly to her new surroundings while making it very clear that no one except Mary was to ride her.

Time passed quickly as Mary learned firsthand how hard ranch life could be. It seemed there was always something that needed fixing, building, or herding. She recognized right away that Gill and Cookie were very important to the smooth running of her new enterprise, and she was happy to see how well the men got along with each other. Gill remained aloof but pleasant, and Cookie would talk as long as she cared to listen. His stories were amusing and helped her relax into her new role as a ranch owner.

Cookie was in the cookhouse preparing to bake the usual four loaves of bread for the next day when he saw two horses cantering down the road to the ranch. He recognized both immediately. Aloysius Grey and his sidewinder hired hand, O'Grady. *Not good,* he thought, and called out through his opened doorway, "Miss Mary, prepare yourself for a visit from two snakes!"

Mary stepped out onto the front porch to receive the unwelcome men. Cookie had coached her in the proper Western decorum of receiving visitors: they should remain in the saddle until she invited them to step down. She did not extend the invitation, but Aloysius heaved himself off his horse and handed the reins to O'Grady, who didn't dismount but turned both horses toward the nearby watering trough.

Grey hid his displeasure at Mary's insult of not inviting him to rest out of the sun, but his voice was smooth. "Miss Mary Ellington? I'm Aloysius Grey. The other gentleman is my assistant, Mr. O'Grady."

Mary's voice held frost. "Yes, I know who you are." She didn't invite him to sit on her porch or enter the house but said instead, "My lawyer in Savannah mentioned you." She said nothing more.

Grey kept his temper when she didn't even offer him a glass of water. He removed his bowler hat and wiped the inside of its rim with a clean kerchief. From Mary's stance on the front porch, he knew immediately that there would be problems buying the ranch from her. She looked a bit fierce with her ramrod straight back and crossed arms. Was that a glare in her eyes? She was no delicate eastern flower! He turned his head and saw three ranch hands drift closer and relax into a half circle behind him. He noticed their hands remained close to their holsters and their faces were grim.

Grey turned towards Mary and tried again. "Well, Miss Ellington, you probably know that I'm very interested in buying your ranch. Yes, I've been turned down before by your Aunt Polly, but I'm now prepared to offer you three dollars an acre and a thousand for the buildings. I'll even buy your stock at a fair price." His shiny face was beginning to show a flush of heat from the hot sun and her rudeness of making him stand outside in its glare.

Her long silence was making him even more agitated. Mary looked straight at him and calmly said, "Mr. Grey, I am fully aware of your past dealings with my family, and I am just not interested in selling my place to you or anyone else. So, if there is nothing else on your mind, please take your leave and take your assistant with you. I wish you good day, sir!" She turned and re-entered the house, firmly slamming the door behind her.

The mockery behind her terse words almost caused Aloysius to miss a stirrup as he remounted his restive horse.

His anger grew the closer they got to Golden. He vowed he would make her pay for her insulting attitude. Nobody, but nobody, stood in the way of what Aloysius Grey wanted. Many men had tried and failed. He drew up to the hitching rail in front the Golden Nugget, dismounted and turned to O'Grady. "Ride out to the camp and bring Big Bill to me. I have a job for him and the boys. Ask him nicely so he agrees to meet in my office day after tomorrow." Two hours later, O'Grady was seen galloping out of town. His observers figured it was just another nasty job for Aloysius Grey.

After they left the ranch, Mary opened the front door to thank her three guardians. Duke, Rusty, and Clint just grinned, and agreed among themselves that it wasn't a bit of a problem as they strolled back to their jobs.

Mary was thoughtful. It was time she did some research and looked for any notes or news articles relating to the ranch. She had already filed the deed and her aunt's will was registered and safely stored in the local bank's vault. Still, she thought, there might be something that was causing Grey to want her property so much. He was a lawyer, not a rancher, for Pete's sake.

After her confrontation with Grey, Mary straightened her shoulders and entered the front office to begin her search. On a tall shelf behind the rolltop desk she found a rather shabby fat envelope tied with string. She had ignored it before because everything else she was doing or learning took her full attention. She sat down at the desk and opened the package. Several old newspaper articles told her exactly what Aloysius Grey was after. The Union Pacific Railroad wanted to build a route from Cheyenne, Wyoming all the way to Denver, Colorado. Mary gasped while reading the final news article about the anticipated route. The right of way necessary for the track would pass right through her Sweetwater Ranch.

Two weeks later, Mary woke from sleep to the sound of rapid gunfire near the front of the house. Galloping horses and rebel yells, punctuated with more gunfire, filled her with alarm as she jumped off her bed and ran to the front window. When she could see little in the darkness, she ran to the side window facing the small corral and bunkhouse. The moon broke through the few overhead clouds, and she saw her ranch hands stumbling out on its porch as they pulled on jeans or shoved their feet into boots. Some already had their guns out but without clear targets, they didn't shoot. After a few more yells and gunshots, the band of rabble rousers galloped back into the darkness and disappeared. Mary looked at her clock. It was after midnight!

She dressed quickly in her riding skirt, pulled a thin cotton blouse over her head, and grabbed her favorite shawl before running barefoot down the stairs. She pulled open the front door and quickly wrapped the red wool shawl around her shoulders. She could hear the men talking as they strode towards her. Several carried kerosene lanterns and were studying the trampled ground around the yard. She stood up and leaned on the porch railing while she caught her breath. She tried to keep her voice from trembling. "What just happened? Did a war start?"

Gill stepped forward. "No, Miss Mary, that was what we call a hoo-raw. Buck recognized one of the horses - belongs to a man called Big Bill - a real nasty fellow. Works for anybody with money. Might mean we got some trouble ahead."

Mary calmed a bit. "Gill, can I speak with you inside for a moment?"

He nodded in reply and said, "Duke, will you stay lookout on the porch? The rest of you each take a lantern and check the barns and outbuildings to make sure there's no obvious damage."

Inside the house, Mary gestured to Gill to follow her back to the kitchen. She poured two glasses of water and sat herself at the head of the kitchen table. Gill sat to her left and waited for her to speak. She was the Boss Lady, and he'd help in any way he could.

Mary didn't quite know how to deal with this type of harassment. Her voice was tentative. "So do you think this was a retaliation by Grey because I won't sell to him?"

He looked thoughtfully at her. "Yes ma'am, I do. And if it's Grey, we can expect more trouble down the road. The man doesn't willingly give up anything he's got his mind set on. He's got money and the folks around here are nervous when he makes it clear he wants something of theirs. It's said that a couple ranchers sold out to him after their range wells were poisoned, barns burned, cattle run off. He bought them out for pennies on the dollar. Sheriff couldn't pin anything on him though, so he got away with it."

She said, "What do you think we should do?" He heard the slight quiver in her voice. Obviously, she was upset, anyone would be.

He kept his voice calm. "The boys will start to keep a lookout at night. I'll have them rotate so nobody loses too much sleep. And we might want to keep Queen in the barn at night. Yeah, I know she doesn't like a stall, but I'd hate to see her get run off or hurt if those guys come back."

And so, it began.

The masked men arrived at irregular times during the month. The Sweetwater crew could never anticipate which night they'd show up. Nerves were becoming frayed. Only Cookie's excellent cooking, Gill's calm disposition, plus their silent loyalty to Mary, kept the men's spirits up and working at the ranch.

Finally, by fall, the bullying slowed, and a tense peace returned to the ranch. She was able to draw a deep breath and make plans to enlarge the kitchen with her private funds and the profits from the upcoming sale of her herd. Branding and culling would start in a week, and she looked forward to her first real cowboy experience.

Before the roundup began, Mary decided to treat herself to a Saturday afternoon of shopping followed by lunch in the Golden Nugget's dining room. Gill insisted that Duke ride with her as protection but once they arrived in town, she went shopping alone. Both agreed to meet at the Golden Nugget for lunch, her treat.

Eighteen-year-old Duke hated shopping and there was this new girl at Miss Flora's (a house of ill repute) who seemed to really like him.

Mary was able to make her feminine purchases in record time but when she entered the town's newest store her heart expanded with happiness. The dense smell of fresh leather and the sight of all the leather boots, belts, vests, tooled leather gun belts with matching holsters, saddle bags and even small purses kept her busy until it was time to meet Duke. She finally exited the store with a grin on her face and a box carrying a pair of brand-new cowboy boots.

CHAPTER 39
SWEETWATER ROUNDUP

Gill and the boys rode north with the chuck wagon to begin the process of rounding up half-wild cattle. It usually took a solid two weeks to complete the roundup and branding and another week to get the herd to the railhead in Denver. He and his crew expected to be gone for almost a month. Mary would be alone at the ranch except for Charlie, her friend from town.

It was hard dusty work and Cookie worked long hours to make sure the men were well fed from his chuck wagon. One week into the roundup, Mary joined them, riding Queen. She brought a canvas bag filled with fresh oatmeal cookies as a treat and she was grinning from ear to ear waving her canvas bag, happy to have found her guys all safe.

When the busy men looked up from their branding fire, they saw a vision on horseback cantering towards them. She had taken to the west with full vigor and wore her gray Stetson with obvious pride. Her newest addition to western apparel was a pair of red, green, and yellow cowboy boots. The men grinned their appreciation. Their Boss Lady was a real winner for sure.

At the end of the roundup, Gill arrived at the house to report on the sorting and branding of the herd. The numbers were lower than expected; rustlers had been slowly stealing cattle from the north end of the property. Since most ranges were still unfenced, keeping count wasn't usually done until branding calves in the spring and according to his tally and compared to previous roundups, they probably lost a hundred head to rustlers. It was a serious blow to the ranch finances.

Several ranches combined their herds for the drive to the Denver railhead and her crew expected to return in about two weeks. She and Charlie had few chores, so she left him enjoying the sun in front of the bunkhouse while she rode Queen out to explore some promising timber stands. If the trunks were of a good size, she would mark and sell some to the lumber mill in Denver. If beef market prices were low, the extra money could be used for ranch expenses and her kitchen plans would just have to wait. She was hesitant to spend any inheritance money just in case the harassment got rougher and emergency repairs were needed.

The men eventually returned from Denver, tired but grinning ear to ear. They told Mary outrageous stories about each other as they relaxed around the outdoor fire pit by the cookshack. The sale of the herd had gone well and would keep the ranch afloat for another year. She told the men about her plans for selling timber and enlarging the kitchen.

Late one night the barn caught fire.

Her men managed to get the horses out safely, but their winter's supply of hay was a total loss. Neighbors saw the smoke in the morning and came as fast as they could, but all that remained of the barn was the blackened shell of charred cross beams and piles of water-soaked hay. The women brought food to share and pitched in to make coffee for the folks milling around discussing Miss Ellington's recent tragedy. The sheriff and his deputies poked around the water-saturated ruins and found two emptied cans of kerosene at the back. Gill confirmed that the containers didn't belong to them.

The newspaper reported the fire two days later as "Arson by persons unknown".

Mary tried to hide her distress over the loss of the barn and the supply of hay, but her mantra of '*I can do this!*' didn't work anymore. She was too tired. Maybe the ranch *was* too much for her to handle. She thought of how much her aunt and uncle fought to make the place work. There was family history at the Sweetwater Ranch, and she was becoming a part of it. She threw back a shot of brandy and shouted at the living room wall as the liquid burned its way down her throat, "No, damn it! I'm not going to quit!"

Aloysius Grey read the newspaper's report of the barn fire as he sat behind his desk in Golden. He smiled and lit another cigar. He figured she would be considering selling out pretty soon. He'd drive over in a couple weeks to make another offer. Didn't want to be too obvious. That girl was too smart for her own good.

CHAPTER 40
NURSE MARY

Summer came early and Mary was humming to herself and happily digging in her kitchen garden when Clint rushed up on his horse. His young voice was breathless. "Miss Mary, Duke was breaking that buckskin and got thrown into a fence and then the dang horse kicked him! Twice! He's busted up mighty bad. We just carried him to the bunk house. Can you do anything for him till the doc gets here? Rusty is already heading to town."

She threw down her garden gloves and ran into the house to get her medical bag. It was only minutes before she ran through the open bunkhouse door, and she prayed she still remembered the lessons and practice from a few years ago.

Duke's bunk had been pulled away from the wall into the center of the room. The men were silent as they stood in a circle around the cot and looked down at Duke with worried faces. Cookie and Gill moved aside to give her room. She could tell by Duke's tightened lips and the sweat on his gray face that he was in a lot of pain and about to go into shock. Mary tried to sound confident. "Somebody heat water and find me something to bandage him with. If there isn't enough, tear up this clean sheet and take his shirt off so I can see what's wrong. Come on guys! Move it!"

Her voice was so commanding the men moved without a word as they rushed to follow her orders.

Boots were pulled off and feet elevated on pillows. She quickly pulled out her scalpel and began to slice through both pant legs and long johns to expose massive bruising high on his abdomen. One knee was swollen and red, but it didn't seem dislocated, only a bad bruise. His right thigh had a six-inch tear that was bleeding so much, she knew it would need stitches. After cleaning the wound, she poured alcohol over a needle and thread and began to sew it closed using the method she learned during the war. She sprinkled sulfa on the area and bound it to prevent any stitches from pulling loose.

After taking a deep breath, she tossed a clean sheet over his naked middle as a gesture to his modesty before carefully running her hands along both arms. On the left one, she felt the fracture, but it seemed like a clean break and should heal straight. She put her stethoscope to her ears to listen to his lungs and heartbeat. "Strong heartbeat," she muttered, almost to herself, "but those lungs may be in trouble now checking for broken ribs." With eyes tightly closed, she ran her hands down his chest to feel for possible breaks. There were two, but hopefully, after binding his chest, they wouldn't pierce the lung.

Sweat ran into her eyes and she blindly reached out a hand to grab something to wipe it from her face. She smiled up at Gill when he pressed a clean, soft cotton cloth into it without comment. "Thanks, Gill," she said and motioned towards a folded blanket. "And please hand me that blanket." He handed her the light blanket, and she laid it completely over the unconscious Duke.

Mary continued to monitor Duke's breathing and heartbeat until the doctor arrived. He looked scandalized to see Mary attending a naked (albeit covered by a blanket) man in the bunkhouse. He was about to say something scathing about a mere woman doing a doctor's job, but after one look at the men standing nearby and another look at how she handled a stethoscope, he wisely kept his thoughts to himself.

Mary stood up from her perch on the bedside and dropped her used instruments into a metal washbasin holding water. She would sterilize them later. The adrenaline rush was leaving her, and she swayed as she bent to pick up her medical bag. Gill rushed over to hold her steady and one of the men pushed a chair closer so she could sit for a moment and catch her breath.

No one said a word while the doctor repeated the same process Mary had used to evaluate Duke's injuries. He seemed fascinated by the neat stitches on the cowboy's thigh and spent a couple minutes looking them over. Finally, the doctor stood up with a "harrumph" and motioned to Mary. "Well done, Miss Ellington. May I ask where you received your training?"

Her voice was firm and clear. "Three years as a medical student, ward nurse at Charleston Community Hospital in South Carolina and four years in various field hospitals assisting the surgeons during the war." The doctor looked at her more closely and thought, why, she's hardly older than my own daughter.

The doctor asked, "Any surgical experience you'd care to tell me about?"

Mary felt a bit defensive but recited some of the things she had been trusted to do during the war. "I cleaned and stitched shrapnel wounds, sawed off too many arms and legs, applied poultices to severe burns and watched too many men and boys die."

She paused to take a breath and with a faint smile said, "I also delivered two healthy babies." Her voice sharpened. "Really, Doctor, I'm not interested in interviewing for a position, but I would suggest that Duke get his arm set and his ribs stabilized before further injury results."

The doctor gave her a small smile and did as she recommended. A short time later he began to pack up his medical bag. He commented that Duke was unconscious from the tiny bit of morphine and wouldn't wake for a couple hours. He shouldn't work for at least two weeks while the bones and stitches healed but he would make a complete recovery. The men nodded their agreement when he complimented Mary on the excellent care given the ranch hand and escorted him to his horse patiently waiting at the bunkhouse hitching rail.

It was twilight before an emotionally exhausted Mary felt able to leave her sleeping patient and return to the house. The ranch hands walked behind her and stood at the bottom of the porch steps. She climbed up and turned around at the door to thank them for their help. Every man had his hat in one hand while giving her a smart salute with the other. Her heart lifted with appreciation at the gesture, and she swore she would do everything she could to keep her special cowboy family together.

CHAPTER 41
LOSING GILL

The rest of the year passed with more nasty surprises. There were tense standoffs between sheep herders and cattlemen and even farmers trying to farm what they thought of as open range. It was late fall when her cowboys found the remains of three dead cattle obviously slaughtered for food. The sheriff questioned all new arrivals, but without proof, he could do nothing.

She was making a pot of coffee in her own kitchen when Duke rode up to the front yard carefully leading Gill's horse behind. She looked out the window and saw a body draped over the saddle. Her heart sank, she knew it was Gill. Already dead. She could even see the partially dried blood stains on his shirt. She flew down the front porch stairs and hugged herself, tears streaming down her face as she wept, "Oh no, not this! Not this!"

Her cries brought the rest of the men running to the yard just as Duke untied the ropes holding Gill to the saddle. The men carefully lowered him to the ground and Mary asked that they turn his body so she might loosen his shirt. She saw two closely spaced bullet holes in the back with lower exit wounds on his chest. With her war experience, she could tell Gill had been murdered by someone shooting from higher ground.

Cookie held back tears as he knelt by the body. He rose, walked over to Mary, and put his arm around her shaking shoulders. His voice rumbled in her ears, "Oh,

Miss Mary, we're so sorry. Now, don't you worry, me and the boys will take care of Gill."

Mary covered her face as she sobbed. "No, I'll take care of h-him please carry him into the front parlor and s-send someone for the sheriff." She pulled away from Cookie and followed behind as Duke and Clint carried Gill's body into the house. The two men returned and stood silent in their shared grief before walking silently back to the bunkhouse. Mary stood in her front parlor and heard Clint ride out towards Golden to alert the sheriff about Gill's murder. Duke drifted away to dig another grave on the hillside and Mary sent Cookie to get clean clothes for his burial.

News of Gill's murder swept through the saloons like news of free beer. Who on earth would kill the Sweetwater foreman? He was a likeable fellow and really looked after Miss Ellington and the ranch. Some folks were even wondering if he would ever pop the question and marry her. They made such a good team. Everyone in town liked Miss Ellington and Gill. She was always willing to fix up a sprung shoulder or a twisted ankle and he was as hard working and honest as the "day was long".

The nodding heads agreed that bad luck had dogged that ranch ever since she started running it. Some had suspicions that Grey and O'Grady were responsible, but the townspeople were too afraid to say anything lest they be harassed too. After a month of searching, the sheriff and his two deputies were not able to discover Gill's murderer and the trail grew cold.

* * *

Mary sat in her office looking at the accounting books opened in front of her. It was no use. She would not make it through another winter. She had lost a dozen cows to a poisoned water hole and there was news that Texas cattle were being destroyed because of hoof and mouth disease. She couldn't find new breeding stock even if she could have afforded it. Yesterday, she tried to lay off Rusty and Carl, but they refused to go and even Cookie was determined to stay. Duke and Clint said they were in for the long-haul and they would stay until she didn't need them anymore.

She felt exhausted as she put her head down and gave way to angry tears. She had tried for almost three years to make the ranch work. It was proving to be too much for her, but she refused to return to Savannah. After she sold the ranch, maybe she would find work at the hospital in Denver.

Another month sped by with more harassment from unknown men. Rusty and Carl discovered someone had snuck out to the little cabin, smashed both windows and filled the well to its top with the cut firewood taken from the side of the house. "A pure bit of meanness" according to Cookie.

Despite the four cowboys swapping nightly watches, no one was seen actually committing the deeds. Mary called the men for a meeting in her kitchen. Cookie brewed up a pot of coffee and all five sat at the kitchen table. Mary wanted opinions from the crew before making the decision that would impact their lives. They all finally admitted that the ranch might be too large to protect against this type of harassment.

"Guys, we're not making it in spite of our hard work. I know I can get a job at the hospital in Denver and if I sell the Sweetwater, I'll make sure you have a job here unless you choose to quit." The idea of leaving the ranch and her crew was galling, but she had to be realistic about choices.

Her voice firmed. "Well, I might have to sell out, but by God it won't be to Aloysius Grey!".

CLAYTON

CHAPTER 42
CLAYTON HEADS WEST

MIDDLE AMERICA - 1866

Clayton decided to travel from St Louis, Missouri to Nebraska on the Union Pacific railroad. He was guaranteed the Nebraska destination but after that, the track was still being laid and schedules were uncertain. Once in Nebraska, he'd figure out where to go next, maybe on horseback, maybe by stagecoach or even by wagon train if it headed further west. Kaliph was used to train travel so loading him into a cattle car was never a problem. Once he made his decision, Clayton resumed his travel west.

It was dusk when the train departed St Louis and after he boarded and surrendered his ticket, he removed the dark glasses covering his light sensitive eyes. The lounge car offered the best views of the countryside and after greeting his fellow passengers, he sat and stared out the window. He overheard some passengers talking about the railroad ending somewhere in Nebraska but lately, it seemed, the Union Pacific had extended another couple hundred miles all the way to Cheyenne, Wyoming. After that, it would be stagecoach, wagon train or horseback. He felt a strong urge to head west, and the faint memory of a woman crying and covered in blood seemed connected to that urge somehow.

The westbound train stopped at small towns along the route for passengers, freight, or supplies and fuel. The dining car provided two meals a day and passengers without meal tickets were able to purchase simple food from carts pushed down the aisles by local vendors.

Time passed until it was full dark. The porters had made up the bunks in the sleeper car just behind the locomotive and many of the passengers had already retreated to their rest. He sat through the night and watched the dark silhouettes of distant houses with their tiny lights glowing like low-hanging yellow stars. His sharp eyes spotted a pack of coyotes running down a frightened deer. Some of the men (most likely salesmen, he decided) fell asleep on benches or chairs. Some continued to quietly talk of the gold strikes in California. Everyone ignored the grit and cinders from the locomotive's belching chimney as it coated everything with a fine layer of soot.

The eastern sky was showing the pinks and grays of dawn, and Clayton felt his body begin to slow. He decided not to ignore it but take advantage of a much-needed rest in his special travel trunk. After confirming there was no one awake he stepped out onto the metal platform at the end of the lounge. With a leap, he landed on the exposed roof of the adjoining car and sped along the other roofs until he found the baggage car below with only the red caboose trailing cheerily behind. He jumped down onto the front platform of the baggage car and opened its door, relieved to see it empty. Explanations would be awkward, and a missing train employee would be a real problem. He stepped in and pulled the door shut behind him.

A faint curtain of golden dust filled the air as the early sun peeked through the slats of the car. He reached out a hand to his iron bound crate and yes, everything seemed safe. He unlocked the hasps holding the cover securely in place, lifted its lid and swung his legs into the box. He quickly seated himself within and grasped the heavy lid to pull it shut. He leaned back and the clasps re-locked themselves at his whispered command.

Clayton stretched out comfortably, crossed his arms over his chest and nestled down into the welcoming earth. The pure relief of lying again in its healing embrace brought a smile to his usually immobile face. Yes, he could move about during the day, but if he stayed in the sunlight too long, his skin would tingle unmercifully until he slept again on earth. His eyes began to close.

But healing sleep eluded him as miles of iron rails unwound beneath the swaying car's studded floor. His dreams were always touched with painful grief. Wisps of memory. A woman covered in blood. Being held in her lap. He tried again and again without success to recall what happened between Charleston and finding himself in Thalia's basement. Those multiple wounds that that almost severed his spinal column came from somewhere but she claimed she didn't know anything.

Thalia was lying and he knew it.

She claimed she found out he had an apartment in Savannah after going through his pockets while he was unconscious. He healed and agreed to close the apartment. He remembered that war was inevitable so he would live with her until he heard from the Navy. The screaming woman and blood? There was nothing. Nothing he could recall about her. Not even her face.

He had so many questions about that missing time, but she wasn't around to answer them. Damn her! He just KNEW she was lying! His anger grew from a simmer to a full boil as his frustration grew. His fractured memory of a woman covered in blood drove him nearly insane. Who *was* she?

When he woke, it was almost dark, and his ears caught the whisper of phlegm-filled breathing in the left corner of the rocking car. He unlatched the hinges on his travel box and emerged into the dusty darkness. He turned toward the sound stalked to the pile of rags trying to wedge themselves further in between the outer wall of the car and a rope-bound wooden box sitting next to it. Two bloodshot eyes filled with fear looked up at him as he bent over the stinking pile.

Renewed anger at Thalia's lies sharpened his voice. "What have we here? Does it speak? Is it fish or fowl or something else? Is it supper?" The utterly cold and emotionless voice chilled the blood of the wretched drifter and caused the remaining warmth of his whiskey comfort to rapidly disappear.

The old man whimpered, "Mister, I ain't done you no harm. Just leave me be an' I won't cause any trouble. Just trying to get by. Be getting off at the next stop." The pleading ended in a spasm of coughing as the man tried unsuccessfully to scramble to his feet.

"Oh, *do* allow me to help you up." Terror filled the man's eyes as a pair of steel arms lifted him from his straw littered corner and yanked him close to an emotionless face that promised hell to come. He couldn't breathe and couldn't look away from the piercing nightmare eyes glaring at him. He became fascinated watching those eyes change from dark blue to red flame and was barely aware of two glistening incisors lengthening from the gaping mouth. Pain at his neck, unlike anything he had ever felt before, burst through him but was quickly replaced with a heated flush of brief ecstasy. He slumped forward as he felt his life's blood being drawn from his neck and his frantic heartbeat begin to slow. Dark swirls edged closer as he managed to whisper, "I never shoulda' hopped this train."

An angry Clayton had fed.

He picked up the near empty husk, stepped to the baggage car door, and using his right hand, easily slid it open. The train was passing through arid desert lands, uninhabited and sterile. He threw the body out the open door with such force that it landed a considerable distance away from the train tracks. He was thinking that the coyotes and buzzards would dine well.

A few brushes to his suit coat, and a hand raking through his hair, made him ready to meet any train passengers who wished for conversation. Quick steps brought him back to the train's lounge car. After seating himself on a padded armchair, he pretended to read a three-day old newspaper. His anger at Thalia had cooled down and he was filled with remorse about how he had treated the old coot. He needed to distract his thoughts, so he put his paper down and began to watch the bleak desert land pass as the train continued its travel west under another night sky.

CHAPTER 43
WYOMING TERRITORY

CHEYENNE - 1866

It was early evening when Clayton and Kaliph arrived at Cheyenne's Pacific Union railhead. After too many days and too many miles by train, both man and horse were more than ready to leave the noise and smoke behind and stretch their muscles. Clayton approached the station master. "Excuse me, I have two pieces of luggage I need to store for a short while. May I leave them with you? I'd be happy to pay for your trouble."

The station master scratched behind his ear, "Well, maybe a couple days at the most. This station belongs to the railroad, and I don't want no trouble. But tell you what, I'll hold 'em until Thursday evening. That's when the next train's due and I'll need the space."

Clayton saddled Kaliph and the two rode south towards the edge of a bustling camp-town of wood and canvas stores and lean-tos. Slabs of rough wood balanced over empty beer kegs acted as open-air saloons. It was quite evident which storefront was the most successful, it had a real door attached to the wooden frame supporting the canvas walls and roof. Partially dressed women with half naked breasts or scantily dressed in corsets and pantaloons posed seductively. The hand painted sign overhead proudly announced '*SALLY'S* – GOLD & SILVER ONLY'. The dust-covered boardwalks were crowded with people talking excitedly of a recent train of more than two hundred covered wagons stopping to re-supply before moving on to Fort Bridger and the Oregon Trail. They had camped just outside of town and would be moving out in a few days.

They continued at a slow pace through the town and rode a rutted trail towards a small stand of trees that had managed to avoid being cut down for firewood. He smiled at the sign posted next to the road: ANYBODY CAUGHT CHOPPING A TREE WILL BE SHOT.

A short distance past the trees he pulled Kaliph to a stop. He couldn't believe the sheer size of the current wagon train. It was so long, the wagons had circled into groups of ten or twelve as temporary barricades against possible Indian attacks. Within the circles, cookfires were being lit, wagons unloaded and excited children ran to find their friends from the neighboring wagons.

As he relaxed on Kaliph's saddle observing the chaos, an older but well-maintained woman (admiring the handsome man on his horse) approached him and invited him to her fire. Conversation ranged from his childhood in India to her leaving England with her husband. The husband died of pneumonia while they were still with a wagon train moving west but she continued by herself, met up with these nice people with similar goals and was headed for Denver, Colorado.

Time passed quickly and the night grew darker and colder as they sat at her fire and talked. She was drinking from a whisky flask and decided to make her move. She said, "I've a very cold bed waiting for me in that wagon. Would you care to warm it with me?"

He liked the fact that she wasn't trying to be coy, so he smiled as he replied, "I never sleep with a stranger. Oh hello Constance." He withdrew from her mind and gently pulled her shivering body onto his lap. He bent his head down and kissed her lightly, savoring the taste of whisky tinged with night air and dust.

It never occurred to Constance that she hadn't told him her name.

His kiss deepened and unleashed a torrent of lust that weakened her legs and settled in her belly. Her need to satisfy the unusual sensual hunger continued to build until she forgot almost everything except her erotic desires. She was even willing to do it next to the fire, but her common sense prevailed. She put her arms around his neck and whispered in his ear, "That bed won't warm up by itself."

He stood up easily with Constance still in his arms and walked to the back of her covered wagon. After he lowered her onto her feet, she climbed up a short ladder and pushed aside the canvas drape. She gestured to him to follow. Once inside, he saw a tidy arrangement of some furniture, several pillows and a thick pallet covered with a goose down comforter. When she hung her lantern from the hook overhead, he looked closer at the fancy roulette wheel tied to the wooden ribs of the wagon's canvas side.

He laughed. "Ma'am, you have my full attention. If I ever reach Denver, I'll look for you."

Constance came out of her dreamlike daze and smiled at him. "I'm all about public relations. My husband and I ran a gambling hall in London, and I mean to do the same again in Denver. I look forward to seeing you in my new place." She paused and putting both hands on his chest said, "Now, if you don't mind, that bed STILL isn't getting any warmer."

Clayton bent his head and clasped her face between his hands as he began to kiss her again. He sensed her eagerness but was determined to make her feel thoroughly satisfied before he was finished. He felt her heart hammering as he slowly opened her vest and shirt. Her breasts were past their prime, but still lovely, and he paid court to both before he allowed her to remove his own jacket and shirt.

She gasped at the sculpted contours of his chest and abdomen. Her eager hands pushed him onto the pallet, and he laid back on his elbows to watch while she pulled off his boots. She was about to work on his belt, when he stopped her with a whispered, "My turn," and easily flipped her on her back.

He slowly removed the rest of her clothing but used half of the comforter to hold off the night's chill. He lay beside her and deepened his kiss with his hand stroking between her legs. Her arousal threatened to cause his fangs to lengthen. As a distraction, he repositioned her on the pallet and pulled the comforter completely over her, undid his belt and managed to slip out of his jeans. He joined her under the comforter and held her close.

He made love to Constance so thoroughly that she was never aware that his body remained cool despite their lovemaking under the covers. He brought her to a shuddering climax and with his quick gesture the lantern's light faded to a glow.

It was time to continue without restraint. His fangs glistened in the semi-darkness of the wagon, but his mind remained separate from their activity under the comforter. He enjoyed the sensation of sliding his cock deep into her heated core, but his mission was not sexual release, but blood. He buried his head at her neck and bit deep as he continued to pound his hardened length into the responding wetness between her legs. Her passion was so aroused and so complete that she welcomed the slight pain in her neck. She felt the slow roll of her climax build and spasm its release again as he carefully drank only what he needed. One final shudder and she fell asleep with a smile not realizing that he had withdrawn without his own climax.

He was dressed and preparing to leave the wagon when she half woke. Her voice was filled with sleep. "Oh, you are the most amazing lover. Thanks for I hope we—" Her head fell back onto her pillow as she smiled up at him with half-lidded eyes. Clayton murmured, "Oh no, thank *you*," as he opened the canvas drape, stepped through, and quietly pulled it closed behind him.

It was a crystal cold morning and the sun had barely made its way above the distant horizon when Clayton walked to where he had ground-tied Kaliph the night before. The horse was loosely grouped with others and had his muzzle buried in a generous mound of hay. He put his hand under Kaliph's mane and felt its healthy warmth. Evidently the overnight cold hadn't bothered him.

A wizened cowboy limped over, "Nice horse you got there. Ain't seen that breed before. Thought he could use a bite to eat this morning." Clayton took the hint, thanked the man, and handed him a dollar. He said,

"Name's Kaliph. He's an Arab I brought west with me. More of a friend than just a horse." The cowboy smiled as he reminisced, "Had me a paint pony for twenty-seven years. That old girl would do anything I asked of her." The garrulous old man continued to praise his wonderful paint pony while Clayton brushed and saddled Kaliph.

He mounted and as they slowly walked away, he smiled when he heard the old dude greeting another early traveler, "Nice horse you got there. Thought he could use a bite to eat this morning."

An exhausted but smiling Constance finally stepped down from her wagon around noon and winced at the slight soreness between her legs as she muttered, "Damn, I forgot to ask his name!"

CHAPTER 44
BEING SHERIFF

STARVING ROCK, WYOMING

The early morning air was crisp, and the ground still sparkled with frost when Clayton decided to continue south following a well-maintained road. When he saw the weathered sign pointing to STARVING ROCK 10 MILES, he had to check it out. An intriguing name, he thought to himself. Must be a story there.

Ten miles later he rode Kaliph into the tiny town of Starving Rock and what looked like the remnants of a small battle. He smelled a lingering scent of sulfur and gun smoke, saw broken chairs, a busted window and a small cluster of people looking down at two dead bodies. There was a man kneeling next to a third body lying on the street. He must be still alive, Clayton thought, since it's being tended to.

Clayton stopped his horse and looked around. Three saloons, two churches, a small restaurant, a dry goods store, and a sheriff's office made up the one-street town. He continued to the sheriff's office, dismounted, and stepped inside. The place was empty, so he returned to stand near Kaliph. He watched a man break away from the cluster of people and hurry towards him, his face full of concern.

"Hey mister, if you're looking for the sheriff, that's him who's been shot dead."

For a minute, Clayton didn't know what to say. There were two dead men lying in the street, and everyone seemed pretty calm about it. *Two dead men for god's sake!*

Clayton found his voice. "Well, no, I was just hoping for a place to sleep and take care of my horse."

The local man looked a little confused. He had thought that the stranger sure looked the part, either gunslinger or professional gambler. Dressed mighty sharp in those black duds, good looking too. Could spark some jealousy between the womenfolk and their men. He cleared his throat and said, "Head for that last saloon, the Gilded Lady, they got some food there and a room that they might rent out. Look, I gotta' go take the bodies to the church for burying." He rushed on, "You wouldn't be looking for work, would you? I happen to be the mayor of this little town and I'll be needing a sheriff pretty quick I'm thinking ahh, are you good with a gun?"

Clayton didn't bother to reply, just shook his head, and led Kaliph down the street to the Gilded Lady. The bored customers were happy to see a new face and the bartender was happier yet to take his money for a room. He looked around the almost empty saloon. After seeing the poor condition of the tables and chairs plus the overall filth of the place, he decided one night would be plenty while Kaliph rested at the livery stable.

He walked back up the street and was relieved to see the bodies had been removed. He entered the cleaner of the two remaining saloons. At least a dozen men were drinking at the bar, and at three of the four tables men were drinking or playing cards. A sweating piano player in a jaunty bowler hat and bow tie was playing show tunes in the corner, but the buzz of excited conversation about the recent gun fight threatened to overwhelm his music.

As he continued towards the crowded bar, the room fell silent, and every face turned to watch him. Even the enthusiastic piano music crashed to a stop as the player turned on his stool to see what was going on behind his back. *I understand what they mean about hearing a pin drop*.

He nodded his head at the curious men, ordered a beer from the bartender and silently moved towards the single unoccupied table at the back. He recognized one of the men at the bar as the mayor he had briefly spoken to. The mayor grabbed Clayton's beer and ordered a refill for himself. Taking both, he prepared to deliver them to the table after motioning towards the remaining empty chair and Clayton nodded his okay, still saying nothing.

The men in the saloon restarted their conversations and the volume returned to its excited state after the piano player started another lively tune.

The mayor felt a bit uncomfortable as he looked at the still silent Clayton. There's something about that man, he thought to himself. Can't put my finger on it though. Oh well, in for a penny in for a pound.

He began to speak. "Welcome to Starving Rock. Not such a good welcome though. That injured fella was taken to jail. We'll keep him there until the traveling judge arrives. I mean we *hope* to keep him there. One of the dead was a gunmen headed to Colorado. I heard both were hired by some rich lawyer fellow down there. The sheriff saw some wanted posters and tried to arrest them in that saloon with the broken window well, you saw the result. I'm sorry you had to see the sad end of a good man."

The mayor continued, "The folks of this town ain't up to defending the jail in case somebody tries to spring him, but you look like you could put up a good fight if you had to. I just need someone to stay at the jail for the next two weeks to act as temporary sheriff. The judge has a couple of rangers and a jail-on-wheels with him, and they'll escort the man to the prison in Denver. You sure look the part and when they see you, maybe troublemakers will think twice before doing something stupid. I can talk to the town council and make sure you get paid in advance the town is usually quiet, and you can make up your own hours."

The last part of the mayor's statement made Clayton perk up his ears. *Okay, 'make up your own hours' just might work out. A local supply of blood for the next two weeks sounds good. Kaliph and I need a break and it's always a challenge to find a blood source out here.*

The mayor was almost breathless as he tried to convince Clayton to act as sheriff. "The jail has an extra room with a bed. Someone in town will deliver the prisoner's meals and pick up the tab, so don't worry about feeding him." Clayton smiled at the wheedling tone of the mayor and after a bit more discussion, they both walked to the jail and Clayton was handed its keys. He was now, the sheriff of Starving Rock.

Once the mayor left the building, Clayton was thoughtful as he looked around. The place was in need of a good cleaning. He walked over to the several rifles locked up in a case bolted to an inner wall and shook his head. Those guns should be cleaned before they backfired and hurt somebody.

There was a potbellied stove at one end of the room, next to a messy paper-strewn desk and its knife scarred chair. It still gave out a tepid warmth, so Clayton pulled several stout pieces of wood from the wood box and built up the fire. He figured curious people would probably be paying a visit to the new sheriff before dark.

There was a hesitant knock on the door and a young man shuffled in at Clayton's response. He looked cold and was too thin. The dirty hair, ragged clothes and sparse beard marked him as someone who had fallen on hard times. Not unusual in this part of the country.

The kid mumbled something as he looked down at his worn boots. Clayton motioned him closer to the warm stove and said, "I just made some coffee, would you care for some?" He had made the coffee but certainly not for himself.

He hid his surprise when the young man responded with a cultured voice, "Yes sir, thank you. I'd appreciate it."

Clayton raised an eyebrow. "What can I do for you? What shall I call you?"

After sipping the burning liquid, the kid answered, "The name is Edgar Simpson and I'm looking for a job."

Clayton thought Edgar looked like he would fall over any minute. It wouldn't be fair to hire him for only the two weeks he'd be here as sheriff, but he could at least offer him a meal and a place to sleep. Best to be clear about the situation.

"Well, Edgar Simpson, I'm only here for the next two weeks until the judge arrives to hold a hearing and take this prisoner to Denver. But if you could use the work, I'll hire you to clean up a bit around here and run some errands for me. I can offer you a place to sleep and a dollar a day to work for me. Does that sound about right?"

Edgar's face split into a grin of perfect teeth. "Yes, sir! I can start right away!"

But Clayton saw how his chapped hands hugged the diminished heat from the now-empty coffee cup and saw the shivers he was trying to hide beneath his threadbare coat.

"Here. Have another cup of coffee and warm up a bit. No need to start working until tomorrow, anyway. In fact, the mayor dropped off a loaf of fresh bread and a plate of beans that I'm not too fond of. I can warm up those beans if you don't mind leftovers."

He handed the plate of re-warmed beans to Edgar and observed the excellent table manners he used as he sat at the desk to eat his meal. Not ten minutes after he finished eating, Clayton noticed Edgar's eyes struggling to stay open in the warmth of the office. He moved to the half-grown man and touched his shoulder. Edgar jerked awake in alarm but settled back with a sheepish smile. "Sorry, I've not been sleeping too good lately. I'll just head out now, but I can be back first thing tomorrow morning."

"No, you will most assuredly not be leaving. It's way too cold outside and frankly, you're not dressed for it. There's a bed in the back room. Help yourself and get some sleep. Use all the blankets you need. I'll be out here so don't worry about a thing."

Edgar stumbled to his feet and tried to smile through his yawn as he crossed the floor to the back room and practically fell, fully clothed, onto the bed. A half hour later, Clayton peeked through the open doorway and grabbed a couple of extra blankets from the pile on the low dresser in the corner. He gently shook them out before laying both on the deeply sleeping boy. *I wonder what his story is.*

It was after midnight. Clayton listened for any disturbances in the town and heard nothing moving in the stillness of the cold mountain air. He adjusted his hat, checked the gun in its holster and quietly let himself out of the building.

He walked throughout the night, quickly learning his way around the darkened buildings. He moved silently into the beech woods hugging the cliffs to the northwest of the small town. But other than the hoots of hunting owls and the distant calls of a coyote pack, there was nothing. He turned back to the jail and let himself back inside. Dawn found Clayton sitting at his desk, pondering his current situation at Starving Rock. He got up, added more wood to the potbelly stove and decided to let Edgar sleep as long as he needed. The kid was worn out.

When Edgar finally woke up, he found a basin of warm water, soap and a clean towel waiting for him on the chair next to the bed. He hadn't even heard the sheriff come into his room. It was clear what was expected of him, so Edgar washed his face and hands and made himself presentable as he could before venturing out into the main area of the jail house.

His new boss was sitting behind his desk with one of the rifles disassembled in front of him. He looked up at Edgar and smiled. "Good morning, I forgot to introduce myself last night. The name is Clayton Masters, and I think we have a busy schedule today, but first tell me a little about your circumstances here."

Edgar Simpson proceeded to tell Clayton of how his father, mother and two sisters left Missouri with a wagon train to come west for the free land the government was giving away. Their dreams ended when a bad fall from his horse killed his father and cholera took his mother and sisters only two months later. He sold everything but kept his horse and continued west with the wagon train. When it passed south of Starving Rock, he decided to stay behind, thinking he could find local work in town or some ranch. He felt pretty stupid about it now. Finally, he had to sell his horse for twenty dollars so he could eat. The money didn't last long, though, and it had been two hungry days before he knocked on the jail door. His stomach growled for attention.

Clayton looked at Edgar after he finished his story and pushed some money across the desk towards him. "This is an advance for seven days work starting when you get back from breakfast. Let the folks know that you're working for me while I'm sheriff. I have no idea what you can find to buy in this town, but if boots are available, you should get them. I've seen what poor footwear can do to a man's feet during the war, so take care of it after you eat something. I've set up an account at the restaurant so eat there if you care to, at no extra charge. If you won't eat there, the cost comes out of your own pocket. I can lend you more money if you need it."

Edgar swallowed. He was a grown man of sixteen but was about ready to cry like a baby. Mr. Masters sounded just like a military man and that slight English accent was really something else. He was being treated like an adult and would try to live up to Mr. Masters' expectations no matter what. Edgar whipped out the door before any tears fell and Clayton sat back in his chair to continue cleaning another rifle. A slight smile crossed his face.

Ten minutes later, a guttural bellow, followed by a string of curses, issued from the jail cell at the rear of the building. Clayton took his time and strolled back to the cell while the man continued to threaten the sheriff's life, liberty, and pursuit of happiness. Clayton stood there and just looked at the bully. He said nothing.

"Hey, what am I doing in here? A man is allowed to have a drink after a cold day in the saddle. A little bit of fun! Don't you know who I work for? When my boss finds out I'm in jail, there'll be hell to pay!" The filthy prisoner stopped to take a breath when he saw something in the glacial blue eyes staring at him through the iron bars of the jail. His eyes shifted away from the emotionless face and his foul expletives stuttered to a stop.

Clayton's response was simple and to the point. "You killed the sheriff by shooting him in the back. A dozen witnesses will testify at the hearing. Should be in a couple of weeks. In the meantime, you'll be my guest in this fine establishment, and I expect you to mind your manners. If you don't, you won't like the results, I can promise you that."

The bully broke eye contact and was almost pleading. "Well, I'm hungry and need to use the john."

Clayton shrugged and opened the door of the cell. "Don't try anything, I don't need a gun to bring you down." Strangely enough, the gunman believed him, and they walked to the outhouse and back again without any problems. Breakfast was delivered as promised and the prisoner was left alone again to shovel it into his mouth. He remained sullen but quiet.

Edgar arrived after devouring his best meal in a month and enjoyed walking with the newly purchased boots on his feet. They weren't brand-new, but they were in good shape and with the new pair of thick woolen socks, his feet felt warm for the first time in ages. He flung open the jailhouse door and threw out a cheery, "Good morning, sheriff! I'm back and ready to work. Where shall I start?"

Clayton pointed to the stove, now empty coffee pot and the wood box. "Fill the wood box, fire up the stove a bit and make some fresh coffee. The rest of the chores, I'll leave to you to figure out. Oh yes, stay away from the cell in the back unless I'm here. We don't want an escaped prisoner on our hands."

Edgar just nodded and went to work while Clayton read through the wanted posters piled on the desk and rummaged through the drawers. The faint sounds of Edgar whistling under his breath had Clayton smiling to himself. The kid might work out just fine.

It was early afternoon before he could hire a teamster with a small freight wagon to drive to the Cheyanne train station to pick up his two travel trunks. The thirty-mile round trip meant a return after dark, but the driver said it was no problem, his team knew their way back to their barn even if he fell asleep on the road.

During the next two weeks, Clayton and Edgar established a routine that felt comfortable to both. Edgar learned how to shoot a handgun and was accurate with bottle targets most of the time. He also learned how to enter a crowded room with little or no notice and watched how Clayton handled drunken miners and rowdy cowboys. Before they knew it, the two weeks had passed, and everyone expected the judge to arrive any day.

The judge did arrive as promised with two marshals and his jail-on-wheels and the hearing was scheduled for the following afternoon. The judge settled several other cases, and shared plenty of news about important political changes being made that would impact Wyoming. He also had exciting news about the Wyoming to Colorado railroad that was supposed to be built, starting the following year. There were two possible routes being considered. One route expected to follow the Front Range along the Rocky Mountains, dip down through Golden, Colorado and continue to Denver. A land grab was going on along the promised route and in some cases, he was needed to settle some ownership disputes. He'd be leaving the next morning for Denver.

The judge, the surly prisoner and the marshals left at dawn. It was late morning when the mayor presented himself and several of the business owners to Clayton sitting inside the jail reading the newspapers left by the judge. The mayor asked Clayton to stay on permanently as sheriff and he promised to increase his salary by ten dollars a month. They appreciated how he handled riff-raff problems without resorting to guns. And who cared if a few of the worst of them left and were never seen or heard from again? As sheriff he was keeping the town safe and that's what mattered.

Clayton considered his options. True, those missing men would never bother anyone again, he always made damn sure the bodies wouldn't be found. But he wasn't really interested enough to continue as the sheriff of Starving Rock. The weather was changing, days were getting longer and at least a little warmer. He might stay another couple of weeks, but he really wanted to be on his way. His dreams of blood and a woman's weeping continued to haunt him and lately, it seemed that ignoring the pull of the open road south gave him a slight headache.

Clayton's plans to leave Starving Rock changed the day a wagon carrying a man and his wife plus their sixteen-year-old daughter rolled into town. Everyone who could walk turned out to welcome them and the women of the town were thrilled to see more female faces.

As the daughter stepped down from the wagon, the males in the crowd were struck dumb. Women were at a premium in the west. The available ones were usually prostitutes past their prime or built like lumber jacks. This girl was very pretty, her face a perfect oval, surrounded by a wavy mass of chestnut hair curling past her slender shoulders. She curiously looked around her but said nothing as she moved closer to the shelter of her parents.

Edgar was leaning against the doorway of the jail when he saw the shy girl step down from the wagon. His mouth dropped open, and his heart raced as he saw his 'goddess in calico' for the first time. Clayton sat in his usual shady spot and watched the girl bewitch Edgar from over fifteen yards away. He smiled and shifted in the shadows thinking he might just stay around a little longer to see what developed between his hired hand and the newly arrived little beauty, headache be damned.

The Williamson family hailed from a small town in Ohio. They'd lost their business during the war and put all that remained into a covered wagon and headed west. They were town people: he a barber and she a seamstress. They hoped to live above the store they were prepared to build before next winter if the town agreed. Their daughter was well schooled and could teach the youngsters of the town how to read. Everyone felt it was a win-win and the chatter of the women as they clustered around the newcomers confirmed their eager acceptance.

Clayton turned to Edgar and said "I'm heading over there to introduce myself as the sheriff. How about if I introduce you as my deputy? What do you think about it? Want the job?"

* * *

Clayton sat back in his usual chair, deeply shaded by the wooden awning he had built the month before. Edgar had rapidly put on weight in the last six months and had grown over two inches to a respectable six feet. He had a reputation as being pleasant and polite and was known to be a hard worker. He made extra money chopping wood and had developed a strong set of arms, a broad back and a chest ridged with muscle. He proved quite handy with a Colt 38 though he didn't wear one. Clayton didn't want trigger-happy cowboys challenging his young deputy. Wearing a gun low on the hip could wait a while longer. In the meantime, his skill with a rifle put many a snowshoe rabbit into some empty stew pots. Clayton felt that the kid's calm demeanor and usual good sense might make him a competent sheriff for Starving Rock after he headed south.

He thought of how he might help his deputy deal with drunks celebrating their Saturday nights. Something unusual, unexpected. Without bloodshed. He remembered his early years in India and the gardener's voice *I am samurai from a far-away country called Japan. You saw an exercise for unarmed combat we used a long time ago. Learning takes time and practice.*

For another year Clayton trained his deputy in a modified form of jiujitsu. He included the twice-daily drills with his ad hoc lessons of Wyoming territory law and proper gentlemanly deportment with women. The two men worked well as a team to keep the town safe for its residents. Five more families moved nearby. Edgar celebrated his eighteenth birthday and had his heart set on marrying his goddess in calico. Clayton knew she felt the same and it was a few days after their wedding that Clayton told the newly married couple that he was leaving Starving Rock for good.

Clayton rode Kaliph behind the teamster and his small freight wagon and when they arrived at the Cheyenne railhead, his boxes, gear, and Kaliph were loaded onboard for the continued trip south. The sun was shining as only a western sun can, while Clayton shook hands with Edgar and briefly hugged his blushing bride goodbye. As the train slowly moved away, he leaned out over the railing of the caboose to wave goodbye to the two friends he had made in the little town of Starving Rock.

Once in the train's lounge, he pulled down the window shades next to him, stretched back onto the padded bench and placed his broad brimmed hat over his eyes. He ignored the slight sting left from his previous exposure to the sun and tried to relax.

He thought of his time in Starving Rock and how much he'd learned about western ways. The people were amazing. Even with the odds against them, they continued to reach for success. There were some nasty sorts, but the rule of law was making itself felt as more and more settlers arrived to make their homes in the west. He wondered what the next hundred years would bring. He looked forward to taking part.

CHAPTER 45
WHERE'S DENVER?

LONGMONT - 1868

Clayton's body felt sluggish as he descended from the train into the late afternoon. Heavy clouds and a recent rain brought a cool sense of relief from the ever-present hot sun, but it turned the ground surrounding the new station into a thick muck of dirt and horse pucky. Passengers greeted family or friends waiting for them on the platform while the train's porters unloaded luggage and maneuvered through the mud to place them at any convenient dry spot. Going almost unheard over the chatter of the excited crowd was the sharp whinny of a horse in its private cattle car. Heavy hoofs threatened to break through the boards separating the excited animal from its freedom.

Clayton understood Kaliph's irritation and walked over to the uniformed man holding a clipboard. He presented papers showing ownership of the horse and said, "Excuse me, my horse seems to be getting inpatient, can he be offloaded immediately?" The man was quick to obey the Englishman's request. He didn't want to be the one underneath that crazy horse's hooves if he managed to break out of the boxcar. Hearing his master's voice, the horse immediately quieted and pressed his nose between the wooden slats of the car.

Clayton slid the doors aside just enough to allow him into the car to make sure his horse was haltered and safe to unload. He pushed the door wider so he and Kaliph could walk together down the wooden dock's incline to the ground. He led Kaliph away from the admiring crowd of onlookers to the small corral behind the train station and tied him to a convenient rail.

The local postal clerk was scratching his head after finding a steamer trunk and a heavily sealed box resting inside the mail car. He read, TO: MR CLAYTON MASTERS, DENVER, COLORADO.

After leaving Kaliph, Clayton hurried back to speak to the postal clerk still inside the mail car. He again provided papers to confirm the boxes were indeed his and he would take delivery.

The clerk shrugged after hearing Clayton's request. His voice was thick with his Kentucky accent. "Well, mister, I guess you be the one named on the box all right but this ain't Denver. This be Longmont, a mite north of Denver. Train can't go any further, no tracks yet. Still deciding that last bit a' route I be thinking. Bout' thirty-five miles away, Denver is."

Clayton was stunned at the news. His sluggish body had betrayed him, and he had dozed while in the dimness of the lounge. He hadn't even heard the porter announcing the town.

He asked, "Can you recommend a hotel nearby? If I can get a room there, could you arrange to have both boxes delivered?"

"Ain't only but one hotel," the clerk replied. "The Longmont Inn is right over there, see it? My sister runs the place and I happen to know there's a room available. Tell Sally her brother Clyde sent yah." Clyde was rewarded with a silver coin for his trouble.

After registering at the Longmont Inn, Clayton collected Kaliph from the small corral and walked him to the local livery stable. Kaliph was skittish, tossing his head and jerking his lead rope, wanting to run but being held back. Clayton was in no mood to deal with this misbehavior and his voice of command was sharp. "Knock it off, my friend. Wait until nightfall and we'll take a tour of the neighborhood." After being reminded of who was in charge, Kaliph meekly entered the vacant box stall and seemed to pretend nothing had happened. Fresh hay and water would keep him busy until nightfall.

The two boxes were already in his hotel room when Clayton arrived. He ignored the room's furnishings except for the drapes surrounding the window. He pulled them firmly shut and turned his attention to the securely bound box holding his earth. He was so tired, and his skin felt on fire from its relentless itching. Yes, he could remain all day in the sun if covered up but the itch from too much sunlight sometimes drove him to distraction. As he unlatched his special box, he noticed small flakes of skin falling from his hands. *These train schedules certainly don't work for me.* He shrugged and climbed into his special box. A final whisper and the lid closed and re-locked above him.

Clayton slept soundly for the rest of the day. When he finally emerged, the damp weather was gone and the cool, clear night sky above was sprinkled with millions of bright stars. His thirst was raging now, but he had promised Kaliph a good gallop. Maybe he could combine the two.

No one on the street saw him dissolve into a dark mist that drifted with unusual speed towards the livery stable and reassemble into the shape of a man. He didn't bother with a saddle, just jumped on Kaliph's broad back and walked him through the stable doorway. Once free of the town, he gave Kaliph his head and both enjoyed the fresh wind created by their quick passage.

A young cowboy, down on his luck, horseless and hungry, sat at his small fire and nursed a pint of whiskey. With no money and few prospects, he regretted the day he left home to dig for gold. Sunk into self-pity, he didn't hear the swiftly approaching horse and rider. Clayton easily leapt from Kaliph's surging back and wrapped his hands around the exposed neck.

Fire embers scattered. The cowboy never knew what bit him. His emptied body was laid to rest in a deep hole a half mile away from the road and a whispered, "I'm so sorry", drifted away- on the cool night wind.

CHAPTER 46
COLORADO

DENVER - 1868

The hot afternoon sun had given way to dusk before Clayton finally strolled along Denver's main street. He was registered at one of Denver's nicer hotels; Kaliph remained in Longmont until his two trunks could be delivered by a hired teamster. His own thirst was manageable, and he felt free to wander about. The gold rush had brought plenty of prospectors and merchants to the town and it seemed that a lot of businesses opened at 6:00 a.m. and stayed open as long as folks were still buying. Saloons were doing a brisk business and their clientele seemed more sophisticated than Starving Rock's. The memory brought a smile to his face.

Earlier, he had found a small church at the edge of town and arranged for a burial plot at the undeveloped western end of its cemetery. The minister seemed a little puzzled by Clayton's comments. A funeral service would not be needed, (it had been held out east) but the deceased wanted his remains buried in Denver and Clayton would hire his own gravedigger for the job. The minister was very pleased with the financial contribution that followed the odd comments and didn't question the handsome stranger.

Clayton continued to walk in a mindless fashion while observing the saloons and fancy-houses where the lightly dressed ladies posed at open windows to display their wares. He was looking for someone who was sober enough and broke enough to be his hired gravedigger. He found the perfect candidate tucked between the wooden sidewalk and a limestone horse trough, snoring blissfully, his sodden clothes and general stench ignored by passersby. He bent over the man and with one hand easily pulled him upright.

Clayton smiled as he asked, "How would you like to earn some easy money?"

A pair of bloodshot eyes peered out of a slackened face and finally focused on Clayton's chin. "Sure, but I ain't ate in a while. Got to eat before I can work. No wait what do I gotta' do? I won't rob nobody or kill nobody—"

The itch from his time in the sun made Clayton irritated but he managed to keep his voice reasonable as he interrupted. "I need someone to dig a hole in the church's graveyard. I'll pay you half now and half when you finish. It must be done quickly, and I'll be there to make sure everything's okay."

"I'm yer' man!" was the slurred response as he shook loose of Clayton's hand, grinned a toothless grin and pocketed two silver dollars. He shuffled off to a cook tent one street over that served the rough crowd of miners or others too dirty or too broke to dine politely. He couldn't believe his luck. Four whole dollars? He would have dug up the whole graveyard for one!

It was full dark by the time the old miner finished digging the hole to Clayton's satisfaction. He stood beside the empty hole and watched his hired hand's slow progress back to town. He shook his head, somewhat saddened when he saw him stumble from saloon to saloon spending his new-found wealth on whiskey.

Clayton continued to watch from a distance, and the old miner's faltering footsteps finally brought him to the town's refuse dump. Rusty bits of twisted iron, clumps of sodden newspapers, emptied cans, glass bottles and discarded pieces of canvas seemed to provide an unlikely place to sleep, but who knew? A piece of discarded oil cloth, folded neatly near the edge of the dump, was unrolled and within minutes the old man fell asleep underneath his makeshift blanket.

Clayton felt truly sorry for the old soak, but his thirst couldn't be denied. His flight back to Longmont before dawn demanded that he take the blood he needed. He moved quietly towards the sleeping body, sat beside it and gently raised the snoring head onto his chest. Fangs pierced the drunken sleeper's throat and he read the faint memories of a daughter's love. He drank deep and pushed a feeling of contentment into the fading thoughts. As he withdrew his fangs and sealed the puncture wounds in the neck, the smiling victim heard a faint, "Thank you", as he died.

During his flight between Denver and Longmont, Clayton stopped twice to "ask directions" from solitary travelers. After a smile and a friendly chat, the beguiled strangers willingly supplied the small drink of blood his body needed, and no one remembered the visit.

A heavy mist drifted down from overcast clouds and through the second-floor window of the Longmont Inn. Once inside his hotel room, Clayton shifted back into his usual self, climbed into his special travel trunk, and laid back on its soil with a sigh of relief. He could feel his skin begin to heal from the assault of the day's sunlight. He looked forward to his sleep. Itching skin was a small price to pay for a day in the sun but still—

Halfway through his rest, his dreams became the repeated nightmare of a woman screaming and a blood-spattered dress. He clawed his way to consciousness. There was something different this time, his view was looking upwards, but he couldn't see her face. It seemed he was being cradled on her lap and it was *his* blood soaking her dress.

The old miner's disappearance raised no alarms. Nobody noticed and nobody cared what happened to the drunken old fool of a failed gold prospector. The bustling town was filled with men down on their luck. A charitable person could only do so much for them before giving up in disgust at their refusal to find the Lord and do His Work.

Later in the week the body was discovered but it was so savaged by animals that no identification could be made. The remains were buried at a pauper's gravesite at the end of town.

CHAPTER 47
THE VAMPIRE ELDER

DENVER, ONE DAY LATER

Clayton's late afternoon arrival in Denver wasn't of any particular interest. It was a common sight to see freight wagons loaded with large wooden boxes rattle through town, though the handsome stallion following behind did cause a few comments. Kaliph was quickly stabled near the hotel and the Longmont teamster generously helped Clayton unload and move his steamer trunk to his reserved hotel room. They moved on to the graveyard and the teamster dropped the special travel box near the empty hole without comment. Clayton paid him well, before sending him on his way with the usual hypnotic suggestion to forget about the final addresses of the delivered goods.

At last, his travel trunk was completely buried beneath several feet of fresh dirt, and Clayton was finally able to seek his rest.

Clayton woke up suddenly with the demand, "*Come here!*" still ringing in his head: His startled heart pounded briefly as he tried to make sense of what had just occurred. It didn't seem like his usual nightmare, and he relaxed back into the soil of his makeshift wooden coffin. The dirt had soothed the skin irritation created by yesterday's sun and he began to drift back into a deeper sleep.

"*Come here*!", again the command pierced his skull like a sharp blade, only this time he felt almost driven to obey. This was something that had never happened before, but he knew immediately that the command came from another vampire. An exceptionally old one.

He quickly barricaded his mind against the strong summons but his curiosity about meeting a vampire Elder, had him ready to respond. He was confident that his own skills would protect him, so he decided to rest until midnight.

At midnight he willed his body to rise from his buried shipping box as a thickened mist and he could feel the slight pull from the other vampire. After becoming solid, he looked around, almost expecting to see someone standing next to the fence surrounding the unfinished cemetery. There was no one, so he began to walk quickly towards the livery stable a short distance away.

He greeted the stable hand forking hay and filling water buckets for a few newly arrived horses. Kaliph whickered his "hello" and stamped a hoof. He wanted out of the stall and into the fresh evening air. The previous day's slow thirty-five miles tied behind a freight wagon was no treat, and he wanted to stretch his legs. Clayton saddled and bridled the horse and after filling several canteens with water, the two headed out of town towards the mountains.

Once away from Denver, the air was so clear, the mountains seemed only a night's ride away, but Clayton knew better. It might take two or even three nights' hard riding to reach the foothills. Again, "C*ome here*!" brushed against his mind, but this time he slightly lowered his mental block and the images of mountains rising in the west provided a mental map.

Millions of stars in the night sky wheeled above as the two traveled west.

He would not allow another being to control him, but he was curious about a vampire Elder being so close. He followed the directions towards an old mine named El Cinco and rode until the morning sun touched the tips of the still distant range.

Clayton knew Kaliph was tired, and the rays of the strong Colorado daylight would make his itchy skin a distraction he didn't want. He figured they both could rest now during the heat of the day and continue at dusk after it grew cooler.

Clayton saw a distant jumble of trees and rocks and rode towards it hoping there would be enough shelter for them both. Once there, Kaliph scented water and pawed at the shale hiding a tiny trickle of water gathering into a shallow pool. He drank at the unusual reservoir as Clayton removed his saddle and bridle. After tending to his horse, he easily dug into the sand and shale to make a depression deep enough to hold himself. With a sigh, he stretched into it while Kaliph munched on the hatful of oats thoughtfully provided for his breakfast. There was no need to hobble the horse, he would never willingly leave his master's side.

Dusk brought a slight relief from the day's heat when Clayton woke. His rest had not been refreshing. Visions of dark tunnels, iron rails, and rotting timber had crowded his dreams and made him restless. "*Come here now!*" The intensity of the spoken command startled his unprepared mind, and he quickly slammed down his barriers. The tiny pool of water hadn't been enough for a thirsty horse, so after dumping a whole canteen of water into his hat and holding it steady for Kaliph, Clayton saddled up. Dusk settled into early evening when they left their makeshift camp. He knew he wasn't being compelled to ride through the desert but once again, curiosity prodded him forward.

The second night of hard riding brought the two into the foothills of the mountain range. The commanding voice in Clayton's head was clearer but no stronger. It was his blood thirst that bothered him the most, and he was worried about Kaliph. Without water or good forage, the horse might die. After two days and nights in the desert, he was losing weight and dried sweat left a white crust on neck and withers. There was still the two-day return to factor in, too. He dreaded the idea that he might have to let his horse go free to fend for himself if there was real trouble ahead at the mine.

Clayton dismounted to spare Kaliph, and they were walking along a rock-strewn severely rutted road when his eyes saw the dark entrance of a mine. It was still another plodding half-hour before reaching the drift of rubble spilling from its mouth. He looked around. A small grove of pinon trees might provide some light shade during the day, so Clayton unsaddled Kaliph, removed his bridle, and spoke softly to him. He dumped a second canteen of water into his hat and held it up so Kaliph could drink. "Well, boy, we're going to part ways for a while. You take good care of yourself, and I'll be waiting for you to join me whenever you can. Stay safe, boy." He gave a final pat to his friend, turned his back, and began to lightly drift up the slope towards the yawning dark hole known as El Cinco. It came to him suddenly, that he could fly back to Denver, and return with grain and water for Kaliph, assuming of course, he survived this odd summons.

"Come!" The voice blasted against Clayton's shielded mind as he stepped onto the loose gravel at El Cinco's entrance and hesitated. Odd, he could hear it but wasn't compelled to act against his will. Further back, the mine shaft was a well of darkness, but his eyes quickly adjusted, and he could easily see moisture seeping from seams in the rock face. Broken support timbers, rusted rails and an empty ore cart fallen on its side confirmed what his dreams had hinted at. This was the place.

The voice was audible now and directed him to the left tunnel. Clayton followed the instructions but stopped when he saw a motionless figure standing at the far end. It was a disheveled specter, gaunt and bent at his narrow shoulders. In all his brief existence he had never seen the likes of this one. He slammed his mind shut against any more intrusions. His curiosity was satisfied.

The vampire Elder's old-fashioned suit hung heavy with dust and when he smiled his unholy welcome to Clayton, a shred of rotted cloth drifted from his jacket to lie at his feet. His long dark hair was streaked with dust and what looked like old blood. He turned and motioned for Clayton to follow him further into the mine and Clayton was willing. They walked for several minutes until they reached a natural cavern. It looked to Clayton as if the cavern hadn't been dug by the miners but had been used by the vampire as his lair. Drifts of small animal bones littered the floor, and Clayton could hear the rustle of vermin as they chewed on anything edible. Two rusted swords were leaning against eyeless skulls, the disjointed remains and rotted fabric telling the story of a fight lost long ago.

The vampire Elder finally turned to Clayton and spoke with a sneer in his rusty voice, "So, you walk in daylight. How nice for you. I've heard of such a thing but was never able to find a way to achieve the same. I expect, no I demand that you share your secret with me. If you do not, your final death will be insignificant but of course, I have time, limitless time to help you decide." The veiled threat was very clear, pain would be used to help with the decision.

Clayton said nothing as he stood still and collected his thoughts. *The sheer arrogance of this man-creature. He looks like the bad character in a children's story book of witches. Still, he appears to be very old, and he's managed to survive so far. This guy looks ready to force the truth from me. By blood, if necessary, but no, that won't work either. Damn, I don't want to fight him but if we* do *fight, I have to win.*

The other's anger at Clayton's silence almost managed to blast past his mental barriers. His response to the failed attempt was cool. "Then, you old fool, you'll have to kill me. I don't know anything that can help you. Not even my blood can give you what you want."

The impatient vampire shrieked and launched himself towards Clayton, grabbing at his neck with both clawed hands, but Clayton shifted at the last second and avoided the grasp. The vampire whirled and sped towards him again with inhuman speed. This time

Clayton unexpectedly stepped into the attack with one arm extended. His closed fist hit the older vampire just above the heart and shattered his ancient ribs.

The Elder gasped and bounded away shrieking over his shoulder to Clayton, "You'll tell me what I need to know! Who gave you this gift? And why you? You're nothing! An infant! A damn pup!" He stood for a brief moment before turning to see how Clayton responded to the insult, but Clayton never hesitated. He launched himself towards the vampire with his leg straight out in a kick that connected with the already healing ribs of his opponent and sent him crashing into the rock wall.

Clayton heard Kaliph whinny in the distance and momentarily lost his concentration. He spun around to the entrance of the cave in response and felt clawed hands on his neck pulling him back. Their strength threatened to crush his bones, but Clayton brought both hands back over his shoulders and gripped the vampire's filthy hair. As he bent low and pulled, the hair acted like a rope around a stubborn steer, and he flipped his opponent completely over his shoulders and onto the rockface floor.

The old one landed on his back but sprang up quickly to cling to the ceiling of the cave, out of Clayton's reach. Screeching again, he shoved himself off the ceiling, and before Clayton could turn to face him, the vampire dropped onto his unprotected back, sank his claw-like nails into his shoulders and bit hard at his neck.

Pain coursed through him from the deadly bite, and with all his strength, Clayton slammed backwards against the cavern wall. The hands loosened their grip, and the fangs withdrew just enough for Clayton to pull away, but his efforts left deep bloody scratches in his flesh, and the claws' putrid venom prevented a quick healing.

The scent and sight of his rich blood maddened the Elder, who forgot about fighting or cracked shoulder blades, instead, fixating his scarlet eyes on the dripping wounds.

In a flash, Clayton turned and pulled the unholy monster towards him. The venom continued to bubble within the scratches on his shoulders and visions of blood, eviscerated humans and screams of the damned began to swarm around the edges of his shielded mind. He knew he must end this fight immediately.

The Elder grabbed him for another savage bite, but Clayton shoved both thumbs deeply into those undead eye sockets. He blocked the elder's hateful vision with one of his own, a crying woman who held his bleeding body while begging him not to die. Someone he had never met but seemed to care for him deeply. A lost love?

The yellowed claws loosened their hold and grabbed at both bloodied eye sockets. Clayton pushed hard to free himself from the blinded vampire, but he was grabbed again and thrown hard against the cold wall of the cavern several yards away. The Elder, maddened at the audacity of the "pup" challenging him, forgot about the possibility of day walking, and flew across the floor of the chamber to deliver Clayton a crushing final death.

Clayton sprang to his feet and braced himself against the wall. With a blur of motion, he pulled his knife from its ankle sheath and stood ready to plunge it through the ancient Elder's throat and deep into the spine.

Instead, he stood amazed at what he was seeing.

A whirlwind of dark blue cotton and lace smashed the flying vampire into the cavern's wall. The crack of his broken neck was loud, and the ancient body slumped to the dirt. The twisted head and sightless eyes left no doubt that he should be dead.

Clayton stepped forward, smiling as he watched the matronly lady dressed in dark blue, bend over the body and plunge a wooden hatpin deep into the rotted fabric over his chest. She was still wearing her dainty white gloves as she effortlessly twisted and pulled the skull from the torso. She tossed it aside muttering, "*There, damn you!*"

Thalia calmly walked towards the stunned Clayton and in a voice tinged with humor, "How many times am I expected to rescue you, silly boy?" He managed to grin at her and muttered to himself, "I'm really getting too old for this."

He reached out a hand, and she grabbed it, immediately hauling him into a quick hug. The two of them looked back at the fallen vampire who was rapidly disintegrating into black dust and shattered bones.

Thalia nodded her head at the stinking pile and said, "Napier and Lillian were siblings, and he was much nastier than she was. I tracked him here when I found out he was in America. I felt your presence in Denver, and you led me right to him. Aren't *you* the lucky one!"

Her leather boot kicked at the disappearing mess on the cavern floor while she smiled with triumph at Clayton.

The two walked arm in arm towards the mine's entrance. The air was cool and refreshing as Clayton's various wounds continued to heal and the venom was overcome by his own ancient blood. He looked down towards the foot of the dangerous slope and saw Kaliph running up and down the roadbed, tail aloft and head held high. Thalia's buggy and livery horse rested beside a small mound of hay and several buckets filled with water.

The two drifted down the face of the mine refuse without effort and they decided the horses were rested enough to begin their return to Denver. With the water and hay, the horses would be fine while he and Thalia hid from the hot sun during the day.

Their nightly hunts for blood were successful and Clayton made sure Thalia was safely covered while she slept. After they reached Denver and settled the horses, Thalia said her goodbyes to Clayton and walked out of his life. Again.

CHAPTER 48
HIS ARRIVAL IN GOLDEN

A week later, Clayton arrived in Golden after a long day in the saddle. He had been in the sun for such a long time, his flesh felt actually sore despite the dark clothing hiding it from neck to toe. He had been riding between Denver and Golden following up on leads for ranch land and had spent some days sheltered in dirt to refresh his system but only when he could find good grazing for Kaliph. An absent farmer's willing wife, a solitary cowboy or two, and one remote military outpost managed to satisfy his blood thirst as he traveled.

The saloons facing Golden's Main Street were busy and faint piano music lilted out of batwing doors several buildings away. The evening air was soft, and the clear early-summer sky overhead promised another hot day tomorrow as twilight bled into darkness.

He rode a tired Kaliph towards an imposing, and very new, three story brick hotel situated at the end of the street. Three large glass windows reflected the gas streetlights opposite the building and the interior of the hotel could dimly be seen from the sidewalk. He continued looking around as he grabbed his saddlebag and tied Kaliph to a convenient hitching rail. He murmured to the horse as he stroked the soft neck and promised to return quickly to get him the best livery the town offered. Kaliph seemed to agree as he pushed his head against his master's chest with a quiet nicker.

The Empire Hotel's lobby was grandly furnished with three chandeliers hanging from an ornate ceiling two stories high. Their glow throughout the richly decorated area highlighted the couches, potted palms and small tables artfully arranged to provide several seating areas for private conversations or other relaxations for the clientele. A stately grand piano stood in a corner of the lobby facing towards the interior. The second and third floors of the hotel created a horseshoe effect with their wrought iron railings along each hallway facing the center lobby. The lobby's desk area was to the side of the room, its long surface covered in highly polished marble.

He approached the registration desk manned by an obsequious desk clerk. It seemed to him that every fancy hotel clerk gave the same response to his questions with a sing-song cadence: *Yes, a room was available for the gentleman, or please sign here, or how long does the gentleman intend to stay, or yes, there is a livery stable close by.* He paid closer attention to the oily voice when he heard, "One of our bellhops will take your horse and see to its care. There is no extra charge, of course, since you are our guest and we'd be happy to send a light snack to your room if you wish. We pride ourselves as being a full-service hotel."

Clayton just smiled, thanked him, signed the guest register, and accepted his room key. Finally, alone in his hotel room, he fell backward upon the plush bed with his itching arms outstretched, booted feet still on the floor. He wasn't the least bit tired, but it felt nice not to be moving, to be completely still. Sounds from the streets began to intrude on his sense of relief and solitude.

Pounding on his door caused him to leap to his feet even as he drew his gun. He threw open the door to a very young and nervous boy who stood in the hallway and stuttered the reason for his panicked knocking. It seemed that Kaliph objected to leaving the hotel without his master. The child's treble voice said, "He almost bit my arm off! He seemed kinda' mad, Mister. You gotta' move him yourself!"

Tears left small streaks down the dirty face, and the little cap with the hotel logo stitched on it was tilted to the side so much, the elastic holding it in place threatened to snap. Clayton put a calming hand on the boy's shoulder and promised to take care of his own horse. He handed the boy a dime and he trotted away with a shaky smile.

After stabling the still anxious Kaliph, he returned to his hotel room. He was washing the dust from face and hands when room service delivered his light snack. Clayton ignored the useless food and moved to the window. His room, as requested, was a corner room on the third floor. The casement window would provide an easy exit if a quick departure were needed. He hoped he wouldn't need to use it.

Feeling restless, Clayton left his room and descended the carpeted stairs to the lobby. He saw the grand piano in the corner and felt drawn to its polished black luster. He remembered sitting beside his mother while she played the classical music she loved. He had clumsily mimicked her playing until finally, she agreed that he could have lessons. The lessons came to an abrupt halt on his eighteenth birthday when his father demanded that he concentrate solely on learning the business of Masters and Sons Shipping. He was told young men should learn the art of fencing and the intricacies of foreign trade. Piano playing was for sissies. He became quite adept at fencing and continued with his martial arts. He also learned the family business as required but he never touched the piano again.

He looked down at the gleaming piano and lowered himself onto its bench. He ran his fingers lightly over the keys and without thought, began to play a Beethoven piece that his mother had loved. It was as if the passage of time had no meaning. Lost in memories of music with his usually strict mother, Clayton flawlessly played other intricate pieces. With a final crescendo, he sat back and stared down at his hands. Applause and a few cheers erupted from the crowd surrounding him. He thought, *Good lord! What have I done?*

Maintaining a small smile he thanked the crowd, bowed with self-mockery, and threaded his way through the admiring hotel patrons towards the stairs leading to the solitude of his third-floor room. Excited chatter followed his retreating back and several of the bolder women tried to intercept his quick exit with inviting smiles and knowing eyes. He ignored them all until a well-dressed gentleman laid a gloved hand on his arm. His voice was well modulated, and he had obvious social skills, but Clayton made a point of looking down at the man's hand. It was immediately removed and replaced with a handheld calling card.

The oily voice attached to the hand said, "Please excuse my forwardness, but it's been a long time since I've been treated to such a talented rendition of some of my favorite music. I'd like to introduce myself,

Aloysius Grey. As you'll note from my card, I'm a lawyer, and if you're new to the area, perhaps I can be of service. Might I call on you tomorrow?"

Clayton swiftly made note of the intruder's attire. The clothing was well made of high-quality material. A gold pin held his tie in place and the shirt looked clean and well starched. The handmade boots were only lightly covered with dust, typical of the west he thought. Yet he felt a small frisson of concern with the man's demeanor. It was a bit off-putting, but since he was new in the area and since he was looking for a small ranch or acreage to purchase, the man's local knowledge might be useful. Clayton put aside his reservations and agreed to meet Mr. Grey at five o'clock the next evening at the Wildcat saloon across from the hotel.

He reached the safety of his room without more interruptions and realized he was truly starving. This kind of hunger would never be satisfied with a sandwich and a glass of beer or even his small drink. He would have to hunt tonight. He put himself into a mindless state and waited in the quietness of his room until the noise of the town faded. He roused himself six hours later.

On catlike feet, Clayton traveled from roof top to rooftop, only descending to the ground when the lack of buildings marked the edge of town. The moon was a quarter full at this time of the month, so the alleyways remained dark with dense shadows. His night vision found the light of a campfire burning almost two miles away. Running into the dark was no problem, his eyes were accustomed to it and the speed of his passage brought him to the campsite within seconds.

Three men sat around the campfire finishing their poor meal of beans and hard tack. Handy cups of whiskey helped wash everything down. Clayton's nose rebelled at the stench wafting into the air from their unwashed bodies. Ten bales of animal hides tied with rope were scattered on the ground by a rickety wagon, showing these were mountain men or trappers. Half drunken arguments and slurred conversation said they would be selling the hides in town tomorrow. Their plans included grabbing a willing woman, getting drunk and getting back to the mountains for more furs.

One by one, the men left their fire and rolled up in their blankets. Snores filled the night as a motionless Clayton watched and waited. Finally, one of the men stirred, rose and shuffled to the edge of a nearby gully. His steaming piss splattered on the rocks below and seemed loud in the night. The man giggled to himself when he finished and tucked himself away. "Now that's a mite better."

Before he could turn and make his way back to the group, Clayton grabbed him by the neck and sank his teeth into the throbbing vein in his dirt lined neck. The man stiffened but didn't struggle, paralyzed by the sheer pleasure coursing through him as the vampire drank deep. A whispered, "Thank you", floated into the darkness as the man's lifeless body was cast deep into the gully.

Three days later, the remaining two men were let out of jail due to lack of evidence for the murder of their partner. The local sheriff decided the broken neck was from a bad fall, the several slashes at throat and wrists looked like animals had begun to tear at the body. Desert winds had dried the remaining blood to almost nothing and without more clues, the sheriff could only have the body properly buried.

The two trappers were happy to leave the town of Golden behind. They knew something odd had happened to their pal. He wasn't likely to lose his footing and the drop from the edge of the gully wasn't that deep. If he fell, he would have shouted for help. Finally, shrugging off their concern, the men rode out of town and headed back towards the mountains.

CHAPTER 49
GREY'S NEXT PLAN

Aloysius Grey reflected on his brief conversation with Clayton Masters from the night before. He thought the man was somewhat intimidating with his stern looks and glacial blue eyes but appearance aside, the man was new to the west, a real "greenhorn" who could possibly be manipulated into a financial deal which benefited himself.

Grey arrived a half hour early for his appointment with Clayton and spied his hired gun slouching over a warm beer at a table across the room. His voice was cool as he hid his contempt, "I have a job for you, O'Grady." Aloysius Grey used O'Grady for some of the unsavory jobs necessary for the shadier side of his legal businesses. The man was stupid but usually effective.

O'Grady rose and strutted towards the bar, both thumbs hooked into the sides of his low-slung gun belt. The look of being a hard ass was ruined somewhat since his expansive beer belly obscured the oversized belt buckle struggling to hold the gun belt in place.

"Yes sir, Mr. Grey, what can I do you for?" Rotted teeth peaked out of O'Grady's grin as he extended his hand.

Grey ignored the man's small attempt at humor and stepped back to avoid shaking hands with the palm being extended. He tried not to breathe in the stench of the unwashed body. "I'm meeting a new client here in a few minutes. I would like you to find out more about him, who he is, what he does, anything you can uncover that would be of value. His name is Clayton Masters. Seems to have money. He's staying here at the Empire Hotel. Got in yesterday I think."

O'Grady looked down at his boots, cleared his throat and waited. Grey took the hint and continued, "And of course, I'll pay you your usual fee." He turned away, signaling that the conversation was over. O'Grady scurried out of the bar and almost collided with Clayton who was entering the bar from the street.

Clayton immediately saw Aloysius Grey lounging against the long bar at the rear of the room. The interior was dimly lit with candles on various tables and glowing gas sconces placed along the walls of the room. Most folks were still at supper, so the bar was mostly empty. His quick glance detailed everything in the room from the liquor bottles displayed on shelves behind the bar's counter to the few customers quietly talking at small tables placed along the walls. He smelled the small mouse scurrying along the floorboard with his supper of cheese. A busy spider floated in the gaslight fixture suspended from the ceiling.

Clayton nodded his head towards Aloysius as he walked forward and said, "Mr. Grey."

"A pleasure to see you again, Mr. Masters," he responded and held out his hand. Clayton hesitated a moment before clasping the sweaty palm in his cool one. He dropped the hand quickly and fought the urge to wipe his own with his handkerchief.

Aloysius gestured towards one of the empty tables along the right side of the dim room, assuring that they wouldn't be overheard by any of the other patrons.

Clayton figured the lawyer might know of a local rancher who wanted to sell out or knew of vacant land. He would also know any rules and regulations pertaining to the sale and transferring of property deeds. *I'll just let him do most of the talking to get a feel for where he's coming from. Maybe he'll recommend some properties or give me some background on the locals and what's going on around here. Worth a closer look.* Clayton gave a mental shrug and prepared to listen to what Aloysius Grey had to say.

"Well now, Mr. Masters, what brings you to our little city of Golden?" Aloysius sat back in his chair, lit a cigar, and crossed one knee over the other. The buttons on his vest strained with their attempt to remain closed. Clayton was fascinated by the war between thread and fabric and wondered briefly which might win.

"I'm looking for a small ranch or land that's not too far from town. Somewhere within a few hours ride. Prefer a good water source, a clean property deed."

"Well, all those things together might be a little hard to find in these parts. Water is at a premium, most of the usable land is already spoken for. Course I *might* be able to find you something," he paused, "if the price is right."

Clayton didn't respond to the hint of a finder's fee but merely nodded his head with a small smile. The two men continued with their general observations and questions until Clayton felt sure his first impression of the man was right. Mr. Grey was untrustworthy.

Clayton had access to almost limitless funds but certainly didn't want the lawyer to know about it. He already felt the man seated across from him was a liar. Here was trouble just waiting to happen. He knew he could handle any trouble that came his way, but why ask for it? "Let the greenhorn beware" was probably the man's motto. He stood and looked down at the self-satisfied smirk on the face of the semi-reclining lawyer.

Clayton was curt, "Thank you for your time, Mr. Grey, but I won't be needing your services after all."

Aloysius Grey scrambled to his feet as his face reddened from the implied insult. "Now just a minute, sir. I'll have you know that I have a good reputation in this town, and nobody will be better able to assist you than I can. I know these parts better than anyone and with my introductions, why folks will welcome you without question!" With his final declaration, the thread lost its war with fabric and a button popped loose.

Clayton hid his smile as he turned away from the lawyer. He didn't need to hear any more of the man's bluster and his horse probably missed him by now. Time to pay a visit to the livery stable to check up on Kaliph who tended to get anxious if he was away too long. Maybe go for a ride around the town. Meet some people and introduce himself and the reasons for his visit. It was still early enough with twilight beginning to fade towards dark. Perhaps start his research at the noisy saloon down the street.

As he entered the stable, Kaliph heard his master's voice speaking to the stable hand and whickered a greeting. The hostler walked with Clayton past several stalls and was telling him how much he admired the horse but didn't admire his tendency to misbehave. Clayton arranged to have Kaliph moved to an empty box stall in a corner area of the barn and promised there would be no further trouble. He walked Kaliph to the box stall with only his voice guiding the animal, and used soothing words as he brushed the shiny black coat and lifted the saddle blanket and saddle into place.

He whispered in Kaliph's ear, "Behave yourself, you have the blood of kings running through your veins. Be proud but not arrogant. Be strong willed if you must, but don't be a bully." He smiled and added, "And be nice to the ladies." Kaliph leaned into Clayton, resting his handsome head onto his right shoulder with a contented snuffle.

Clayton and Kaliph rode down the main street, seeming not to notice the stares from the townspeople grouped on the wooden sidewalks. The incredibly handsome stranger sitting on the incredibly handsome horse stopped some of the women in their tracks as they watched. Kaliph used his best parade prance and tossed his head as he acknowledged their silent praise. Once at the end of main street, Clayton allowed the horse to have his way and they galloped into the night. Both enjoyed the fresh air and freedom of the open road beyond the town, but a half hour later, it was time to return to the lights of Golden.

After visiting the second tavern, Clayton struck paydirt in the third. He asked the bartender if any of his customers knew of a ranch or vacant land for sale. The bartender aimed his chin at an old cowboy leaning forward with his elbows on the bar, one boot hooked on the railing below. Clayton noted the clean clothes and the bright and intelligent faded blue eyes as the man turned towards the newcomer.

Clayton introduced himself and asked his question again. The response was thoughtful and still held the hint of southern gallantry. "Well, I do know of such a place. Worked out there when I was younger. Owned by a really nice lady, and if you ride out there, you tell her Charlie sent you. And bring a shotgun for protection. She's a might quick with her trigger finger." Charlie started to laugh at his own joke.

Clayton bought Charlie a beer, hoping to hear more about the ranch. Charlie drank the stranger's offering as he thought, *I want to like this handsome fellow but he's a strange one. Something about him. Well-dressed, high-class English accent, clean, well spoken. Educated for sure but different.*

Clayton and Charlie continued to talk for the rest of the evening. Charlie drank enough to swamp a boat but kept his wits and his humor. He never noticed that Clayton drank very little or just touched the rim of his glass without drinking. Clayton appreciated any man who could drink and still hold his liquor and Charlie's sense of humor was quite entertaining.

CHAPTER 50
SELLING SWEETWATER

The next morning, Charlie rode down the street to meet Clayton in front of the hotel. After a hearty breakfast of ham and eggs at Jennie's Café and feeling the effects of three cups of her strong black coffee, Charlie barely felt the cold air of the pre-dawn morning. They had a two-hour ride ahead of them and he knew his old bones would be grateful when the sun finally rose behind with its light and promised heat.

Charlie was never a quiet man and his garrulous nature reasserted itself as he began to tell Clayton about the current owner of the Sweetwater Ranch. Charlie held forth, "Troubles started a bit after she inherited the place from an aunt out east, Georgia, I think. Even her barn was burned with a winter's worth of hay. She kept holding on, but Miss Mary never really recovered after some outlaws murdered her foreman."

Charlie swallowed the lump in his throat before continuing with his recital. "Never caught em' either. A couple of months later, after the funeral, a water tank was poisoned lost almost a dozen steers. Heard she tried to lay off her hands, but they refused to go that's loyalty for sure. She's got nothing now except a wish to leave and maybe start over out east or even Denver. Can't keep up the ranch by herself but, to give her credit, she refuses to sell to just anybody." He finally paused for breath.

Clayton's eyes sharpened as he turned in his saddle to look at Charlie. "Anybody? She's refused all offers? That's unusual if she's almost broke, isn't it?"

Charlie shrugged. "Yep, word is a lawyer feller from Denver just made a third offer a couple days ago. Can't possibly be wanting the ranch for hisself. He's a city guy what doesn't know a ranch from a lady's front parlor, and I don't know who he's working for."

Charlie ran on, "That lawyer feller you met last night has been trying to get that land for a couple years. Tried to buy it from the aunt, and after she died, tried again with Miss Mary. But she wouldn't sell even when he raised his first offer. After that, things started to go bad at the ranch. Started out with gunshots after midnight. Two hired hands disappeared at the same time, never heard from again. Stock went missing. Nothing ever came of it though. Couldn't prove anybody was guilty. That land sure is pretty and there's plenty of water, a small spring fed lake. Grazing is good all year if the herd is kept small enough but with no help, she just can't keep it. Yah know, folk hereabouts help when they can, but she's mighty prideful and won't accept much."

He leaned over to spit and continued, "One piece of livestock she's kept though, a truly be-u-t-full Arabian mare. A dark dappled gray that glows in the sun. And feisty? Whew! Brought her along when she arrived planned on breeding her. Remarkable animal. Let's *her* ride but nobody else gets too close unless they've been *introduced properly*."

Charlie's emphasis on the last words and careful pronunciation made Clayton smile. Charlie shifted in his saddle and said, "That mare is a sweetie but with a temper, to be sure." He grinned sideways at Clayton. "Course her and I are good friends now Queenie just *loves* carrots."

A friendly silence fell between the two men while Charlie rested his jaw and reached into his shirt pocket to withdraw a small sack of tobacco. He built himself a smoke while guiding his patient mount with his knees, the reins looped casually around the saddle horn. After taking a drag off the lit cigarette, he continued, "We'll be riding about another half hour towards that flat topped hill. It's an easy ride to the top and you can see Sweetwater Ranch from up there."

Moments passed until Charlie looked over at the silent Clayton and grinned, "Not much for talking, are yah?"

The two men turned away from the dusty main road to follow a well-worn track heading towards a low mesa. Clayton looked back at flat yellow grassland that seemed to stretch to the horizon. Ahead, the rough road disappeared, and he could see mountains beginning to stretch their massive girth up to the heavens. The sun was still behind them, but early morning and its heat was beginning to make itself known. He casually reached into the saddle bag behind him and put on the smoked glasses he knew he'd need.

Clayton smiled at his new friend. "Nope, not much for talking right now but I'm looking around and admiring what I see." Charlie chuckled in response.

They paused at the hill's summit to rest the horses and Clayton was mildly surprised to see a wide valley displayed below. He would never get used to how the land spread and folded in upon itself with hidden gullies and low rises that tricked the eye into thinking the terrain was completely flat.

Some late morning haze still covered distant trees, and a small lake in middle of the shallow valley's center reflected the clear blue of the sky above. An unpainted two-story ranch house and several outbuildings showed mild neglect but the small corral to the side of the house seemed to be in good condition. Clayton's sharp eyes saw a magnificent horse near the fence, the dainty head lowered to gently accept the attentions of the woman stroking its dappled cheek and smallish nose. He saw her look up at them, a startled expression crossing her face.

As the men slowly rode down the track towards the house, she turned and walked quickly to its front porch. The horse snorted and began trotting around the corral, her tail a bright banner in the sun. Her whinny was loud, and Kaliph jerked his head up and lengthened his stride in response to the mare's siren call.

Continuing to follow the track down towards the house, Clayton's scanning eyes saw a small log cabin near the trees on the far side of the lake. Despite its shabby appearance, there was a neat pile of cut wood stacked on its north side and from the looks of it, the well in the cabin's front yard might still be serviceable.

Charlie stood up in his stirrups and waved his hat at the woman standing by the front door with a shotgun pointed directly at the two men. He called out, "Miss Mary, it's me, Charlie!"

She raised her hand over her eyes to shade them and a wide smile crossed her face as she lowered the gun and leaned it against the open doorway. A few minutes later the two men entered the yard in front of the unpainted house.

The woman continued to smile. "Charlie! Well, I'll be. What brings you out here? And you even brought a guest. I'll put on the coffee pot, and I've got lemonade in the icehouse."

As she stepped off the porch into the dusty yard, her beautiful southern accent pulled at Clayton's memory. The exotic scent lilac and jasmine overwhelmed his nose and almost blew away his self-control. His cock hardened and would have embarrassed him if he hadn't been in the saddle. He wanted to thrust his hands in her hair, pull it free of the pins and lose himself in the glory of her blood as he fed from the slender column of her neck. What on earth? He was sure they hadn't met before, or he would have remembered such a beauty.

His mouth had dried completely, so he said nothing as he touched his hat to acknowledge her greeting before turning back towards the small corral and dismounting. He tied Kaliph lightly to the corral rail and settled his hat forward to shade his face.

Charlie was dismounting and still explaining things to Mary Ellington, speaking at his usual speed of a mile a minute. Both seemed to forget all about Clayton as they chattered to each other and returned to the porch. Finally, Mary picked up her shotgun and re-entered the house.

Clayton's hands were shaking slightly as he took his time watering both horses and loosening saddle cinches. He had to get himself under better control. Who was this woman and why did she affect him so strongly? *Oh yeah, she was his idea* of *perfection wearing a cowboy hat.*

Charlie called to him, interrupting his scattered thoughts. He joined him on the porch and the two men used hands and hats to brush the road dust off jeans and shirts. Charlie was first to enter the dusky interior of the house and began to speak at his usual rapid pace. "Miss Mary Ellington, I'd like you to meet Mr. Clayton Masters. He's looking for property around here, so I told him a bit about your Sweetwater Ranch. Hope you don't mind that I brought him out without letting you know first, but he's in town only a little while and he sure seems to like it around here." He looked down at the hat in his hands and finally took a breath.

Mary was stunned as she looked up into the face of the man she had loved and thought dead several years ago. She ducked her head as she wiped her shaking hands on her jeans, willing herself to remain composed, but words stuck in her throat when she realized he didn't recognize her. *Oh, he is even more beautiful than I remember, but have I changed so much he doesn't recognize me? Or is he trying to hide our earlier relationship?* She felt the blood leach from her face and took a deep breath before forcing a polite smile.

Clayton heard the rapid beating of her heart and was puzzled by her strong response to him. His voice was grave. "My pleasure to meet you, Miss Ellington. I've enjoyed the ride out from town, the country around here is beautiful." He nodded at Charlie. "Of course, Charlie kept me entertained practically the whole way."

He held out his hand. She hesitated before allowing him to take her cold hand in his. "Please call me Mary and yes, I truly love this place." She quickly dropped his hand as a pretense to gesture towards the kitchen. She needed to put space between the two of them and moved to the pine table saying, "Please take a chair and I'll re-heat some coffee. Hope you don't mind, I made it this morning." Her voice trembled as she forced herself to continue. "My family put a lot of years on this land so it's quite special to me. But it's become too much for me to handle and it's time to sell. As soon as the right buyer comes along, I'll sell and move."

Her voice strengthened as she gripped the back of the nearest kitchen chair. "Are you looking to buy an existing ranch, Mr. Masters, or are you looking for vacant land?" He noticed she still refused to look directly at him as she grabbed the coffee pot and began to pour the hot liquid into ceramic mugs.

The scent, sight and the *perfection* that was Mary. stirred Clayton's lust as never before, but he had to keep it controlled or it would be a disaster. He was grateful for the shelter of the table while he forced his building erotic thoughts aside. He sincerely hoped his cock would behave itself and return to normal, it had become so hard that even sitting in a chair was uncomfortable. He swallowed a small sip of coffee and said, "I'd prefer a working ranch, but if that's not possible, I'm ready to buy acreage. If you'd like references, I can put you in touch with my solicitor in Savannah."

Solicitor? This is my Clayton but how could he not know me? What we shared together was real, damn it! His kisses didn't lie, and I said "yes" *to his marriage proposal. Well, he better make the first move because*

Oh no, what if he's married now? She willed away threatening tears and swallowed the lump in her throat.

Mary's voice was warm but controlled. "Why don't I just show you two around? It should only take an hour or so since the sale doesn't include any branded stock. Those might be sold at auction or to the buyer if any are found. Only the buildings, water rights and acreage are included if you're ready, I'll saddle up Queen's Pride and we can be on our way."

Seeing Clayton's raised eyebrow, she explained, "Queen's Pride is my Arabian mare. More royal than I am, and she agreed to be called Queen." She smiled before taking a sip of coffee and continued, "I rescued her from a slaughterhouse in Savannah, she was obviously ill-used, and I just couldn't turn away. I brought her out here and thought of breeding her but never found the right stud." She smiled faintly down at her hands folded in her lap and sighed. "Of course, that won't be happening at Sweetwater after all." She paused and swallowed. "She's not included in the sale I would never part with her."

She shook her shoulders, straightened up and smiled at the two men seated at the table across from her. "Enough of crying over spilled milk! I can even make you supper before you head back." She smiled at Charlie. "Charlie, you won't refuse some of my cooking, will you?" Mary rose from the table, put on her hat, and moved out the door. She figuredt the men would not turn down a home cooked meal.

She forced her memories of Clayton Masters away and quickly saddled Queen at the small corral and led her mount towards the two men waiting for her in front of the house. Queen started to dance sideways, pulling on the reins. "Calm down, girl." Mary's voice tried to soothe the suddenly fractious mare.

Clayton removed his smoked glasses and sent a mental command to Queen to behave herself. The startled horse calmed and allowed Clayton to approach. Using a soft voice and running his ungloved hands along the horse's neck and shoulder, he assured the animal that he was a new friend who respected and appreciated her. Queen's Pride snuffled through her nose and thrust her head into Clayton's chest, nearly knocking him over.

Charlie stood with mouth open, pulled off his hat and scratched at his sparse hair. "Never seen *that* before." Mary stood at Queen's side with a mystified look on her face. "I guess she's made up her mind to accept you, Mr. Clayton Masters."

Kaliph, on the other hand, did not appreciate all the attention being lavished on the beautiful female a few yards away. He threw up his head, pulling the loosely tied reins from the corral gate. Backing up, he danced and pivoted in place to show that mare just who was the king. He pushed closer to Queen who was becoming nervous with his obvious intentions. Mary stood between the two and had no way to avoid being stepped on or knocked over.

Kaliph was about to grab at the neck of his chosen bride with his teeth to place her properly for his lusty mounting when Clayton whistled sharply, grabbed his reins and mentally commanded Kaliph to behave himself.

Kaliph was angry, and pulled at the tight reins, but he obeyed, and Clayton pulled him further away from temptation. Both horses settled and pretended not to notice each other after their adolescent display. Two humans stood dumbfounded, not sure of what they had just witnessed. With only a whistle, Clayton had just stopped his stud from covering the mare.

An embarrassed Charlie cleared his throat. "Well, I guess we might as well get started on that tour, Miss Mary." The quiet group left the front yard and rode towards the little cabin nestled between huge cottonwoods at the rear of the property.

Mary regained her composure and turned to Clayton. Her smile was blinding and turned his thoughts from ranching to blood-filled hope. "What's the name of your horse? Obviously Arab and he's a beauty I also think he knows it." She laughed again that the memory of the chastened look on Kaliph's face after Clayton's scolding.

Clayton's voice was thoughtful. "Bought him in England after the war and brought him to New York by steamer. Since then, we've been traveling west." *Who is this woman who is driving me crazy? Quit thinking about her obvious charms! Just stop it!*

Clayton, Mary, and Charlie spent the afternoon touring the ranch property. Clayton was making mental notes about what might need his attention, but all signs pointed to careful and thoughtful maintenance. He could tell that the only drawback seemed to be lack of funds, not lack of interest or skill. The trio returned to the ranch late in the afternoon after taking a break on the shore of the small lake.

Charlie offered to look after Queen (he had carrots in his saddlebag) so Mary could start to cook the promised meal, and both thought it a very fair exchange. Clayton unsaddled Kaliph and put him in the small corral with Charlie's paint, a gelding well along in years, while Charlie led Queen into her usual box stall, safely away from the amorous stallion. Queen smelled the carrots in Charlie's sack and followed closely, trying to nip the treat before it was offered.

Clayton entered the house and removed his hat as he took a chair at her kitchen table. He sat quietly and watched Mary bustle around the kitchen as she heated fresh coffee and put loaves of sourdough bread into the oven. He admired her efficiency and the quick movements between the sink, stove, and table. The stove's heat brought a light shine to her forehead, and damp tendrils of dark honey-blond hair escaped the loose knot pinned at the back of her head. He thought she looked absolutely adorable but also noted that she refused to look at him and barely spoke.

She placed a cup of black coffee on the table within easy reach before resting both hands on the back of one of the chairs. "I forgot to ask earlier, do you take cream or sugar?"

He looked down at the cup while trying to gather his thoughts. "Uh, no thanks, this is fine." He felt an odd sense of knowing her from before, but that was impossible. He would never forget such a woman. He wanted her so badly he could barely think straight.

He took a breath and said, "Miss Ellington, I'd like to make an offer for your ranch. It's in a great location, not too far from town, not too close. The water, those mature hardwood trees at the back of the property, the corrals and bunkhouse the ranch is in pretty good shape and would be perfect for me."

Mary caught her breath. She would have to look straight at him now while they came to terms. She already knew she'd sell to him. Absolutely. But what came afterwards? She managed to keep her voice calm. "Sure, I'll sell to you but there are a few conditions."

Her hands clutched the back of the kitchen chair while she continued. "The ranch hands have worked here for years, and they've been very loyal. Even Charlie used to work for my aunt until he retired a few years ago. I'd like you to keep Rusty, Carl, Duke, and Cookie employed. They're good men to have around and you can already see there's plenty of projects and repairs to be done. I'd also like to delay the actual sale until the railroad decides its route from Cheyenne to Denver. They'll either offer to buy some of my property, or the route will bypass my land all together. If they need the property, there may be less than what you want. You can write me a note of your intent to purchase, and I'll just keep it in my safety box at Golden's bank until you decide."

She turned away from him and began slicing cucumbers and tossing greens for a salad. Clayton thoroughly enjoyed watching her firm bottom in the snug jeans as she washed and cut tomatoes. Even the homey smells of baking bread, hot coffee and beef stew teasing his nose seemed, somehow, to be just right. Her natural fragrance of jasmine and lilac was a perfect blend and she smelled so wonderfully good it was hard for him to ignore the urge to jump up and pull her into his arms. He ached to feel her against his body and as his groin tightened, his fangs threatened to lengthen.

Clayton realized, sitting in her kitchen, that he also wanted to share these feelings with her. He didn't want to conquer her, he wanted to love her. He cleared his throat and asked, "Do you have any plans for after the sale? Maybe return east to family, or settle in town?" Finally, he dared to ask the dreaded question. "Is there someone special waiting for you?"

She put down her knife and held back the tears that threatened. Without turning around, she replied, "There was a man once, back home, but he seems to have disappeared. I've made my peace with his loss, but I've never been with someone who even came close to what we shared. So, to answer your question. No there is no one waiting for me."

Clayton tried to feel sorry for the guy who had left this woman alone, but he enjoyed the flood of happiness cascading through his heart.

He needed to change the mood and hoped he could seal the deal so he said, "Miss Ellington, I could really use your help. Would you consider being my housekeeper until the sale is final? At that point, you may look for other options or decide to stay. Who knows what will happen in *our* future? I-I mean, *the* future."

Mary smiled down at the sink. O*h, yes, Mr. Clayton Masters, I'll most definitely stay around until our future is sorted out!* She turned towards Clayton, leaned back against the counter and didn't even try to hide her satisfaction. "Yes, Mr. Masters, that sounds just about right."

Mary and Clayton quietly ate their meal while the still talkative Charlie spun yarns about local history in between bites. When he finished eating, he left the table to bring the men in from the bunkhouse. While he was gone, Clayton agreed that an offer of employment should also be made to Charlie. The man was older, but he had a steady hand with horses, and both knew he could use the money.

The ranch hands cheered the coming sale and promised to keep it a secret. The men returned to the bunkhouse and a very happy Charlie looked forward to spending the night with them, under a solid roof and with a full belly.

Two days later, Clayton and Mary rode into Golden and settled their financial arrangement. The bank's representative was cautioned not to publish or speak of the pending sale and purchase of the Sweetwater Ranch. The clerk took one look at Clayton's closed expression and decided he would never want to be on the man's bad side.

Clayton moved his gear into the bunkhouse but explained to the men, he probably wouldn't sleep there too often. He had insomnia and didn't want to disturb anybody's rest. They accepted his excuse without question, and he knew he'd find himself in Mary's bed if he didn't distance himself while she slept.

Before long, a routine was established. Charlie mostly sat in the sun with a new puppy he was training as a watchdog. Mary, as his housekeeper, discovered she had a knack for growing flowers and vegetables in the newly expanded garden next to the kitchen. The ranch hands continued doing their work for a new owner that seemed to know what he was doing.

* * *

The moon was full, giving Clayton a perfect view of the house as he sat on the grassy hill overlooking the ranch below. Kaliph was grazing nearby and seemed quite content to be near his master. Clayton jumped up, angered at himself and where his thoughts kept taking him.

Why does this woman affect me so much? I want to pull her into my arms and hold her tight. I want to feel that beautiful honey hair as it tickles my nose. Ahh, what am I saying, I want to make love to her so much it hurts. I can't keep pretending I'm not aware of every breath she takes. That woman is so sexy she drives me crazy, and her blood must be so sweet.

Kaliph snorted as he lifted his head at Clayton's sudden movement. He rubbed the soft nose. "Sorry boy, didn't mean to startle you." He saw the dim light in Mary's window and watched her shadow pass back and forth. The light went out and she moved to the open window, leaning out to gaze up at the full moon.

Clayton's heart stopped when he caught her scent and realized she was wearing nothing between her and the night air. His groin tightened and his fangs dropped unnoticed while he gazed at the perfection of her breasts glowing like twin pearls in the wash of moonlight. His pupils dilated and dark heat thrummed through his veins. *So easy to approach her now.*

Mary enjoyed the cool velvet air bathing her shoulders as she stood at the open bedroom window.

The men were in town, so she felt free to indulge herself. To feel the night air caressing her bare skin. She lifted the heavy mass of her hair off her damp neck and closed her eyes. She moved away from the window and lay, still naked, on the bed's gold and white quilt. She needed to think about her relationship with Clayton, the man who treated her as a friendly stranger might. A few minutes later, she fell asleep, one palm lightly cupping her breast.

Clayton couldn't resist getting closer. His dark mist reassembled itself at the foot of her bed. *I'll just watch her breathe for a minute.* He inhaled her warm woman's scent of lilac and jasmine deep into his lungs and felt himself helplessly drawn to her side. *I can lie next to her, and she'll never feel my touch.* His hand reached out and lightly stroked her sleeping form from neck to slender ankle. Red heat blasted within him and the urge to drink, even the smallest sip, slammed into his consciousness. His body demanded to be released and he quivered with the effort to control himself. *Just one small sip—*

Mary's dreams became erotic but all wrong. She wasn't some wanton female sharing her body's secrets with a stranger. She was asleep but her soft "no" stopped Clayton even as his mouth was about to kiss the warm column of her neck. Cold anger at himself drenched the heated fires in his blood and he withdrew as fast as possible from her bedroom, back to safer reality next to Kaliph. A quiet, "What the hell am I doing?" drifted down the hill.

CHAPTER 51
MEMORIES AND RUSTLERS

SWEETWATER - 1869

It was almost a year since Clayton had made his offer to purchase the Sweetwater, and the best part of Clayton's week was the long ride and picnic with Mary. Today, he met her at the kitchen door and grabbed the small basket already packed with sandwiches and a bottle of wine. They usually rode until they felt like stopping or when they found a particularly nice view. But today was different. He wanted to tell Mary that she had become special to him. Would they continue down the path and find love together, or would she decline in favor of that damn lost love out east?

He had his plan all set for their route today. He said, "I'd really like to see how Queen and her new foal are doing in the west pasture. Okay with you?" Of course, Mary was thrilled with the idea. Queen's Pride and Kaliph bred true to form and their brand-new offspring was a perfect little Arabian filly.

As they rode, Mary chattered on about the ranch projects and started to give a detailed account of her current fundraising efforts for a new school. Clayton had promised to match any funds raised during the town's events and her excitement was growing as their goal grew closer.

Clayton had difficulty listening to her recital while trying to remain calm. Her scent always drove him to distraction. He wanted to bury himself within the circle of her arms, rest his lips on her willing neck. He wanted to spread her naked body beneath his and feel her respond to his lovemaking. He felt almost dizzy as his lust mixed with an intense longing to know her even better. He hadn't felt these emotions since— When?!

He felt his blood pulse with a strange rhythm, and he rode without thought as a kaleidoscope of scenes flashed before his sightless blue eyes. Breakfasts and long walks with *this* beautiful woman, nights with tender kisses that changed quickly to heated lust for *this* woman. His proposal of marriage to *this* woman!

He remembered Savannah and brief but blinding pains in his neck and body. Screams. Dripping blood coating a diamond and ruby ring. His spinal injury in Savannah! Kaliph stumbled on a partially buried rock and quickly recovered, but Clayton was lost in his past and couldn't fight the dizziness that overwhelmed him. He slumped forward and slid sideways off the saddle onto the ground at Kaliph's feet. Seconds later he opened his eyes, but his thoughts were muddled. *What a beautiful blue sky. Did I just fall off my horse?* He raised his head slightly and saw Kaliph's black leg shifting near his boot. A pair of knees in tight jeans rested next to his shoulder and a small hand was patting his cheek.

Mary's face was at an odd angle. "My god, Clayton, are you okay?"

He realized he was lying flat on his back and looking up at her. He saw the concern in her eyes and *remembered*. He remembered loving her so much, life without her meant little.

"Mary? Savannah? I know you. I *remember* you!" He clutched at her arm as he rose to a sitting position on the ground.

Tears were welling up and spilling down her cheeks. "Yes, Clayton. It's me and I've been waiting for you," she whispered with a sob.

He scrambled up and without effort, pulled her up to stand beside him. He wrapped his arms around her and pulled her into his embrace. Her hat loosened and her glorious honey dark hair spread on the shoulders of his jacket.

He breathed in the scent of lilac and began to kiss her. Her deep and fiery response caused his blood to roar with its need to take the final step and make her completely his. Without thought, he began to brush her neck with his lengthening fangs when Kaliph shoved his head hard against Clayton's shoulder blades causing him to lose his balance.

Realization of what had almost happened flooded his mind with guilt. A memory and a promise made long ago: to never take the blood of someone he loved.

Both stepped away to catch their breath and Mary almost giggled with happiness after they agreed to continue their ride to see Queen and her baby. After spreading the picnic blanket and unpacking their lunch, they began to share the stories of their years apart with frequent pauses for more intimate explorations and re-discovery. Clayton held himself in check and ignored his body's growing thirst and the almost constant itch on his skin from the sun.

It was dusk and time to ride back to the ranch and its responsibilities. Clayton and Mary rode side by side into the ranch yard holding hands. The puppy was fully-grown and bounced and jumped a joyous welcome while Charlie stood up from his favorite bench by the bunkhouse. After they dismounted, Mary grinned and said, "Charlie, meet Clayton, my fiancé from Savannah."

With a huge grin poking through his whiskered face Charlie marveled, "Well, don't that just beat all!

CHAPTER 52
ANGRY BLOOD

It was after ten o'clock and Mary had retired to her bedroom, but Clayton was restless. He needed to feed and absolutely would not endanger his crew on the Sweetwater. He decided to drift towards the far boundary of the ranch after he scented smoke and burning cowhide. Rustlers were still a constant threat and he wanted— No, he needed to stop them and he was hungry.

He changed into mist and followed the faint smell of smoke to the property rising along the foothills of the mountains. A small fire glowed within a cluster of scrub pinon trees, and he saw three horses tethered nearby. A hushed conversation was taking place.

"Hey, Johnnie, do you think Grey will need us some more? This cow stealing is getting a little old and I'm getting nervous. They still hang rustlers around here."

Johnnie had no patience with lily-livered partners. "I heard he wants to put a real scare on Mary Ellington. Something more *physical*. I sure wouldn't mind tossing her around before screwing her. Let her know what a real man can do for her Geez I get horny just thinking about it." Johnnie threw another piece of wood on the small fire. "Sully, bring that calf over here, the night ain't getting any younger."

Clayton became solid and waited with unnatural stillness in the shadows. His anger was building when he recognized the rustlers. Mary had hired the three of them two weeks ago to help with their growing herd, but this was obviously not what she expected. He sped past the two men hunched over the body of a bawling yearling calf and stopped behind the third man holding the branding iron with its red-hot tip.

Mike heard a slight sound and whirled around in surprise, "What th—"

He never finished his question as Clayton gripped his throat with one hand and the arm holding the branding iron with the other. Bones snapped. Mike tried to scream but his larynx was crushed, and he crumpled to the ground, almost falling on the still glowing iron clutched in his nerveless hand. The other two men jumped up from the bawling calf and faced Clayton. Their eyes were wide with fear, but Clayton knew they would fight. They recognized him and they had no other choice.

His voice was low and cold. "Gentlemen, you are on my property, and I believe that is my calf you're treating so poorly."

Sully, didn't hesitate but pulled his gun from its holster and aimed at Clayton. He was about to pull the trigger, but his finger never completed its mission as Clayton flashed across the fire and completely crushed all the bones holding the gun. He bent the man's neck to an almost impossible angle and bit deep, his fangs piercing the thick vein below the carelessly tied bandana. The iron-rich blood laced with adrenaline gushed into Clayton's mouth and he took a satisfying swallow. He looked directly into the third man's stunned face as he continued to drink from the pulsing fountain before dropping the emptied husk to the ground.

Johnnie, the remaining rustler stood immobile, shocked into frozen stillness by what he was seeing. His mind couldn't process the dark evil that had invaded their temporary camp. *Vampires don't exist, do they?* He didn't wait to find out but gave a short yell, turned, and tried to run away from the horror he saw in the wavering light of their dying campfire.

Clayton sent a bolt of command for the rustler to stay where he was. He was extremely angry about all the harassment Mary had endured before giving up and selling her beloved ranch. He was angry when the harassment continued unabated, as though she was considered an easy target, as though there was a sign that read "Welcome Rustlers". But now, they were stealing from *him.*

His anger grew hotter, and his sapphire eyes turned scarlet as he glared at the third cowboy. His mental touch told him all he needed to know. Johnnie wanted to assault Mary and Johnnie's memories held a very dark history of abusing women.

He decided to play with his food.

His steps toward the remaining rustler were slow and measured, and he made sure the other man could see the vampiric red glaze of his eyes. He raised a hand and began to stroke it along the shivering shoulders of the fright-frozen cowboy. He sent erotic scenes tinged with sensual pain into Johnnie's mind and the response below his belt was immediate. The man groaned when Clayton stepped closer and rubbed his hand against the tight hardness beneath his jeans, and his eyes became glassy with the mixed messages of lust and fear.

Clayton whispered into Johnnie's ear, "I can promise that you'll never steal another man's work or harm another woman *ever*." He yanked the dark blue sweat-stained shirt away and skin gleamed fish-belly white in the moonlight. His head lowered to bite deep and drink the rich blood tainted with lust and fear. It slipped smoothly down his throat until the heartbeat warned of death. Clayton dropped the corpse and wiped his mouth thinking; *I'm not going to waste one bit of sympathy on this animal.*

The still unbranded calf was set free, and the small fire buried in dirt before he walked to the three horses that had been tied nearby. He loosened their reins and let them drop. It had to look like the horses had broken loose on their own, keeping the three was not an option. Horses were easily recognized, and like cattle rustling, horse stealing was a hanging offence. He slapped their rumps to start them headed for home and wished them well. The wolves in the nearby foothills had developed a taste for domestic meat.

Within a half hour, Clayton had carried the three drained corpses up into the foothills. He dumped each one at least a mile apart and he knew that scavengers would finish the messy job of disposing of their remains. He decided to feel no remorse for what he had done. He would protect Mary against anyone and anything that might cause her harm.

His preternatural hearing caught the distant sounds of a feeding wolf pack. He chose to ignore it as he returned to mist and drifted through the trees and back to the darkened shadow of the Sweetwater's barn. He could sleep now.

CHAPTER 53
GREY'S FAILURE

Aloysius sat behind his desk smoking his usual after-lunch cigar and staring blankly at the ceiling. His mind was fixed on the events of the last year and how things were slowly but surely trending in his favor. Opportunities to create havoc had slowed down a bit, and he didn't want any accusations made against him or his band of bullyboys. It was amazing how that little hothouse flower kept the ranch going. Being jinxed with minor but repetitive problems hadn't caused her to give up and sell. Gill was dead and without him, she would be vulnerable even with that greenhorn Englishman she hired. Might have to rachet things up a bit.

His thoughts turned. Another possible problem had recently surfaced. While drinking at the Wildcat saloon, he overheard talk that the engineers and owners of the railroad were still trying to determine the best route between Cheyenne and Denver. There were two possible routes and he had spent a lot of money and called in a lot of favors to ensure the track would run through the Sweetwater property and south through Golden.

He knew he was financially overextended with setting up and buying the expected rights-of-way for the Cheyenne-Golden-Denver route, but if he could just nail down one more investor or maybe offer a partnership? Most of his own investment would be covered and with the later re-sale of the properties to the railroad company, he and a partner would make a very nice profit. It was a good plan, but he needed to move fast.

* * *

Aloysius was in his hotel office when a letter was hand delivered asking for his attendance at a landowner-railroad meeting in a week's time. He was nervous. He hadn't been able to convince anyone to partner up with him. Everything was on the line now and he knew it.

If he won, he'd be a rich man, but if he lost, he had a hunch that most of the land would be practically worthless to the railroad, and he'd be forced to sell at a loss. Well, he wouldn't think about it now. Maybe a night out with Red Della would help set his head right. As he heaved himself out of his chair, visions of Red Della's special tricks with tongue, hot candlewax and handcuffs stiffened his cock to a throbbing salute.

The week had passed quickly, and Aloysius sat at the polished mahogany table with a stunned look on his face. He had just been told the Union Pacific Railroad would bypass Golden completely on its way south to Denver. He was ruined! Through the roaring in his ears, he barely heard the director's explanation for their choice of route. The route through the Front Range presented just too many geographical hurdles for the engineers to overcome. The voice droned on, maybe in a couple years a short spur could be built from the mainline over to Golden, but for now, the deal was done. And dead, dead, dead.

His fortune was gone, and his creditors would likely be lining up to take their pound of flesh. He continued to sit at the table staring sightlessly down its polished length. Other (and smarter) Union Pacific Railroad investors wouldn't look at him as they silently rose from the table and quickly left the room.

White hot rage filled Aloysius as he stood and kicked an office chair into the wall behind him. He was being denied the opportunity to become the richest and most powerful man in Colorado. All the deals and arm twisting, favors asked for and granted, all the long hours and financial risks he took had resulted in nothing. Nothing. Just dust beneath his feet.

He gripped the edge of the table with his meaty hands, their knuckles stretched white. The focus of his anger shifted and sharpened when he thought of Mary Ellington. A scowl crossed his face deepening the fat folds around his lips and eyes. *It's all her fault, and by God, if I can't win the railroad battle, I'll make sure she doesn't win her battle to keep Sweetwater. I'll make sure she's looking me in the face when I pull the trigger.*

CHAPTER 54
A WEDDING AND A GUNFIGHT

SWEETWATER - 1869

After a hectic two weeks of preparation, their friends came out to celebrate the wedding held at the ranch. Mary and Clayton stood before their minister and said their vows, the cheering and rice throwing afterwards confirmed true happiness being wished for the newly married couple.

Long tables were covered with checkered red and white tablecloths and decorated with clay pots filled with flowers and small pine boughs. A young steer provided the main course for the outdoor barbecue and the women donated a seemingly endless amount of food. Not to be outdone, the men set up kegs of beer and a nearby table held a crystal bowl filled with punch for the ladies. The three-tiered wedding cake was a confection of white frosting and spun sugar flowers but the miniature bridal couple resting on its top caused plenty of smiles and a comment or two. The tiny statues were dressed in western garb! Clayton grinned when he saw it, he was sure his men had swapped out the traditional cake topper and replaced it sometime during the service.

Local musicians played their hearts out for the dancing that followed the feast. Kids ran about, narrowly missing tables still full of dessert trays and bottles of homemade wine. A huge mound of hay near the barn provided a semi-private get-away spot for any young men who had enough nerve to court their hearts desire.

Thalia arrived after dark to give her congratulations to them both before she pulled Clayton into a brief hug. Mary was puzzled by the warmth of the greeting but not the least bit jealous when Clayton hugged her back. It was obvious they shared a history she knew nothing about, and she knew Clayton would tell her at the right time.

Thalia gifted Mary with a beautiful cameo to wear at her throat. When she looked closer at the fine detail of the engraving, she realized the stone was carved into a startling likeness of Clayton. She looked from Clayton to Thalia and back to Clayton. She smiled at both and spoke words from her heart. "You've been friends a long time, haven't you." She nodded to Thalia and her voice was hesitant. "I hope we can become friends too."

Thalia recognized Mary's sincere warmth and looked over Mary's shoulder at Clayton. Both knew that someday Mary would have to make a decision. One that would change her forever.

It was after midnight before the couple could break away from the raucous celebration by the bunkhouse. Clayton rode Kaliph with both arms securely holding Mary before him on the saddle, the horse already knew his way towards the little cabin by the lake and needed no guidance. The night was crystal clear, and a full moon washed the cabin in silver, highlighting the details of fresh cut pine boughs and strings of pinecones and popped corn decorating the front of the little porch.

They would spend their wedding night here, and Clayton could think of nothing better than smelling rich pine scents while making love to Mary without reserve. How lucky he was to have found his Mary and the perfect place to spend his lifetime with her. *Time. Time. Never enough time. I'll just take whatever she can offer and let her go when—*

He pushed away the intruding sadness.

After Clayton and Mary dismounted, he loosely tied the reins around the neck of his horse, slapped his rump and gave the command for him to return to the barn. Kaliph nudged his shoulder, whickered, and wheeled away to trot back to Charlie and his guard dog, both waiting patiently on the bunkhouse porch.

Mary stepped inside the cabin to wait for her bridegroom. She was not one to be carried over the threshold. Nope, she wanted to get ready for her wedding night, *now.*

Clayton stood alone in the darkness and gazed upward at the points of light overhead. Millions of stars glittered like diamonds, and he stood admiring their cold beauty. He mused that in all his years he had never met or loved such a remarkable woman. He prayed that his love for her would help him hold strong against the darker, secret side of his nature, his other self.

A soft voice called from inside, interrupting his thoughts. "My husband, are you joining me inside or should I get dressed again and join you out there?" Her soft laugh followed the almost breathless questions.

Clayton shook off his revery and jumped from the darkness outside, through the open doorway and into the cabin. He took one look at his new wife standing before him and forgot all thoughts of a slow seduction. The blazing fire behind her highlighted the sweet curves of her body as she stood proudly before his heating gaze. He pulled her into his arms, swept her up and carried her to the waiting bed. She looked up at him with a smile as she put her arms around his neck and whispered, "My husband, what a perfect word."

He smiled down at her in his arms, "My wife, that word will always be in my heart."

He laid her on the bed and started to undress in the wavering light of the crackling fire. She watched him, admiring the view as she leaned on an elbow and thought, *What a magnificent body. And it's all mine!* His back was turned as he pulled his shirt overhead and tossed it on the nearby chair. The muscles bunched and stretched with each movement until he sat on the edge of the bed to pull off his boots.

She decided that she was done waiting for him. Just as the second boot hit the floor, Mary grabbed his shoulders from behind and pulled him flat on his back, his feet still resting on the floorboards. He grinned as he looked up at her but said nothing as she swung her long legs astride his jean covered lap and grabbed each of his hands to move them above his head. For the briefest of moments, she read concern in his eyes but as quickly as she saw it, the look disappeared. She stretched along his body and felt the hardness of his cock through her sheer nightgown. She rubbed hard against the straining bulge and tiny jolts of pleasure raced through her blood to pool beneath her belly. She leaned down to kiss him and as she did, her grip on his hands loosened and he was able to reach forward and hold her as the kiss deepened. He pushed his way further onto the bed and managed to maneuver them both into a more comfortable position.

He was surprised when she actually began to undo his belt buckle. He smiled to himself as he helped her loosen the belt and undo the buttons at his waist. *The little minx, she wants this as much as I do!* In a matter of seconds, his jeans joined the shirt on the chair, and he helped a blushing Mary out of her nightgown.

Clayton easily flipped Mary on her back and stretched next to her on his side. He ran his thumb lightly and slowly along her jaw and down the slender column of her neck. To shoulder. To breast. To hip. To the softness between her thighs and up again, retracing his path. He lowered his mouth to her breast and teased its pink bud with his tongue as his hand cupped and caressed the other. She gasped with pleasure as his mouth moved to worship lower on her body, inserting his tongue into the tiny well of her naval.

She was on fire with his caresses and heat pooled at her pelvis as his tongue moved to the hot wetness between her legs. She jerked in surprise at his soft invasion but immediately wanted more. Her hands stroked the hard muscle of his shoulders and buried themselves in his hair as she tried to hold back a low moan. She wanted him to stop not stop stop.

She panted, "You're driving me crazy, come back up here."

She pounded lightly on his shoulders as if to get his attention. He was more than willing to return and plunder her swollen lips with his tongue. He paused with a faint smile and looked into her eyes, prepared to kiss the sweet spot of the pounding vein nestled between her neck and shoulder. He moved to cover her willing body with his own. His muscles tightened and his fangs threatened to drop with his desire to mount her. He managed to hold onto his control as he entered her heated wetness slowly and partially withdrew several times. She was breathing heavily and grasped his waist, urging him to enter her. Moments later he was sure she was ready to receive his hardened length. He gave a final push, and it was done.

Her startled gasp caused him to pause, but she wrapped her legs around his waist to pull his length deeper. He obeyed the unspoken demand, and her hips rose to match him thrust for thrust. The warm tension below her belly continued to grow and demand its own release. She moaned softly as she felt a rush of pulsating pleasure wash through her. Clayton pushed up on his arms and with a final thrust, growled low in his throat as he buried himself completely in her heated core.

The sheer intensity of his climax surpassed anything he had ever felt before, and without conscious thought, he fell on her glistening body as his mouth closed on the pulsing vein of her neck. He bit, and the thrill of her blood welling into his mouth brought a never before feeling of excitement, love, and glorious satisfaction.

He swallowed the scarlet gift before his reason returned with a crash, bringing him to the cold reality of using her, the woman he truly loved, to satisfy his lust for blood.

He reared back, his erection still impaled in her heated sheath. His mind screamed as he saw her pallid face resting on the pillow, her eyes closed, blood trickling from the bruises on her neck. *Oh no! What have I done?* He damned himself as a reckless fool but couldn't help slowly licking away the sweet honey and ginger remaining on his lips, savoring its unique flavor before he sealed the small punctures closed with his kiss.

He adjusted himself on the bed and moved her to rest in his arms while sending a hypnotic suggestion that she forget his blood-kiss. Seconds later she looked up at him with a sleepy smile and sighed as she stretched her cooling length against him like a satisfied cat.

"Did I just fall asleep for a minute?" Her eyes cleared and her face bore an expression of false innocence. "Can we do it again?"

Tonight was special for them both, so he shut away his guilt, knowing he'd think on it later. He looked down at Mary reclining in his arms. "Woman, you'll be the death of me. Wait a bit while I grab that bottle of wine over there. Have you ever had wine in bed before? No? Well, it's one of life's little pleasures."

For the next hour, she enjoyed the wine and the attention of her new husband. Finally, an exhausted and thoroughly loved Mary fell deeply asleep, her head on the pillow of his shoulder. Clayton remained awake and in agony at what almost happened. He must never *ever* allow his blood lust to take control when making love to her.

Clayton was dozing but woke up completely alert to the soft scrape of footsteps outside the cabin. He quietly threw back the tumbled quilts and picked up his jeans from the chair. He pulled them on and reached for his loaded gun. The fireplace held only embers, and moonlight threaded through the gaps of the closed lace curtains hanging from the open cabin windows.

Mary turned over in her sleep and reached for him but felt only a cooling emptiness. She sat up, pulled the quilt to cover her breasts and was about to ask him what was wrong, but Clayton held a finger to his lips for silence. She nodded acknowledgement. After crawling off the bed, she pulled on her nightgown and its matching satin robe. He motioned her to the side of the heavy oak door where the stout log walls of the cabin would protect her if necessary. He motioned with his arm for her to stay low and she nodded.

A dark shadow moved past the window as Clayton and Mary stood against each side of the door in the darkness of the room. Both watched the slow turning of the doorknob. A hand slowly appeared from around the semi-opened door and pointed a gun directly at the piled pillows on the disheveled bed. The gun thundered even as Clayton's hand slammed down on the extended arm. The crack of a breaking bone was followed immediately by a sharp yell and a curse. The intruder tried to step back, but Clayton flung open the door and grabbed the man's arm, tossing him into the far side of the room without effort. The heavy body crashed headfirst into the sturdy log frame of the bed and remained motionless on the floor. Mary could tell from the unnatural slant of the neck that it was probably broken.

More gunfire came through the still open door and several bullets hit the unfortunate man on the floor. Blasts from another location confirmed a second would-be killer. Clayton motioned again for Mary to stay low and safe as he crouched over and ran with inhuman speed through the door into the darkness beyond. Silence.

A gunshot. A soft grunt and the sound of fists pounding flesh. A second gunshot. The silence seemed to drag on until Mary thought she'd die from fear.

"Mary, it's okay." The sound of Clayton's calm voice brought tears of relief but as she was about to step through the door he continued, "Stay in the cabin. I think there's one more out here somewhere."

In the darkness he withdrew his mouth from the rapidly emptying vein of the dying man's throat. He figured from the rancid body odor and small size it must be Big Bill. He was taking a chance with his timing, but there was already blood everywhere and he needed it. He carefully wiped his mouth and used his saliva to seal the other's neck wound. The stomach's gaping bullet holes would account for the massive loss of blood slowly dripping onto the dirt.

Mary continued to kneel in the darkness. She wasn't frightened any more. She was damn mad. This was her wedding night, and her man was out there trying to protect her! She crawled towards the sprawled body by the bed and groped around for the gun. She knew how to use one but hoped she wouldn't have to. She was so intent on searching near the body, she didn't see the dark shadow climb through the window. A gloved hand grabbed her hair from behind just as she found a skinning knife laying partially wedged underneath the twisted corpse. She held it close to her side as she was roughly pulled to her feet.

A voice hissed in her ear, "Make one move or say one word and I'll kill you." Mary slumped within his hold but held tightly to the knife hidden in the folds of her nightgown. The man began to push her towards the door with one hand while he held his gun pushed firmly into the small of her back. They reached the open doorway and the gunman called out, "I've got your woman here Masters! Come out or I'll kill her where she stands!"

Mary almost forgot to breathe. She knew that voice. Aloysius Grey!

Clayton remained hidden in darkness. His voice was low and deadly. "You really don't want to do that Grey, or you'll regret it for the rest of your short miserable life." Mary could feel Grey's shiver through her satin nightwear and heard him swallow convulsively. The rank stench of his nervous sweat filled her nostrils. *The man's a coward and a bully!*

She shifted her weight, slightly away and to the side, while making a little whimper of discomfort and Grey reacted by shifting his weight for balance. Mary wasted no time repeating her mantra but plunged the skinning knife up to its hilt into the man holding her. Her determined strength pushed it through Grey's stomach and lodged it against the vertebrae of his spine.

She managed to yank the knife free before Grey fell like a ton of bricks at her feet. He sprawled motionless, his blood dripping past the cracks in the floor and onto the thirsty dirt below. Clayton leapt through the door towards her and grasped her shoulders to steady her as she slumped forward, her long hair hiding her face in shadow. The bloodied knife was still clutched in her shaking hand, but he could tell she was unaware of it. He could feel her chest heaving as she struggled to gain control of emotions torn apart by the killing of a human being, one who had tried to kill them both.

His hands crushed the bloodied silken robe as he roughly pulled her limp body into his. Anger, that she had put herself in harm's way, battled with the sheer relief that she was unhurt. She said nothing as she sagged against his chest, her face still lowered and heart beating erratically.

His eyes glazed and pupils dilated as the smell of cordite and blood saturated his nose. His fangs began to lengthen with the strength of his desire to take the richness and exotic flavor of her blood once more. Without thought, he lowered his mouth to the pulsing vein in her neck. Clayton's mind whirled, and emotions roared with the dark desire to make her completely his. His mouth was open, and ready to draw the first drop of blood, when he became aware of her sobbing quietly into his chest. The knife Mary had been clutching dropped to her feet and her arms reached around his waist in a frantic bid for comfort and relief.

His mind stuttered and fangs withdrew as reason returned. *I could make her safe forever. But not this way.* His hand reached under her chin to lift it. His voice was calm and gentle. "Mary, look at me look at me. We're okay. You're safe and these guys can't harm us anymore."

Mary silently nodded and moved away from the shelter of his arms. She drew a deep breath, and her voice was adamant. "I absolutely *refuse* to sleep in here tonight."

Clayton bit back a laugh as he grabbed the quilts off the bed and led her to the cottonwoods near the lake. He wrapped her against the night's chill before pulling her onto his lap. He leaned against a tree, and she nestled in his arms while they watched the night fade into the dawn.

* * *

Golden's sheriff arrived in the late afternoon to take statements about the gun battle. He stood over the three corpses laid out in front of the cabin and shook his head. "Okay, who shot who? Not that there will be much of an inquest. I already know who these men are and good riddance."

Clayton kept his arm around Mary as he replied, "The one on the left, O'Grady, was shot by me when he came shooting at us through the door. He landed hard. Guess he broke his neck. Mary managed to find and grab that skinning knife from under his body and when Grey snuck through the window to hold her hostage, she acted in self-defense and stabbed him."

The sheriff bent for a closer look at Grey, "Well, Mrs. Masters, I'd say you were a real professional with that knife blade. So, who killed Big Bill? Body is a real mess."

Clayton responded, "That was kind of a mistake, Sheriff. I wanted to just knock him out and tie him up for you to question, but he had a gun and we wrestled. The gun fired and well, I guess you'd have to say he shot himself in the gut. Twice."

The sheriff looked hard at Clayton, shrugged, and turned to his deputy. "Well, I guess that'll do. Jim, we'll load up these losers and drive them over to the undertaker in town. Leave these good folks alone so they can go back to what remains of their honeymoon."

CHAPTER 55
WOLF PACK

SWEETWATER - 1879

Clayton was sitting alone in the living room reliving the day and making plans for rebuilding the pump and windmill at the back of the south pasture. He was mentally adding the costs and amount of time needed for this latest project when his ears caught faint rifle shots from the closest mountain range. Two more shots close together. A pause. One more shot. Silence.

He rose from the cowhide-covered easy chair and walked lightly across the polished plank floor to the front door and opened it. A biting chill swirled into the room carrying a few snowflakes that caressed his face. Lord, he thought, it must be at least ten degrees below zero tonight. The snowflakes on his face were slow to melt as he stood in the doorway and sharpened his hearing. Late winter was the time when hungry wolves would attack anything with warm blood. He'd better check it out, there might be someone in trouble up there.

Without waking up Mary, he changed into thicker clothing and smiled to himself. He didn't need the heavy jacket and mittens, or the bright blue scarf Mary had knitted him for Christmas. *But I love this scarf - it smells just like her.* He wrapped the long scarf around his neck, opened the door and stepped out into the winter darkness. A minute later his preternatural speed brought him to the nearest edge of the forest surrounding the wide valley that made up Sweetwater Ranch. He drew in a breath, settled his thoughts, and changed.

There was no sound to break the brittle crystal night. Clayton moved wraithlike through the old growth pines, drifting up in a silent advance that left no tracks on the snow that had fallen late the previous afternoon. By evening another foot of fresh snow had swallowed the rocks and snug winter dens of sleeping wildlife. It was approaching midnight when he smelled the slight tang of woodsmoke coming from a stand of stunted cedar trees hugging the tree line at the top of the three-thousand-foot-high mountain. The faint woodsmoke, combined with the scents of fresh blood, acted as a homing beacon for his nose.

The smell grew stronger as he stopped and morphed quickly into his more acceptable form. He could see charred grass where the remains of a huge fire still smoldered slightly. The fire had melted the snow underneath and there was a wide swath of trampled snow and churned earth surrounding the shallow pit. Deep heel marks ground into the softened soil were filled with small pools of livid red. A trail of blood connected two dead wolves to a bearded trapper sagging against a low shelf of granite, an empty rifle lay across his lap. He looked directly at Clayton and gave an exhausted smile through his unkempt and blood-matted beard.

Clayton stood in the melted snow next to the fading embers of the fire. He could clearly see long slashes on the man's neck. Half of his face looked like it had been torn apart by sharp teeth. The torn shoulder of the trapper's woolen jacket was soaked with blood, so fresh it hadn't had time to freeze. The now-empty rifle was pressed tightly to the man's stomach as if to hold his belly in place.

"Can I help?" Clayton asked as he moved a little closer to the downed stranger.

"Wished you could'a gotten here sooner, is all," was the ironic reply.

"Me too, but I'm here now and I might be able"

The trapper broke in with a wheeze, "Mister, them devils got me good. My stomach is cut open stem to stern so now, I'm just wait'n to move on, so to speak. Ain't much you can do for me except keep me company for a while I won't keep you long." The effort to speak caused the man to cough, and a gout of blood spilled from his mouth onto the open wound by his throat.

Clayton kept his voice confident. "Well, let me build up this fire again to keep the rest of the pack from coming too close."

He quickly snapped branches from several cedar trees and tossed them onto the dying coals. The red and orange flare of the newly kindled fire showed canvas packs heaped nearby, next to a pile of iron traps. A broken camp shovel leaned against them, more proof of a hard-fought battle. All were lightly covered with snow and blood spatter.

There was no reply from the old trapper except strained gasps for breath, punctuated by an occasional soft moan. Clayton hurried over to the figure, sat beside him in the snow, and reached over to cradle the man's bloodied head against his shoulder. He looked deeply into the fading eyes of the dying trapper and said softly, "I can help you begin your last journey."

The old man shuddered as he whispered, "You do that, Sonny. I'd be grateful."

Fangs glistened in the moonlight as they descended and pierced the wrinkled neck of the dying man. He sent feelings of warmth and contentment into the darkening mind as the salty sweet taste of aged blood flooded his mouth. The heartbeat was slowing to a halt when the dying trapper murmured, "Sweet Jesus." It was heard only by Clayton, the wind, and the pines.

The frozen snow-covered ground was no match for Clayton and the broken camp shovel. In seconds he was past the permafrost and deep into the gravely soil. He buried the old man deep, dropped in the bags and traps and quickly refilled the hole. A few large pieces of granite and some heavier tree trunks were casually thrown over the grave, and in a short while it would become unnoticeable. He carried the two wolf carcasses up to the wind-bared summit of the mountain and threw them as far as he could. He hoped that scavengers would feast there instead of hanging around the blood-churned snow. He was saddened to think the trapper might have died alone in such a manner and in such a wilderness but felt a little better knowing he had been able to ease his passing.

The fire was out but Clayton continued to listen to the wind whisper through the trees. He decided to clear his head and walk the several miles back to the ranch. His mind continued to imagine what the old trapper must have gone through fighting off the wolves. He was half-way home and wasn't paying attention to the area, when he heard the deep growl of a wolf behind him. He stopped and turned towards the sound and saw the rest of the wolf pack quietly gathering to surround him.

He counted six rail-thin adults, some with bloodied muzzles, and two cubs. All of them began to circle, heads lowered, and teeth bared. An impatient youngster dashed forward to grab his ankle but with lightning speed, he grabbed the pup by the neck, easily broke its back and flung the carcass into the surrounding trees. The pack leader's hackles raised as he growled his challenge and lunged at the hated man-thing that faced him. The rest of the pack stopped circling and rushed from all sides at once.

Clayton's sadness at the old trapper's untimely death turned to rage and fueled his energy as one adult tried to hamstring him even as a second larger wolf charged at his throat and a third one landed on his back trying to bite through his neck. He fought with strength and speed that the wolves did not expect, but they were committed to win this battle.

He inserted his hand into the dripping maw of the wolf going for his throat and with the other, pulled both jaws apart hard enough to break them. A gagging scream and the animal fell to the snow. The snarling wolf on his back almost managed to sink his teeth into Clayton's neck but the gift of Mary's thick blue Christmas scarf prevented it from gaining purchase. He reached back and grabbed the front claws digging into his shoulders and flung the remaining thirty-pound animal straight over his head and into the slavering jaws of the pack leader charging forward to disembowel him. Both animals rolled with the impact before regaining their balance to charge again. Clayton spun and his solid kick crushed the skull of the wolf that had tried to bite through his neck.

He pulled his knife from its boot sheath just as the pack leader lunged for his unprotected hand. It was still midspring when Clayton reached out, snagged the slavering muzzle, and pulled the twisting animal closer.

Before the surprised wolf could react, he pushed his knife into the wolf's chest, sliced deep and slammed the shocked animal onto the frozen ground. With his free hand, he reached deep and pulled out its still beating heart. Steaming blood sprayed the fur of the remaining pup who became frenzied and began to snap in hysterical confusion when the heart landed at its feet. The alpha female growled and gave a sharp bark as she backed away, hackles still raised in defiance. The pup turned away and faded into the trees.

Now, only the alpha female remained to challenge Clayton. She understood her role but the man-thing in front of her didn't smell right and she became confused. Her mate was dead! She wanted revenge for the loss of her mate and her other pup. She was about to lunge for a kill when the figure in front of her stooped low, glared with frost blue eyes across the trampled snow and straight into her own. She skidded to a full stop in the bloodied snow and sat. Time stopped. A low whine crept past her teeth. Finally, she turned and with her tail drooping, walked away into the fresh snow to disappear into the dark woods surrounding the battlefield. Minutes later, sounds of her grief echoed down the mountain side.

Clayton looked down at himself. His clothing was shredded beyond repair and blood, his and the wolves', saturated his jacket, scarf and gloves. He became aware of several sharp pains and saw blood continuing to well through the multiple rips in his jeans created by sharp teeth and nails. He managed to find his hat, but it was torn and crushed so badly, using it again was out of the question.

Dawn was less than a couple hours away and he was too messed up to use his skill to drift through the forest towards the house. Some of the bruises and slashes caused by sharp teeth began to heal as he tramped through the deep snow towards home, but a few deep gashes continued to leak into the frigid air. The idea that Mary might see him like this filled him with dread. The men were in town on a shopping mission for their New Year's Eve party, so if he got to the bunkhouse and managed to clean up before walking into their own kitchen, he might be able to pull it off.

Most of his blood had stopped flowing and the minor scratches had already healed themselves, but Clayton was still limping as he eased open the bunkhouse door. He shuffled to the sink and poured cold water over one of the clean towels hanging nearby before pulling off his now useless jacket. He stared down at his shirt front. Most of it was shredded and stuck to his chest with frozen blood. His attempt to remove it broke open some of the deeper scratches and blood began to trickle down to the belt of his jeans. He swiped the scratches he could reach and decided the rest would just have to heal on their own. After soaking and wringing out the towel again, he wiped his face and hands as clean as he could and started to pat at the bloodied flesh beneath the shreds of his pantlegs. He ran his fingers through his hair and used a curry comb to tackle his muddied, half frozen boots. It wouldn't do to track mud into Mary's clean kitchen.

He was about to open the bunkhouse door and sneak into the house, when it flew open with a bang and Mary stood there, her trusty shotgun primed and ready, held to her shoulder.

Her face froze as she beheld her husband wearing shredded clothes covered with blood. Her arms went numb as she released the shotgun's hammer and lowered it to her waist. Ignoring him, she walked stiffly to the pinewood table and carefully laid the shotgun on it.

Clayton gulped in his suddenly dry throat. Shook his head. Looked down at the floor. Shuffled his feet. Tried twice to speak before he finally was able to say, "Mary, I'm so sorry. I didn't want to worry you. I-I wanted to check if wolves were getting to our herd on the upper range. Guess I wasn't alert enough and a couple got me good. But I'm fine really. Managed to kill some of them before the rest ran off." His voice regained its usual confidence as he continued to spin his tale.

She didn't believe him for a minute, not after seeing the tattered remnants of clothing on the husband standing in front of her.

She sighed and shook her head, but her voice was steady. "Okay. Just come up to the house so I can take a good look at you." She grabbed the shotgun and left without looking back or saying another word. Through the open door he realized the sun was lifting over the horizon creating a hazy but sparkling light over the stark-white snow. Time to move inside before all the scratches and bruises healed themselves.

A silent Clayton followed Mary into the warm kitchen at the side of the house. A table large enough to seat eight hungry people dominated the kitchen and she motioned to the chair at its head as she reached for her medical bag under the sink.

"Take your shirt off," she commanded. Her back was turned while she ran hot water into a ceramic bowl and grabbed a fresh washcloth. When she turned back to face him, her eyes filled with tears at the obvious destruction done to Clayton's chest and back by the wolves.

"My God, Clayton! What—" Her throat tightened as she approached him and began to wipe at the claw marks and bites that crisscrossed his muscles. She was in nursing mode thinking; *this deep slash will have to be stitched and maybe this one.*

Clayton grabbed her hand and quietly said, "Mary, I'm okay. I don't need stitches. Just clean the wounds, wrap me up like a Christmas goose then let me rest for a while. I'll be fine."

Arguing with him about scrapes and scratches was futile, Mary knew, but this was so much worse. And what was hidden beneath those rips on his pant legs? She remained quiet as she continued to clean his chest with soap and water, followed by swipes of antiseptic. After bandaging chest and stomach she moved her attentions to his hand and shoulder. Finally, she helped him shuck out of his wet, previously frozen jeans and pressed a fist to her mouth as she saw the damage. It was worse than she feared.

Once again, Clayton soothed her mind with words of comfort and promise as she washed and wrapped the bloody gashes on his thighs and legs. Less than an hour passed before he rose and circled his arms around her, carefully pulling her into his embrace.

Together, they climbed the stairs to their bedroom. Once there, he suggested that she close the special blackout curtains in their bedroom before returning downstairs. He used a light touch of control and promised (with crossed fingers) to sleep there until suppertime. She shouldn't worry about him, but just let him sleep undisturbed for the rest of the day. He released his light touch, and she followed his instructions without question. He could feel some of the lesser injuries healing already but knew he'd need to relax in dirt to complete the process. The guilt over his mind control of Mary continued to simmer even when he tried to justify it as a means of avoiding an explanation of what he *really was.*

Mary was in the kitchen cleaning up when it occurred to her that Clayton hadn't told her the whole truth. He was hiding something from her. She felt a little confused about the last hour but felt sure he would explain everything once he got up. She kept herself distracted by making him a light supper of beef broth, toast, and canned peaches, her usual meal for the sickroom.

She shivered when the mournful howl of a wolf drifted down the mountain.

CHAPTER 56
WHITE LIES

Mary sat in her favorite spot at the kitchen table with her chin resting on her hand. The earlier cup of coffee she had poured herself was cold, and her thoughts were so deep she was unaware of the growing coolness of the room.

Just *what* is going on here? For the first time since her marriage to Clayton she was ready to admit that there was something off about her husband of ten years. Off? No, not *off*, what about *strange*? Not that either. But she had to admit that her handsome husband had a certain glamour. Yes! That was the word. Extremely fast when he had rushed towards an accident about to happen (hadn't thought about that in years), never ill, the incredible sex they continued to share (certainly couldn't complain about *that*). It was hard to put a finger on why he seemed different than other men of her acquaintance, but she had to admit that it was time to acknowledge something else.

She had aged. He had not.

She was a weathered forty-plus with arthritis making itself known in the knuckles of her hands and one knee. He still looked as fresh as the day they first met in Charleston. She abruptly straightened up in the chair. *Now, wait just a damn minute!* She was sixteen at the time and to her youthful eyes he seemed so handsome but so much older! Her face grew cold at where her thoughts were taking her.

Her old mantra came to mind once again: *'I can do this! I'm a nurse and I can handle anything!'* She got up from the table, grabbed a pen and a tablet of paper from their junk drawer, and began to list the oddities she had chosen to ignore over the years.

After writing for what seemed like hours, she reviewed the long list. But what did it mean? Rather than drive herself crazy, she decided to return to the darkened bedroom with her list in hand and have a good discussion about this very thing.

She tiptoed up the stairs and quietly opened the bedroom door. The darkness of the room was lit only by the open door of the hallway. "Clayton? Sweetheart, are you awake?" There was no reply. She moved towards the bed and looked down. The bed was empty, the sheets un-rumpled. Clayton had lied to her.

Anguish filled her but she bit back her cry. She ran from room to room opening doors, looking into closets, even under the beds. Fear had her almost staggering by the time she reached for the doorknob to the cellar. She remembered Clayton insisted on digging one when they had added an extension to the house. With its unfinished floor, the dirt acted as a coolant for the kitchen, and its cross ventilation prevented any musty odors wafting up through the floorboards overhead.

She held a lit kerosene lamp high as she descended the stairs. Other than a bit of roughed up earth in the far corner of the room, and shelves filled with canned food in mason jars, she could see nothing to alarm her. She turned around and remounted the stairs to the kitchen and shut the door behind her.

It had become full dark outside, and she hesitated to leave the house to search further. If he returned When he returned She should be there waiting. She finally noticed how cool the house had become so she built up a crackling fire in the living room. The light of the flames cast shadows near the walls, but the room had always been a cozy one. She poured herself a healthy measure of brandy, curled up on the couch with her favorite knitted Afghan throw, and stared into the flames.

The room was warming up nicely and the brandy was beginning to slow her churning thoughts. She heard Clayton softly call her from their bedroom upstairs. *Upstairs? What on earth!* The empty glass fell from her hand and bounced on the wide plank floor. Her heart thundered as she swiftly climbed the stairs ignoring the aching arthritic stiffness in her right knee.

Clayton sat on the edge of the bed, cocooned in a soft comforter wrapped around his naked hips. He held out his perfectly healed arms to her and she flew into his embrace with a stifled cry.

He smiled at her tear-stained face, the one he loved so much. He crooned, "Hey now, what's this? Why are you crying? I'm right here. Nothing to worry about. I told you all I needed was a rest."

He loved how her hair was upswept in a careless knot on top of her head, its damp tendrils escaped to frame her jaw. He leaned forward to kiss her perfect lips. *Oh, the scent of her!* His body immediately responded, but he pushed away the idea of lovemaking, and his hardening cock subsided under the softness of the comforter. *Now is not the time and something is going on in Mary's head.*

Mary stood between his knees and put her hands to each side of his dark hair, raking it back to fall in its usual slightly messy way (her favorite look). She looked into those dark blue eyes and almost gave herself over to those sapphire depths. Her hands moved to his naked shoulders in a soft stroking motion, and with a start she realized there wasn't a cut, a slash, a bruise, or a tooth mark on that glorious marblelike skin. She looked closer at his neck to check for a possibly hidden wound but what she found there was a small bit of fresh dirt clinging to his hair behind one ear.

She jumped out of his embrace and backed away. Blood drained from her face as she forced her frozen lips to speak. "Clayton, we n-need—" Her voice failed her as she saw the concern and love in his eyes.

He took over her attempt to speak. "Yes, darling girl, we *do* need to talk." His mouth quirked. "Can I get dressed first, though? A man feels totally exposed without his pants on." His rueful chuckle escaped as he reached for her and pulled her back between his knees.

Mary cleared her throat, "Sure. Put your pants on and come downstairs. Heaven knows, you are very distracting right now." *I could never resist his humor, I'm so in love with this man I can wait a few minutes longer to hear what he has to say.* She left the room and started down the stairs.

Clayton pulled on clean jeans and his favorite flannel shirt, thinking that the love of his life had quite a pragmatic streak in her. *Must be the nurse part of her. But oh, that mouth and that body! Perfect for love making.* He looked down. *Damn, if I'm not getting hard again just thinking about her.*

He knew it was time to have "the talk" with her. She certainly deserved the truth of him, and it would be her choice to continue together or apart. He shuddered at the thought of losing her, but he still appeared to be a smooth faced thirty-something and she was a magnificent forty-plus.

He joined her on the living room couch but left plenty of space between them in case things went south. She looked over at him as he settled and gravely handed him the paper listing the odd things she had noticed during their time together. She said nothing as he quietly read the paper that had details listed all the way back to Charleston when she was sixteen years old.

The last item was heavily scribbled and underlined in pencil. Penciled doodles surrounded the last entry: Heals completely without scars—and way too fast.

He nodded towards the paper in his hand, sighing as he looked thoughtfully at her. His voice was soft. "What is it you'd like to know?" It would be all or nothing for them both.

She hesitated with her reply but straightened her spine, repeated her internal mantra, looked him straight in the eye and asked in a firm voice, "Are you a vampire?"

"Yes I am."

His response shocked her, and she fought against the dark sparkles floating around the edges of her vision. She took a deep breath. *I will not faint.*

She collected her thoughts, shifted a bit, and said, "Okay, I've read Mary Shelly's *Frankenstein* and my mother read me Irish tales of blood suckers, and I guess people have thought of this before. So do you kill people and drink their blood? Like the vampires in the old stories? And just how old *are* you anyway?"

Mary's voice had a forced calmness to it, but Clayton easily heard the staccato pounding of her heart underneath her heavy sweater.

Again, with the pragmatic approach. His response was thoughtful. "Not exactly like those blood drinkers in the Irish tales and I'm very young in vampire terms. I'm only a hundred-twenty-five years old, give or take a year or two. Mary, I've lived a remarkable life, but most of it has been doing the ordinary stuff like other people do." He continued, "I'll tell you anything you want to know, and I will tell you my complete life's story, but right now, the one thing you need to know is that I love you with all my heart and I will never let anything bad happen to you." He paused and with a softened voice said, "Or for as long as you choose to be with me."

She gazed at his earnest face as if searching for a clue to his existence. *Who is this man sitting beside me?* Light from the gas lamps hanging overhead brought out the strong cheekbones and narrow nose of the handsome face. His fabulous eyes widened a bit as he looked at her and she watched his jaw muscles clench. She got up and grabbed the decanter of brandy. She poured a generous dose into her glass and looked back at him with a question in her eyes.

He smiled. "Yes, thank you for asking, I would love one."

The teasing in his voice made her smile back. *Yes, this man is my husband and I adore him no matter what he is.* She had trusted him for a lifetime and knew that would never change. She rejoined him on the sofa, sitting much closer than before, and handed him the filled glass.

"Okay," she said, "tell me everything or at least anything I need to know. And make it good, mister. Your life depends on it."

His bark of surprised laughter filled the room as they simultaneously put down their glasses, turned towards each other and kissed with a passion and knowledge that nothing had been broken between them.

After talking late into the night, an exhausted Mary was ready for bed. As she climbed the stairs, Clayton followed closely behind, admiring the tight jeans and trim waist of his bride of ten years. He vowed to just hold her close while she slept, keeping his lusty thoughts buried deep. Poor gal needed her rest.

Mary had other ideas.

Clayton quietly opened the front door to the early morning sun spreading its dim glow onto freshly fallen snow.

He fought against the usual tiredness creeping up his body as he breathed in the clear crisp air. *Years. Years behind. Years ahead. What kind? How many? Mary is in her forties and the clock can't be turned back for her unless—*

Clayton's dark thoughts were interrupted by a throaty "come hither" call from Mary, still warm and nestled in the blankets. He grinned as he sped up the stairs to their bedroom.

She sat in the middle of the bed surrounded by her warm nest of blankets and decided the man standing in the middle of the open bedroom door was still stunning to behold. The light stubble on his chin made her think of a handsome pirate and she wanted to have his sword sliding into her sheath. She crooked a finger, and her heavy-lidded eyes completed the invitation. Clayton easily jumped the distance from doorframe to bed and landed lightly amid the tangle of covers.

His eyes darkened with desire as he reached out to pull the blankets over them both. Within an hour Clayton fell heavily asleep, his arms still holding Mary against his shoulder. She decided to let him rest until late afternoon, after all, it was Sunday and she could tell the guys were already up and taking care of the horses.

CHAPTER 57
SNAKEBITE

TWO YEARS LATER

"Clayton!" Mary's voice called from the kitchen. He didn't respond immediately so she called again, with a little more force. "Clayton!" He put down his weekly newspaper, stood and strolled towards the kitchen. He already knew what she wanted because he could hear her cutting bread for sandwiches. Bet she wants a picnic, he thought. He walked into the kitchen and put his arms around her, hugging her from behind. He began to nibble her earlobe.

"Yes, darling girl," he drawled into her ear, "what are you yelling about?" He turned her around to face him but kept her within the circle his arms. The breadknife still in her hand, Mary smiled and said, "Hey, it's a beautiful day, let's ride out to Lupin Pointe and have a picnic. And say "yes" or this knife will be buried where it'll hurt the most!"

He raised his hands in mock surrender. "Okay, okay! Sounds good, I'll get the horses while you finish up here. Do you want to ride Queen or Peaches?"

"I'll use Peaches today. She needs some exercise. I think somebody is feeding her too many treats." The remark was addressed to Clayton, a known sneaker of treats for the horses. If he brought an apple or sugar cube for Kaliph, Peaches was sure to be given her share.

Duke was already working in the barn and helped Clayton saddle the horses. As they finished and led them outside, Mary showed up with her saddle bag filled with sandwiches, fruit, a thermos of coffee and extra water. Duke tied the bag behind Peaches' saddle after Mary mounted her and settled. She rode slowly past the corral and headed towards the rocky outcropping in the distance known as Lupin Pointe. From there, the view of the surrounding land was spectacular, and it had become their favorite picnic spot away from the busy ranch. Clayton mounted Kaliph and hurried to catch up. The bright sun was already causing his sensitive skin to itch a bit, but he figured his sunglasses, broadbrimmed hat and long-sleeved shirt would keep it within tolerable limits.

Mary called over her shoulder, "Ready for a race? Last one to the Pointe, unpacks the picnic!" Clayton responded with a whoop and put heels to Kaliph who immediately sprang forward. Within two strides, he was at full gallop, trying to catch up with galloping Peaches.

The horses ran eagerly, Kaliph slightly behind due to a light but firm hand on his reins. Clayton loved seeing Mary's long honey blond hair blowing out behind her hat as she leaned forward on Peaches, urging her horse to win. They pulled far enough ahead to alert Mary to the possibility that her man was throwing the race on purpose. She looked back with a grin and full-throated laugher at the idea that Kaliph would ever allow himself to lose an honest race.

The horses slowed to an easy canter with Peaches still in the lead. Clayton was about to speed forward when Peaches leaped high to the side and bucked hard.

Mary was unprepared and desperately clung with one hand to the saddle horn to keep from falling but Peaches reared in panic again and Mary lost both stirrups. She was flung off the panicked horse and landed heavily on the stony ground. Clayton clearly heard the sound of a snapping bone and the buzz of a startled rattlesnake. Peaches ran a short distance and finally stopped with lowered head and heaving sides.

"Mary!" Clayton shouted. He was about to pull Kaliph to a full stop when he again heard the clear buzz of a rattlesnake almost hidden in the rocky soil. The five-foot rattler was poised and ready to strike when Kaliph let out an outraged scream and attacked the snake with iron bound hooves. Clayton was still astride when the horse reared a second time to smash his enemy. Rather than try to stay in the saddle of an angry stallion, Clayton lightened himself and flew the twenty feet to Mary's unconscious body crumpled in the dust.

He knelt next to Mary, "Oh please God, please, please—." With a shaking hand he gently smoothed her hair away from the raw scrape on her temple. He knew headwounds bled freely but he had heard a bone break too. He ran his hands lightly over both arms and her jean covered legs. He easily confirmed her left arm was broken and the bloody wound on her head still seeped down the side of her face in the hot acrid air. Her eyes remained closed, but he clearly heard her faint whisper, "Snake bite left boot."

He pulled his knife from its sheath and quickly slit the denim fabric stretched over her boot. After pulling apart the material, he saw the two deep puncture wounds on her calf left by the king-sized rattlesnake. He knew that the venom from such a large snake could kill an adult in a matter of hours of extreme pain, sweating, and vomiting followed by a difficulty breathing and death.

Unless he could do the unthinkable. His heart twisted.

His voice was soothing and floated its way into Mary's nightmare, calming her. "Mary, I need to draw out the venom within your blood. Be very, *very* still, I'll try not to hurt you. I love you so much lie still now." His beloved voice faded into the fog.

Clayton lowered his face to Mary's leg. The scent of her blood trickling from the two punctures did little to stir his usual vampiric reaction. He lowered his fangs, and gently bit into the puncture wounds to draw out the venom-blood mixture. The venom's flavor was noxious, tasting unbearably rank as he spit and sucked again. After drawing and spitting out several mouthfuls he couldn't detect more venom, but his vampire curse slammed past his control and demanded that he drink deeper.

Without conscious thought he responded by biting deeper and sucked strongly at the wound. Her blood tasted of a fine red wine mixed with honey and ginger. It caressed his tongue as it slid to the back of his throat, and he swallowed in reflex. His blood lust burst past his control, and he drank deeply a second time. The taste and scent of her rekindled his awareness and his mind screamed for him to stop but with mindless passion he drank again. And again.

But this is Mary! No, no, no. I cannot do this, I will not do this! He forced himself to pull away from the slowly pulsing injury on the lightly tanned leg resting in his lap. He wiped his blood reddened mouth on his sleeve, and hurriedly closed the wound with a swipe of his mouth and bloodied fingers. His hands shook as he wrapped a clean kerchief around the leg and tied it off.

His voice was pleading, "Mary, open your eyes. Can you hear me? Please open your eyes and look at me."

Mary's eyes slowly opened, and she looked blearily up at Clayton. "Hi there, hero! Hey, you have pink colored tears! Lord, I feel so tired, can we go home now? Something bit me, damn it! And my arm really hurts!" She fainted without another word.

Clayton stood, carefully picked her up, and walked towards Kaliph. "Well, boy, you're going to have to carry double back to the ranch. Now, stand still." Since holding Mary and mounting Kaliph would be very awkward, he leapt high with Mary in his arms and landed centered in the saddle of the patient horse. Kaliph swung his head around to view the strange method of getting on his back but didn't move. Peaches approached and brushed close to Kaliph as if asking his forgiveness for her earlier panic.

"Okay boy let's go home. Nice and easy, we have precious cargo here!" Kaliph's pacing gait was a comfortable rocking chair and Clayton was able to hold Mary safely while using his knees to help guide the horse around any obstacles and back to the ranch.

Duke came running across the yard when he first saw Peaches trotting towards the corral with an empty saddle. He ran up to Clayton and looked up with obvious concern. "What happened? Is she okay?"

Clayton gave a tight smile. "I think so, but her arm is broken, and she was bitten by a snake. I think I got most of the venom, though. Send one of the boys to town and bring Doc soon as you can, and I'll put her to bed. If Kaliph allows, put him in his stall, if not, I'll see to him later. And make sure Peaches is okay, that snake really scared her."

The ranch hands came running to help, so Duke sent Rusty into town and instructed the others to take care of the horses. Clayton carefully handed Mary down to Duke's waiting arms and swung down himself thinking how easy it had been to lift himself into the saddle earlier. *Too bad I couldn't dismount the same way.*

He made sure to give Kaliph a quick pat and after taking Mary back into his arms climbed the stairs to their bedroom. He laid her on the bed and pulled off her boots and spread a coverlet over her. He shuddered at the dark bruising around her arm. A minute later she woke up with clouded eyes. She tried to sit up against the pillows and pain crossed her face as she bit down to muffle her sharp yelp.

Cookie came stumping up the stairs and entered the bedroom with a washbowl of hot water, several clean towels graced his forearm. He glanced at Mary, "Here you go Missus." Then he looked over at Clayton. "Do you need anything else right now, boss?"

Clayton took the washbowl and set it on the dresser. "Nothing right now, but maybe some hot tea and honey later or whenever you can. I'll get her settled and ready for the doc. Let the men know that Mary will be fine." He walked Cookie to the door and closed it.

He turned to look back at Mary propped on her pillows. He thought she looked much better than before. Her eyes were clear and razor-focused on him. With her "no nonsense" nurse's voice she spoke. "Okay, tell me everything. What happened after Peaches threw me? I can't seem to remember a thing."

Clayton managed to focus on her shoulder, unable to look at her while he thought of a few white lies that might satisfy her demand.

Mary read his avoidance and said, "Look at me, Clayton!" Her hand touched the scab and dried blood on her temple and grimaced. He was quick to rinse and squeeze a cloth, gently wiping her forehead and cheek before he answered.

He was thinking, how much to tell, how much to gloss over. She already knew of his "otherness", but he had never shown her his fangs or let her watch him drink (which he still hated). But she also deserved the truth of it or at least *most* of it. He shuddered to think of what had happened and guilt over the loss of his control burned deep in his belly.

He sat on the edge of the bed and held her uninjured hand as he began, "Well, you remember Peaches was startled by a rattlesnake and after you got thrown, Kaliph stomped the hell out of it. *That* was a sight to see. But when you landed, you hit your head and you broke your arm and I I—."

His mouth felt dry as dust and he swallowed before continuing. "You said, "'snake bite'" that five-foot rattlesnake bit you above your boot right after you fell." Clayton wanted to be anywhere except under the unblinking gaze of his wife. He tried distraction, "You should have seen Kaliph stomp that rattler. It was really something."

She interrupted his hesitant recital with a question. "And how am I still alive?"

Clayton forced a smile. "Yes, well, I managed to get most of the nastiness out of the wound pretty quick, so I think you'll be okay." He refused to acknowledge how he had sucked it out.

Mary settled further into her pillow and looked at him eye to eye. Her voice remained calm. "Clayton, you had to bite me didn't you to get the poison out. That was *my blood* you drank, tainted or not."

He could barely look at her, "Well, there was a moment, but it passed quickly. And you're here and you're safe. No harm done really."

Mary closed her eyes to avoid looking at the shaken man sitting beside her. She knew in her heart that something more had occurred, but she wouldn't pursue the whole truth of it. It would have to be enough that he kept her safe, brought her home and loved her without reservation. Her mind began to drift. *I'll bet he drank an extra mouthful or three or twenty. he's a vampire for God's sake!* She fell asleep.

Clayton was stretched out on the bed next to the sleeping Mary when Duke knocked on the bedroom door several hours later. His voice was low. "The doc's here, do you want to come down and talk to him first or shall I just send him up?"

He climbed off the bed as he answered, "Just send him up. Can you check to see if Cookie has any beef broth or soup around? She'll probably be hungry after that bone gets set." He heard Duke's "Okay," as booted feet stomped down the stairs for the doctor.

Mary was not a good patient and kept trying to tell the doctor how to set and wrap her arm properly. Finally, in self-preservation, he gave her a half-teaspoon of laudanum and she quickly fell asleep. Now, he could finish his work without interruptions. He began to closely check the snakebite site on her shin. He took out his magnifying glass and held it steady. Sucking venom from a snakebite was almost the stuff of legend. It seemed that this injury would be one for the books.

The sun was setting, and shadows grew longer around the outbuildings of the ranch. Clayton stood alone in the barn and leaned against Kaliph's warm shoulder. He couldn't seem to stop the shakes that racked his body after Mary's close call with death from snakebite. *I drank her blood! I drank her blood and almost couldn't stop! I didn't want to stop! But I can't lose her! Not now. Not ever! As long as she's alive and needs me I want to be by her side.* Anguished tears threatened as he looked up at the barn's dusty cross beams. *I'll just have to wait for her to decide. Will she, or won't she?*

He felt emotionally drained and at last said, "Goodnight boy, thanks for listening." Clayton fed Kaliph his nightly treat, gave him one last pat and left the barn. Too restless to return to the house, he turned and began to walk towards the small cabin, deciding to check on it as an excuse to stretch his legs. Once there, he sat in his favorite chair, his hands holding his head in the darkness. There was a choice to be made. Should the two of them have the conversation about eternity? Or was it still too soon? Should he wait until she brought up the topic and together, they would list her options? A slight smile crossed his lips, his Mary loved to make lists. They still had years together and he knew they could be very good years. Clayton finally decided to say nothing about turning Mary into someone "other".

Mary's leg was sore from the snakebite and her broken arm hurt like hell, but she managed to get out of bed and limped towards the dresser. Her hands gripped the edges as she peered at herself in its mirror. *I don't even recognize this face anymore. When did I get so old? What does Clayton really see when he holds me? This damn western sun doesn't do any favors for a woman's skin and my hands! Just look at those freckles. By the grace of God, the arthritis hasn't gotten any worse might have more problems with my knee though. What happens when I can't ride anymore? Does Clayton wish I were younger? Prettier? Will his attention wander to someone younger than me?*

If I want to be with him, I will have to choose someday. I'll have to make a decision. The most important and unchangeable decision of my life! How can I choose? An eternity with him or his without me?

* * *

Ranch life on the Sweetwater had its highs and lows the same as any other ranch. Good years resulted in profits which were used to buy more land or improve the herd. Mary got the kitchen she had always wanted, and Clayton brought her to England and France. A bad year due to drought or low cattle prices only meant Clayton's wealth was used to make up any financial shortage.

Duke turned out to be an excellent foreman for the ranch. Rusty and Carl worked well as a team and took their responsibilities seriously. Cookie continued to fill empty bellies and Charlie made "guard dogs" out of any stray that showed up in need of a free meal. Their life together was good.

CHAPTER 58
TIME

The sun was beginning to set when Mary and Clayton rode their horses out to their favorite picnic spot at Lupin Point. He spread a blanket for Mary to sit on and lowered himself to sit next to her. She poured herself a cup of coffee from her travel thermos and grinned at him over the cup's rim. "Clayton, don't you sometimes miss the 'finer things in life' like coffee or a big slice of apple pie?" He smiled but his reply was thoughtful, "Not really. The smells are more than enough and indulging in solid food ends in disaster, you *know* that."

He reached out a long arm to circle her shoulders and pulled her against his side. She said nothing as she continued to sip her coffee and enjoy the last glow of the setting sun. She tried to ignore the piercing joint pains caused by the ride out and sitting on the hard ground. She looked at Clayton and thought, how did I get so lucky to be with such a good man? And still so handsome. He still hasn't aged a bit—

Clayton closed his eyes, trying to delay the next conversation. It was time for "the talk", and he was nervous about her possible response. He felt her put down her coffee cup and place her hand on his thigh as she leaned back onto his shoulder. Her arthritic hand covered his, and the difference between the two was obvious.

Her voice was soft but clear. "Do you have something to say, Clayton? Something is on your mind so it's best to get it out there so we can talk about it."

He could barely say the words past the lump in his throat, "Mary, would you consider remaining with me forever?"

Mary leaned over and kissed him. "Of course, my answer is yes. What else would it be?"

CHAPTER 59
MARY DECIDES

THE LITTLE CABIN - 1896

It was 10:00 p.m. and in the little cabin, Clayton stood before the bedroom fireplace, one arm rested against the stone mantle as the glow of the fire's dying embers created shadows that danced around the corners of the small log room. Fifteen years had passed since Mary had been bitten by the rattlesnake, and Clayton still shuddered to think he almost lost her to his blood lust while pulling the venom from her veins.

Mary sat before her dressing table snugged into the corner of the south wall. Several oil lamps shed their light on the silver gleam of her hair as she thoughtfully pulled the hairpins out, unbraided the loose coil and slowly brushed it. Her eyes sought him in the mirror's dark reflection, and she smiled faintly at him. Her face glowed with a mature beauty as the tiny flames of the fire's embers highlighted the planes and angles of her face. She shook her head in mocking rebuke when she caught his eyes roving over her still slender body. She was dressed in his favorite French robe, and he was admiring its crème-colored lace covering her still generous breasts. He moved toward her, and his hands trembled slightly as they rested on her shoulders. He slowly leaned forward to kiss the sweet space between her neck and shoulder. His voice was low and husky. "I will love you forever."

She smiled into his mirrored reflection and turned toward him shifting in the chair to grasp his hips. She pressed her head against his waist and murmured, "And I will always love you." There would be no more dark secrets, no more white lies between them.

Clayton was still a handsome thirty-something with an unlined face under a shock of dark hair. His sapphire eyes were clear, and his body remained firm and youthful, the muscles sharply defined across chest and stomach. But time and the brutal western sun had weathered Mary's face, her arms were freckled, and arthritis had enlarged the hard-working knuckles of both hands. She still rode around the ranch but there were no more overnight rides and camping.

One long afternoon in the saddle meant getting up late the next morning while she worked the kinks out of strained muscles and angry joints. At almost sixty, she was still an attractive woman though it was evident to strangers that she had married a much younger man.

The twenty-seven good years together had not lessened his desire for her and as he drew her up from the chair and pulled her body close, her familiar scent triggered his usual response. This one was difficult to ignore. Taking a deep breath, he asked, "Are you sure about this? Once done, it can't be un-done. You'll never walk in the sun again. It will mean a life of deception. Secrets and more lies."

Her hands spread against his chest. She could feel his cool incredibly strong body and beneath his loosely tied silk robe, the swelling of his cock. Grasping its pulsing length in her hand she replied, "Clayton, we've talked about this many times. I'm sure very sure."

His right hand cupped the back of her neck as his left encircled her waist. He held her tight against his coolness as he raised his hand to smooth away the silk of her dressing gown. As it dropped, dark excitement swept through him and erased all thoughts of denying her – or himself.

She felt his lips trail a hot burn down the side of her neck to the softness beneath her bared collarbone. She knew from his descriptions that the neck provided a meal but drinking from above the heart sealed his vampiric commitment to her forever. And she knew she was his first. Her heart thundered and ecstasy filled her as his fangs gently pierced her skin. The slight pain mingled with her immediate arousal, and he began to drink deeply of her blood. She felt her skin begin to warm as he continued, and his arousal became hers.

She moaned low in her throat as she reached to pull his head tighter to her. A crimson veil drifted over her half-closed eyes and mounting passion thrilled her as he continued to drink. She felt her heart stutter and almost stop its rhythm. She collapsed in his arms with a faint smile.

He carried her to their bed and laid her on her side upon the coverlet. He quickly removed his robe and lay next to her, using his knife to slash his chest above the heart. His hand dropped the knife and reached for her, gently but firmly holding her head with her lips pressed against the scarlet blood pooling there. Would she accept his blood and her rebirth, or would she slip peacefully away from him forever? He felt the black agony of unknowing.

It seemed to him that time stopped and only restarted when her pale tongue crept past her lips and touched the ruby slash on his chest. She licked at it lightly, and again with more force. She began to suck. His ancient blood flooded past her tongue and his mind began to link with hers as it slipped down her throat. Both were lost in a mindless whirlpool of lightness and desire. At the continuing touch of her lips, lust raged through him, and he shifted until he was completely underneath her, still holding her mouth to the slow fountain of his blood. He had waited so long for this moment.

Finally, he pulled her mouth away and effortlessly flipped her on her back. He covered her swollen lips with heated kisses that deepened until, with almost savage fury, he drove into her pulsing liquid heat. She almost screamed her pleasure and clutched him tighter as their climax rolled to a crest and surged. He remained buried in her intimate space and pushed again deeper than before. His slow movements promised another wave of ecstasy until their climax surged again.

Both were breathless in the aftermath of their intense coupling. She smiled up at him as he slowly withdrew his still hardened cock. He leaned over and licked the wound at her breast closed. He could only smile when Mary did the same for him.

Returning his thoughts to the present, he shifted aside and explained the process; how it would feel and what would happen afterwards. As expected, she eliminated the waste from her former self, and he gently wiped her glistening body with towels soaked in warm water. Afterwards she lay quietly in his arms, and he marveled at how special she was to him and how much he loved her. He continued looking down at her as the moon gently bathed them both in pearls of light.

Her silver-streaked hair was lengthening and returning to its lustrous dark honey. The wrinkles at her eyes and throat disappeared and a pale smoothness replaced her sun-damaged skin. Her lips grew lush and deep pink, and the faded blue of her eyes became dark sapphires surrounded by long thick lashes. The thickened knuckles on each hand disappeared. Age spots retreated, and her arthritic knees healed with small bursts of heat. The early-stage (and undetected) cancer in her breast dissolved and completely disappeared.

They lay quietly together with hands clasped and stared at the ceiling thinking about what had occurred between them. Clayton's voice broke into the silence but was soft and clear in the cabin's darkness. "I've been thinking that to make this work, we have to make sure our deaths look good. The guys will be back the day after tomorrow, so we only have two days to burn the cabin and disappear."

Mary sighed and said, "I'm going to miss this cabin, but I guess it has to be done. Any ideas about finding two dead bodies to replace us? I don't mean to sound cold-blooded, but this only works if we're found burned so bad everyone will think it's us."

Clayton's reply was quick. "I've got some ideas but first, you must be starving, and you need to be fed."

Mary gasped, "Oh, this is real, isn't it. I truly didn't think—" She forced herself to continue, "What if I can't do this after all? I mean I want to but what if I can't drink?"

He hugged her close and murmured into her ear, "I'll be with you and will help you until you feel comfortable. You may hate its necessity, but you also may find it irresistible after a while."

In the first dark of her new "otherness" Clayton carried her in his arms as they passed near Denver in a blur of dust and wind. He left her standing alone in an alley and jumped easily up to a nearby roof and disappeared. Being alone made her nervous, but she willed herself to remain completely still and realized it wasn't difficult at all. She stared at the streetlight at the end of her chosen shelter and entertained herself by watching changing patterns of dust flit through its glow. Dripping water from a leaking tap one street away captured her attention, and after a few minutes she was reminded of her building thirst. The thirst continued to grow until she thought she might be hungry enough, crazy enough to just pounce on the next passerby. Damn the consequence!

A pebble dislodged by a man's boot created enough racket to make her heart leap until she realized it was Clayton carrying a dark bundle slumped in his arms. The body remained covered with only its pale neck exposed and he continued to hold it as he said softly, "Don't think about it, just drink." She *didn't* think about it as her small fangs descended and her hands pulled the unconscious neck towards her waiting mouth. She pierced the skin easily and her fangs began to drink her first meal. S*alty sweetness, iron, some kind of alcohol?* Her nurse's training was shoved aside as the rich blood filled her. *Nice! Perfect! More, I want more!*

Clayton watched closely and pulled the nearly drained body away before Mary made the beginner's mistake of drinking from the dead. He knew without a doubt that his tough Mary would survive her transition. "Wait here." he said and flew into the dark with the now lifeless form. He easily buried it deep in Denver's surrounding desert.

After returning to the alley, they made another stop, several miles away, which gave Clayton the opportunity to slake his thirst with a small drink while Mary observed from a distance. The cowboy sitting alone by his campfire would never remember the nightmare that descended on him.

Their thirst was quenched and now they needed two bodies for the fire. Needed someone already dead. Clayton was very familiar with all the homesteads within a hundred-mile radius, so he bypassed those and continued towards the mountains. He already knew of an obviously abandoned ranch twenty miles from Golden in the barren foothills. He had discovered it and its two dead bodies a week before and wondered why anyone would choose to live in such a desolate place. There wasn't even evidence of water.

Inside the weathered shack, the couple of homesteaders lie side by side, holding hands in front of their empty fireplace. The hot dry air of the desert winds whistling through the open window and partially collapsed roof had completely mummified the bodies. Clayton thought they must have succumbed to overwork and starvation. These bodies were the perfect solution for their final deception so he needed to remain objective knowing they would be burned inside the little cabin.

Mary's nursing instincts took over and she looked closer at the two. The man had a severely broken leg that had been poorly set. She thought gangrene probably led to his death, but the bullet's massive exit wound at his back certainly hastened it along. Three empty bottles of tincture of laudanum and a gun lay next to the woman's hand. Mary stood straighter and said, "I think the man died of his injuries and a bullet. His wife may have committed suicide in her despair." Clayton nodded to her, and carefully placed both bodies onto a tattered sheet. She remained quiet as she helped Clayton carefully wrap the sheet around the couple. Memories of her wartime experience choked her voice, but she forced herself to accept the need to burn the bodies. She barely heard Clayton say, "Hold onto me and I'll fly them back with us."

Back at the Sweetwater cabin Mary fought tears while she proceeded to carefully dress the two bodies in clothing she and Clayton usually wore around the ranch. He slipped his ring on the dead man's finger and after kissing her cameo Mary pinned it to the neck of the blouse covering the second corpse. She said a prayer, and both silently thanked the couple for their help.

Dawn was only an hour away when they entered the mine shaft Clayton had found earlier. Heavy sleep was already overtaking Mary while he finished boarding up their side tunnel against the brightness of the morning sun. In the welcoming darkness, Clayton lifted Mary in his arms and gently laid her on the blankets waiting there. He sat in the dark for a while and felt the usual daytime fatigue begin to steal into his body. He shook himself awake, no time for that now, he thought. He had almost forgotten to have a drink with Charlie in the bunkhouse. It was very important that Charlie slept through the cabin fire if their exit plan was going to work. He flew to the back of the barn, grabbed the bottle of whiskey hidden there and proceeded on foot to say hello to Charlie and Ringo, the current floppy eared and friendly watchdog.

* * *

The cabin had been prepared the day before with dried resin-saturated wood. Stumps and branches left over from logging done years ago provided a natural fire starter and shredded piles had been arranged throughout the cabin. Clayton tossed a burning turpentine-soaked rag onto the pile. The dry wood caught quickly, and he retreated as the intensity of the fire grew. The fire was far enough from the bunkhouse and Charlie was sleeping off the whisky so he figured it wouldn't be noticed too soon. He launched himself into the late noon day sun and flew towards the mine shaft and his sleeping Mary. He was smiling as he lie beside her, took her in his arms and fell into the best sleep he'd had in over a hundred years.

CHAPTER 60
EXIT STRATEGY

After a successful roundup and sale of Sweetwater cattle, the cowboys enjoyed a long weekend in Golden. Whiskey, women, all night poker games and a friendly bar fight or two made for the perfect change to some rough weeks in the saddle. Sunday evening meant a return to the ranch, so the men gathered at the livery stable and got ready to head back. The two-hour slow ride was made easier with a couple pints of bourbon passed from hand to hand while the men exchanged riotous stories about previous escapades in town.

As they neared the top of the low hill overlooking the Sweetwater, they smelled smoke coming from a distant pile of glowing embers. Only burned timbers and a few charred roof beams remained of the little cabin. Instantly sober, the stunned ranch hands urged their mounts into a full out gallop and headed towards the gutted building. Duke yelled that he would check the Big House for the Boss and the Missus. If not there, he would check the bunkhouse and meet up at the cabin.

Duke called out as he approached the house, but there was no response. He dismounted quickly and ran up the porch steps, slamming open the front door as he continued to call. The house remained dark and empty, so Duke took off running towards the bunkhouse.

He called again as he entered the common room and almost collided with Charlie's watchdog. Ringo was whining and pawing at Charlie's mattress. He looked at

Duke and barked, ran back to Charlie and barked again. There was a loud snore followed by an "umnph" when Ringo decided to leap on the sleeping man's chest. Charlie's bleary eyes looked at Duke as he managed to sit himself on the cot's edge. Twenty pounds of frantic black and white dog jumped off the bed and charged through the open bunkhouse door.

Charlie's voice was slurring a bit. "Hi yah, Duke! What's going on? Back kinda late ain't cha?" He rubbed his whiskered face with a shaking hand.

"Charlie, there's been a fire at the little cabin. Did you hear anything?" Duke was trying not to yell at the old man, but it was hard to remain calm. Charlie mumbled to himself as he tried to make sense of what he was hearing. Thinking clearly wasn't easy when shaken out of a sound sleep by a barking dog. Duke interrupted the mumbles as he handed Charlie his boots, "Here, put on your boots fast as you can let's go!"

Charlie was still trying to understand what all the shouting was about when he smelled the smoke. He ran as quick as he could towards their hitching post as Duke flung himself onto his saddle and hauled Charlie up behind him to ride double. They rode hard towards the faintly smoking ruin.

The ranch hands had left their mounts tied to the cabin's hitching posts away from the remaining heat and smoke of the dying fire. They all stood silent as they looked at the glowing heap of embers. They knew there was nothing to be done until everything cooled enough to be approached. Calling out for the boss and his wife produced no results and they had already made a quick search around the cabin and small lake without discovering anything unusual. Not even a footprint.

Finally, Duke assigned two of the men to remain with the cabin to make sure the fire remained contained and Cookie volunteered to bring coffee and sandwiches for them in a little while. Duke looked around and saw Charlie leaning against the shoulder of his horse, his shoulders were shaking with quiet sobs. Duke approached and put his hand on the old man's shoulder.

Charlie turned toward him his voice sounded old and cracked. "Honest Duke, I'm not sure what happened. The boss came to visit a bit, we had a couple of drinks and and next thing I know, Ringo's barking and you're hauling me out of my beauty sleep. I'm so sorry I just didn't hear or smell nothin'. I coulda' helped put out the fire or somethin'." Charlie's voice broke and he covered his grizzled face with his hands.

"Charlie," Duke's voice showed his understanding, "You're not to blame yourself for anything. We'll figure out what happened, I'm sure. Maybe the boss and the missus took the horses for a ride you know they loved to do that all the time. Go on back to the bunkhouse and rest a bit or help Cookie rustle up some grub for us. "

"I'm going to get a fresh horse and ride back into town. It's too dark to see anything so I'll bring the sheriff out here to look around first thing in the morning. He might spot something we missed. Okay? You get some rest now. I'll be back quick as possible."

Sunday night had fallen, and a tired Duke found himself in the sheriff's office giving him an accounting of their weekend in town. They left for home in the late afternoon after their heads had cleared because it was a two-hour ride that didn't go well with hangovers. He had found old Charlie sound asleep in the bunkhouse. Seems the old man and the boss had shared some whiskey earlier since Charlie hadn't felt up to joining the carousing bunch in town two days before. Charlie had never smelled the smoke from the burning cabin.

Duke and the sheriff arrived at the ranch just after dawn and rode directly to the little cabin to be met by tired cowhands. No one had touched the debris and no suspicious clues had been found nearby. The men had searched the surrounding area without results. One of the men rode out to Lupin Pointe. Nothing found there either. Only one fact had made itself known: both horses were still in their box stalls, which meant the two hadn't gone for their usual ride.

The sheriff stepped carefully onto the cooling ashes and broken glass of the cabin. The hand-built furniture had been almost completely burned and the pine floor was dangerous with hidden holes and weak spots. The brass headboard was blackened, and the spring mattress had only its coils and some ashes remaining. The sheriff moved to the bed and bent over to look closer, he carefully touched what remained there with a gloved finger and whistled his dismay. He brushed carefully at the pile. There was barely enough left of the skeletons other than two skulls and some bones, but the signet ring on one finger and the soot covered cameo resting near the second skull, suggested the remains could only be Clayton Masters and his wife Mary.

The sheriff carefully picked up the jewelry and handed both to Duke. "Here, hold onto these for me." Later, he stood near the horses and looked at the burned husk of what had been a nice little cabin used mostly by the Sweetwater women. He figured the couple must have died from inhaling too much smoke in their sleep before the fire took hold. That's what he would tell the undertaker in his report.

* * *

Their friends in the small city of Golden were in mourning. Mr. and Mrs. Masters had been well liked. Her nursing knowledge drew the respect of everyone, and both helped their neighbors whenever and wherever needed. Friends donated enough money and time to place a grave marker on the low hill by the lake. The cameo and signet ring would remain with the buried bones. All agreed it had been one of the couples' favorite places.

After services had been held in the church, everyone gathered at the town park for a light lunch. Questions and gossip kept everyone busy while they ate. No idea what caused the fire? What would happen to the Sweetwater Ranch now? Did bandits set it on fire? Any family out east? One of the town gossips just had to have a last word. "You know, ain't it something, her being so much older than him. Wonder what the attraction was?"

The sheriff strolled over to Duke. "How about you, Cookie and Charlie, come with me to my office. We can talk there away from flapping tongues. There's a fellow from out East waiting to meet you. Says he knew Clayton and Mary."

When they arrived at the office, a well-dressed stranger was seated next to the sheriff's desk. He stood and introduced himself as Thomas A. Wilson III, the grandson of Admiral Thomas A. Wilson from North

Carolina. The two families had held strong ties back east. Thomas was also the Masters' lawyer and would be presenting the will at their convenience. The three men were dumbfounded. What will? Duke spoke for the other two, "Well, we don't know anything about a will. Right guys?" They nodded in response. "But, if you want to read us something, it might as well be now, I reckon."

Thomas read the document to the three stunned men. Cookie and Charlie received two thousand dollars each. Duke received the Sweetwater Ranch and five thousand dollars "seed money". Clint and Rusty would have their pick of the horses and five hundred dollars each in appreciation for their sticking it out during the lean times. There was a caveat to the will: Duke should continue to live on the ranch for ten years and try his best to make it prosper.

Duke remained dumb with shock. He and Clayton had spoken many times about running the ranch and both enjoyed making the improvements together. He had joined Old Boss when he was just an orphaned kid and decided to stay on when Mary took over.

Duke said softly as he pointed his finger upward, "Old Boss took me in when I had nowhere else to go, and now, Mr. Masters is giving me even more of a chance for a good life. Guess I'll stay on. I can't imagine living anywhere else. He grinned at Charlie and Cookie and said, "Course you two old guys gotta' stick around too, wouldn't be the same without you." Duke continued, "And there's that widow gal in town that I been courting for the last year. I ain't getting younger, maybe it's time to tell her I'm serious."

Charlie wiped tears from his eyes and said, "As if I could hire out anywhere else." Cookie cleared his throat and in a strangled voice, "I've worked for so long in those kitchens, I guess I gotta stay. Couldn't cook nowhere else, nobody could eat my cooking."

Duke shook hands with Thomas Wilson and all the men agreed to the conditions and signed the paperwork. After everyone had signed, the sheriff pulled a bottle of whiskey from a desk drawer, poured out five drinks and said, "Gentlemen I toast your good fortunes and I know we'll never forget those two mighty fine people, Clayton and Mary Masters." Duke's heart expanded with thoughts of a good future ahead, all due to Miss Mary and her Englishman.

They drank and left the sheriff in the temporary solitude of his jail. He knew it wouldn't last long so he hiked up his gun belt, grabbed his hat and headed back out into the Colorado sunshine.

It was dusk before the Sweetwater ranch hands were ready to leave the park and escort their burden back to the ranch for burial. They headed towards the livery where their horses waited with the buckboard that would carry the casket..

The church was almost dark inside and the simple casket still lay untouched in front of the altar. Clayton moved silently towards it and hoped to hell and back that no one saw him easily lift its lid and remove both his ring and Mary's brooch. He re-sealed the casket and with only a whisper of movement, left the church and sped towards the mountains where Mary waited for him.

Two months later, Charlie had a mild heart attack.

After feeling better, he rode out to the lake and looked around. It's nice and quiet here, he thought, even when the wind carries the sound of the herd. He dismounted and sat in the cottonwood's shade, closed his eyes to relax and fell sound asleep instead. When he woke up, it was twilight, and his old eyes didn't see the two figures standing motionless at the top of the low hill overlooking the ranch.

The taller of the two held his arm around the figure of a woman in tight jeans and a big gray cowboy hat. His heavy signet ring glinted in the rising moonlight and the cameo at the throat of her shirt gave off a pale radiance. She moved her arm around his waist to hold him closer as he bent down to kiss her.

If Charlie had been watching, he'd have seen the two figures fade into a heavy white mist before disappearing into the gathering dark.

Together forever.

EPILOGUE

Clayton and Mary stood on the balcony of their New York penthouse apartment overlooking Grand Central Park. The weather dome over Manhattan had been programed to allow a light snow to fall as if to celebrate the new year. The electric self-driving buses below tried to avoid running into the inpatient crowds of celebrating pedestrians at every intersection and their distant cacophony of blaring horns seemed at odds with the quiet frosted night sky above them.

Mary wore her favorite fur lined cape with its matching knee-high red leather boots. Her hand held a half-filled wine glass. Clayton stood close to her, his right arm around her shoulders as snow continued to drift lazily down from the sparkling darkness above. Some of the flakes began to melt on his black tuxedo as he raised her left hand to kiss her knuckles.

"Let's go back in and light the fireplace. It would be a shame to waste such a fine evening without it." They retreated to the apartment's warmth and the city sounds became muffled as he slid the balcony door shut behind him. He gestured with an index finger toward the fireplace grate and the gas logs caught fire in an instant.

Mary was waiting on the couch as he leaned over her, pouring the last of the vintage wine into her glass (upset stomach be damned). He mock toasted her. "Happy New Year, darling girl. I'm thinking we should fly the jet to visit our High Lonesome retreat. It's been a while and I miss the Rockies and the Sweetwater. We can go skiing at Eldora's ski resort if you like." His voice became teasing, "That moonlit snow at midnight is always spectacular and you look so good covered in frost." He sat on the couch next to her and pulled her into his arms.

"Sounds good, so how about visiting the London flat in the spring? The place really needs some upgrades."

Clayton shifted away and looked at her with alarm. "Hey, wait a minute! I don't want you to start a "honey do" list! I just want a little ski vacation and some downtime!"

Mary grinned at him, "Oh, well in that case, maybe in the fall? Give me a few minutes and I'll start packing." She paused as she set down her glass and reached for him. Snuggling closer, she looked into his sapphire eyes and with a teasing voice responded to his earlier toast, "And a Happy New Year to *you,* my love. I have a feeling that 2100 will be the beginning of a very good century!"

THE END

Printed in Great Britain
by Amazon